I0600038

F. R. E. KINNEY

Bone Touched

Copyright © 2025 by F. R. E. Kinney

All rights reserved. No part of this publication may be reproduced, stored or transmitted in any form or by any means, electronic, mechanical, photocopying, recording, scanning, or otherwise without written permission from the publisher. It is illegal to copy this book, post it to a website, or distribute it by any other means without permission.

This novel is entirely a work of fiction. The names, characters and incidents portrayed in it are the work of the author's imagination. Any resemblance to actual persons, living or dead, events or localities is entirely coincidental.

F. R. E. Kinney asserts the moral right to be identified as the author of this work.

Imputing this work or any parts of it, including any amount of the text and any art on the cover or inside the book, to an AI without the express, written and signed permission of the copyright holder is ILLEGAL.

First edition

ISBN: 979-8-9991498-0-0

Editing by Jeff Hart
Cover art by Em Kinney

This book was professionally typeset on Reedsy.
Find out more at reedsy.com

For everyone who has ever been hurt by or in the name of religion.

Trigger Warnings

This book contains depictions of panic attacks and physical injuries/trauma, as well as allusions to religious trauma that may be upsetting to some readers. Read at your own discretion.

1

One

I was no more than a piece of blown glass sitting on the bench outside the administration office. Something on display that one of the students passing by might pick up and examine only to quickly lose interest and put me back. They would say, 'Yes, it's pretty,' and nothing more. They would only care enough not to completely break me.

I was tired of being stared at.

The scenery of Mortorous Academy made a much better view. The grounds were lovely despite being shrouded in mist and shadows from the ever-present cloud cover. All of the buildings featured gothic architecture that made the school look like a series of small cathedrals. Admirable, but occasionally a little unnerving, especially when the sun set and the fog rolled in.

"Ms. Ravena, your guide will be here momentarily," one of the administrators popped her head out of the office to inform me for the third time.

If only they would let me sit *inside* the office. There were a few empty chairs in a corner that I'd noticed when I went inside to get my schedule. But they told me to wait outside. They probably wanted to see what I would do. If the welcome I'd received so far was any indication, they thought of me as more of a specimen or a pet than a human. Perhaps that's what I was now.

I couldn't remember being anything else.

The woman in the office had seemed nice enough. She'd smiled and said, "Here you go, honey. Your schedule, your campus map, your ID, and some fliers for clubs. You should really check some of them out. Oh, and that top one is the calendar for the school year, lots of exciting events to help you make friends and get settled in. There's a girl in your grade who throws end of the week parties every other Friday. I hear they're a great place to make new friends."

I had nodded, knowing full well that I probably wouldn't even look at the calendar or the club fliers and definitely wouldn't be attending any parties. As much as I wanted to adjust to life here, I wasn't looking to get involved. At least, not until I stopped feeling like a freshly reanimated corpse.

The lady had directed me to the bench to wait for my tour guide with that same smile, which felt less and less genuine the longer she kept it stitched across her face. Sitting outside the office on the white wooden bench with the words *Mortorous Academy* carved into the back didn't make me feel very welcome.

But instead of complaining about the lack of punctuality or comfortable seating, I nodded politely to the administrator. Better not to antagonize them after they had already gone through the trouble of procuring me a room, a uniform, and more supplies than I could possibly want or use. Better not to let them see how much I didn't want to be here. They hadn't exactly given me a choice. Neither had *he*.

I tucked into a ball, my most comfortable position. My black-slack-clad legs pressed into my chest, crinkling my white button-up shirt. The heels of my black sneakers perched on the edge of the bench. My chin rested on my knees. My thin arms snaked around my shins. My eyelids drooped. I hadn't tried sleeping like this yet, but I wouldn't be surprised if I could.

Sudden drowsy spells had characterized the last few days. They'd gotten less frequent, but sometimes I nodded off in strange positions that only the dead should be able to sleep in.

The front doors opened, and a chorus of giggles and chatter filled the entry hall. Up until that point, I only caught snippets of the other students' conversations as they came in for classes. But there were so many feet and so many voices coming my way, I couldn't make out more than a disconnected word or two. It sounded like a stampede. So many clicking heels like the clopping of undead hooves on the elaborately tiled floor.

I was almost disappointed when the four horsemen didn't come riding in. I would have welcomed the excuse to run. Instead, a group of students rounded the corner. Mostly girls with a handful of guys. One painfully attractive boy occupied their center.

They all hovered around the boy like flies around a carcass. They stood so close together I could hardly believe they weren't stomping on each other's toes. I'd seen this kind of phenomenon in movies. Popularity.

Look away and they won't bother you.

I sighed through my nose and lowered my head to stare at

my hands gripping my calves. Out of the corner of my eye, I watched the flock of students as they focused on their leader, the black-haired boy with a jawline sharp enough to strip flesh from bone.

No, not bone. I regretted the thought the instant it entered my mind. My fingers clenched around my legs, knuckles going even whiter. *Anything but bone. Bone. Bone. Bone...*

"Hey."

The voice was gentle, but I startled anyway. The boy stood in front of me, gazing down with eyes blacker than grave dirt. I cast a glance behind him to where his entourage was dispersing with murmurs and furtive looks.

"Are you Sylvan Ravena?" He asked.

I nodded once.

"I'm supposed to show you around." He flashed me a smile that probably got all the girls purring in contentment and held out a hand the pale brown of a freshly built gallows. "Nicholas Ater."

My fingers tightened their grip on my legs. "Nice to meet you."

Nicholas dropped his hand but recovered with that smile again. "Not much of a shaker, eh?"

I shook my head, wintery white waves of hair flowing around my shoulders. I knew what his hand would feel like. It would envelop my slender fingers and squeeze with enough force to crack my bones.

Bones. Bones. Bones.

At least, that's how it would feel to me. That's what the handshakes of the administrators felt like when I first met them. To him, it would probably just be a brief touch.

"Well, shall we get going? There's a lot to see." Nicholas

4

took a half-step back.

I stood silently and secured the strap of my satchel over one shoulder.

"We'll start with the foyer since we're already here," Nicholas began. "Mortorous Academy likes to show off their trophies and such out here." He gestured to the black trophy cases set into the wall. "Mortorous has gotten national acclaim for its STEM curriculum. We've churned out enough renowned scientists, technicians, engineers, and mathematicians to attract the interest of parents who want their kids to grow up and get high paying jobs. The admin thinks it's inspiring to walk in and see all our accomplishments, but I think it's a little much."

He paused as if waiting for me to agree. I kept my eyes fixed on the doors to the school proper. A keypad clung to the wall beside each of the two sets of double doors. I got my ID card a few minutes ago which was supposed to open the doors to most of the buildings on campus. The woman who gave it to me waxed some poetic about how important security was to the school. Considering how remote and gloomy the campus was it didn't seem necessary that Nicholas had to swipe his card before leading me inside. Who would want to come out here?

A scream strangled itself in my throat when we passed into the circular hallway. Standing on a dais inside an alcove in the opposite wall was a giant skeleton, human except for the head. It was topped with the hornless skull of a antelope but with lethally sharp teeth. Its empty eye sockets stared down at us. The skeleton leaned forward slightly like it was about to climb down the dais steps and grab us by the throats.

Around the middle from behind once you pass is more likely.

Then squeeze the air from your lungs while your fear-choked mind fights for life. Then the black room with the white tub and ages alone with only your terror for company, until he comes in and—

Nicholas chuckled as if I were a puppy scared of my own reflection. "Don't worry. It's just plaster."

"What is it?" The words escaped like a last breath. My back was pressed against the door which had closed behind us—a pull door, of course, which didn't open when I leaned heavily into it.

"Our school mascot, *the Boneman*." He waved his arms and warbled his voice in a mockery of a ghost's moan.

When I kept staring at the statue without reacting to his joke, he stuffed his hands in his pockets and straightened his face.

"He's real, you know." His tone became far graver. He gazed at the enormous figure. "That's what people like to say anyway. No one has been able to prove that they've seen him. As the legend goes, he wanders this area watching over Mortorous Academy. Lots of students have claimed to see him in the forest. Though they most likely make it up for the street cred. The Boneman only lets his chosen ones see him. And if he chooses you, he marks you and grants you eternal magic. They call it being—"

"Bone Touched," I breathed.

Nicholas looked back at me. "So, you *have* heard the stories. But have you heard the catch to being Bone Touched? That you feel such unspeakable, paralyzing fear when he blesses you? That he breaks apart your body and turns it into what *he* wants it to be? That he empties your head of everything that happened before you met him, so you have no previous attachments? That you are considered, from that day on, to

6

be one of his disciples and must obey his every order?"

My lips pressed into a line thinner than the crack between a coffin and its lid.

"Some of the students go looking for him in the dark of the night so that they can have a piece of his magic and become one of his elite." I didn't care for the way Nicholas was watching me, too intense and focused.

The sound of bones cracking echoed in my mind. "Why would anyone want to endure that just to be haunted by him?"

Nicholas shrugged. "It's not like he really exists. It's just a fun story to scare new kids with. People tell stories about how he saved the school from having to close a long time ago and that's why we dedicated our school to him. But like I said, no one has any proof. The Boneman is just a figure in some long-gone society's mythology that we like to play around with."

I wouldn't want to go looking for proof a creature like that existed.

"Have your eyes always been that color?"

I finally looked at him, taken aback by the question. I hadn't thought my silvery-white irises would be a problem in a place like this. Not when his pitch-black eyes weren't exactly normal either.

"What other color would they be?"

Nicholas shook his head. "Sorry, that was rude of me. Let's get on with the tour."

He took the hallway that curved to the right. I watched the statue of the Boneman until it was out of sight around the corner, but I could still feel the chilling gaze of its empty sockets.

Nicholas showed me the cafeteria, the gym, the main

buildings where classes were held, and the rec center. The whole time he made jokes, which I didn't respond to, over and over. So, he was probably as glad as I was to be done with the tour when we finally stopped at the girls' dorm.

"You won't have any classes today, so you can spend the rest of the afternoon getting settled in, maybe take a walk around the grounds to familiarize yourself with them. The admin as well as the dorm supervisor will be available if you need anything," Nicholas said. "You know where your room is, right?"

I nodded. Room 300 on the third floor.

Nicholas regarded me for a moment with a faint smile. "You're a little strange, you know that?"

I didn't respond.

"You don't really talk. You don't shake hands. You're afraid of a statue."

"He's a monster," I said softly.

Nicholas's eyebrows shot up. "Don't let anyone else hear you say that. He's a *god* around here."

I turned away, muttering under my breath. "Funny how often the two words are synonymous."

My room was on the top floor, away from everyone else. *It's for the best.* That's what the faculty had said. I had the room all to myself, also for the best. It was surprisingly well furnished with a queen-sized bed, a nightstand, desk, dresser, and closet, as well as my own bathroom. Everything was black with white accents, just like the rest of the school.

I set my satchel down on the desk and turned in a slow circle to survey the room. A pair of armchairs sat in the corner by a window that overlooked a stretch of perfectly manicured lawn that ended at the edge of the forest. Mist clung to the ground in a low, creeping bank. The trees were so thick I could only see a little way in before they became an uninterrupted wall of trunks large enough to be living coffins.

Lots of students have claimed to see him in the forest.

I lurched forward and whipped the black curtains over the window. My eyes didn't leave the inky fabric until it stopped swaying from the momentum and my hands stopped shaking. I drifted into the bathroom. A quick check of the drawers and cabinets revealed enough toiletries to last until I turned thirty. I wouldn't be here that long, would I?

And then there was the bathtub. Its two eye-like knobs stared at me. The gaping mouth of its rim waited to swallow me whole. Just like a different tub had not long ago, drowning me in its milky waters. All of that white porcelain, smooth and polished...

I nearly tore down the white-and-black polka dot curtain when I swung it between me and the tub. I stumbled out of the bathroom.

It's fine. I told myself. *I showered this morning anyway.*

It took me until after dinner—a meal of snacks from the bottom drawer of the dresser—to work up the nerve to go back into the bathroom long enough to brush my teeth. Afterward, I hurtled onto the black-clad bed, wrapping as many blankets around me as possible, as if they were layers of armor. My exhaustion spells had *conveniently* stopped. It took me half an hour to relax enough to close my eyes.

Hopefully, the rest of the school year would be more enjoyable. The last few days had been a dream compared to... before.

2

Two

Tiny bubbles escaped my lips as I breathed softly, slowly, almost sleepily. My eyes stayed wide open, barely blinking, even if all they saw was the milky white fluid I'd been trapped in for what felt like an eternity. Time was hard to grasp when the only thing to break up the minutes were his visits.

He didn't talk. Not audibly anyway.

That made it worse.

His silence crushed what little composure I had into dust. His presence was enough to set a breakneck beat in my heart even if I couldn't do anything about it. He would come in, sit at the edge of the tub, and watch me the way a vulture watches a dying animal. It's not like I was doing anything interesting. I couldn't even move.

He rarely came to visit though. I spent most of my time in stone-cold silence, rooted to the bottom of that tub by a fear that made my muscles lock up and my breathing turn shallow.

How I could breathe through the pearly substance surrounding me was a mystery. The cool liquid flowed into my lungs as smoothly as air. Small bubbles floated in the stream that blew *back out. When I let out a stuttering sigh, those little pockets of air raced from my mouth and breached the liquid's surface with soft pops.*

That was the only noise breaking up the long hours until the sound of a door opening drifted down to me through the white water.

I dreaded that sound. My breathing trembled with the desire to scream, to cry, to beg. But I could only blink as his skeletal shadow fell over me.

A hand descended into my bone-white stew and took my left arm. I tried to yank it back, to return to my loosely curled ball, to save it from him. My muscles refused to obey me.

When he took my finger and broke it, the pain could not overcome the paralyzing terror. Either my bath or the immobilizing fear dampened the ache. A soft flow of bubbles continued to blossom from my nose and lips as he pulled the joints out of alignment and broke the bones of my finger into tiny fragments in his fleshless hands. I was glad for the small mercy of having been set on my side so that I couldn't watch.

But then he started to massage the shattered finger as if he were working a lump of clay. Vaguely I felt it lengthening, becoming more slender and delicate, more skeletal.

His thoughts floated around me in the white water. He communicated like that. Not in words, but in the whispers of feeling that carried through the air and water. This time, they were wrought with concentration accompanied by little sparks of frustration or triumph and finally satisfaction when he finished.

I breathed an inward sigh of relief. He was done. He would leave now.

Please let him leave now.

He didn't. His hands found the next finger and began the same process. Breaking, tearing, remolding. I wished I could cry. It might have made this more bearable if I could let out the fear and pain into whatever fluid I'd been stewing in since he had captured me and brought me to this place.

I didn't remember much from before his bone arms closed around me from behind, squeezed until I couldn't breathe, and the world went black. I remembered that I'd had a family, a big one. We ran an inn. I'd gone outside to get firewood when he took me.

Sometimes I wondered if they knew what had happened to me or if they even cared. I couldn't recall if they had loved me or simply put up with me. If our family were big, maybe they didn't care that they had one less mouth to feed.

"She's gone. More for the rest of us now," someone would say.

"Rest in peace, little—" They would say my name at the end there.

What was my name? I wasn't sure if I was comforted or distressed that I couldn't remember. A name might have given me something to cling to in those long stretches of time when I lay alone in the tub. But some part of me knew it was pointless to hope.

I wasn't going to leave here unless the giant skeleton man with the skull of a sort of wolfish antelope picked me up and carried me out—and he was too busy disassembling my fingers. There was no way I could escape on my own. My ability to fight or fly had been broken with my bones.

At long last, he lowered my arm back into the fluid with a gentleness that belied his disassembling of my bones. It landed on my side and slid to rest atop my right arm, completing my fetal position.

He had destroyed and reshaped all the bones inside my hand. Now, my left hand felt wrong against my right like it belonged to a stranger, or a skeleton, all long and boney.

He wasn't finished with me yet.

He reached down again and took my face in his hands. Smooth, weathered bone gripped my cold skin as he pulled my head above the liquid's surface. I gasped at the cold air that rushed into my lungs when I emerged. Fluid dripped out of my mouth and nose.

I blinked to clear my eyes and found myself face to face with those empty eye sockets and that elongated snout full of sharp teeth. The face that haunted my nightmares–waking nightmares.

As he rotated my head, examining me, I got a view of the room.

It was tiled completely in black with a simple, black, wooden chair that the skeleton man sat in beside my white porcelain tub which squatted in the middle of the room. Soft yellow light glowed from fixtures in the ceiling. The room was empty except for us, the tub, and the chair. I didn't see the door.

He turned me back to look him in the eye sockets. His thoughts echoed in my head nearly as loudly as my own.

My student, my creation, my daughter.

He lowered me back into the tub and carefully arranged my body so that I lay on my side with my legs tucked beneath me, arms curled up to my chest. The door opened and closed, and I was alone again in the white expanse of the water with nothing but my fear.

3

Three

I woke up shivering, despite the many layers of blankets wrapped around me. My pulse took a moment to calm itself. I slowly stretched out my muscles, making sure the nightmare memory wasn't real. I could still move. That was air in my lungs, not the white solution from the enormous bathtub. No Boneman lurked in the corner of my room.

My eyes wandered to the window. The thick, black curtains were open. The sun crawled over the horizon through thick grey clouds that threatened rain.

Hadn't I closed those?

Yes, I had.

As the legend goes, he wanders this area, watching over Mortorous Academy.

Chills spider-walked down my spine. I kicked off the blankets, shot across the room, and yanked the curtains closed again. My hands fisted in the dark cloth. My forehead rested against it. The cold from the glass leached into my skin.

He can't get me. He can't get me. He can't get me.

But what if he could?

No. You must have opened them in the night and forgot to close them.

And forgot you opened them.

I had to stay here, then I had to believe that the Boneman couldn't get to me for the sake of what remained of my sanity. It wasn't like I could leave this place. I had nothing and no one outside of the handful of gothic structures that made up the school.

Identical copies of the white shirt and pants I'd worn yesterday occupied the small closet beside the bathroom door. I dressed quickly, pausing only to grimace at the sight of the three black fingerbone marks below the left side of my collarbone. As if it hadn't been enough for the Boneman to remake my body, he had to put his signature on it too. Like I was a work of art for him to claim.

I braved the bathroom again to brush my teeth, keeping as far away from the tub as possible. In my mind, it crouched behind its deceptively cheerful, polka dot curtain, full of white water, prepared to snatch me into its depths and hold me there forever.

I shouldered my satchel before heading down to get breakfast. I had lost interest in the snacks in my drawer after the curtain incident. I should be safer in the cafeteria with all the other students around.

The Boneman only lets his chosen ones see him.

There weren't as many people roaming between the food lines and the white tables as I had hoped but it was still pretty early. I joined the more populated line for pancakes.

They smelled good. I couldn't remember the taste of food

before I was taken. I had no idea what my preferences were, or if I'd even had the luxury of preferences. The admin had fed me well enough the last few days that I stayed in a small cottage at the edge of campus while they got everything in order. But I only ate what they prepared for me—mostly oatmeal and frozen dinners that tasted as bland as wood. They never asked what I wanted. Perhaps because they knew I wouldn't know what I liked.

Hopefully, I didn't have an allergy to anything here. I prayed that would be the one perk of getting kidnapped by a living legend. I didn't care about whatever magic the tour guide had babbled about yesterday, but being able to live long enough to forget the monster who supposedly gave it to me would suit me just fine.

"You know that's a boy's uniform, right?"

I turned toward the harsh voice. It wasn't hard to recognize a pair of Nicholas's groupies. One, probably the girl who had spoken, had curly, shoulder-length blonde hair and eyes the color of a hangman's noose. The other, standing behind her friend, had long, straight, black hair and a ridiculous amount of eyeliner that made her green eyes pop like the grass that covered barrows.

"Girls are supposed to wear black skirts and heels not pants and sneakers," the blonde continued, gesturing to herself as an example. I highly doubted the length of her skirt was part of the dress code.

"Ok." I turned back around.

"Aren't you going to go change? You'll get in trouble if you're not following the rules. Mortorous Academy is very strict about that sort of thing."

I turned just enough to watch her out of the corner of my

silvery-white eye. "I planned on getting breakfast first."

The blonde huffed but, having nothing else to say, turned to her friend and started talking. As I swung back around to face the front of the line, their ceaseless chatter buzzed in my ears like mosquitos, hovering at the edge of my attention. Homework, which teachers sucked at their jobs, who to invite to a party this weekend.

There was no way I was going to change. The admin had given me this uniform which had to mean that it was perfectly fine for me to wear, even if I was the "wrong" gender for it.

I collected my food and found an empty table in a corner to occupy. One eye monitored the open expanse of the cafeteria. The other focused on my food. The pancakes were as delicious as they smelled. They replaced spaghetti as my new favorite food.

Priorities. I needed to get those straightened out.

A chorus of cackling drew my gaze to the table where the two girls from the line were joined by a few others. They sat all the way on the other side of the room, but between their increasing volume and the relative quiet I could almost make out what they were saying.

I sighed and ate faster. *It's better than* him, I told myself. *Anything is better than* him.

Priority number one: Never see the Boneman again.

Priority two: Stay away from those girls as much as possible. People like them were nothing but trouble.

If I was to live a quiet, peaceful, normal life—and that's why I was there—I'd need to surround myself with those who wanted the same. That was priority number three.

Class didn't start for another hour after I finished eating, but I sure wasn't about to go back to my room with its self-

17

opening window curtains. So, I wandered to the library instead. I remembered the large ornately decorated building from the tour primarily because it had been nice and quiet. Even though the tables had been populated with students, they were all too busy doing their work to chat.

The shelves reached up a foot above my head—made of black wood, of course—creating the perfect aisles to get lost in. I couldn't remember if I liked reading or not before I was taken. Maybe I hadn't even had time to read before. I certainly had time now. Maybe I could find something to occupy my mind. Something other than trying to figure out what to do if I ever ran into the Boneman again.

I chose a shelf at random and started browsing. It was mostly nonfiction, history, and biographies. A couple aisles over was fantasy. A few more were realistic fiction and horror. I was just bending to examine a book with swirling gold and silver on the spine when someone crashed into me.

There came a thin squeak and a thump as the person hit the ground along with several books they'd been carrying. I picked myself up in time to see a small girl leap from the ground and go scrambling after the books all over the floor. She muttered to herself about damages and mint condition copies.

I crouched and picked up a book thicker than my arm. *Bone Spinner*. The cover was a tangled mass of spider webs with arm and leg bones caught in them, forming the letters of the title. Why did everything here have to involve bones? *Bones. Bones. Bones.*

"Oh," said the girl.

I peered up at her. If I stood up, she would be a head shorter than me but, from down on my knees, she towered over me.

Her oak-brown hair was woven in a thick braid that swayed as she bent down and held out a hand.

"Sorry for bumping into you. I can take that now."

I looked back at the book. My free hand clenched into a fist at the sight of all those bones. *Bones. Bones—*

A breath shuddered in and out of me. *Leave him behind. Leave all of that behind and move on. Think of priority number three.* What better way to escape than with someone else?

My gaze returned to the girl. "Is it any good?"

"*Bone Spinner*? Any good?" The girl's sea-green eyes lit up behind a pair of similarly colored glasses. "Why, it's only the best fantasy novel written this *century*. How have you never heard of it?"

"I've been a little… distant recently," I replied. She had five other books in her arms already. "Do you need help?"

"Oh no, I'm quite used to this. Thank you though." She grabbed for her stack as it began to tilt dangerously toward me.

I stood and placed *Bone Spinner* atop the rest of her books.

"You're new here, aren't you?" the girl asked.

"How could you tell?"

"For one thing, you're wearing a boys' uniform. And for another, your appearance is way too… distinct to forget." The girl looked me up and down.

"Oh." I lowered my gaze. Barely a day in and the body the Boneman gave me was causing trouble.

"Not in a bad way," the girl rushed to amend. "It's just not every day you see a tall girl with hair that long and white. It's pretty. Is it natural or did you dye it?"

I curled a lock around my slender finger. I couldn't remember what its color had been before, but clearly mine wasn't a common shade. I hadn't seen evidence of more naturally colored roots in the last few days I had been free, though.

"Natural," I decided.

"Cool. I'm Wren Mentis, year three." She didn't offer me a hand, not that she had a free one anyway.

"Sylvan Ravena, year three."

"Wow, your parents must have really been a pair to name you Forest Raven." She chuckled, then stopped abruptly. "That sounded meaner than I meant. I'm named after a bird too, so I don't have much room to talk. It's a nice name, just auspicious."

I shrugged, not sure how to respond. It wasn't my parents who had given me that name. It had been written on a black tag tied around my wrist with a similarly colored ribbon when I had been found outside the school. I didn't know what my name was before the Boneman took it.

A high tone echoed through the library. The bell for class.

"Well, that's five minutes," Wren said, beginning to back away. "Better get going. Nice meeting you. Sorry again for running into you."

I watched her go. Interesting girl, but someone who spent as much time in the library as it seemed like she did was bound to be.

4

Four

My first class was near the library, so I didn't have to rush to get there on time. Despite my short trip, everyone was present by the time I walked in. A group of girls chattered near the door. A couple of boys clustered around the middle of the room, looking collectively at something on a phone. A few loners sat on their phones or frantically scribbled on what was probably homework that was due today.

Most of the desks were occupied or had backpacks plopped in them. Thankfully, there were a pair of empty seats—the desks were pushed together in twos to form thick columns facing the front of the room—at the back corner near the wall of windows.

My new classmates only spared me a few passing glances as I took the spot nearest the windows. I pulled my hair back into a ponytail and stared out into the courtyard as I secured the black scrunchy at the base of my skull. It looked like the perfect place to sit and do homework despite the gloomy weather. Some grassy hills had been carved for sitting as well as plenty of chairs and tables and benches. Purple flowers sprouted on low bushes and creeping vines clung with leafy fingers to the walls around the courtyard. A circular fountain took up the center of the space.

"That's usually where I sit."

I looked up into a set of charcoal-black eyes undercut by sharp cheekbones. *Bones. Bones. Bones.*

"But I guess I can let it slide since you're new and no one sits in this seat anyway," Nicholas continued with a conspiratorial smile as he set down his bag.

I turned away while he sank into the neighboring desk. Of course, he would be in my class. One day with his deadly confidence and outgoing attitude wasn't enough. I was stuck with it for the rest of the school year. My fingers knotted around themselves. I did my best to stare straight ahead and not acknowledge him.

I was the only one it seemed. It took all of two seconds for others to take note of his presence. The blonde from the breakfast line stopped by his desk, accompanied by her black-haired friend and a brunette who I thought might have joined them after they got their food.

"Good morning, Nick," she chirped. The others murmured similar greetings from behind her.

He flashed them that smile of his. "Morning, Nina, Lily, Vanessa."

The girls grinned wolfishly as he addressed them by name. I sat still as petrified wood. *Don't notice me. Don't notice me. Don't notice me.* I started to tuck my knees up but banged them loudly on the bottom of the desk, startling myself and the others.

"Oh!" The blonde made a big deal of exclaiming. "I didn't

know you were in our class."

Great. I looked at her.

"What happened to changing your clothes?"

"No time."

"Hm, well." She turned a blistering smile on Nicholas. "I'm having a party in the girls' common room tomorrow night and I would *love* for you to come, Nick." She dragged out the word 'love' the way a dead body is dragged into a mass grave. "We're planning to take a trip into the forest at midnight to look for the Boneman."

My jaw clenched. I had hoped that Nicholas was kidding when he said the students wanted to find the Boneman. They clearly didn't know what would happen if they found him.

"I should be free unless Professor Tilns decides to give us another packet of homework to do over the weekend," Nicholas replied, a smile in his voice.

"Terrific!" The blonde—Nina, I thought—cheered.

I rolled my pencil to and fro across my desk slowly enough that it didn't make much noise.

"How do you know Sylvan?" My hand froze at Nicholas's question.

"Who?" the blonde asked dubiously.

Don't do it. Say nevermind. Tell her to go away.

"Sylvan." Nicholas jerked a thumb at me. "You act like you've met before."

"Oh." The chipper chirp returned. "We met in the cafeteria. I gave her some wardrobe advice that she *said* she was going to take."

Nicholas turned his gaze on me. His pity was tangible. I refused to look at either one of them.

"I don't see anything wrong with what she's wearing. After

23

all, it's the same thing I'm wearing."

Nina emitted a strained titter. "Yes, and you look wonderful in it. I'll see you at the party then."

"See you around."

The trio walked away, and Nicholas turned his attention back to me.

"I'm sorry about them. Nina can be a little high and mighty. Her parents have a lot of money, so she was raised—"

"I don't need you to comfort me." I stared at my pencil on the desk with tired eyes.

There was a moment of silence, but the smile returned. "Of course not. You can fight your own battles."

I didn't move.

Another moment of silence. He had no idea what to do with me. "So, why *do* you wear a boy's uniform? I was curious yesterday but thought it might be off-putting to point out when we'd only just met."

And yet he'd had no problem asking about my eyes. "Admin gave me two options. I chose this one. Pants are more comfortable." *Easier to run in.* I hoped that ended the conversation.

No such luck. "The school gave you uniforms?"

A nod.

"Are you here on a scholarship?"

I swallowed. *No. I was delivered to the doorstep of this school at midnight four days ago, wearing nothing but a wrapping of white silk sheets, still so terrified that I couldn't move except to blink. The headmistress nearly tripped on my body on her way out the door after a staff meeting.*

"Alright, class," the teacher, a round woman with thick brown hair, called.

24

The room quieted and everyone made their way to their seats. Nicholas focused his attention on the front of the room where the teacher was looking over a piece of paper.

Thank goodness.

"First order of business, which one of you is Sylvan Ravena?"

Oh no. I raised my hand as discreetly as possible. Several eyes wandered to me anyway.

After an unrealistically long moment of looking around, the teacher found me. "I'm assuming that's where you would like to sit for the rest of the year."

I glanced around. There weren't any other seats available. I nodded, clutching my pencil with white knuckles. The last thing I wanted was to be stuck next to Nicholas the chatterbox charmer for the rest of the year, but it didn't look like I had much of a choice. The teacher grunted and marked something down on her paper.

"Don't worry about Dr. Shalm. She acts like she doesn't care about any of us but then she throws us class parties on the holidays," Nicholas muttered to me.

I pressed my lips together and focused on my pencil again.

"We'll start the class reading tonight. Everyone has their copy of the text?" Dr. Shalm asked.

"Yes." The class answered with one voice so loudly that I jumped.

Nicholas chuckled. When I glanced at him, he was grinning with all those white teeth. So many bones. *Bones. Bones. Bones.*

Class passed in a slow-motion blur of Old English and figurative language like bloody water swirling down a drain. When I glanced around, the three girls from the beginning

25

of class were watching me like hawks. It was a relief when the bell finally rang, and I was free of all of them.

"What's your next class?" Nicholas asked as I swiftly shuffled my things into my satchel.

"History."

"With Professor Tilns?" Was that hope in his voice?

"Yes." I wished I could say no.

That smile lit up his face. "That's my next class too. Let me walk you."

I stood. "I can find it on my own." He'd already shown me around the school once, I didn't need to repeat that experience.

"I wasn't trying to say you couldn't." He stood as well. "I just find that walking with a friend makes the journey so much more enjoyable."

I looked at him sharply. "Friend?" I couldn't remember having any. Surely, making one took longer than this.

He stood at the opposite end of the pair of desks, watching me. "Yes, friend."

"You met me yesterday."

"Maybe but I feel like—"

"Nick!" The blonde girl, Nina, darted to his side. "Come walk with me and my friends to class. I want your opinion on the menu for tomorrow night."

She twined her arm through his and started pulling him toward the door. These boy-crazy girls might work in my favor. I wasted no time scurrying to the door as Nicholas gently extricated himself.

"Thanks, but maybe we can talk at lunch. Your class is in the opposite direction from mine. Besides, I was going to walk with—"

And just like that, I was out the door and lost in the crowded hall before he knew I was gone. I had only a few minutes of reprieve, but I planned to enjoy them.

I made it with three minutes to spare and was greeted by a familiar face. Wren, the girl from the library, sat in the last row with her nose buried in a book. The seat beside her was open and the one on the opposite side of it was occupied by a mousy boy scribbling in a notebook.

I slid into the seat and peered at Wren, trying to get a look at what she was reading. After a moment, she frowned up at me.

"What are you looking—? Oh, it's you." Her face lit up a bit.

My expression softened in response. "Me."

"I was wondering if we would have any classes together—"

I cut her off. "Do you know where Nicholas Ater sits in this class?"

"Nicholas?" She didn't look that surprised. "Why do you want to know where he sits?"

"We... met yesterday. He talks too much." This was probably the first time I'd volunteered more information than absolutely necessary.

Even when the school staff had interrogated me, I'd barely spoken enough to answer their questions. They brought me inside following my delivery and got me as comfortable as possible after what I'd been through, but still I wouldn't open up for them. After spending so much time in that tub with my lips glued shut, the silence had become a part of me. At first, I wasn't even sure I'd still be able to speak after going so long without saying a word.

The admin hadn't pressed too hard though. The main thing

they impressed upon me was the urgency to keep what had happened a secret. No one could know I was Bone Touched. If they did, it would only lead to chaos and massive witch hunts to find other Bone Touched. The governments of the world would get involved and I would never be free again.

And freedom was the only thing I wanted.

"Oh." Wren pointed toward the front of the room. "He sits in the first row next to the door."

That was about as far from where I sat as it got.

"What do you mean he talks too much?" Wren asked. "All the girls love it when he talks to them. *If* he talks to them." The last part was muttered almost wistfully.

I shook my head. Yes, he was pretty. Yes, he had girls like Nina hanging off him. But for someone who couldn't remember having a consensual conversation, he was way too talkative. I couldn't take it. I needed someone more like Wren who was quiet and would do most of the talking when she did speak.

"I guess even guys like him can't get every girl," Wren answered her own question. "Speak of the devil." She jerked her chin at the doorway.

Nicholas strode through. I ducked my head and prayed that he wouldn't notice me. Why did I have to have such distinctly colored hair? I wondered if I could find dye for it.

You're worried for nothing. There's no way he can sit near you. A girl had just taken the seat in front of me and there was a student on either side of her, walling me off.

"Wow, you really don't like him," Wren muttered, taking note of my posture.

I forced myself to straighten a bit.

"I suppose it makes sense given how little you talk." She

paused. "Do I talk too much for you?"

The corner of my mouth tugged upward ever so slightly. "No. You talk just the right amount."

She grinned at me and then her eyes widened, fixed on something beside me.

"I thought we were going to walk together."

I stiffened at the sound of his voice. I almost didn't dare to look. When I did, Nicholas was sitting beside me instead of the mousy boy.

"You left without me." He smiled playfully.

"You had Nina."

"Nina isn't as much fun as you are." He flashed me one of his trademark grins.

"Isn't that Dan's seat?" Wren asked, leaning forward to peer around me.

Nicholas turned his smile on her. "He has graciously allowed me to sit here to keep my new friend company on her first day at Mortorous Academy." He leaned closer to me, which wasn't necessary because the desks were already so close, I could barely walk between them without hitting a hip. "It helps that Scarlet sits next to my usual desk."

I glanced at the seat Wren had indicated as belonging to Nicholas. A gorgeous redhead was just sitting down beside it. The mousy boy, Dan, watched adoringly from his new place next to her.

Terrific.

"The two of you act like you know each other," Nicholas commented. Why was he so interested in who knew me? We weren't actually friends. We were barely acquaintances.

Thankfully, Wren answered him. "We met this morning before class."

"Good to see you're making friends that aren't me." Nicholas pierced me with those pitch-black eyes. *What was his deal?*

One good thing about him being so popular, he attracted other students like dust to an old tomb. A half dozen swarmed him after class, letting me and Wren escape together.

"I bet he thinks you're playing hard to get," she declared. "Boys like that take rejection personally whether it's meant that way or not. If you ignore him long enough, he'll lose interest. Even the greatest players will quit a game once they know they can't win."

I huffed a breath and hoped she was right. I could only handle worrying about one person—thing?—stalking me at a time.

5

Five

The whole day went like that. Nicholas was in all of my classes. Every. Single. One. And in all of them, he finagled his way into sitting beside me.

I only got a break during lunch. Nicholas got ambushed by Nina and the rest of his fan club before he had the chance to see I was there. I slipped out into that courtyard I'd seen during English. The cloud cover had thinned enough that rain no longer looked imminent. Several students ate at the benches and on the grassy hills, but it was much better than the deafening noise of the cafeteria.

Wren found me out there. I scooted over on the bench to make room for her and her tray.

"Looks like we have similar preferences for eating locations," she commented. "I'm sure it helps that a certain someone is being detained in the cafeteria."

She leaned forward to peer around the bush that hid us from the cafeteria windows. I had picked this spot for that exact reason. We were safe from prying eyes here.

The two of us spent the rest of lunch in comfortable quiet.

But when I had to go to the gym without Wren and ran into Nicholas on the way, my moment of peace ended. I was ready to give up hope that I do anything at this school without Nicholas by the time the final bell rang. At least I could go to my private tutoring without him.

I understood my...circumstances weren't conducive to picking up learning in the middle of the school year. But I didn't understand why they told me not to tell anyone where I was going after school. They grossly overestimated my social skills. I didn't have anyone to tell except maybe Wren, but that was still new.

The room marked on my campus map was on the top floor of the science building. It reminded me disturbingly of one of those towers that maidens got locked inside of in faerie tales. From the moment I stepped inside I saw no one, and it wasn't a short hallway. The room itself was no better.

Rows of tables each sporting two chairs faced a wide countertop at the front of the room. The walls were lined with shelves upon shelves stuffed with jars. I squinted at one. The glass was cloudy so all I could make out was a mass of green leaves and stems. A terrarium held a large, black, and red spider with legs so thin, I could barely see them against the dark dirt covering the bottom of its home.

I rested my back against the wall near the shelf, my head tilting back. What was I doing here? Was this the wrong room or just the strangest classroom I had ever seen? Not that I'd seen many. What kind of science did this professor teach? My eyes drifted to the ceiling and a shriek exploded out of me.

Hundreds of bones hung from the rafters. Some of them were suspended as partially finished skeletons. Some dangled by themselves. *Bones. Bones. Bones, bones bonesbones.* So many of them.

My fingers shook as I whirled and grabbed the doorknob. Private tutoring or not, there was no way I was staying here with all those fleshless corpses hanging over my head.

"Ah, Ms. Ravena. So glad you were able to find the classroom."

I spun back around. A man with hair the color of blood streaked with silver hobbled toward me out of a door on the opposite end of the room. He might as well have been a skeleton too for how thin he was.

"Wrong room," I breathed barely loud enough to be heard.

The old man chuckled and shook his head. "No, this is the right room. I'm Professor Tumulus, the first- and second-year biology teacher. It's nice to meet you." He was right in front of me now. At least he didn't offer to shake my hand. "I'll admit I was excited to receive a new student. It's not every day we get deliveries from the Boneman himself. How have you been adjusting to everything?"

I shook my head and looked up at the ceiling. Professor Tumulus followed my gaze.

"Oh, I see you've become acquainted with my collection. Those who are Bone Touched tend to cross paths with dead things. Have you found any mouse carcasses yet? Those seem to be the most common around here."

A hollow squeak escaped my throat. What little color my skin retained drained away. I shook so hard the door rattled in its frame behind me.

The professor frowned at me. "Is everything alright, Ms. Ravena?"

My eyes were fixed on the bones. *Those who are Bone*

Touched tend to cross paths with dead things. My breathing quickened. My vision blurred. Distantly I heard Professor Tumulus talking to me, calling my name. The world went black.

* * *

I sat up in a nest of pillows when I regained consciousness. Professor Tumulus sat cross-legged on the floor in front of me. My eyes went up, looking for the bones, but this wasn't the same room. It must have been the one Tumulus came out of when I first saw him. An old man like him couldn't have dragged me far by himself.

The office space was cluttered, to say the least. There were desks and papers and filing cabinets everywhere. Empty jars occupied the shelves of a bookcase to my right. A wilting plant gazed sadly out the tiny window in the back.

The door drew my attention. I shot to my feet only to go crashing back to my knees. Spots swam in my vision. Was the room spinning?

"Easy," Professor Tumulus soothed as I swayed on my hands and knees. "You fainted."

"Have to go," I panted. I needed to get as far away from those bones as possible.

"Ms. Ravena, you're in no condition to walk, and we haven't had our lesson yet."

I shook my head. I couldn't stay here, but I couldn't walk with the ground tilting under me.

"Why don't you tell me why you fainted? Did you have lunch? Are you tired?"

My hands gripped the cushions beneath me. "Bones," I

whispered.

Based on how old he looked, he shouldn't have been able to hear me. But when I looked at him, he was nodding contemplatively.

"They remind you of him, don't they?"

I sat back and tucked my arms around myself.

"I see. I can put up a tarp, so you don't have to see them," he offered.

I heaved a breath and looked around for my satchel. "I should just go."

"But I'm supposed to teach you how to use your bone magic."

My eyes shot to his. "What?"

"You are Bone Touched, Ms. Ravena. That much I'm sure you know. And being Bone Touched means you have been imbued with certain gifts. My job is to teach you how to use them. That's why you're at this school. That's why the Boneman brought you here."

"No." It was the first time I had put any real power in my voice.

I didn't care if the Boneman brought me to Mortorous Academy to learn magic. I didn't care that I was Bone Touched. I didn't care that this man talked as if he were Bone Touched too. I was, under no circumstances, going to do anything with what had been done to me except shove the experience into the darkest corner of my mind and forget about it.

I stood, no longer unsteady, grabbed my bag, and started out the door.

"Ms. Ravena!" Professor Tumulus called, hurrying after me as best he could. "Stop! You must do this. You can't just sweep what you are under a rug."

But I was already out of the office, across the classroom, with my hand on the doorknob, pointedly not looking at all the bones in the rafters.

"Yes, I can," I said and slammed the door shut behind me.

I didn't register that I was on my way to my room until I had already set my satchel beside my bed. I collapsed on the rumpled comforter. What a nightmare.

I needed to wash off the day's disasters. But there was no way I was going to use the tub. I gathered my things and started for the gym. The girls' locker room was deserted when I used my ID to get in. No one wanted to be here after such a long day at school.

After a steaming hot shower, I felt a bit better, if only because the heat relaxed my muscles. Until the door banged open, and a familiar voice barked into the room.

"—not even interested," Nina was saying.

I snatched the rest of my things and darted into the forest of lockers to hide from them. I didn't need any more contact with people like her today.

"She is pretty, though," a softer voice said.

"For someone who's hair has gone prematurely white, I guess she's ok," Nina snorted. "She's just something new. Boys like playing with new toys. Once Nick realizes she's no fun to play with, he'll look for a more... stimulating partner."

The girls cackled. I wound around the lockers, heading for the doors.

"What if he's into the silent and submissive thing? It wouldn't really surprise me," a third voice interjected.

I glared at the lockers I passed. I may have been relatively silent so far, but I was *not* submissive. I never would be again after what the Boneman did to me.

"He's not," Nina snapped. "Otherwise, he would have gone after Wren when she tried to get him to notice her last year. No, he's into real girls. I just need to change my makeup look a little and his interest'll turn. This *Sylvan* doesn't stand a chance."

The doors closed behind me, sealing away the sound of their echoing laughter.

Go after him all you want. I don't want him.

I had bigger things to worry about than the attention of some random boy. I might be looking to rebuild my life and finally feel safe, but *that* was more than I was ready for. He would lose interest in me once he realized that and go right back to his brood of petty admirers. Those were his people.

The curtains were mercifully still closed when I trudged into my room. I retired early, climbing into bed before the sun was anywhere near the horizon. I needed to forget this day as soon as possible.

6

Six

He had remolded all four of my limbs. They lay against one another like a pile of spindly twigs. These new arms and legs were foreign compared to the main trunk of my body. I had no idea how long it had taken him to do it all but now it was finished.

But, if it's finished, why is he visiting again?

A fresh wave of terror washed over me as those skeletal hands dipped into the liquid.

This time he pulled my whole body up and propped me against the edge of the tub facing out into the rest of the room. White liquid dripped down my face and out of my mouth as my breath stuttered through the acclimation to breathing air again. From where I sat, exposed from the chest up, my skin was freezing cold, but I couldn't muster the nerve to even shiver.

His wisps of thought combed through my mind as he stepped into the tub behind me. Contemplation, decision, resignation. I had a moment to wonder what this could mean before his hand entered my back.

A heavy huff burst from my mouth. His hands felt like snakes, cold and smooth under my skin, sliding around my bones and organs. He grabbed hold of one of my ribs and broke it. I whimpered. It was barely more than a single note that lasted the smallest fraction of a second, but it was there.

I might have been proud of myself if the pain hadn't distracted me.

It hurt so much more than when he broke my arms and legs or when he reconfigured my hands and feet. It burned deep in my core, but I remained incapable of movement. I wasn't sure if that was the ever-present incapacitating terror or the new fear of having his hands inside my body, shifting things around. One wrong move and he could end my life.

What was left of it, anyway.

His hands broke the rib in a different place. I whimpered that single note again. He did it over and over until the rib was in pieces and then he started to mold it just as he had done with my limbs. I wanted to scream from the pain, but a new wave of fear engulfed me, silencing me as he worked.

My gaze locked on the tiles at the edge of the tub. My lips remained slightly parted, huffing every once in a while, in place of the whimpering. He remade every single rib and then he did the same to my pelvic bone, my sternum, my shoulder blades, and my clavicle. I couldn't feel much difference in how they sat in my body afterward, but it took a long time to shatter such large, complicated bones.

And then there was my spine. All feeling in my legs and hips vanished the first time he broke a vertebra, crushing one low in my neck in his fist. I slipped to the side—the first time I'd moved without him intentionally shifting me around.

He caught me and carefully repositioned me so I wouldn't move again. I slumped heavily into the tub when he got a few bones *higher. All sensation was gone. I supposed that was a good thing. I didn't have to endure the pain anymore.*

It was an eternity before his hands retracted from my back. I felt dead, like someone had flipped a switch and my soul wasn't attached to my body but still floated around inside it, trying to stay anyway.

He turned me over and lowered me back into the white bath. He arranged my body in its usual fetal position and stood beside the tub. His shadow hovered over me. He waited there for a long time, not thinking anything at me, just watching like he thought I might sit up and start staring back.

Gradually, the feeling returned to my extremities. My muscles still refused to work, but I could feel the rightness in how my new body settled into place with my limbs. They were evenly matched, like they belonged to each other.

A glimmer of relief flashed into my mind from his. He lowered a hand into the water and rested it on my head for a moment before he stood. The door opened and closed, and I sighed inwardly.

My body ached where he had reshaped me. It felt like being squeezed into a too-tight space. I hated it. Though I couldn't exactly ask him to put me back the way I had been. I couldn't even remember how I had been. With every moment I spent in this tub, more memories spiraled down the drain.

How much more would be gone before I got out? Would I ever get out?

* * *

I was greeted by pitch black when I opened my eyes. I blinked. No, not pitch black, just very dark and… outside? Trees rose around me, dark and formless, blending together into one big silhouette. The ground was soft and cool beneath me. Leaves and grass pressed into the side of my face.

I tried to sit up. That's when I heard it. A rattle like sticks clacking together but deeper. I knew that sound. I knew the accompanying wave of petrifying fear that swallowed me whole. And there he was, standing maybe twenty feet away, watching me with the hollows in his skull where eyes should have been.

My breathing fell into that tense, slow rhythm it had taken when I lived in that tub. As if my lungs were terrified to give me away. He started toward me. His gait was slow. He circled around behind me and crouched. I stared at the spot where he had first appeared, unable to even move my eyes.

His hand came to rest on my head. His thoughts fluttered like moths around a flame in my head. Disappointment, frustration. His fingers combed through my long white hair. Then words.

You must learn it.

My breath caught. He knew. He knew I ran out on my tutoring and had come to express his displeasure. This was a warning. He knew where I was and how to get to me. If I didn't want to incur his wrath, I had to learn bone magic.

I wanted nothing to do with whatever *gift* he had given me. I wanted no connection between the two of us. But what I wanted even less was this. The terror overwhelming me, his hands on me, his empty eyes watching me.

He knew that somehow. All he had to do to get me to comply was threaten to show up. Because if he had to come back, if I disappointed him, he wouldn't hesitate to return me to that black room and put me back in its white tub for however long it took to soak up my new memories,

41

maybe even remake my body again. He would turn me into a different person and release me back into the wild as many times as it took for me to obey him.

He was the one in control. He made the rules. He might have let me out into the world, but he could take me out again just as easily. If I wanted to stand a chance at having a life, it would have to include him.

I squeezed my eyes shut, the only muscular control I retained. I had no choice.

Good girl.

When I opened my eyes, that grey, cloud-diluted sunlight streamed in through my window. I lay on my bed in the morning, not on the forest floor in the dark of the night. The curtains were wide open again. I buried my face in my pillow. Tears burned my eyes. I thought I was free, safe, but he was there the whole time, watching. I couldn't escape him.

7

Seven

I couldn't bring myself to go to breakfast. I didn't want to get out of bed at all, but the Boneman already proved he didn't take kindly to truancy. I got dressed and went straight to class. The room was the same, populated by a bustle of students chatting before the day began. I sat in my back corner and stared at my desk.

Everything else faded. Was I doomed to remain tied to the Boneman for the rest of my life? Would I ever be able to sleep without fear of waking up in the forest with his fingers in my hair? After I learned bone magic, what would he demand of me next? Because surely this wasn't the end. He wanted me to learn it for a reason.

"Sylvan." A hand slid onto my shoulder, the fingers long and slender. Like *his*.

I jerked away. Nicholas sat beside me. I hadn't seen him come in and sit down.

His dark brows furrowed as he lowered his hand. "Are you ok?"

I faced forward and tucked my knees to my chest. It wasn't

easy to do with the desk attached to the chair, but I was desperate for any measure of comfort. My chin rested on my knees.

"Do you want to talk about it?" His voice was gentle, with no hint of charm, just concern. Somehow it made me feel worse. This wasn't any of his business. He didn't need to get involved.

I put my forehead against my knees, tucking my chin to my chest.

"Do you need to take the day off?"

My eyes closed.

"I want to help you."

"Please," I whispered. "Leave me alone." Whatever knight-in-shining-armor move he was trying to pull, I was in no mood for it. He couldn't defeat this dragon. No one could.

Somehow, that worked. Nicholas didn't talk to me for the rest of class. We read our books silently and filled out a worksheet. I collected my things when the bell rang and started for the door.

"Nick!" Nina exclaimed as she stepped between him and the door. "We never got a chance to talk about the menu for my party tonight. It's not too late for me to get something special if you want."

Nicholas gave her a smile that lacked its previous brightness. "I'm afraid I'll have to leave that in your capable hands. The food you usually have is fine. I've got a lot of work to do and—"

Vanessa, the brunette, cut him off with a laugh. "You work too much. Don't you know this is the time of our lives when we're supposed to have fun and goof off?"

I was already past them and nearly at the door, but I still

heard the slight hiss Nina directed at her friend. Like a dog lifting its leg, she was trying to claim Nicholas for herself.

"Sorry, I have to go," Nicholas said, more forcefully than I'd heard from him before.

The girls tried to call out to him, but he darted to my side as I made my escape. He didn't open his mouth once the whole way.

Wren only had to look at me when I sat down next to her to figure out that something was wrong. Her eyes went to Nicholas who shrugged. They had some kind of silent conversation while I stared straight ahead.

We got a minute into the lecture Professor Tilns had planned for the day before I tucked back into a ball.

Nicholas bent over to rummage around in his backpack. "Dark, milk, or white?" he whispered to me.

I frowned. *What?*

"Chocolate. What kind of chocolate do you like?"

I shrugged and set my chin on my knees. I hadn't had a chance to try any yet. Though the people in the movies the admin had given me to watch while I stayed in their care glorified it like some kind of ambrosia.

He muttered something under his breath. His hand emerged from the depths of his bag full of crinkling wrappers. I tensed when it came to rest on my desk and dumped its contents in front of me.

I leaned forward slightly. The little balls of sugar wore different colored metallic wrappings. I poked at a red one. It rolled a little.

"When I'm upset, chocolate usually cheers me up," Nicholas murmured.

Wren leaned over a bit to survey my pile. "You shouldn't

45

encourage such bad habits," she said to Nicholas. "I'm going to have to confiscate these."

She snatched a dark blue sphere and peeled it open. The covering came off with a hissing noise like a snake shedding its skin. Wren grinned as she bit into it.

"Perfection."

"Those aren't for you." Nicholas smirked as he tried to reach around me to swat at her, but she leaned away and pointed at the front of the classroom.

He followed her gaze to where Professor Tilns glanced back at the class to ask a question. Nicholas snapped back upright in his seat so fast the breeze of his movement tugged at a few strands of my hair.

The corner of my mouth twitched. I looked over the glittering trove and picked up the red one I'd played with a minute ago. I unwrapped it and popped it in my mouth. I went still as the flavor melted on my tongue. Pancakes were overrated. Chocolate was now my favorite food.

Nicholas and Wren smiled as I reached for another.

"Thank you," I whispered.

Nicholas's smile turned incandescent. "You're welcome, Sylvan."

"What was that, Mr. Ater?" Professor Tilns asked, turning around.

A faint color bloomed on Nicholas's cheeks as the rest of the class turned toward him. "Nothing. Sorry, sir."

"Nothing? Well, maybe you'd care to answer the first question in your book on page 287, then." The professor turned his watery eyes on me as Nicholas furiously searched his textbook for the right page. "I realize you're new, Ms. Ravena, but that's no excuse to be breaking school rules. No

46

food in the classroom. You can wait a couple more hours for lunch. Bring those here."

My heart stopped in my chest. All eyes focused on the chocolates still sitting on my desk, then on me. My throat constricted when I tried to swallow.

"Come on, now. I'd like to get back to my lesson." Professor Tilns waved me forward.

"Professor—" Nicholas started.

"Excellent, you can answer the question while we wait on our new student."

I slowly uncurled from my ball and stood. My hands shook while they gathered my treats. Nicholas tried to catch my eye, but I stared down at the colorful candies as I drifted like a lost ghost to the front of the room and set them on the professor's desk. Everyone's gaze burned into me as I made my way back across the black tiles speckled with white.

My dead weight fell into the chair and my knees instantly tucked back against my chest. Nicholas had finished answering his question, and Professor Tilns had gone back to lecturing the class while scribbling something on the chalkboard.

No one dared say a word for the rest of class.

I moved mechanically for the door once the bell rang.

"Sylvan." Nicholas touched my shoulder, barely more than a brush of skin against fabric, but I jumped anyway. "I'm sorry. I wasn't thinking about you getting caught with the chocolate. I should have only given you one, so he wouldn't see."

I glanced over my shoulder at the desk where Professor Tilns sat down, picked up one of my chocolates, unwrapped it, and stuffed it in his mouth.

47

"It's fine," I mumbled, turning my gaze to the floor.

Wren murmured a few words of encouragement before peeling off to go to her next class. Nicholas hovered nearby, mercifully remaining silent.

The rest of the day passed like that. He walked beside me in the halls but didn't talk anymore. I almost felt bad for him. He probably blamed himself for what happened.

I didn't speak to anyone. I did my classwork, packed up, went to my next class, unpacked, and repeated the whole thing over and over. During lunch, I escaped to the courtyard to sit in moderately comfortable silence with Wren. She tried to offer me some of the small slice of chocolate cake they served with lunch, but after what happened in class, my mind was too occupied with what happened the last time I broke the rules.

Would something like this bring the Boneman back?

* * *

I didn't have another "lesson" with Professor Tumulus until next week. So, I ended up circling back to my dorm room after classes ended. The sight that greeted me when I opened the door to the common room of the girls' dormitory building made me stop though.

Everything was clothed in vibrant blues and greens from the streamers strung between the pillars to the plastic table-cloths on the coffee tables bedecked in blue and green confetti. It was the most color I had seen since coming to the school, since as far back as I could remember really. The marine life cutouts taped to the walls and columns tied everything together.

Standing in the midst of all that with my black uniform was like dropping a rusty, old anchor on a patch of coral. Girls—Nina's friends in varying shades of blue and green—scuttled about, putting up more decorations and setting out food platters on the tables. They glanced at me as they passed, almost scowled.

I got the message loud and clear as a death knell. I wasn't wanted.

Good thing I didn't want to be involved in their party in the first place. These weren't my people. I didn't have people.

Wren was the closest thing to a friend I had, but I'd only met her yesterday. I didn't know much about her other than her bookish habits and what she thought of each of her teachers. Nicholas didn't count, either. I had no idea what to think of him or how to classify our relationship.

I climbed the two flights of stairs to my room.

Professor Tumulus leaned against the wall beside my door. My feet rooted themselves to the spot.

Had I done something wrong? Was he going to tell the Boneman that I wasn't ready to be out in the world yet? That I needed to go back to that black room with the tub full of water as white as bones? *Bones. Bones. Bones.*

"Ah, Ms. Ravena," he said warmly as he turned toward me. "I was beginning to think you wouldn't come."

My hands twisted the strap of my satchel in a white-knuckled grip. *"Where else would I go?"*

"I think we need to talk. Come with me." He waved for me to follow with a placating smile and turned toward the opposite end of the hall.

What choice did I have? I drifted after him like a ghost reluctantly trailing the Grim Reaper.

Tumulus took me down to the second-floor office where the dorm supervisor resided. She wasn't there when we entered, probably at Tumulus's request.

He closed the door behind me and gestured for me to sit in the chair on the near side of the desk. I plopped down and watched him sit opposite me. He sighed in relief as his weight left his feet.

I waited silently, fighting the urge to bolt for the door. *Stay and endure. He'll leave after he's said his peace.*

Tumulus leaned forward to rest his forearms on the desk. I sank as far back in my seat as possible. The more distance I could put between us, the better. "I feel like we got off on the wrong foot yesterday. I should have anticipated your reaction to my… decor. I'm sorry I didn't take your position into consideration."

Sure, you are.

"I'm well aware of what you went through prior to your arrival at Mortorous Academy. Being Bone Touched myself, I have a bit of experience, even though it's been a while. So, I'd like to start over if we can." He took a deep breath and smiled softly at me. "Hi, I'm Professor Tumulus. During our weekly lessons, I'm going to instruct you on how to use your Bone Magic. I'll assume it was you the Boneman was after last night."

The blood drained from my face. "How do you know about that?"

"Those who are Bone Touched always feel his presence. I can only assume he wasn't happy with your refusal to learn about the gifts he has given you."

I frowned at the desk's black wood. *"More curse than gift."*

Tumulus's scrunched brow and placating tone told me just

how much he pitied me. It made me feel even worse. "He chose you for a reason, Ms. Ravena. Whatever that reason may be, he did not put all that time and effort into turning you into who you are now just for you to run away from who you are supposed to be."

My fists clenched in my lap and I met Tumulus's gaze. "Why does *he* get to decide who I am and who I'll become?"

I never wanted him to drain my very self out of me and replace it with something that would always belong to him. I just wanted to be *me*. Even if I didn't know who that was, I wanted the space to at least figure it out before he tormented me. More.

Tumulus pursed his lips. "I know you don't want to have anything to do with him. I've been where you are. But from my experience, it's easier to accept once you start learning about it. Staying where you are right now only lets those wounds fester. You have to move on, and this is how you must do so."

I resisted the urge to argue more. It was the only way to make him stop talking. My legs tucked themselves to my chest. My gaze fixed on the desk. I was ready to escape to my room.

"The Boneman made you for a purpose, Sylvan Ravena. He gave you magic because he believes you are special. Do you understand that?"

No. "Yes."

Tumulus gave me that gentle smile, which I might have appreciated had it not followed everything he'd just said. "Good. I hope you grow to enjoy learning with me. The last student I had did."

My eyes snapped to his face. He'd had another student?

I supposed it made sense. The faculty and the Boneman arranged for me to learn with him. I should have known he would have had prior experience. And the admin who told me to keep what I was secret made it sound like there were a lot of other Bone Touched out there.

"Who else is Bone Touched like me?" Maybe they could help me get out of here.

"Like us," Tumulus corrected.

No. Tumulus may have been Bone Touched, but he was nothing like me. He worked for the Boneman. If I had somewhere else to go, I would leave this place and the Boneman and never look back.

But saying so would just make Tumulus lecture me even more.

"There are many of us all over the world, but you don't need to worry about that right now. All you need to do is focus on studying your bone magic."

My fists clenched so tight in my lap that my fingernails cut into my palms. He really wasn't going to tell me anything? One of the few pieces of information I truly wanted, and he wouldn't let me have it?

"Well, if you don't have any other concerns, I'll let you go now. I'm sure it's been a long day and you're eager to get to that party downstairs." I must have wrinkled my nose in disgust because he laughed. "I wasn't really a party person either. Whatever you end up doing, enjoy the weekend, Ms. Ravena."

I stood when Tumulus did but waited for him to walk out the door before darting into the hall, up the stairs, and to my room. I only breathed easily once the door closed firmly behind me.

52

8

Eight

I drifted in and out of sleep for several hours, waiting to open my eyes and see the trees and the Boneman towering around me.

Morning found me groggy and unwilling to get out of bed until my stomach howled its hollowness at me. At least it was Saturday. No school, no dealing with people. I could find a nice quiet spot and do whatever I wanted with my sleep-addled self. The half-open window curtains cut any chance of me staying in my room for the day to bloody ribbons. I had definitely closed them before I got in bed.

I packed my satchel with a few things and trudged down the two flights of stairs. The common room had returned to its monochrome color scheme. Bits of blue and green confetti hid under tables and chairs, the only evidence of last night's festivities. At least they had mostly cleaned up after themselves.

The cafeteria was pretty deserted. Only a handful of stragglers milled around. It meant fewer people to contend with, but also more deserted corners for things to hide in.

I wouldn't put it past the Boneman to watch me from an alcove.

The cafeteria was enormous, made for many more students than I usually saw there at one time. Plenty of individual tables hid behind low walls, meant for privacy while doing schoolwork. The dark paint made every shadow look alive. I picked the most open spot to sit, with my back against one wall, and as wide a view of the rest of the space as possible.

I struggled to place the waffles I got from the one open line in my list of favorite foods. Were they better or worse than pancakes? Maybe the same. They tasted similar. You put butter and syrup on both. The shape was the main difference.

Chocolate was still the best though. Nothing could top chocolate.

Chocolate, waffles, pancakes, I decided. The squares made a perfect guide to cut the waffles into little bite-sized pieces.

A tray glided over the table across from me. I glanced up into Wren's ocean-green eyes. They reminded me of the party decorations from last night.

"Morning," Wren said.

"Morning," I replied in a much quieter voice.

"Please don't take this the wrong way, but you look terrible."

I shoved a forkful of waffle into my mouth. "Didn't sleep well." She, on the other hand, looked great in a short sleeved turquoise blouse and pale grey shorts that made me wonder if she'd been at the party. At least her clothes had some color to them. I wished I had more to wear than my school uniforms.

"Did Nina Regine's party keep you up? I thought they were remarkably quiet this time around, but that's probably because they got in trouble the last time they were too loud. The admin came and broke it up. It was kind of funny to

54

listen to from upstairs. It just went completely silent all of a sudden." She smirked to herself. "The staff only lets her have those parties if they aren't disruptive and are chaperoned by the dorm supervisors."

Maybe she hadn't gone to the party. She didn't seem fond of them. "I had a lot on my mind." A lot of deep ceded fear.

"I hear you. It takes me a while to fall asleep sometimes too. But I'm glad I ran into you. It occurred to me yesterday after class that I don't have your number."

"My number?"

"Your phone number," Wren said. "I mean, I know we just met a couple days ago, but you seem way cooler than a lot of the other people here. And we probably both need more friends."

My head tilted slightly. I liked the idea of having a friend, of having a life outside of the Boneman.

"Soooo, what is it?" Wren prodded as she pulled out her own phone and started typing. Its forest green case reflected my image back at me. My face looked too vacant, too hollow, too haunted.

I looked down at the tiny puddles of syrup on my plate to avoid my own stare. "I don't have one."

Wren's fingers halted their tapping on the bright screen. "What do you mean? You don't have a phone?"

I shook my head.

"How do you not have a phone? What do you use to tell your parents you aren't dead and haven't blown through your bank account because you accidentally bought a bunch of new books?" That sounded incredibly specific and personal.

I didn't have *anything*. I didn't even know if my parents were still alive. Had they come looking for me after the

Boneman took me? Had they held a funeral when I didn't return? How long had it been since I'd seen them? I couldn't remember a single thing about them other than a vague feeling that I'd *had* a mother and a father before I was taken.

"Well then," Wren pushed to her feet, picking up her half-eaten breakfast. "We need to change that."

I blinked. "What?"

"We're going to get you a phone."

I stared for a long moment. "I don't have money."

"That's fine. My dad just gave me my allowance. I can get you something and you can pay me back later. Come on." She started walking off to get rid of her tray.

I looked down at my empty plate, then back at her. I *had* been thinking about how much I wanted to escape this place. My feet followed before I overthought it.

I trailed Wren as she wound behind the administration building, where a parking lot full of cars lay half-hidden in the early morning mists. The rolling hills of metal and glass shimmered with a crust of dew. My eyes darted between the rows as Wren glided to a sleek, forest-green vehicle that looked capable of cutting through the air like a knife through flesh. The car chirped a greeting when she pressed a button on a keychain.

She bowed and gestured toward the car in a grand sweeping motion. "Your carriage awaits, milady."

The corner of my mouth twisted upward. "You are too kind."

Wren giggled as she opened her door and slid in. I found a place in the brown leather seat beside hers.

"We're going to have so much fun today." Wren practically vibrated with excitement as the car purred to life.

It was like sitting in the belly of an enormous beast. Its sound rumbled through me. The crisp smells of leather and metal filled my nose. Even the smooth interior felt like the skin of an eldritch creature.

Fascinating.

"Hang on," Wren ordered and slammed her foot down.

The car lurched out of its parking space so fast, I was sure we would hit the vehicle in the row across from us. My legs braced against the floor as we spun at the last minute and hurtled down the empty, car-lined aisle. I seized the handlebar above my head and held on for dear life when we careened to a stop at the red light suspended above the entrance to the lot.

Wren glanced at me. "Sorry, was that too fast for you?" My short, sharp breaths and wide eyes must have been answer enough for her. "I'm just a bit excited. Mom put a limit on how much shopping I could do after I came home with twenty books following a trip to the bookstore this summer. But, if I'm out with you, I have an excuse. 'Philanthropy is medicine for the soul' as Dad would say. They couldn't fault me a few missing dollars if it was to help out a friend." She winked.

Friend.

The light turned green, and we sped out, not quite as fast as before, but still quick enough to keep me stiff in my seat.

"Where are we going?" I managed to ask once we hit a stretch of open road with no other cars.

"To Noxier, of course. They don't have the best tech stores, but it's the only place within twenty miles of the Academy."

Twenty miles. It was just me, the Boneman, and a school full of people I didn't know for twenty miles. I swallowed.

He won't come for me while Wren is here. He doesn't show himself to anyone he hasn't chosen.

I inhaled deeply through my nose and exhaled in a small huff from my mouth.

"What are you looking for in a phone?" Wren asked after a long moment occupied only by the empty road. "Good camera? Big storage? Small size? What?"

"I don't know." I hadn't the foggiest idea what she was talking about. I knew what each of those things separately meant, but not in relation to a phone. Weren't phones for calling people?

"That's not a big deal. Even with the limited selection they have in town, I'm sure we can find something good. It might just come down to a choice between what you want most."

What I wanted most...

I opened my mouth to ask questions, but an approaching set of buildings caught my eye. They were squat, little things all crammed so close together they blended into a single structure on either side of the small road winding between them. Their grey fronts boasted brightly painted letters labeling each set of glass double doors.

I leaned forward. My eyes devoured the colorful window displays flashing past on either side. White lights illuminated lively interiors beyond. Tiny parking lots and thin alleyways spaced out the crowded buildings in a handful of places. A bright blue truck drifted past us heading in the opposite direction.

"You look like you've never seen a town before," Wren teased.

"I didn't think so much life could exist so close to the morbid Mortorous Academy."

Wren laughed raucously. "I knew under that quiet exterior you had a sense of humor."

I had been entirely serious. It didn't make sense that such a happy little place could exist so close to the Boneman's territory. Unless this wasn't part of his territory.

I hardly dared to hope that I could escape him with just a short car ride. The last time I'd been convinced I was free, he'd shattered that illusion so fast it hardly had time to form. I shivered at the memory of two nights before.

But those were houses down that road to the left. They probably held families and children safe in their walls. Surely, the Boneman wouldn't come for me here, where so many people lived and moved.

Will he be upset that I left the Academy?

The thought gnawed at me. No one had told me I had to stay on campus. But no one had told me I had to learn bone magic until the last minute, either. I bit my lip hard.

"Hey, are you listening?" Wren shouted. I hadn't realized she was still talking.

I jumped so badly my seat belt locked into place.

Stuck. I was stuck. No, I was trapped. Like in that tub. Like on that forest floor.

The belt turned into a pair of skeleton arms, holding me tight while I drowned in my own terror. I thrashed against it, pinned to the seat where I couldn't escape, couldn't run, couldn't defend myself. The car suddenly looked too much like a tub with a lid over it. My breathing turned shallow.

"Hey, hey, calm down." Wren.

She grabbed my shoulder and pushed me back against the seat. I jerked forward against her. The seat belt gave way. I punched the release button, yanked on the door handle, and lurched out of the car like a zombie fresh from its grave.

Wren had parked in a small, deserted lot. Only two other cars populated the plain of black asphalt. I staggered out into the middle where I wasn't surrounded on all sides. My breaths came in jagged huffs. I stood on shaking legs for a long moment while my heart raced like a deer fleeing a forest fire.

Eventually, my breathing evened out and my heartbeat slowed. My fingers trembled as I straightened and dragged them through my hair. I wasn't in that room anymore. The Boneman wasn't here right now. I didn't have to worry about any of that. I was here with my friend, who would keep the nightmares away because she hadn't been touched by them.

Friend. Friend. Friend.

I took one more deep breath and turned around to face Wren. She stood with the driver's side door half open around her like she was ready to jump in and drive away. Her eyes were so wide I thought they might roll out of her head.

I opened my mouth, searched for some plausible explanation, and found none. I settled on a soft *sorry*. I'd had a friend for maybe a day, and I'd already scared her off.

"No!" Wren held up both hands. "You don't have to apologize."

"I scared you."

"Only because I didn't know what to do. I thought you might… I don't know. I wanted to help, but I didn't know if me helping would make it worse." Her voice dropped off into a mumble at the end. She glanced at the ground.

"You did fine. Before I came to the school—" *How do I tell you what happened without telling you what happened?*

"You don't have to explain if you don't want to. It's not

60

anyone's business but your own. Not if whatever *it* is caused *that*." She gestured vaguely at me.

My shoulders sagged with relief. She understood. "Thank you."

Wren offered a tentative smile. "Do you still want to go get a phone?"

I nodded.

* * *

The store Wren led me to was small with an open floor plan and thin tables displaying phones and tablets and other things that glowed and made soft little noises. I stood and stared at a device slightly bigger than my hand for a long time, picking it up and looking at it, prodding it with a finger. The cable connecting it to its stand was annoying, but I had a feeling that if I asked Wren about it, she would laugh at me for not knowing its purpose.

"Seeing anything you like?" a young man in a dark blue shirt and khaki pants asked. "Do you need any help?"

My gaze shifted to him, and he visibly jumped. I tilted my head at his strange reaction.

"Sorry," he chuckled. "It's just your eyes…"

He leaned forward to get a better look. His rich brown eyes, the color of a hanging tree, speared into mine. I put the phone down and took a step back.

The man held up both hands in surrender. "I don't mean any offense. They're nice. Were you interested in this model?"

I glanced at it. It would probably work as well as any other phone here. I couldn't see a difference between it and the others besides the dimensions. So, I nodded.

"It's a good choice, lightweight, small, and a surprising amount of storage for its size. It's an older model though, so if you're interested in what's new, there are a few different options over here." He gestured for me to follow.

Wren examined a large tablet and spoke to a woman in the same uniform as the man on the other side of the store. It would probably be best not to disturb her. Besides, who better to explain the products than an employee? I didn't know what to look for, but maybe he could help me figure it out.

I drifted after him and let him drone on about the different brands and their advantages and disadvantages. He reminded me of Wren. Talking but not expecting me to respond. It was nice.

"So, what do you think?" he finally asked, looking for an answer this time.

He'd laid out so many choices. It wasn't like picking which line to get food from at mealtimes where there were only a few alternatives. I had no idea why Wren thought this store wouldn't have a good selection. There were plenty of options here for me.

"There's no rush," the man—he'd introduced himself as Mallor—assured me. "Take all the time you need. Picking out the right device is an important decision that shouldn't be made hastily—"

"This one." I picked one up, tiny compared to some of the others, but that's why I liked it. It wasn't flashy. It didn't take up too much space. It flew under the radar the way I wanted to.

Mallor smiled. If my contradiction and interruption

bothered him, he didn't show it. "Excellent, I like that you're decisive. I'll walk you through getting it set up real quick. Then we can get payment out of the way, and you'll be ready to go."

Getting everything right with the phone proved easy since I didn't have to transfer any information from a previous device. Wren stood on her tiptoes to peer over my shoulder for the last half of it.

"That's a cute one. You should pick out a case while we're here."

"Case?"

"So, it's protected if you drop it."

"We have a decent selection." Mallor gestured to a wall of colorful, phone-sized rectangles entombed in coffins of plastic and cardboard.

"If you ladies are from Mortorous Academy, I suggest our bone collection." The woman who had helped Wren indicated a series of black and white cases with skulls and bones and little cartoon images of the Boneman on them. "Very popular among the students when they come into town."

My jaw clenched. Wasn't it bad enough that he haunted my dreams? Did he have to be attached to my phone too?

I snatched a case with a multicolored mandala pattern, as much of an opposite to the black and white of the school as possible.

Behind me, Mallor laughed. "Looks like your sales charm is wearing off, Rachel."

Rachel rolled her eyes at him before turning back to me. "Why don't I get you checked out?"

A few minutes later, Wren and I walked out with a bag of

accessories and manuals for my phone.

"Let me see it." Wren extended a hand for my phone. "I'll put my number in."

I fished it out of my bag and watched her fiddle with it.

"Come here." She swung the screen around, so it reflected both our faces and snapped a picture. "And there you go."

She returned my phone. 'Best Friend Ever' captioned a picture of the two of us as her contact name. Wren grinned widely in the image while I hovered behind her like a phantom with a mildly surprised expression on my face. It looked ridiculous. A half-smile curled one corner of my mouth up.

"Thank you," I told Wren as I slipped my phone into my pocket.

She waved a dismissive hand. "Don't mention it. I can't have my only school friend be unreachable. Someone has to make sure you can get help if you get lost in the forest or something."

My jaw clenched. "I won't get lost." The forest was *his* domain. I wouldn't be caught dead going in there voluntarily, much less losing myself in it.

"I'm not saying you would," Wren rushed to amend. "I was just joking. I'm sure you have a great sense of direction. Just… if you ever need help on homework or want to talk to someone. I mean, I know you don't like to talk much, but texting is different. You might like it. And now you have the option."

I liked having options. I also liked the idea of help only being as far away as my phone. Maybe it would deter the Boneman, or I could call for someone to save me from him if he came back for me—if I could move enough to do so. It was my best, my *first* weapon against him.

"So, where should we go next?" Wren eyed the storefronts as we passed.

"Next?" I thought we were going back to the Academy now that we got what we came for.

"We're in town, and it's a Saturday. We might as well poke around, do some window shopping." She halted in front of a window populated by plastic mannequins in a variety of orange, black, and yellow outfits. "I don't suppose you have any clothes besides your uniforms."

"No." The staff only gave me uniforms.

Wren's crazy, ear-to-ear grin might have sent me running if I didn't know her. "We *have* to get you a new wardrobe. Come on."

She darted into the store before I could say a word. I sighed in amused exasperation and followed her in. It might be nice to get some clothes that didn't label me as the property of Mortorous Academy. Having more than one choice of outfit was yet another chance to find freedom.

Besides, Wren was my ride. It wasn't like I could leave without her.

Wren clearly knew what she was doing. She herded me through a labyrinth of metal racks boasting more clothes than they could hold. Wren plucked out pieces, seemingly at random, and tossed them into my arms. I could barely see over the top of the pile by the time she nudged me into a dressing room stall.

"You have to come out and show me everything," she insisted from the other side of the door.

I surveyed the small mountain of clothes Wren had gathered. We would be here a long time if she was going to make me try all of this on. I weeded out anything that had large amounts of white or black. The size of the pile looked much more manageable after that.

A few hours later, laden with shopping bags heavier than a casket, we trudged back to the little parking lot where Wren's car waited.

"You looked fantastic in everything, but if you ask me, red is one hundred percent your color," Wren chattered. "The subtle kind, though, almost orangey. Makes you look like a cloudy sunset."

I gave a light snort. She had gushed over a red and orange tie-dye tank top and insisted on going to find more clothes with a similar color scheme. It extended my internment in the fitting rooms by at least half an hour. But I became rather fond of the look too.

"I'm serious. I mean, you're gorgeous to begin with, even when you're not wearing those kinds of warm colors." She waved an arm decorated with bags. "You should take advantage of that kind of thing."

My lips pressed together. My looks weren't high on my list of priorities—especially when they weren't the ones I had been born with. Did I retain *any* of my original features? Did I look anything like either of my parents, wherever they might be now?

"If you did, I bet you could—" Wren stopped when I whirled around and looked back down the sidewalk behind us. "What?"

I stared hard, eyes darting from buildings to roofs to windows. Nothing more than a few birds perched on store signs and other shoppers milling around. I frowned.

"Sylvan, what is it?"

I felt something. But there was… "Nothing." I shook off the sensation.

Wren shrugged and we started talking again. I only half-listened to her continued chatter. I focused more on my surroundings, ears straining, eyes scanning.

And…*there.* A tickling at the back of my mind like a whisper of wind through a freshly opened tomb. I glanced over my shoulder again, more subtly this time. I could have sworn I saw a shadowy figure following us a moment before it darted into a tiny alley.

Not the Boneman. It was too small and quick. I'd only ever seen the Boneman move in long, deliberate strides like he had all the time in the world. And this was too public for him.

Who else would follow me?

Nicholas had been persistent in his efforts to engage me, but he didn't seem like the kind of person who would resort to stalking. He just wanted attention. Nina and her friends were a bunch of bullies but only offered underhanded insults.

I faced forward again, no longer listening to Wren at all as we entered the parking lot. Wren unlocked the car and tossed her bags into the back seat. I followed suit.

"*Terror touched.*" The whisper was so quiet I almost didn't hear it.

All my attention went to the low wall surrounding the lot. *Where are you?*

"Hey!" I jumped half out of my skin when Wren poked me in the arm. "I asked you if you wanted to get lunch while we're out."

"Sorry," I muttered, turning back to scan the wall again.

She followed my gaze. "What are you looking at?"

I shook my head, that feeling still wriggling at the edge of my perception. *Just get in the car and drive away.*

"I think we should go." Whoever was following us couldn't have good intentions.

"What is a disciple of death doing so far from its nest?"

I leaped away from the trunk. The voice was louder, and it came from the front of the car.

"What?" Wren demanded. "You're acting weird. Not your normal weird. Like scary weird."

"Did you hear that?" I breathed.

"Hear what?" She slammed the trunk closed. But her hands were shaking. She caught me looking and shoved them in her pockets. "You're making me nervous."

"You feel it too." I realized.

"Feel what?"

"Harbinger of endings."

My head snapped around. There it stood. A boy, perhaps my age—whatever age that was supposed to be. Long, stringy brown hair hung in his eyes, concealing them from view. He wore a plaid button-up shirt and light-wash jeans. He just stood there, near the back of the car parked next to ours, watching.

"What do you want?" I whispered.

Wren practically stomped her foot. "What do you think? I want to go back to the Academy and for you to stop acting like you've lost it."

"Not you." I nodded at the boy. "Him."

She looked around. "Who are you talking about?"

How could she ask that? He was in plain sight—

My eyes widened. She couldn't see him. And if she couldn't see him...

The boy cocked his head to the side, hair shifting over his face. *"You don't know, little Bone Touched. You don't know."*

"Get in the car," I ordered Wren in the calmest voice I could manage.

"Sylvan, what do you see?" She gripped my arm, hands like vices around my slender bones. *Bones. Bones. Bones.*

"Car. Now." The same steel from when I refused Professor Tumulus hardened my tone.

She obeyed that time, jumping in and shutting the door on me and the boy. I would have to get closer to him to get to my door. I inhaled slowly like I had when I'd lived in that tub. And stepped forward.

The boy smiled.

I took another step.

And he lunged.

His hair parted to reveal wholly black eyes. Not black irises like Nicholas's. These had no whites. His body turned translucent around the edges as if he was starting to fade away. I dove out of his path, skinning my palms on the asphalt as I tumbled.

He slammed into the car. Wren screamed from inside as the vehicle shook. But his focus stayed on me.

"You have so much life inside you. Give it to me!" He shrieked and leaped forward.

My arms went up to shield myself a moment before something hurtled over my head and collided with the boy. He went down. It only took him a moment to shoot up and let out a keening cry, ripping at a band of white around his upper arm that hadn't been there before. I stared as he writhed and tugged, completely forgetting me.

"I'll take it from here." A figure in a black sweatshirt with the hood pulled low and a pair of familiar khaki pants stepped around me from behind. "You get your friend back to school."

He glanced down at me, and I stared into the face of Mallor, the phone salesman.

"Don't worry. I've handled worse than him. But you need to leave now. You're not trained to handle this kind of threat."

I frowned at him. In response to my unspoken question, he pulled down the collar of his sweatshirt to expose three black lines that looked like human finger bones pressed into the skin below the left side of his collarbone.

The mark of the Bone Touched.

I put a hand over the same spot on my own chest where an identical mark marred my otherwise unblemished skin.

"Go." Mallor jerked his chin at Wren's car.

I scrambled up and raced for the passenger door. Wren didn't need to be told to drive. I didn't mind how fast we swerved out of the parking lot that time.

"What the *hell* was that?" she shouted as we rocketed down the street at illegal speeds.

"Ghost," I breathed. "I think."

* * *

We didn't speak for the entire ride back to the Academy. We were too busy monitoring the trees on either side of the road as if they might leap into our path.

The jitters only faded once we got inside the girls' dorm. A handful of people sat on the couches, talking, or reading, or doing homework. No ghosts. No Boneman. Just normal people.

I'd managed to fit all my bags of clothes on my arms, so I

could take everything to my room at once. But Wren paused on the second-floor landing.

"If you want, you can come to my room." Her voice was soft, a little shaky. "I mean that was pretty freaky."

It had been. A ghost *attacked* me. I wanted time to myself, though, to sort through everything I'd seen. My hesitation must have been answer enough for Wren.

"It's ok. You probably need to go wash all of that." She gestured to my load.

"Thank you, Wren." *For the clothes, for the phone, for understanding.*

"No problem. Don't be surprised if I have to call you to the witness stand once my parents see the credit card bill though." Her smile didn't quite reach her eyes.

I nodded.

"If you can't sleep tonight after all… that, I'm in room 216. My roommate usually goes home on the weekend, so you wouldn't be bothering anyone."

"Thanks."

"See you on Monday, I guess." She chewed her lip and turned away. I hoped she wasn't too shaken up.

My footsteps thunked on the wooden stairs like a corpse knocking on the inside of a closed coffin. My room was just how I'd left it, bed rumpled, curtains half open. I heaved my clothes onto the floor in a pile.

One rumble from my stomach was enough to drive me back to the cafeteria where lunch was being served. A handful of Nina's friends slumped at a table, looking like they hadn't slept at all the night before.

I almost sympathized with them. After my ghostly encounter, I was more than ready for some rest.

The drowsy spells hadn't quite left me alone. My dead weight fell into bed, and I was out before I had the chance to worry about my still-open curtains.

9

Nine

I didn't leave my room much the next day. The curtains fully covered the windows when I shuddered awake from another dream of the Boneman's torture tub in which he'd sat there at the edge, hovering over me. His massive shadow floated in the water while I lay paralyzed.

I didn't know what to think of the sudden privacy he allowed me, maybe he thought the ghost from the day before scared me enough. But the curtains stayed closed for the rest of the day, even when I left to get food from the cafeteria. So, I stayed and clipped all the tags off my new clothes, leaving briefly to throw loads of them into the laundry down the hall.

It was a nice, quiet day.

Monday brought back the noise of school.

Students' voices echoed in Dr. Shalm's classroom louder than they would in a set of stone catacombs. Nina's pack clustered in one corner, making the majority of the noise. Little groups interspersed between the desks contributed their fair share, though.

My desk swallowed me like quicksand. I tucked one leg up and pulled out the weekend's homework. I had plenty of time to take care of everything yesterday. It hadn't been as difficult as I'd feared to start in the middle of the year. The Boneman seemed to have only taken my memories, not any of my knowledge.

One less thing for you to worry about. Ghosts and the Boneman are more than enough.

I started doodling on the back of my homework.

The thump of Nicholas falling into his seat alerted me to his presence. He sighed and raked his fingers through his hair.

Please don't talk to me. Please don't talk to me.

"Good morning, Sylvan," his voice was soft as a ghost's whisper.

No. Not ghosts. No more ghosts. At least he was being quiet.

"Mm," I replied, one eye on my paper, the other on him.

"You're looking better today. Enjoy your weekend?"

"Mm." *If you can look past getting attacked by a spirit and meeting another Bone Touched.* I needed to find a way to speak to Mallor again. He might have answers, or better yet, a way to escape.

"Is that position actually comfortable? It seems like you're always curling up."

He grunted as he swung his leg up into his seat in an imitation of my pose. I paused my drawing to watch him struggle. He was by no means overweight, but he didn't have my slender figure either. The finished product appeared more than a little awkward. He had to hunch over a bit to fit between the back of the chair and the desk.

"I don't get it," he declared.

I snorted lightly, my face softening. I had to put a hand over my mouth when he almost fell out of his seat in his attempt to unwedge himself from behind the desk.

Nicholas was laughing too by the time he righted himself but stopped when he glanced at my drawing.

"Sylvan, how did you know Lucas?"

I blinked. "Who?"

He pointed at my paper. "Even if you weren't so good at drawing, I would recognize him anywhere. He was in this class. Used to sit where I'm sitting now. Really nice guy…" He trailed off.

"Used to?"

Nicholas looked away. "He was a bit of a party boy. He went into town one Saturday night about a month ago and got drunk at the bar. On his way back to the Academy, he stepped into the road. The officers said he died the instant the car hit him, and he didn't feel any pain." He cleared his throat and turned fully away from me before whispering. "*Really* nice guy."

I swallowed the lump in my throat and looked down at the paper, where I had drawn a remarkable likeness of the ghost boy who had attacked me and Wren on Saturday.

My eraser was moving across the image before I realized it was in my hand.

Nicholas was uncharacteristically quiet during the walk to history class. It felt more like a funeral procession.

Wren smiled when I sat down. "Did you get all your new stuff washed?"

I nodded. I'd filled the extra hangers we bought to hold my new wardrobe. They made a stark contrast beside the devouring black of my school uniforms.

"Good, I can't wait to see you in them. I think you should wear the red top next weekend, and we can go back into town again. My birthday is on Saturday, and my parents are busy until next Friday, so they're sending me extra money as an apology. I would *love* to take you to a bookstore."

I wasn't particularly keen on the idea of going back into town after encountering Lucas. But maybe I could use the opportunity to find Mallor. I had questions than a cemetery had bodies.

"You went into town?"

I glanced at Nicholas. He stared hard at me with those eyes darker than an empty grave.

"We had to. Sylvan didn't have a phone," Wren answered. "How else was I supposed to contact her?"

"Did you… enjoy your trip?" he asked me, hardly looking at Wren.

"Mostly." My eyes found my desk and stayed there. I wasn't in the mood for an interrogation.

Wren glanced between the two of us. I would have to ask her at lunch what she divined from this strange interaction. I certainly didn't know what to think of the sudden intensity in Nicholas's gaze. "It started out good, but something strange happened when we were leaving."

"You saw Lucas."

Both knees huddled close to my chest. My chin rested on them.

Wren recoiled like she'd been struck. "Lucas Penumbra?" Her focus shot to me. "That would make sense actually. Sylvan said it was a ghost. Do you really think it was him?"

"She was drawing him before English and as far as I know, they've never met."

76

I hated that they both stared at me like I was a cadaver they would carve open to discover what secrets it might hold.

Please let class start. Please let class start.

I didn't care for Professor Tilns after what happened on Friday, but at least he was strict enough to not tolerate talking during a lecture.

"Sylvan." Nicholas put a hand on my desk. I cringed away from it despite his gentle tone. "What happened with Lucas?"

"Nothing fun." I didn't want to talk about this. Not with him.

I wanted to put it as far from my mind as possible. Just like the Boneman. If I could push it down far enough, I could forget all about it. And then I would be ok. I could be happy. The faint scabs on the heels of my hands from skinning them in the parking lot ached from how tightly I gripped my legs.

"It's ok if you don't want to talk about it," Wren murmured, shooting Nicholas a look that had him retracting his hand from my desk. "It was terrifying for me in the car when I couldn't see him. I can't imagine what it was like for you having to face him."

My breath stuttered in and out as I raised my face enough to see Professor Tilns walk in. End of conversation. At least, I thought it was until Tuesday afternoon.

I had gym right after lunch. Nicholas had to branch off to go to the boys' locker room, so I had the last minute or so to myself before I plunged into the girls' locker room. None of the others paid me much attention as I made for the nearest bathroom stall.

Aside from modesty, I couldn't change in front of others when it risked exposing that mark on my chest. They might write it off as a tattoo, but if the students here took the

Boneman legend as seriously as it sounded like they did, I wasn't taking any chances.

Nicholas had said people went looking for the Boneman to raise their social status, but what if it slipped out that I was what they longed to be? What if someone believed them and took me away? What if I spent my life as a test subject or a weapon?

Even if it didn't get that far, I wasn't particularly interested in advertising my Bone Touched status. The memories were enough of a burden. I didn't need anyone else treating me like a specimen in a jar.

At lunch the previous day, Wren taught me how to braid my hair. It kept everything out of the way much better than a plain ponytail. And seeing as this was the first day I would wear my gym clothes and participate, it would be essential. The last three days, the coaches had let me sit in the bleachers and watch since, they had to order a gym uniform for me.

So, I sat in the stall and braided my hair before pulling on the grey shorts and shirt that both had the Mortorous Academy logo stamped on them. I rubbed at that three-fingered mark on my chest once it was hidden by my clothing.

There was someone else, someone nearby, who also bore that mark, who knew what had happened to me because they'd been through it too. Someone who wasn't actively trying to make me bend to the Boneman's will.

I took up a place at the top of the bleachers to wait for the rest of the class. Nicholas trotted out of the boys' locker room, spotted me, and climbed up to sit beside me. I had my legs crossed but folded them up and away when he slid down beside me.

"Your hair looks nice in a braid," he said.

"Thanks," I waited for the coach to tell us to get up and start performing the warmups I'd seen the others do.

Back then, Nicholas had kept busy with whatever sport they had us doing. He had no time to bother me. I had a feeling that would change now that I had to participate alongside him.

"I don't mean to pry or anything…"

Yes, you do.

"But when you saw Lucas, Wren made it sound like she couldn't see him, but clearly *you* did."

Get to the point, please.

"Did anyone else see him? Anyone who recognized him for what he was, I mean."

I shrugged. "Maybe." I wasn't going to tell him about Mallor. I didn't know if there was any kind of code between the Bone Touched, but this seemed like the kind of thing I should keep to myself.

"How did you get away from him? Wren made it sound like he was attacking you."

I didn't remember Wren saying anything like that, but maybe they talked after class.

I turned and met his black gaze with my icy white one. "I just jumped in Wren's car, and we drove away."

Nicholas sighed. "I'm glad you're ok. It would suck if my friend got hurt by my other, dead friend."

"You have plenty more. Everyone's your friend." He had so many friends. Who knew how he kept them all straight.

"Everyone except you?"

My lips pressed together.

"That's what you're thinking, right?" He slumped back against the wall. "Is there a reason you don't like me? Did I do something wrong?"

I chewed the inside of my cheek, looking away. I couldn't tell him that my issues with him had just as much to do with things that were completely out of his control as things that were. Everyone else seemed to love him and hang off his every word. Maybe it was something wrong with me, something the Boneman broke along with my bones.

Bones. Bones. Bones.

"If I did, will you please tell me?"

"Why do you care?" I asked. *Why does this matter so much to you? You don't know me.*

"Because I was the new kid once." I glanced at him out of the corner of my eye. "I know how hard it is to move to a school where you don't know anyone. It took me a while to build up to the person I am today. That was without help from anyone else. So, I guess I want to help you the way no one ever helped me."

Help. Friend.

I had Wren. Wasn't that enough? Did I need Nicholas to sweep me into a world of drama and shallow friendships with dozens of people? Definitely not. Not when they could never know the truth. Keeping it from one person was enough.

There was Mallor. He was Bone Touched too.

Tumulus just wanted me to learn bone magic and do what the Boneman wanted, but maybe Mallor was different.

One of the coaches blew a whistle and shouted for everyone to start jogging laps around the gym. I stood. I didn't want to be associated with the kind of person Nicholas was, always around people, always talking, always giving everything of himself to them, just like he was trying to do with me. It was enough work to take care of myself.

"I'm fine on my own," I told him and climbed down to join our other classmates on the finely polished dark wood floor.

10

Ten

When Thursday rolled around, I found myself outside the door to Professor Tumulus's classroom. I had to stand there for a few minutes to psych myself up. Last time I'd set foot in that room, I passed out after seeing all the bones in the rafters. Losing consciousness had been humiliating enough but doing it in front of a stranger in a strange space didn't sit right with me. It reminded me too much of the times when I was at the Boneman's mercy, unable to move or fight back if something happened to me.

It wasn't an experience I was eager to repeat.

Tumulus had seemed understanding enough about my fainting spell last week. Hopefully, he would have the bones covered.

After several deep breaths, I worked up the courage to open the door. Professor Tumulus looked up from the long counter in the front of the room where he was jotting down some notes. But my eyes skipped over him and went straight up.

A black tarp hung below the rafters from a series of ropes messier than a cobweb. My heartbeat steadied. At least there was a barrier between me and all the bones lurking up there.

Satisfied, I focused on Professor Tumulus.

He smiled. "Ah, Ms. Ravena. Good to see you again."

I stopped at the edge of the counter and planted my hands on it. "I have questions."

"Oh, I'm sure you do. I will do what I can to calm your curiosity."

I rallied my courage. "I saw a ghost."

"Ah, yes." Professor Tumulus nodded gravely. "I heard."

My brow furrowed. *"From who?"*

"Mallor contacted me a few days ago. He's a former student." Tumulus scratched at his cheek. "I believe his exact words were 'what were you thinking letting her out of the school before she's dry'."

"Dry?"

"It's slang referring to the time you spent in the tub. You're considered 'wet' when you don't know how to use your powers to defend yourself. Dry is what we call those who *have* learned and are living out in the world."

Terrific. Even the language here revolved around the Boneman. But even more worrying…

What were you thinking letting her out of the school?

"I'm not supposed to leave?" No one had told me. The Boneman hadn't come to scare me into staying on campus in the handful of nights since the incident. The admin hadn't mentioned it. Maybe they assumed that I wouldn't have the means to leave since I didn't have a car or know how to drive and walking all the way to town wasn't realistic. But if this was the case, someone still should have told me.

Tumulus winced as if he knew how I would react to being confined to school grounds. "Not unless you have an experienced Bone Touched with you. It would keep things like what happened on Saturday from occurring again. And if they still did, you would have someone to protect you."

No more shopping trips with Wren, then. No more escaping into that world of color and life. No more freedom. And Mallor had turned me in, taken that away from me.

"You see, the Boneman uses his magic to protect this campus and the immediate area from ghost attacks so that young Bone Touched have a safe place to live and learn. If you travel outside the border of his protection, you risk a ghost sensing your magic and attacking you to get it."

"What would a ghost do with my magic?" If they wanted it, they could have it. I had no interest in using it.

"Your magic is tied to your life force. It keeps you alive. Ghosts sense that and think if they take it, they can live again. Unfortunately for them, it doesn't work that way. Bone Touched magic resides in the marrow of our bones. It can't sustain life outside of the confines of a bone. And since ghosts have no bodies, consuming our magic only makes them stronger, harder to contain, and more deadly. It can drive them mad. As I'm sure you can imagine, it's not pleasant for the Bone Touched either, having their bodies ripped apart and their marrow drunk from inside their bones, sometimes while they're still alive—"

"I get it." I didn't need that imagery. "Ghosts are bad and only the school keeps me safe from them." No matter how much I might hate being stuck here.

Tumulus nodded. "Yes, if it's an emergency, you can let me know and I'll coordinate with Mallor to take you into town.

He's our guard, so to speak. He keeps an eye on the town and stays on hand if he's needed at the school."

Going out with a friend for fun probably didn't count as an emergency.

He leaned forward. "I know it's not ideal, but believe it or not, the Boneman cares about you, and wants you to be safe."

My hands twisted in my lap. If he cared, he never would have taken me in the first place. Destroying me, mentally and physically, wasn't conducive to my safety. He only wanted to make sure all the work he put into remaking me didn't go to waste.

Tumulus reached across the table to set a hand in front of me, the closest to touching me he could get without actually doing so. I eyed his wrinkled fingers distrustfully. "He genuinely wants you to be happy, but you have to follow his guidelines."

My hand curled into a fist. If the Boneman wanted me to be happy, he never would have taken me. I would have a family and a normal life, completely oblivious to the world of the Bone Touched. I would give anything to only have the problems of the high schoolers in those movies the admin showed me during my early days at Mortorous.

"You aren't very good at this," I muttered.

Tumulus laughed and withdrew his hand. "That's not the first time I've heard that, and it probably won't be the last. But we have more important things to discuss. You saw the ghost."

Yes.

"Mallor has been after that ghost ever since it first appeared a couple weeks ago. He should have had it contained long before you even arrived at the Academy, but the spirits of the

85

young are always slippery. I'm sorry you had to deal with it at all. Usually, ghosts don't come near the school or Noxier, but when someone dies in the area, it's hard to avoid."

Like me, Lucas probably didn't have anywhere else to go.

"I should give you the background that I would have given you if you hadn't run away last week. Honestly, I've been trying to track you down for a couple days, but…" He waved a hand around. "Everyone seems to need my attention."

He stared hard at me. I stared right back. I wasn't sorry for leaving, just sorry I didn't have a choice about coming back. If it weren't for the Boneman holding my leash, I never would have returned.

"Souls are supposed to move on once their bodies die. But in some cases, they don't. The Boneman is the god of death. In the beginning, he would hunt these rogue ghosts down and take them to the afterlife himself. But as the world's population grew, so too did the number of restless dead. That's where the Bone Touched come in.

"You see, in order to keep these spirits from wreaking havoc in the realm of the living, the Boneman needed some help. So, he took a man and imbued him with death magic. This first Bone Touched learned how to use his new abilities and joined the Boneman in his crusade against ghosts.

"Over time, more and more Bone Touched were created and joined our ranks. We are spread across the globe, living anywhere people live and subsequently die. You, Ms. Ravena, are the newest and, as the younger generation says, the wettest of our number. After you master your magic, you will be posted somewhere in the world to watch for ghosts and continue to keep the living and the dead where they each belong."

Tumulus sat back in his chair, looking satisfied with his little tale. I continued to watch him silently.

The Boneman was a god? And this was what he enslaved and tortured me for? If I didn't know it would bring the Boneman knocking, I would have gotten up and walked out. I didn't care about ghosts being in the world of the living. No one should be forced to endure what I had and then be put to work battling the supernatural just because some "god" couldn't keep up with his workload.

"Any questions?" Tumulus prodded once the silence became too much for him.

"Why me?" He could have taken anyone. There are probably plenty of weirdos who would love to do this sort of thing. Why did he pick the person least likely to obey him?

Tumulus heaved a sigh. "That is one of the few questions that I don't have a definitive answer to. Who becomes Bone Touched is entirely up to the Boneman. All I can tell you is that the Boneman saw something in you that convinced him you could not only do this job but do it well. Something that told him you should be one of us."

"What was it?" What could the Boneman have possibly seen that made him think it was a good idea to do what he did to me?

Tumulus chuckled. "I don't know. You'd have to ask the Boneman."

I shuddered. That was absolutely *not* an option.

Tumulus clapped his hands and straightened. "Now, if you're done asking unanswerable questions, we can begin, then. Take a seat at one of the tables."

I sat as he shuffled to one of the shelves lining the wall. *Begin what?*

When he returned, he held out a tiny white bone to me. I stiffened.

"It's not going to hurt you." Professor Tumulus smiled softly. "Come on now."

I scowled at the tiny thing. These lessons were going to be torture if Tumulus forced me to interact with bones. I reached out and took it. The bone couldn't have been from anything large. A bird or a rodent of some kind. My skin itched where it rested in my palm. I hated it.

"Now I want you to close your eyes and tell me what you see."

I raised my eyebrows at him. He wanted me to *close my eyes* while I held this ominous object? Did he remember how I fainted after seeing so many of them above us?

"I know how it sounds but you'll understand in a moment. Close your eyes."

I obeyed, clenching the bone in my fist so it wouldn't jump out of my hand while I wasn't looking. There was just darkness on the inside of my eyelids. It was nice and quiet, but I didn't *see* anything.

I shook my head. "There's nothing."

"Think about the bone. Where has it been? What did it do? Who did it belong to?" Professor Tumulus coaxed. "Don't think about it too hard. Let the answers come to you."

I sighed. *Let the answers come to you.* Yes, very helpful. Not cryptic at all.

I sat quietly with my eyes closed for so long, I thought I'd drifted off into a dream when the haze of an image swam into my mind. In the vision, I looked through a set of bars, painted red as spilled blood, into this very room. There were fewer jars on the shelves and no tarp covering the bones hanging from the ceiling, but it was the same place.

My eyes flew open. "It was here," I breathed. "Behind red bars."

Professor Tumulus grinned, the wrinkles around his mouth and eyes pulling tight. "Very good. What you saw was correct. This is the leg bone of a pet rat I had about ten years ago. His cage was painted red, and he sat right over there." He indicated a shelf to my left. I practically threw the bone onto the table. It had belonged to his *pet*. Gross. "Very well done, Ms. Ravena. The last student I had took an hour to see anything."

I heaved a relieved breath. Then the Boneman should let me sleep easily tonight.

Tumulus wasn't finished with me though. "Shall we try again and see what else you can find?"

I cringed at the bone lying on the table. Knowing where it had come from made touching it worse, like I was intruding on the little rodent's life, even though it was only an animal and not even alive anymore.

"Just one more attempt, and then you can go," the professor promised.

He *might come if you don't*. Chills raced down my back like mice in a mausoleum. I sighed and reached for the bone.

The lesson left my head spinning. By the end of an hour, I only managed to see more of the same picture from before. Sometimes things were slightly different— items on the shelves moved, more bones hung from the ceiling, students sat at the tables—but it was always that same view.

"I think that's enough for today." Professor Tumulus reached for his dead rat's leg.

I jerked it away. I hadn't seen anything new. Our deal

had been one more vision, and I hadn't delivered. If I hadn't progressed then—

"If you're concerned about the Boneman, I can assure you, he will be as proud of your progress as I am. You've done well and you need to rest now before you exhaust yourself and collapse again. I can tell you for a fact that the Boneman doesn't want that. Please, go back to your room, eat, rest, and be ready for next week."

"It's not enough." It couldn't be. I'd barely done anything at all.

"If it would make you feel better, I can package up a different bone for you to practice with until next week." He offered.

I nodded. The Boneman couldn't be mad at me if I was actively trying to improve outside of lessons. Even if I didn't really want to.

Tumulus shuffled away and came back with a small box. "See what you can do with this." He handed it to me.

I gave him the other bone, followed him to the door, and left him standing in the doorway, watching me walk away down the hall.

I only took enough time to go eat dinner before heading back to my room. One of the curtains was open when I set my satchel down in the desk chair. I should have been used to them moving on their own and left it alone by now, but I still marched across the room and closed it. I wanted to have this one space where I didn't have to be afraid of the Boneman watching me. Was that too much to ask?

I sat at my desk and opened the little box Professor Tumulus gave me. Inside, wrapped in a little square of red fabric, sat a skull a little bigger than my palm. It had to be from some kind of rodent, judging by the teeth that only grew in the front of its mouth.

My mouth went dry at the sight of it. Its empty eye sockets seemed to stare up at me. Just like another eyeless skull I was all too familiar with. I shut the little box with a snap and pushed it to the furthest corner of my desk.

I rubbed my hands over my face as I got up. *Why did I think I could do this?*

I wriggled out of my uniform and into the soft, black tank top and shorts I had for sleeping. The darkness swirled around me as I settled into bed.

What if it hadn't been enough? What if I woke up in the forest again with those empty eye sockets staring at me through the trees? The Boneman didn't seem like the kind of creature that believed it was the thought that counted.

My chest shook when I inhaled. I couldn't do this if he kept turning up. Tears leaked from the corner of my eye as I stared into the black of my room.

Ghosts, and the dead, and bones, bones, bones.

A small sob escaped from me like a grave robber fleeing from the scene of his crime. My face turned into my pillow to quiet my crying.

This was too big for me. No one would help. No one would free me from the Boneman. Tumulus treated me well enough, but he was pulling me deeper in. Mallor, who I had thought might be an ally after he saved my life, immediately ratted me out to Tumulus.

There weren't any other Bone Touched that I knew of, and I doubted the two I *did* know would tell me where I could find others. I couldn't talk to Wren, because she wasn't one of us. And the admin only wanted me to pretend everything was normal.

So, that was it. I was alone.

But maybe I didn't have to be.

When Wren got me a phone, she showed me how to use it to access the internet, which according to her had the answer to any question you could possibly ask. Would it know where my family might be?

There was only one way to find out. I reached for my phone.

11

Eleven

I lost count of the number of times he had come into my little room and rearranged my bones, shattering them one fracture at a time and molding them into new shapes. My body didn't feel like it had when I recalled first laying in the tub of white liquid. It was longer, thinner, more delicate, as if he had made me into a skeleton just like him. The sides of the tub still didn't touch me but from what I had seen, they never would. The tub was too big, and I was just a rock sitting at its bottom.

The sound of the door opening brought a familiar wave of dread. What else would he do to me? Rearrange my organs? Stretch my skin? I was tired of being afraid. I should have gotten used to it by now, but the fear never lessened, never loosened its grip on me.

Bone fingers hooked around me and pulled me into a sitting position against the side of the tub. The skeleton creature knelt before me, waist-deep in the milky fluid, empty eye sockets regarding me carefully. A sense of contemplation emanated from him as if he were considering his work. His fingers traced my cheekbone, my jaw, the arch of my forehead.

More contemplation. Planning. Decision.

He pressed his palm to my forehead. Terror stuffed itself down my throat, into my ears, up my nose, flooding me more completely than the contents of the tub ever had. It oozed out of my pores and leaked out of my eyes like tears.

My mouth opened in a silent scream before my eyes rolled up in my head.

When I rested in my milky bath my eyes were always open, gazing at the smooth side of the tub. I could blink or hold them shut but it never lasted long. My eyes felt restless when they were closed.

When I came to, I realized I had actually fallen asleep for the first time. Granted I had passed out from fear, but I had slept. I had been unconscious. What an odd feeling, to have a gap where nothing happened, and I hadn't been there to witness the nothing happening.

It was comforting to know I was still capable of sleep.

That brief reassurance lasted only a moment. Because the next thing I became aware of was a splitting headache. Despite being once again submerged in my white bath, my head was on fire.

My skull, *I realized.* He destroyed my skull.

He'd remade every single one of my bones, saving the most important one for last.

His previous alterations had only hurt when he was in the middle of breaking my bones. As soon as he fully submerged me again, I felt fine. But this time it hurt beyond that. The fear was strong enough to keep me silent, but it felt like a herd of stampeding horses had trampled my head.

Closing my eyes didn't help. I couldn't go back to sleep. I couldn't escape this waking nightmare.

If this was how it felt afterward, how much must it have hurt while he was breaking and remaking my skull? I was grateful for

94

that small mercy whether that's what my torturer had intended or not. Depending on how long I had been out, it could be much worse. I might have already recovered a good bit, and this was just the lingering pain.

I shut my eyes and though I was submerged in water, the tears came.

What was left of who I had been before was gone now. He'd taken everything. I couldn't remember my family, my life, or my name. And now I wouldn't even be able to look in a mirror and recognize myself. I would only see what he made me into.

His student. His creation. His daughter.

Whoever I'd been had died. He had taken her from me. I was his now. Neither my mind nor my body obeyed me anymore. I couldn't do anything unless he wanted me to. And if he wanted to break me again and remake me all over, nothing could stop him.

I couldn't escape. I couldn't recover what I'd lost. There was no going back.

I knew that. But it didn't stop the tears.

* * *

The Boneman didn't come that night, but it hardly mattered. I stayed up long enough searching my phone for any piece of my past—which turned out to be useless—to exhaust myself for the next day. I barely had time to run down to the girls' locker room and shower before class. I didn't bother with eating. After yet another failure, my stomach didn't want food anyway.

Nicholas beat me to class for once. He watched me walk up the aisle to my seat the way a lion watches a wounded antelope cross an open field. He'd barely said anything to me since that day in the gym and paid more attention to his old friends.

Nina loved that he came to her desk and talked to her and her gaggle of girls before class while I sat in my chair, by myself, trying to ignore how happy and normal they all sounded.

I came in late enough that everyone had already taken their seats, and Dr. Shalm was writing something on the board. I managed to slip by her as the late bell rang.

I sat and pulled out my things. Dr. Shalm started talking about Old English language.

I was taking notes silently when Nicholas set a small, napkin-wrapped parcel on the edge of my desk and nudged it toward me until it bumped against the edge of my notebook. I eyed him, but he stared straight ahead as if he hadn't done anything.

I turned my gaze on the package. The last gift he'd given me had backfired. But the smell coming from it had my stomach churning. I carefully unwrapped the napkin. A fluffy biscuit sat amid its creases. I hadn't thought I was hungry until I laid eyes on it and my mouth started watering.

A glance at Nicholas revealed nothing. He continued to pay full attention to Dr. Shalm like she was performing a funeral service, copying down the occasional sentence on a loose sheet of paper.

I eyed the biscuit and swallowed hard. Nicholas wordlessly slid a folded-up piece of paper onto my desk.

I can hear your stomach growling.

My lips pressed together. What would it mean to him if I ate his peace offering? Would he think we were friends?

My stomach protested my indecision loudly.

"Please eat it before Dr. Shalm hears that and confiscates your breakfast," Nicholas whispered out of the corner of his mouth, using his hand to block his lips from the rest of the room.

Fine. I was hungry anyway. Professor Tumulus had told me to take care of myself. This wasn't about Nicholas. This was just about me and my needs.

I bit into the biscuit. Its buttery layers melted on my tongue. I had to close my eyes to keep from making a contented noise. It was almost as good as chocolate. I mentally rearranged my list of favorite foods while I polished off the rest. Nicholas whisked the napkin away, crumpling it and throwing it in the trashcan in the corner behind us in one smooth, lightning-quick move.

"Thank you," I breathed.

He returned to his casually slouched position with his chin propped up on his fist. A satisfied smile lurked on his face, half hidden by his hand.

Nicholas let me leave the classroom in peace. He let me walk by myself to our shared classes. He sat quietly beside me during them. He left me alone while we played volleyball during gym. But the whole time, his eyes followed me wherever I went.

I did my best to ignore him. He'd done something nice for me, but that didn't mean he was entitled to my time and attention.

"You look tired today," Wren declared when I joined her at our usual lunch spot in the courtyard.

"Didn't sleep well."

"Hm. I suppose that means you aren't interested in coming to my room later and watching a movie."

"Movie?"

"You know, the moving pictures. The talkies. How old are you again?"

I rolled my eyes. "I know what a movie is."

The admin filled my time with them before I started school. The ones they showed me were all high school dramas. I had a feeling they thought it might prepare me for school. It only partially worked since none of the films featured a Bone Touched girl desperate to escape the Boneman.

"I was thinking something exciting. Like an action movie. It should inject a little energy into us after the monotony of classes. Not that school can't be fun sometimes. It just seems like it's the same thing over and over and over these days."

The corner of my lips tugged upward. "Sounds nice."

"Excellent!" Wren clapped her hands together, making me jump. "You can help me pick something after class. Just come to room 216. My roommate stays with her family on the weekends, since they live in Noxier. We'll have the whole place to ourselves. I'll microwave some popcorn, maybe scrounge up a few snacks."

Wren continued plotting as we finished off our pizza. She seemed excited to see these cheesy triangles on the menu, but I couldn't get past how much grease dripped off of them. It coated my lips and fingers. Pizza went somewhere in the middle of my food list.

I looked forward to the end of the school day more than usual. Who knew what Wren had in store for me? She always seemed determined to go above and beyond my expectations. Granted, I didn't have much in the way of expectations but based on the one other time we'd done something outside of class together, Wren didn't do 'small-scale.'

The anticipation was almost enough to make me forget about Nicholas. He waited until statistics, our last class, to make his move.

"Nina's throwing another party tonight."

Of course, she was. Nina didn't do small-scale either.

"She and her friends have been bothering me about going, but I'm kind of tired of parties. They're all the same, no matter what different themes or decorations they have. It's always the same people, the same activities, the same food and drinks. I'd rather do something new."

What does that have to do with me?

"What are you doing tonight?"

Ah. There it was.

"I have plans." It was nice to have a legitimate excuse.

Nicholas's brows rose. "Really? What are you doing?"

"Something with a friend."

"Wren?"

I nodded. I didn't have any other friends.

"That sounds nice." His voice came out in a wistful breath.

The bell rang. I packed my things and stood. The usual suspects clustered around Nicholas. His expression changed from that vague longing to his blinding smile. My knuckles paled as I gripped the strap of my satchel in a stranglehold.

"Nicholas." The group didn't pay me much attention until he looked at me. "You don't have to do things you don't want to do."

It was like I'd pulled the lever at the gallows. His smile vanished, and he stared with those depthless black eyes. I held his gaze for a moment before turning and hurrying out into the hall.

There. We were even. I'd paid him back for the biscuit

99

with a bit of advice he probably needed. We didn't owe each other anything anymore.

12

Twelve

The common room in the girls' dorm was decorated less extravagantly than last time. Only a few multi-colored streamers hung around the space. Nina's crew wore different variations of the same shorts and sleeveless shirts. I kept my head down and made my way toward the stairs.

Nina materialized out of nowhere like a ghost in front of me. I had to backpedal a few steps to keep from running into her.

"Sylvan," she cooed like we'd been best friends for years. "I was hoping to get a word with you."

She reached for my arm. I stepped out of her way. "What is it, Nina?"

She scowled at my rejection, but her saccharine smile didn't take long to return. "Don't be like that. I just wanted to have a little girl talk."

I seriously doubted that. She'd been nothing but dismissive and condescending toward me from the moment we met.

"So, listen, here's the thing." She drifted closer. My hands fisted around the strap of my satchel. "I know Nick has kind of taken an interest in you. And I know you're stringing him along by playing hard to get."

Absolutely false.

"But there are some things you should know about him before you two really get involved."

"You're misreading—"

"First of all, he was a transfer student, and while that might appeal to you since you're one too, you should know that he was really awkward and weird when he first came here. He's gotten better about it, but every once in a while, he'll disappear completely off the grid and no one will be able to get a hold of him, not even me. I don't know what he does when he disappears, but that's a big red flag if you ask me."

I frowned. This was absolutely ridiculous. Was she trying to convince me to stay away from a boy I wasn't even interested in? What did I care what Nicholas did in his spare time or if he decided to take a much-needed break from Nina's obnoxious personality? We weren't involved, so it didn't matter.

"Second, even when he's acting normal, he's always super busy. I've asked him to go to stuff so many times, and aside from the parties, he always has something else going on. So, he doesn't even have time for a relationship."

Maybe Nina should take her own advice. If he didn't have time for her, why was she still pursuing him?

"Not to mention the fact that he's way out of your league in the first place. He's probably just interested in you because you're the new girl. I've seen it happen before. Guys like fresh meat, but if it doesn't suit their tastes, they drop it like *that.*" She snapped her fingers in front of my face. "And given the crowd he usually runs with, you're probably not his type."

How jealous was she to insist upon all of this?

"I'm just telling you, so you don't get hurt later on. There's enough drama going on around here as it is. You should probably just stick to that Wren girl and be happy with that."

My lips pressed together. This was exhausting. I just wanted to get up to Wren's room.

"You understand, right?" Nina pressed. "I'm trying to spare your feelings."

Yes, I'm sure it has nothing to do with your obsession with getting Nicholas to like you.

"Yeah, thanks," I mumbled.

Nina clapped her hands together and started to drift away. "Great! I'm glad we had this talk. Us girls have to stick together."

My teeth clenched. Right. Stick together.

"I don't suppose you want to stick around for the party. It's tradition to send new students out into the woods to see if they can find the Boneman, and I'm willing to bet you haven't gone yet."

My heart felt like it was about to punch clean through my ribs. "Actually, I have." Except that the Boneman had come to me instead of me going to him.

"Really?" Nina raised her brows. "Did you find anything interesting?"

My hands curled into fists so tight my nails bit into my palms. "No."

"Figures," Nina sniffed and sauntered away.

I couldn't get upstairs fast enough. Wren answered my soft knock on the door to room 216 almost immediately.

"Welcome to my humble abode!" she crowed and gestured

with a flourish of her arm for me to enter.

The room beyond was certainly not humble. It had all the same basic elements as mine: desk, chair, bed, closet. But there were two of everything. One set for Wren and one for her roommate.

In addition to that, there were soft touches everywhere. Pencil holders and little knickknacks cluttered the desk. A big, fluffy, blue rug took up most of the floor. It matched the sheets on the beds and the curtains on the window. Everything in my room was black and white, like the rest of the school.

Those curtains were open to look out on the school grounds at the front of the building. Students wandered along the sidewalks. Trees and bushes grew in their designated spots. There was no deep, dark forest or mist covering the ground. It felt so open. And safe.

"Well, what do you think?" Wren asked.

"I wish this was my room," I said softly as I looked over the colorful paintings on the wall. "Did you do it all yourself?"

"Well, it took some coordinating with my roommate. She brought the rug and the wall decor. We couldn't leave it all black and gloomy. We're both more creative souls. We need the color, the energy."

That sounded really nice.

"I'm guessing you haven't had the chance to outfit your room. Maybe we can go shopping tomorrow and look for something you like. What's your favorite color?"

I chewed my lip. "All of them?"

I had no idea. Blue was nice. So were green, and orange, and yellow, and just about every color. As long as it wasn't black or white.

"Well, we can figure it out later. Right now, it's movie time." Wren clapped her hands excitedly.

She darted over to a large flat screen hanging against one wall and pressed a button on the side. I jumped as an advertisement for toothpaste blared out from the speakers.

Wren winced and quickly adjusted the volume to a manageable level. "Sorry, we like our shows loud sometimes, especially when people are being noisy out in the halls. It makes it so much more immersive. You forget everything else that's going on and live in the story. Not that real life can't be fun. It's just so much less interesting more often than not."

The corner of my mouth tugged upward. I understood the need to escape reality more than she knew. To lose myself in something that wasn't tainted by the Boneman even just for a little while sounded amazing.

And forget about Nina and her drama.

I scowled at the floor. It wasn't my fault Nicholas attached himself to me like a knife to flesh. I never asked for his attention. But I was starting to get the feeling Nicholas never really asked for Nina's or anyone else's attention either. That wasn't any of my business, though. His life was his own, and my life was my own.

Wren flopped on the bed across the room from the TV and glanced at me. "What's wrong with your face?"

My eyes flicked to her.

"It's just that you were glaring at the floor so hard, I thought you might have seen another ghost down there or something." She pulled her feet up and eyed the carpet.

Right. I hadn't stopped scowling. "Just…" I sighed. "Nina."

"*Oh*." Wren patted the bed beside her. "Come and tell me

all about it."

I obeyed, setting my satchel down next to the bed. "She thinks Nicholas and I are together."

"Mm. And she doesn't like that because she's been trying to seduce him for as long as he's been at this school."

My eyebrows rose.

"Yeah. He got here two years ago. Middle of the year transfer student. Kind of like you. And…" She let out an appreciative whistle. "It was like every girl within a five-mile radius had some kind of built-in homing device to detect him. They all wanted a piece. He was a lot more shy back then, though. Didn't really know what to do about it. Kind of awkward, but that only made him cuter."

I leveled a knowing look at Wren.

"Fine!" She threw her hands up. "I'll admit it. I was one of the girls who was attracted to him. But I'm not the kind of girl he'd notice." She picked at the blanket underneath her. "I've always been too quiet and bookish for guys to approach me."

"You'll find someone," I tried to reassure her. All the characters in the teenage dramas I'd watched said things like that.

She smiled. "Thanks, but honestly, it's probably better this way. I've been alone for so long I wouldn't know how to act in a relationship."

I got the strange urge to put a hand on her shoulder. Until the sound of my bones breaking the last time someone—or something— touched me for more than a moment speared through my memories. My fists clenched in my lap. Physical contact was off the table.

Wren cleared her throat. "But listen to me droning on

about my failed love life. The whole point is that Nicholas is highly desirable, and it kills all the girls who thought they were getting close to him that you just show up and he's suddenly obsessed with you. They're jealous. Don't let it get to you. I mean, you don't even actually *like* Nicholas, right?"

"Right," I echoed, staring at my fists in my lap.

Even if I *was* interested in him, Nina was right. He was out of my league and from a whole other world. One without any death gods. We would never last as anything more than friends.

"So, I thought we could start out with a heist movie and see where the night takes us from there," Wren said, aiming a remote at the screen and flipping to the right setting.

I nodded. That sounded interesting.

The movie transfixed me through its entirety. I barely touched the popcorn and candy Wren brought over in little bowls for us to snack on. Despite the fact that I jumped at just about every loud noise that came out of the speakers, I rather enjoyed it.

This movie was so different from the ones the admin showed me. I could feel my heart pounding in my chest for nearly the whole two hours. Wren laughed at one point because I leaned so far forward on the bed that I nearly toppled off.

When the end credits rolled, I sat there for a moment, blinking, and confused. I had to reel myself back into my body and remember that I was in the real world, not the one shown on the screen. I didn't think I could be interested in anything more than getting the Boneman to leave me alone. But I'd gotten so invested in the band of thieves stealing priceless museum pieces, I hadn't thought about anything

107

outside of that little box of light and sound for the duration of the movie. It felt strangely freeing.

"So, what did you think?" Wren asked as she moved to take the disk out of the player.

"Fascinating," I breathed. "Is there another one like it?"

Wren grinned.

We went through two more movies. All of them captured my attention more effectively than a public execution enthralled an angry crowd. But by the time the last one ended, my eyes had started to hurt. I massaged them in my sockets, annoyed that I had to look away from the screen.

Wren yawned loudly as she put the movie away on a little shelf above her desk. "It's getting late. Are you ready to go or...?"

My gaze darted to the window. Night had fallen over the school grounds, but a few lamps lit the walkways, so it wasn't as dark as it always was outside the window of my dorm. I didn't want to go back to that shadowy room where the curtains opened by themselves and the Boneman stole me from my bed to terrorize me in the woods.

Wren shifted on her feet. "I mean, like I said earlier, my roommate isn't here. You could just... stay, if you wanted."

I turned wide eyes on her. "Really?"

"You'd have to sleep on the floor, cause I don't want to violate her space or anything, but you can stay."

Hope bubbled in my chest. "Yes." Anything to keep the nightmares and the Boneman away. If I was with Wren, he wouldn't come after me. He wouldn't risk her seeing him.

Wren grinned. "Awesome! I'll get the spare blankets."

My makeshift bed was little more than a mound of sheets and a large comforter laid out on the rug. It wasn't nearly as comfortable as the bed in my room, but it was really warm once I snuggled down in it. The pillow tried to swallow my head. I got the feeling I looked more like a poorly concealed corpse than a living person.

"If you need anything, the bathroom's through that door there, and snacks are in the cabinet," Wren said. "Good night, Sylvan."

"Good night, Wren."

I burrowed into my bedding. I had a good feeling about tonight.

13

Thirteen

My head had stopped hurting. My body relaxed as much as it could at the bottom of my tub. He hadn't come to visit in a while. Maybe he'd forgotten about me. Maybe this was the way I would live my life from now on. It wasn't too bad as long as he left me alone. I couldn't remember anything before this, so I had no idea what it might be like to be free, how much better it could feel.

I wished I could move, though. My muscles didn't cramp, but they wanted to move anyway, wanted to test out my new body, wanted to run far away from this place and never look back.

The door creaked open, and my heart pounded in response. What more was there for him to do? He'd already broken all of me apart and put me back together in the shape he wanted. Why had he come back? Wasn't it enough that he'd ruined my body and stolen my memories?

The familiar, enormous shadow loomed over me and paused for a moment. His thoughts circled the drain of my mind. Thoughts I couldn't quite grasp before they disappeared forever. He was thinking long and hard about something. It scared me more than *those times he thought about how to remold me. At least then I could try to brace myself for the bone-deep pain.*

Bones. Bones. Bones.

I was so tired of them. I wished I could rip them out from under my skin and live as a gelatinous blob in the bottom of this tub. Maybe I'd get washed out with the water, down into the ocean, where I could float among the fish for what remained of my life.

Long, hard, bone arms dipped into my translucent bath and scooped me up. I gasped as my head came out of the water, and I breathed air again. My fingers numbed with the sudden cold that wrapped itself around my dripping skin.

The bone creature knelt and set me down on a fluffy, white towel beside the tub. He picked up another towel and started drying me off.

I hardly dared to breathe. This was it. He'd spent all that time remaking me for something and now it was time to find out what. I didn't know whether to be thankful that I was finally out of the tub or terrified about what came next. I still couldn't move. I still couldn't fight back. I still didn't know what was going on. But at least I was dry. At least I breathed air. That had to count for something, right? Either way, life as I knew it was coming to an end.

Goosebumps bloomed across my skin. The skeleton set aside the towel and lifted me into his arms again. We crossed to where a long bolt of white fabric covered the black tiles.

He situated me on top of it and gently wrapped it around me, lifting my feet or shoulders when necessary, until I was just a long, white worm. He only paused once to tie something around my right wrist, some kind of black tag.

My curiosity surged. Whatever the tag said, it had to be important. I wished I could move enough to read it. A corner of the fabric obscured a good portion of my vision, but I watched him tuck me in and pick me up once more.

He held me close to his chest, my cheek pressing against the smooth, hard surface of his shoulder. His ribs dug into my side. The deep rattle of his bones clacking together as he walked echoed in my ear. He let go of me with one arm and the door creaked open.

My heart pounded in my throat. This was it. I was leaving.

The skeleton glanced down at me long enough to pull the cloth completely over my face, blocking everything from view, before he stepped out of the room.

I wanted nothing more than to reach up and throw back my makeshift blindfold. I wanted to see what was to become of me. He could at least afford me the dignity of meeting my fate with open eyes, couldn't he?

Was I about to be buried alive? Sacrificed in some occult ritual? Burned to death on a pyre? I wanted to know. I wanted to scream that he'd kept me in the dark long enough.

But I stayed frozen, unmoving, unspeaking, as we walked and walked and walked. If it weren't for the ever-present dread that kept my eyes wide open and my body tense, I might have fallen asleep. Only the sounds of the skeleton's footsteps interrupted the quiet. I had no idea where we were, where we were going, or how much longer until we got there. But at least it was warm and dry inside my little cocoon.

Finally, we stopped. The creature set me down on a hard surface. Cold leached through the fabric. A skeletal hand rested on my covered head.

Be good.

I hardly had time to wonder what he meant before the hand retracted. The rattle of bones faded, leaving me alone on the *ground.*

I blinked.

I still couldn't move, couldn't speak. But he was gone. What now?

The faintest sounds of the wind blowing reached me, making the fabric over my head twitch, and branches rustle, but nothing else. I was more confused than anything. Had he just left me here? What was supposed to happen now?

A door opened somewhere in front of me, and voices spilled out.

"Yes, I'll see you all bright and early for the monthly staff meeting on Monday. Have a good night."

The woman's voice was so loud compared to the quiet I'd lived in for so long that I flinched slightly. It was the barest tensing of muscles, but I'd done it. I moved on my own!

I was so excited I completely forgot about the woman until her foot connected with my arm. It didn't hurt, though the sudden contact startled me, making me jump again. The woman swore, paused, swore even more colorfully, and yelled at someone.

"I need help! Hurry!" She lowered her voice, and it sounded like she crouched down beside me. "You poor thing. I can't believe he just left you out here." The fabric over my head lifted and a brown-haired woman stared down at me with wide hazel eyes. "Are you alright? I didn't hurt you, did I?"

Footsteps pounded behind her, and more people peered over her shoulder. Light poured from an open doorway behind them, turning most of them into dark silhouettes. I blinked and my eyes moved for the first time since I could remember, trying to take in all the new faces.

Who were these people? Why did he leave me with them?

"Here, get her up. She probably can't move yet," the woman was saying. "Bring her to the cabin. We can get her cleaned up and

settled there." To me, she said with a smile that showed too many of her teeth, "Don't worry. You're safe now. We're going to take care of you."

Her words didn't do as much to quell my anxiety as she probably wanted them to. But I was out. I'd survived. At the moment, that was all that mattered.

14

Fourteen

I woke up shivering on the floor of Wren's room. I'd managed to kick my blankets mostly off while I slept. They tangled around my feet like skeletal hands holding me to the ground. I struggled against them, thrashing wildly when they wouldn't let go. I finally ripped myself free and scrambled away from the offending fabric until my back was pressed against the wall. My chest heaved, stealing air as fast as possible.

After several moments, I managed to calm down enough to remember where I was. My eyes darted to Wren's bed, but she was nowhere to be seen.

"Wren?" My voice came out scratchy and hoarse like I'd been screaming. "Wren?"

My ears finally registered that the water was running in the shower.

Oh.

Of course. Wren wasn't afraid of the tub in her bathroom like I was. She actually used it.

I curled my knees to my chest and dragged my fingers

through my tangled hair. Good thing she hadn't been here to see that. It was bad enough when I freaked out over the seat belt in front of her. What would she think of me if I lost it over a couple blankets?

By the time Wren got out of the shower, I had picked myself up off the ground and perched on the edge of her bed.

"Morning, sleepy head," she called.

"Morning." My voice was still a bit raspy.

"I hope they have something good for breakfast this morning. They like to do special stuff on the weekends, but you've probably already figured that out." She was already on her way out the door.

I drifted after her, clutching my satchel. The sun had finally emerged from the clouds and shone through the hall windows in swathes of warm, yellow light. It was the first time since I arrived at Mortorous Academy that it hadn't been completely gray and overcast.

Breakfast was waffles again, now my third favorite food. *Chocolate, biscuits, waffles, pancakes—*

"—into town again today."

I snapped back to reality. "What?"

Wren raised an eyebrow. "I said we should go into town again today, it being my birthday and all."

"Right, happy birthday." She'd mentioned it before, and I'd completely forgotten.

She grinned. "Thanks. So, what do you say?"

I stared blankly at her.

"About going into town? Did someone scoop out your brains while you were asleep?"

Something like that. "I don't know."

Professor Tumulus told me I wasn't supposed to leave

campus. I doubted he or the Boneman would approve of this impromptu trip, even if it was to celebrate my friend's birthday. And the last thing I wanted was to deal with another ghost.

Wren nodded. "I get it. Last time was a little…scary. Nothing like that has ever happened to me before." She paused and stared into space for a long, silent moment. "Honestly, the more I think about it, the less I want to go. I mean, what if that ghost is still running around?"

I breathed an inward sigh of relief. Telling her that someone had taken care of it would sound suspicious, but at least *I* could take comfort in knowing it was gone.

"Maybe we should just go to the library. I have some books to return anyway. And they always have good reading material. I can recommend something to you." Her excitement returned in full force.

"Ok." I might as well have a look around. So much had happened between trying to settle in and getting dragged into Bone Touched business, I hadn't had a chance to explore the library after running into Wren on my first day.

"Yay!" She clapped her hands together like a child and jumped up with her empty plate.

I followed.

The library was quiet at this early hour. Only a handful of students sat at tables in the corners, reading or doing classwork. After depositing some books in the return slot, Wren took the lead, winding through the stacks like she was perfectly at home among them. She paused every once in a while to pluck a book off the shelf, tell me something vague about how good it was or what she'd heard about it, then hand it to me.

I had a sizable stack in my arms when she halted right in front of me, and I bumped into her. Wren grabbed my arm and hauled me around a corner. It took some quick maneuvering to keep my tower from falling.

"Don't look now," she whispered, "but you-know-who is sitting at the table around the corner."

She peered around the book stack. I followed suit. A familiar head of black hair was bowed over a thick textbook.

Wren nudged me back. "I just said don't look. I mean, unless you *want* to go talk to him."

I blinked down at Wren. "Then why were you looking?"

She ignored my question. "*Do* you want to go talk to him? It's just that now would be a great time to tell him you aren't interested in him. If you want to."

There was a strange mixture of hope and encouragement in her voice. I couldn't help remembering that she, like so many others, was attracted to Nicholas. Despite what she'd said about being better off on her own, if she had the chance to catch his attention, I didn't doubt she would take it.

"Maybe *you* should go talk to him," I said.

Her cheeks flushed. *I knew it.* "What do you mean? You want *me* to tell him to leave you alone?"

"No, just talk to him. Not about me."

Wren peered around the shelf again. "You mean, like, flirt with him?"

I shrugged before I remembered that she wasn't looking at me. "You can."

"Do you really think I should? I mean, I'm probably not his type."

"I didn't think I was either."

Wren turned back to me and chewed her lip. "You're right.

118

Other than being super pretty, you don't seem like the kind of girl he'd go for given the crowd he usually hangs out with."

I flushed at the compliment, but Wren was too busy staring at the ground in thought to notice.

"He's probably tired of girls flirting with him, though," she mused. "And the ones who do probably actually know what they're doing."

I rolled my eyes. "Then just ask if he likes books and see how it goes."

"I don't know." Wren frowned. "I might come across as desperate. Boys don't like that, you know."

I sighed and leaned back against a shelf. "Just do it. I don't think he likes girls like Nina, so maybe he'll like you."

"You have a point. I don't think he's dated any of those girls since he got here. Maybe I *should* give it a try."

I nodded.

"Ok." She huffed a breath. "Do I look alright?"

I nodded again.

"I don't know if I can do it. Can you come with me? Maybe if you make it clear you aren't interested and then I swoop in, he might take more of an interest in me."

I didn't know about that, but I could give it a try. "Alright."

Wren beamed. "You're the best. Ok, let's go. But we have to play it cool. Like we just happen to find him. Which we did. Follow my lead."

She turned the corner toward Nicholas and started perusing a shelf a little too intensely. I rolled my eyes but copied her as best I could around the stack still in my arms. We shuffled down the aisle pointedly not looking at Nicholas. He didn't take note of us. He might not even know we were there, being as absorbed in his studying as it seemed like he was.

Wren echoed my thoughts. "I don't think it's working. We need to try something else."

Like what?

"Sylvan?"

I went still at the sound of his voice.

"That works," Wren muttered. She turned toward him and gave a little wave. "Hey, Nick! What are you doing up here so early in the morning?"

Nicholas gestured at his book. "Just a bit of research. You might actually find it interesting. It's about ghosts. Since you two saw one last weekend, it might be worth your time. It certainly piqued my interest."

"Really?" Wren wasted no time scurrying over to him and peering at his book.

I took my time following her, focusing on my own precarious stack of books.

"Did you get this from the library?" Wren asked. "I don't think I've ever seen it in here before."

"I ordered it from the bookstore in town. They have some good stuff like this. I guess given our school's supposed patron it's not that surprising. People love the myth of the Boneman and the other gods."

Other gods?

"Huh." Wren turned the book toward her and flipped through a few pages with hazy images on them. "What kind of stuff does it have to say?"

"It categorizes the ghosts and details a few methods of contacting or exorcising them. It even lists some haunted locations, like this one hotel down south that used to be a hospital where a lot of people died."

"Fascinating."

I didn't realize I'd been peering over Wren's shoulder until Nicholas nudged a chair toward me. "You can sit down, you know. There's no need to crane your necks like that. You'll strain a muscle or something. Especially with all those books you're carrying."

Without looking away from the book, Wren pulled out the chair across from Nicholas and plopped into it. I set my stack on the table with a relieved sigh and sat beside her. Wren hunched over the book so far that I couldn't make out most of the words from where I sat.

Wren was absorbed in the ink, sinking into the words like quicksand. She didn't seem aware of us at all. That must have been what I looked like last night when we were watching movies.

"The thing about that book is that it's mostly speculation," Nicholas grumbled. "I know life after death is a mystery and all that, but you'd think that after all this time we'd have a better grasp on what these spirits are and how normal people can deal with them without needing a professional exorcist or psychic."

I wished normal people could deal with ghosts, too. Then there wouldn't be a need for the Boneman to steal children in the night and torture them into becoming his minions. I wouldn't have had to suffer those long hours in that tub while he broke apart my bones.

Bones. Bones. Bones.

"I think Lucas was a poltergeist," Wren declared, snapping me out of my thoughts. "It says that those are the most dangerous. Though it seems like they mostly interact with inanimate objects. So, maybe he was just a different kind of bad ghost."

Nicholas scowled. "The Lucas I knew wasn't bad."

Wren winced as she glanced up. "I didn't mean it like that. Maybe he was just angry."

"About what?"

Wren shrugged. "I don't know. Maybe dying. But there has to be a reason he attacked Sylvan."

Nicholas's eyes snapped to my face. "Did he talk too or...?"

Terror touched. Daughter of death. Harbinger of endings. That's what he called me. Like he knew the Boneman owned me. Not ominous at all.

"He was probably just mad that his life ended so soon," Wren mused. "Or maybe he was upset before he died. Who knows? Like you said, it's hard to pin these things down since they're no longer alive and don't follow the rules of the living." So, she *had* been paying attention to us when she was reading. She pushed the book in front of me. "Do any of these look like they might be what you saw?"

I studied the grainy photos. Lucas definitely had a full body. The depictions of poltergeists sounded similar.

I frowned. "He just looked like a person."

Wren sighed as she pulled the book back toward her. "I wish I'd seen him."

I pressed my lips together. *No, you don't.*

"He didn't hurt you, did he?" Nicholas asked.

"I'm fine." I'd scraped my hands a little on the pavement, but it was only skin deep and had mostly healed already.

Nicholas smiled softly. "Good. I'm glad."

I swallowed hard and focused my gaze on the table. Wren nudged my leg with hers. Now was as good a time as any to have this talk.

My eyes stayed on the table. "Nicholas—"

Wren's phone went off so loudly that all three of us jumped. It sounded like monkeys screaming.

"Sorry, sorry." Wren wrestled it out of her pocket and checked the screen. "It's my mom. I've got to take this. I'll be right back." She darted off through the shelves as she answered the call.

"Bit of a weird ringtone to have for your mom, but..." Nicholas shrugged. "I'm sure it's some kind of inside joke."

Probably.

"I took your advice, by the way."

I raised an eyebrow.

Nicholas pulled the ghost book back to his side of the table and closed it. "I didn't go to Nina's party last night. I just stayed in my room and did my own thing. Honestly, it was nice. There were no expectations, no one complaining about petty drama, just me and my thoughts."

That did sound nice.

He drummed his fingers on the book's spine. "Nina's probably going to ask me about it in class on Monday, though. I don't usually skip out on social gatherings. I hope she doesn't take it personally."

"Why?"

He stared at me. "Why do I hope she doesn't take it personally?"

I nodded. In my opinion, Nina could use a little humbling. She saw herself as above everyone else. Her ego was big enough to crush anyone around her.

Nicholas sighed and ran a hand through his hair. "I don't know. I guess I just want to play nice. It's better to be on everyone's good side than to be on their bad side, even if it's only until we graduate. It makes everyone's lives easier."

Everyone's? Or just everyone else's? "But you didn't go to the party."

He huffed a laugh. "No, I didn't."

"And you enjoyed that."

He grinned. "Yeah."

Good. I didn't care what Nicholas decided to do or not do with his life, but it was nice that he made a decision for himself instead of letting others pressure him into it. I was sort of proud of him.

The light pounding of feet heralded Wren's return. "I'm so sorry to leave like this, but my parents are actually in town. They came to surprise me on my birthday." She let out a squeak of excitement.

"It's your birthday?" Nicholas asked. "Happy birthday. You're seventeen now?"

"Yeah, thanks." Wren blushed slightly. "But they're here now, so I need to go. I wish I could stay and talk about that book. It seems really interesting. I might need to get my hands on a copy at some point. Or maybe I can borrow it."

Nicholas offered her a brilliant smile. "Only after I'm done with it."

She grinned. "Of course, then we can talk about it."

Nicholas nodded. I glanced between the two of them, trying to read their collective thoughts. It was hard to tell anything for sure, but things seemed like they were going in the right direction.

Wren turned on me. "Do you have all your stuff out of my room? I don't know when I'll be back."

"I do," I assured her. "Have fun."

"Thanks, you two have fun." She winked at me before

darting for the doors.

That must be nice— to have someone surprise you and spoil you for a special occasion. I had no idea if my parents were still alive, who they were, or what they even looked like—no amount of internet searching had yielded any results. If it hadn't been for a tag the Boneman tied around my wrist, I wouldn't even know my age. I wished I had something of them to cling to, just one thing from my past to carry with me into this uncertain future.

"Wow," Nicholas said. "You *almost* have an expression on your face."

I pressed my lips together and stared pointedly at my hands in my lap. I knew Wren wanted me to officially friend-zone Nicholas—as the teen dramas would say—but I honestly wasn't sure how to go about doing that. Was I supposed to just blurt it out? Or ease it into conversation?

"It's ok to show that you're happy, you know. No one's going to crucify you for it," Nicholas teased. "Besides, Wren is great and very deserving of your smiles. She's definitely one of the better girls in our grade. Down to earth while still being enthusiastic about life."

"You know her well?"

Nicholas leaned back in his chair and shrugged. "She's been in at least one of my classes every year I've been here. And she's always kind of stood out, in her own quiet way. She doesn't try to blend into the crowd, but she doesn't go over the top to be unique either. She just does her own thing. I wish I was a little more like that."

"I think she likes you." I'm not sure where the words came from. They just spilled out of my mouth like a flash flood after a heavy rain. I wished I could stuff them back in. This

125

wasn't how this conversation was supposed to go.

Nicholas stared at me with eyes so wide the whites stood out all around his black irises. He let out a nervous laugh and fidgeted with his hands, adjusting the book, popping his knuckles so loud it sounded like necks breaking one after the other.

"No matter how many times I hear that, it still catches me off guard," he muttered.

I raised my eyebrows.

"I don't want to sound conceited or anything, it's just that, since I started going to school here, I've had a lot of girls ask me out or tell me they were interested in me like that." He watched me out of the corner of his eye like he was looking for a reaction.

I stared placidly back.

"It's flattering and all, but it always seems to come when I least expect it. Like there's a conspiracy going on between all the girls here where they're trying to catch me off guard long enough for me to say yes before I can really think it through."

"Have you?"

"Have I what?"

"Said yes."

He swallowed and held my gaze. "No."

"Why not?"

"I don't know." He was still trying to pop his knuckles. "I guess I was never interested enough in any of them."

That's not what Nina told me last night. But naturally, she wouldn't think there was a problem with his interest in *her*. Of course, it had to be because he was too busy.

"Do you want a relationship?" I continued.

His eyes drowned me like tar pits. "I wouldn't be opposed

to one if I found the right girl."

"Is Wren the right girl?"

Nicholas's face slowly split into a grin. "Sylvan, are you trying to set me up with Wren?"

Heat crept up my neck and swallowed my face.

He laughed, clapping a hand over his mouth to keep from being too loud in the library. "I never thought you would be so conniving. What happened to the shy, quiet girl I found sitting all by herself on a bench outside the admin office two weeks ago?"

I was fairly sure my face was as red as spilled blood. "Nevermind," I muttered. I grabbed my satchel off the floor and got up to leave.

"Wait." Nicholas shot to his feet and snagged the cuff of my uniform's sleeve, dangerously close to touching my skin. "I'm sorry. I didn't mean to make fun of you." He let go of my sleeve.

I glanced at him over my shoulder. Debated leaving. I might as well see this through. For Wren at least. My satchel stayed on my shoulder when I sat back down. Just in case.

Nicholas leaned back on his heels. "I think it's great that you're trying to make your friend happy. I'm just not interested in Wren like that. I think she's great and I'd like to be her friend too, but she's not my type."

Oh. Of course. He'd known Wren for a while now. If he liked her like that, he would have talked to her about it already. Poor Wren. I'd built up her hopes for nothing.

"Did she ask you to talk to me?" he asked.

Sort of.

He rubbed a hand over his face. "Can we go somewhere else? We can just walk around campus. I'd rather no one

127

overhear anything."

I looked around at the seemingly deserted library. While I couldn't see anyone, that didn't mean people couldn't be lurking between the shelves. The last thing I needed was anyone eavesdropping, but that didn't mean I wanted to go anywhere with Nicholas.

"I know a nice cozy place that serves food way better than the cafeteria and its chairs are way more comfortable too."

Good enough. I could always clarify my intentions. I stood up and waited for Nicholas to collect his things.

He flashed that brilliant smile at me as he rounded the table. "Let's go."

15

Fifteen

I trailed Nicholas out of the library, abandoning my stack of books on the table. That smile never left his face. I tried to fall back a little once we got outside, but he matched my pace, staying right beside me as we made our way down the sidewalk.

"So, here's the thing," Nicholas said. "Attention is nice until you get too much of it. You know what I mean?"

Definitely. I'd spent every day that I could remember wishing a certain someone had given me less attention. While our two situations were nothing alike, I could see how having people constantly hovering around you like flies over roadkill would get annoying.

"Like I've told you before, I only got here two years ago. It was kind of like how you arrived. These people already had most of the school year to form relationships and figure out their internal dynamics. So, it was strange for them to suddenly have to deal with a complete unknown."

That tracked. Other than Nicholas and Wren, none of my fellow students had given me anything resembling a warm welcome, but they seemed plenty friendly with each other in their little cliquish circles.

He shrugged. "They took an interest in me, each in their own way. The guys were a little skeptical, mostly because I got a lot of attention from the girls. But the last thing I wanted was to be the new kid that they bullied, so I just became their friend and didn't get involved with any of the girls. Through all of that, I figured out how good I was with people. I kind of liked the way people saw me. So much so that I found myself playing that part more and more."

"You lost yourself," I murmured, watching the tiny cobblestones pass under our feet.

He chewed his lip. "Yeah, something like that. The worst part was, I didn't even realize it. I thought I *was* that guy. I didn't understand why I felt so alone when I was around all of them. I thought it was just part of becoming who I was supposed to be, but it was just my real self, trying to tell me that I was doing too much, trying to be everything for everyone."

"But you *did* realize it."

We headed toward a small building painted a warm shade of brown, rather than the dark grey of the other structures on campus. Soft yellow light spilled out of the large windows at its front, mirroring the rare day of sunshine we were having. The inside held little wooden tables and chairs and even a few couches. It looked so much more inviting than most of the other places I'd seen around the Academy with their sharp edges, elegant carvings, and monochromatic color scheme.

Why couldn't we have more of this and less of the cold gothic architecture? I would settle for an occasional green or yellow.

"Yeah, I did," Nicholas said softly as he grasped the door handle and pulled. "And I think it was mostly because of you."

I stared at him for a moment. He held the door and gestured for me to enter. Watching him out of the corner of my eye, I stepped inside. Soft music drifted out of unseen speakers. A handful of people occupied some of the seating around the edges of the room, but they didn't pay us any attention. They were too absorbed in their books or phones.

Nicholas stepped in and gently nudged me toward the counter at the far wall. Half of it had a glass case full of pastries while the other half held a pair of registers and an open counter corner.

"I don't have money," I protested as Nicholas urged me forward again.

"That's ok." He produced a wallet from his pocket and held it aloft like it could ward off the plague. "I was going to pay anyway."

"You don't have to."

He skirted around me and headed for the pastries. "But I want to. Come on, you're holding up the line."

I figured it wouldn't matter if I pointed out that no one waited behind us. So, I approached the glittering glass case and its bounty of baked goods. They all seemed to glow under the bright lights.

Nicholas hovered behind me and peered over my shoulder. "What do you think?"

I had no idea what any of them tasted like, but they all looked delicious. Too many choices. I liked picking my own path, but the paths were too numerous this time.

I chewed my lower lip. "I don't know. You pick."

He stepped back and raised his eyebrows. "Really? Are

there at least a few that you've narrowed it down to?"

I shrugged.

"Hm." He went silent for a long minute while he contemplated his options. "Ok. Do you want a drink with your food? Coffee, tea, hot chocolate, water?"

I shrugged again. "I've never tried them." Except water, of course.

"Hot chocolate is probably best then. Not everyone likes coffee or tea, and water is a little boring." He spun on his heel and marched to the register, where a boy who looked like a student, waited to take our order.

My gaze wandered the little shop while Nicholas secured our food. I couldn't reconcile it with what the rest of the school looked like. Why was this one, little cafe the exception to the black and white of literally everywhere else?

"What are you thinking about?" Nicholas's soft voice in my ear made me jump and whirl around. He stood right behind me, watching with those eyes dark as a moonless night, holding a paper bag in one hand and a drink tray with two paper cups in the other.

"Why isn't this place black and white like everything else at Mortorous?" I asked.

"Because it's not owned by the school." Nicholas gestured for me to follow him to a small table with two tall chairs facing one another beside one of the large windows lining the wall. "They rent this building, but the business owners, a trio of former students, get to decide the décor. This is the most popular atmosphere for coffee shops. Besides, eighteenth-century gothic architecture is expensive to replicate. The school board lets them have their freedom because this place brings in decent money and helping support a small business looks good to the public."

I gazed around as Nicholas unpacked the bag of food and arranged the pastries on separate napkins. "It's my favorite spot on campus. It's so calm and relaxing. Even if there are groups of students here studying, they're usually pretty quiet. The food's really good too. Try it for yourself." He gestured at the spread between us.

I eyed it. "Which ones are yours?"

He waved a hand as if the question was silly. "I'll just eat whatever you don't want."

I stared at him. He stared back, completely serious. I was starting to think coming here with him was a bad idea. The biscuit had been one thing. This felt way too intimate. Almost like a date.

Nicholas pushed one of the muffins toward me. "How about you start with that?"

I picked it up, peeled back the wrapper, broke off a piece, and stuck it in my mouth. Nicholas watched like it was the most fascinating thing he'd ever seen. A steady heat built in my cheeks.

"Well?"

I licked a crumb off my lip while I considered. His eyes tracked the motion. I put a hand over my mouth, self-consciously.

"Good," I finally admitted.

"*Just* good?"

"Really good." Better than waffles and biscuits. Sweet and fluffy and mouth-wateringly delicious as little blueberries popped between my teeth.

His smile practically glowed. "I knew you'd love it. Try another."

I swallowed hard. "You were saying something about being yourself."

"Oh, yeah." He glanced out the window. I took advantage of his distraction and pinched a chunk out of the scone. "I was saying that I have you to thank for helping me see the light, I guess." Was he blushing? It was hard to tell in this light. "Meeting you reminded me of all of that and made me want to get back to what really matters."

"What really matters?"

He braced his elbows on the table and laced his fingers under his chin. "Being authentic. I know it sounds super cliché, but we lose ourselves more easily than we think, and it takes a lot to get back to who we were. If we ever knew in the first place."

All my focus went into peeling apart the buttery layers of the croissant to keep from smiling. It was a nice sentiment. I could only remember a few weeks of my life, not including my time in the Boneman's tub. All I wanted was to have a chance to make a life for myself and live it.

"Sylvan, are we... ok?"

My eyes flicked up. *"What?"*

Nicholas scratched at his jaw, keeping his eyes fixed on the half-eaten food on the table. "We had a bit of a rocky start, and I never know how you're going to respond to me and the things I do and say. One minute we're friends and sharing chocolate. The next it's like you've hollowed out, like you're not there anymore, and you want nothing to do with me. I realize you have your own life and your own stuff going on that I'll probably never understand. I just... like being around you and it would be nice if you liked being around me too." He finally looked up at me.

I set the dismembered croissant back on its napkin while I tried to form my thoughts. I still wasn't sure how I felt about Nicholas. He certainly had his moments, but there were times when it seemed like he wanted more out of me than I wanted to give. Like he was trying to dig me out of a cave I was perfectly happy staying in.

"You like being around me?" I finally said, stalling for time.

"Yeah, I think you're interesting and funny in a really dry, honest sort of way. You don't seem to have a lot of life experiences and it's fun to be there when you do experience things. Like parents recording their baby's first laugh or first bite of real food."

I raised my eyebrows. "Am I the baby in this scenario?"

He held up his hands in surrender. "That's not what I meant. I'm trying to say that it's exciting. I think you see the world differently from most people because of it. You make me want to be more like that."

I chewed the inside of my cheek. I supposed I could understand that. All these new things were exciting for me, too. Wren always acted so eager to do things with me, like get my first phone, or shop for my first real set of clothes. She didn't know the extent of my newness to the world, but she enjoyed spending time with me anyway. In his own way, Nicholas was the same.

"Sooooo," Nicholas drew out the word like he was measuring a rope for his own hanging. "Can we be friends? Is that ok?"

I studied him for a moment. He might be a good friend. It would be nice to have someone other than Wren, someone I saw more often. I glanced down at the half-eaten food covering the table. If nothing else, I would never go hungry

135

having him around.

"Yes," I agreed. "Friends."

His grin just about split his face in half. "Thank you."

I rubbed my hand over my mouth to conceal my half-smile.

"So, which one is your favorite?" He nodded at the wreckage of the pastries.

"This one." I picked up the blueberry muffin and took a large bite. *Chocolate, blueberry muffin, Danish, cinnamon muffin, waffles, scone, croissant, pancakes—*

"And the hot chocolate?"

"It's great. Thank you, Nicholas." I folded my legs up on my chair and cradled it in my hands.

"Any time, Sylvan."

Half an hour later, we cleaned up our table and left.

"We should go again sometime, maybe get Wren to join us. I've seen her in there a few times," Nicholas said.

Right, Wren. She was going to be disappointed to learn that Nicholas wasn't interested in her.

Nicholas leaned toward me. "You've gone all quiet again."

"I'm always quiet."

"But you've got this look on your face too."

"It'll be awkward," I said. "With Wren. Since you don't like her."

"Oh." Nicholas frowned. "You think she wouldn't want to come?"

I shrugged. She might want to come, but how would things be between the two of them if he knew about her unrequited affection for him? Especially if she saw that Nicholas and I were friends. Would she get jealous? No, she was better than that. Right?

"You don't have to invite her. I just thought it would be

nice to have her along too since she's one of your friends. It wouldn't be awkward for me. I'm kind of used to hanging out with girls who are interested in me. Ultimately, that's up to you and her."

Right. He had experience with this. That was his life.

"Maybe," I conceded.

"Great." He smiled. He did that a lot.

I didn't have the heart to tell him that I didn't think it was a good idea. I didn't know if I should even tell her about our conversation. She would probably just get all embarrassed and never want to talk to Nicholas again. I'd said too much to him. Maybe I should say less to her.

"You've been more talkative than usual today," Nicholas said. "Do I have Wren to thank for that, or are you finally getting more comfortable around here?"

I shrugged. Finding my voice was an ongoing quest, but at least I was getting better at it.

"Well, whatever the reason, it's been nice. You have a beautiful voice."

My eyes darted to him. His face was expressionless, and he faced forward. "Thanks."

"What are you going to do now?"

I raised an eyebrow. "What do you mean?"

"Well, Wren is off celebrating her birthday with her parents. I was wondering what you were going to do for the rest of the day."

"Homework." At least for some of the time. Maybe try looking for my parents again.

Nicholas grimaced. "That's right. We have that packet of Statistics work we're supposed to have done by Tuesday. I'm not looking forward to that." He cast a sidelong glance at me.

"Maybe we could work together on it."

I winced. Nicholas and I were on good terms now, but that didn't mean I wanted to spend the rest of the day with him. This friendship felt new and fragile, like a freshly hatched bird. There was no reason to push it out of the nest before it even grew feathers. I needed to at least sleep on this development before we went about testing boundaries.

"I like working alone," I told him.

"That's fine. We all have our own ways of getting things done. I guess this is your stop then."

We paused in front of the girls' dormitory. The gothic structure made me suddenly long for the softer, warmer space of the cafe. This was where the Boneman watched me. Where I was often afraid to fall asleep because I might wake up deep in the forest with only the sound of his rattling bones to keep me company. Where dreams of the worst time in my life plagued me. I could barely stand to be in the bathroom long enough to take care of business because of the tub that lurked behind its polka-dot curtain.

"Unless you'd rather go somewhere else," Nicholas continued.

Like where? I could go to the library, but that felt too alone without someone with me. Like I might catch the Boneman watching me from around the corner of a shelf. Maybe the common room would be populated enough to assuage any anxieties. That seemed like my best bet.

"This is my stop," I repeated.

"Alright, I'll see you in class on Monday." He flashed me one of his trademark grins. "Thanks for coming to the cafe with me, and talking to me, and not running away screaming."

I tilted my head. *Why would I run away screaming?*

"And." His smile softened. "Thank you for being my friend."

I blinked. "You're welcome." I didn't think it would be that big of a deal. He was good at making friends, wasn't he?

Nicholas took a few slow steps back while keeping his eyes on me. "Bye, Sylvan. See you soon."

"Bye," I echoed.

He turned away, smiling to himself, and started back the way he'd come.

* * *

I'd almost managed to forget about the skull sitting in its little wooden box on my desk. I hadn't been able to bring myself to do anything with it on Thursday night, and I spent last night in Wren's room. But now that I was back in my own dorm, even though it was pushed to the farthest corner of the desk, I couldn't ignore it, no matter how much I wanted to.

Tumulus gave it to me to practice reading memories, so the Boneman wouldn't be disappointed enough in my performance to visit me in the middle of the night again. I had to try at least once.

Walking to the desk chair felt like marching to my own grave. Sitting down felt like climbing in. Pulling the box closer and opening it felt like scooping dirt over myself.

Wide, empty eye sockets stared at me as I delicately picked the skull out of the box with two fingers like it might come alive and bite me. I set it on the desk and stared at it for a long minute, trying to muster the courage to actually hold it.

You're not going to get this done if you just keep staring at it. My fingers trembled slightly as I reached out and laid it across

139

my palm. *It's not going to come alive. It's not the Boneman.* I laid my other shaky hand over the top of the skull and tried to calm my racing heart. I needed to concentrate.

My eyes slid closed. I waited for the memories to come.

It took longer than I expected. There were a lot of images of the insides of some kind of burrow. Very dark but not pitch black. The best visions were of fields and wooded areas. Whatever animal this skull came from could run fast enough that it looked like it flew across the ground.

I watched as many of the memories as I could access, hoping for more of those wild moments and wide-open spaces. When they ran out, I opened my eyes, blinked the tension from my face, and went back in.

It was fully dark by the time my stomach growled loud enough to snap me out of my trance. I tucked the skull back in its box and closed the lid.

That was enough for today. It might be enough until my next lesson with Professor Tumulus. I definitely felt better about taking a break from bone magic than I had after only a couple hours on Thursday. I could spend the weekend not worrying about waking up on the forest floor.

16

Sixteen

I was idly sketching a tree in my notebook on Monday morning when Nicholas slipped into his chair beside me.

"Morning, Sylvan."

"Morning." I kept my eyes on my paper. Thanks to my phone, I'd discovered some videos online about how to draw and was focused on trying out some of the techniques I'd seen.

Nicholas leaned over to look, his head practically resting on my shoulder. "You're pretty good at that. Is it something you like to do often?"

"Sometimes." I shrugged. I'd only just started. The first thing I'd ever drawn was that portrait of Lucas. This was a much more pleasant turn for my art career.

"Well, listen…" He steepled his fingers in front of his face. "I read something interesting in that book I was showed you on Saturday and I went to text you about it when I realized that I don't have your phone number."

No one had my phone number besides Wren, and that was

mostly because she was the one who bought the phone for me. Aside from a handful of messages from her, I didn't use it to communicate with anyone.

"So, I was hoping I could have it or at least give you mine."

"Ok."

He blinked as if my response surprised him. "Great. I thought you might be some phone number gatekeeper who hates having too many contacts."

I only had one number in my phone, so that wasn't a problem. I produced my phone from my pocket, unlocked it, and slid it across the desk toward Nicholas.

He picked it up like it might explode in his hand and passed me his. We entered our respective information, but when it came time to swap back, Nicholas frowned at my screen.

"You only have one other contact in here."

"Yes."

"And it's Wren."

"Yes."

He tried for a laugh. "Don't you know anyone else? Where are your parents' phone numbers?"

"I don't have parents."

I shouldn't have said anything. I should have kept my mouth shut like I always did. The words tumbled out and rolled around on the ground like severed heads. Nicholas's reaction was instantaneous.

His black eyes opened wide. "I'm so sorry. I didn't mean to joke about—" He cleared his throat. "My condolences. Were you close?"

"I don't remember." *Stop talking!*

"It happened a long time ago?"

I managed to sew my mouth shut and simply nod. I had no

idea how long ago it had been. It could have been months or years. Who knew how long I was the Boneman's experiment after he stole me from them. It certainly felt like a long time.

"Who takes care of you now? Are you a ward of the state, or do you have relatives that look after you?" His voice was gentle, but the questions were still too much.

"Nicholas."

"Yes?"

"I don't want to talk about it."

"Right, sorry. It's not my place to pry." He gently set my phone down beside my elbow on my desk. He swallowed so hard I heard it and whispered. "I don't have any parents either."

Stillness crept up my feet, engulfed my legs, clawed up my torso, and infected my arms, like rigor mortis setting in on a dead body. He was an orphan too. How curious, this sensation that bloomed in my mind at his soft words. Somehow it eased the loneliness that draped itself over me like a burial shroud every day by a fraction. A different kind of grief than I was used to tugged at my heart.

It took me a moment to make my mouth form words. "I'm sorry."

"It's ok. It happened a long time ago too. I don't remember them."

Like me.

I moved to pick up my phone, but a well-manicured hand shot out and snatched it away. Nicholas and I both spun to see Nina eyeballing the little device.

"You've got good taste in phones, Sylvan," she said. "Though your preference in contacts is a little wanting."

"Nina," Nicholas said in a low voice that I'd never heard

out of him. "You can't steal people's personal belongings."

"I'm not stealing it." Nina pouted as she typed something in. "We're all exchanging numbers."

She tossed back my phone. I snatched it out of the air with a dexterity I didn't know I had. Nina raised her eyebrows at me. She must have wanted to send it crashing to the floor. A quick check of the screen revealed that she had indeed input her contact information. And sent herself a text.

Great. Now she knew my number too. One more way she could torment me.

She fixed her gaze on Nicholas. "Speaking of phone numbers, you never answered the messages I sent you this weekend."

He smiled, but it looked strained. "I've been busy."

Nina rolled her eyes and sighed dramatically. She looked at me when she spoke. "See? I *told* you he's always got something going on. He was even too busy to come to my party, and he *always* comes to parties when he's invited." She turned back on Nicholas. "Don't you, Nick?"

His smile turned even more brittle. "Like I said, it's been a hectic weekend. It feels like all of my teachers decided to assign a boatload of homework on the same day."

Liar. We had all the same classes together and except for the packet from Statistics, there had only been a bit of reading to do for Dr. Shalm's class. It was easy to knock out in one day. Was he just looking for an excuse? Did he always do this kind of thing to avoid social engagements or discourage girls?

Honestly, it wasn't a terrible strategy. It made him look studious instead of rude.

"Really? Cause Lily saw you at the cafe with *her*—" She

stabbed a finger at me. "—on Saturday. She said you were there for a long time, too."

Nicholas's smile made a brighter return. "I happened to run into her at the library, and we talked about some math homework." He shrugged. "If it had been you I ran into, we'd probably have had a similar discussion."

Technically none of that was a lie, at least not about what happened on Saturday. We did run into each other at the library, and he did mention the math packet. Nicholas was good at this. Had he spent the last two years cooking up excuses and half-truths to preserve his image *and* avoid the judgement of the people he'd fallen in with? Such a precarious balancing act seemed like more trouble than it was worth. Especially if he got caught in a lie like he almost had and needed to backpedal fast.

Nina looked a little skeptical about this development, but she calmed down enough to lose the accusatory tone in her voice. "Well, I can't have a party this week because of the basketball game, but you're going to come next Friday, right? You owe me for missing out this last time without telling me first."

Nicholas gave her his most blinding smile. "Yes, of course. I wouldn't miss it for the world."

"Good." Satisfied, Nina turned away and went back to her seat with her friends.

Nicholas sagged a little as he faced forward again. "You see what I have to deal with?"

It looked tiring, having to care that much about what people thought of you. I gently tore out the drawing of the tree I'd finished and passed it to him.

He took it like it gently. "For me?"

I nodded. I couldn't seem to get the ends of the branches to look the way I wanted them to anyway.

His smile was so wide it looked like it hurt. "Thank you."

I was glad Dr. Shalm started class before I had to respond.

* * *

We had Nicholas as an audience in history class, but Wren began her interrogation the minute she sat down on our usual bench at lunch. The air was starting to chill with the onset of autumn—the cloud cover didn't help keep the temperature warm—but it was still nice enough that we didn't have to retreat indoors. The heat in Wren's gaze kept our little corner of the courtyard especially warm.

"How did it go with Nicholas on Saturday?" She leaned so close, the faint scent of breath mints wafted into my face.

"Good."

"That's it? Come on, Sylvan. I know you don't talk much, but this is big. Tell me everything."

I hated having to answer so many questions. "We're friends."

"Ok. Just friends? He didn't try to make a move on you or anything? You made it clear you just wanted to be friends, right?"

"Yes." I wasn't sure if that was entirely true. I hadn't outright told Nicholas that I didn't want to be anything more, but it was implied. We were on the same page. At least, I thought so.

Wren nodded. "That should get him to not bug you so much. What else did you talk about?"

A lot. Maybe too much. Honestly, I was still trying to process our conversation.

"So, this is where you run off to during lunch."

Both of our heads jerked up.

Nicholas smirked down at us like he'd caught two cats playing with a dead mouse on the carpet. "I should have known you'd like it where it was less crowded. Mind if I join you?"

Wren smiled back. "Sure, no problem." She scooted over almost on top of me, hardly giving me time to move, so he could sit on her other side.

I didn't complain. This was their moment. I hadn't told Wren what Nicholas said about him not being interested in her. But it would probably sound better coming from him anyway. I'd mess it up and Wren would get the wrong idea if I told her. I would give them their space to sort this out.

"How was your birthday?" Nicholas asked as he cut up the marinated pork on his tray. "Did you have fun with your parents?"

"Oh yes, it was really fun. We had lunch out at that seafood place in the middle of town. Then we went to the bookstore, and they let me pick out whatever I wanted. Within reason, of course. If it were up to me, I would have had them buy the whole store." She laughed at her own joke. "I practically have one at home anyway."

Did her family really have that kind of money? Enough to buy a store? She hadn't batted an eye at buying me a phone, one that wasn't even the cheapest model, or all those clothes. So, maybe they did. Her parents had to at least have good enough jobs to afford to send her here.

"What did you end up getting?" Nicholas prodded.

"Mostly fantasy novels. Some of my favorite authors had

new books out that I'd been hoping to get my hands on. They also had some adorable book-inspired mugs and totes and things like that."

She kept going on, detailing every purchase her parents had made. I focused on my food. The potatoes were a little clumpier than usual today, but everything still tasted good. Not as good as the pastries from the cafe. Nothing would ever top those. I made a mental note to find a way to get my hands on some money so I could get more when I wanted.

That might be a bit difficult, though. I didn't know how to get a job or even where to look for one. I couldn't exactly go off campus. And what would the Boneman think of me working at anything besides bone magic?

I pressed my lips together. Mallor had a job, but he was grown up. He'd graduated and had full control of his powers. He knew what he was doing. He wasn't still reeling from his time in the tub. He probably didn't hear the sound of bones cracking in his ears whenever someone touched him like I did. I was so new to everything, even life itself.

I gritted my teeth. This was getting really old, this helplessness. Why couldn't I have control over even a fraction of my life? Why did I have to be held down by everyone else's decisions about what I was supposed to be?

"You ok, Sylvan?"

I glanced up. Nicholas and Wren were staring at me.

Nicholas tilted his head at me. "You've been stabbing your food almost the whole time Wren's been talking." He tried for a lopsided grin. "Did the lecture in science get you fired up, or what?"

"Yeah," I murmured and set my fork down on top of the remainder of my mutilated pork. "Sorry."

"You don't have anything to be sorry for. The periodic table gets me fired up too."

Wren glanced between the two of us and smiled tightly. "You know, I'm really glad you and Sylvan are friends now. She could use some bad humor in her life."

"I beg your unbelievable pardon!" Nicholas huffed exaggeratedly. "There is nothing wrong with *my* sense of humor."

Wren rolled her eyes, but her smile was genuine this time. "You're trying to make chemistry jokes."

"Chemistry is hilarious. You can spell 'funny' with fluorine, iodine, two nitrogens, and yttrium."

Wren tried and failed to hold back her laugh. I had to stuff the rest of my food in my mouth to keep from doing the same. This was one perk to having Nicholas around, I supposed.

"You didn't tell her," Nicholas said during gym that day as we put up the equipment.

I raised an eyebrow.

"About me friend zoning her. You didn't tell Wren."

"Neither did you," I replied as I tossed a volleyball into its cage in the back of the closet on the side of the gym. It wasn't like he hadn't had plenty of chances. They'd hardly stopped talking all through lunch.

He massaged the back of his neck. "I thought it would sound better coming from you since you guys are so close. I don't want to make things awkward or hurt her feelings."

That makes two of us.

"Besides, you were the one who was trying to set us up. You're her wingman—er, wingwoman. Shouldn't you tell her?"

I spun on him and crossed my arms over my chest. Good thing we were the only two selected to pick up.

I stared him down across the ten feet of poorly lit closet space. "She thinks you like me. Romantically."

His eyes went as round as twin drops of poison. "And you think she'd be jealous?"

I tucked a wisp of hair that had escaped from my ponytail behind my ear. "Everyone is. They all think you like me."

"Do *you*?"

Nicholas took a step closer. I became aware that we were alone in this closet and Nicholas stood between me and the half-closed door. I stepped away. My back hit the metal mesh containing the volleyballs. It felt like a lattice of delicate finger bones waiting to curl around me. My heart rate picked up.

He moved toward me again. "Sylvan, do you think I'm interested in you the way Wren is interested in me?"

My breath came in shallow gasps. "I don't know."

His voice was deathly quiet when he stopped a foot away. "Are *you* interested in *me* like that?"

He was too close. I couldn't move away. *Trapped.* Trapped in a white tub filled with white water that bleached my eyes and my hair white. White like bones. White like *him*.

My knees gave out and I went crashing to the floor. I barely felt the impact. My body curled in on itself. I couldn't breathe. The air itself choked me, clawing up the inside of my throat and lungs. Everything closed in on me, pinned me down, spun me around.

Someone was talking near me, but the inside of my head was too fuzzy to pick out their words. They might have been saying my name, shouting it, shouting for someone to help, help, *help*.

I moaned and covered my head with my shaking hands.

And then other hands were on me.

"No." I tried to get away, to escape, but the hands scooped around me, picked me up.

No! Don't take me back, please. I can't go back. I can do better. Please, leave me alone, please.

The arms disappeared after setting me down on a soft surface. I continued to gasp for breath, my hands clutching my head. My eyes shut tight. White light bled through my closed eyelids, but I refused to open them.

I couldn't be back in that terrible room. It would break me to return to that silence and stillness and fear.

Soft voices drifted around me. There weren't any voices in the Boneman's room. Just the sound of my own breathing and the low rattle of him moving. My breathing slowed a bit. I dared to crack open an eyelid.

The polished planks of the gym floor reflected the bright overhead lights in my face. I moved my arms just enough to glance around. Someone had laid out a handful of yoga mats on the ground. That's what the soft surface under me was. People conversed softly behind me. I slowly uncurled and turned toward them, propping myself up on an elbow.

The two coaches stood in a huddled circle with a handful of people I recognized as members of the administration I met during my first few days here. There was the school nurse, and—Professor Tumulus?

I groaned softly as I sat up. My muscles were stiff and sore, like I'd overworked them.

The nurse noticed me first and rushed over. She crouched a good yard away, giving me plenty of space. "Hi, sweetie." She gave me a patient smile. "How are you feeling? Any dizziness or nausea? A headache?"

I swallowed the lump in my throat and shook my head.

"Good, good. You should drink some water, though." She handed me a plastic cup.

I took a sip and rested it in my lap. My focus went to the others, who hovered behind the nurse as if I might combust, and they didn't want to be in range when I did. Professor Tumulus had no such compunctions. He stepped in, closer than the nurse, to sit on the yoga mat in front of me.

His smile was much more genuine than the nurse's. "Nice to have you back, Ms. Ravena."

I blinked at him, glanced at the other staff members, and looked back at him.

"There's no need to get frazzled. We were just having a brief conversation." He turned to the others. "Thank you for fetching me. Would you mind giving us some privacy?"

They nodded and muttered a handful of goodbyes before drifting out the door. They kept casting glances back at me as if I might start convulsing. How humiliating to have them witness me in such a state.

"Give a shout if you need anything," the nurse called. She was the last one out and took it upon herself to usher the stragglers away. She seemed nice. I wished I could remember her name.

With everyone else gone, I focused on Tumulus. "What happened?" My voice was scratchy like I'd been screaming.

"You had a panic attack," he said it so casually it took me a moment to register. "I'm going to take a stab in the dark and say you aren't fond of confined spaces."

I shook my head.

He nodded. "As I suspected. You should probably stay out of any cramped closets until you get a little more used to that sort of thing."

Right. I took another sip from the cup in my lap.

"It reminds you of being trapped in the tub, doesn't it? Of not being able to move?"

"Yes," I whispered, staring into the clear depths of the water.

"I'm sorry." He sounded genuinely remorseful. "This is one of the harder parts of being Bone Touched. The trauma leaves a mark that is hard to overcome. It will get better with time, but I've seen other Bone Touched, years after they graduated from this school, who still hate being in large crowds because they can't move easily."

I scowled into my lap. *Years.*

"At least Mr. Ater was here to get help. You calmed down pretty fast once we got you out of that tiny closet."

The plastic of the cup creaked in protest as I gripped it harder. Part of me knew I shouldn't blame Nicholas for what happened, but that didn't change the fact that it wouldn't have happened if he hadn't boxed me in.

"Is this the first time this has happened to you?" Tumulus asked.

"No." There was the time with Wren when the seat belt got stuck. I'd survived that on my own, though. I'd been aware enough to get out of the car before things got bad. The same thing happened with the blankets getting knotted around my legs when I stayed in her room.

"Well, you're just fine now. You've been excused from the rest of your classes as a precaution though. The admin doesn't like taking chances with us Bone Touched."

It was weird to think of Tumulus as being Bone Touched. I had yet to see any indication of his bone magic or the mark that probably lurked under the collar of his black button-up shirt.

"Since you have the spare time, I would like to show you something, if you don't mind." He got to his feet with much groaning. "You can stand without any help, can't you? I'm afraid I won't be able to do much on that front. I can barely lift myself."

I carefully unfolded myself from the floor. Other than the mild soreness in my muscles, I felt fine.

Tumulus beamed. "Excellent. Shall we?"

I glanced down at my gym uniform. "Can I change first?"

"Oh." Tumulus looked me over. "Yes, of course. Take your time. I'll wait outside."

We headed in separate directions. Thankfully, the locker room was empty. I didn't know what I would have done if there were still girls in there. Did they know what happened to me? There was a back door to the locker room for emergencies, but had this counted as an emergency?

I hoped so. I could only imagine what some of the other students would say if they found out about my episode, especially Nina and her crew. My hands scrubbed over my face. How embarrassing. I hated being Bone Touched.

17

Seventeen

Tumulus moved at an unbearably slow rate. I had to drag my feet to keep from outpacing him as we wound around outside, between buildings. The muscles in my legs kept twitching like they wanted to run. This was a different kind of confinement, a quiet, frustrating kind. It didn't send me into a panic though. So, at least there was that.

"I assume you were given a tour of the campus when you got here," Tumulus said.

"Yes."

"And on that tour, you were told that the main office faces in the direction that the Boneman came out of the woods to first issue his decree that this school would house and teach his pupils?"

"Yes."

I'd hated that part. That first half of the tour had been mostly about the urban legends surrounding the Boneman and his connection to the school. I didn't care about that, and the whole time I wished that Nicholas would stop talking about him.

"That's a lie."

Oh?

"They tell that story for dramatic effect. It always gets people's blood pumping. No one really knows where he walked out of the forest, but it probably would have been closer to here." He gestured as we turned a sharp corner.

Just past the science building, the ground opened up to a field that ran for a decent way before ending abruptly at the tree line I knew so well from the view outside my dorm room window. I tried to calm my breathing as we stepped out into that field. Mercifully, Tumulus stopped a few feet from the path. I couldn't handle approaching the forest, especially not after what had just happened in the gym. Even being this close made my heart rate pick up again.

"He likes forests, but you've probably already figured that out."

Fresh night air, fallen leaves pressing into the side of my face, mist cooling on my skin, and the rattle of bones, bones, bones.

"The academy was in its early years. No one really knows exactly when, but it was a while ago. At the time, there was a Baron who ruled over Noxier and a few other small towns in the area. He was the one who built Mortorous Academy in order to educate children of the nobility from across the country. He and the board he assembled to run the school thought it would do well. With the scenic location, the promised academic success, and the beautiful campus, who wouldn't want to send their children to learn and grow here?"

Beautiful campus. Right. With the sun only coming out once every two weeks and fog rolling in thick enough that it was hard to see all the way down the sidewalk on some mornings.

"It turned out a lot of people didn't. I suspect it was a combination of the remote location and the newness of the school. None in the upper echelons wanted to risk that kind of money without proven results, and they could just as easily send their kids somewhere closer to home. The gloomy atmosphere probably didn't help either. Superstition was rampant back in the day, and people kept saying the place was haunted."

He sighed. "The school cost more much money to maintain than it made on tuition. The Baron was close to closing it completely and selling the property. As the tale goes, the board members were in a meeting to decide on a date to shut down, when the Boneman came knocking. Literally."

My blood chilled.

"No one saw him enter the building. They just heard bones rapping on the door to the boardroom. I can imagine their shock and horror when the giant bag of bones walked in." Tumulus chuckled to himself.

My face went pale. Wasn't he afraid of badmouthing the Boneman? Especially so close to his usual haunt.

Tumulus went on, unaware of my apprehension, staring into the forest as if he were telling it the story. "After they managed to calm down, he said he had a deal for them. He would save their school. In return, all he asked was that they welcome whatever students he delivered to their doorstep. To instruct them both in matters of the world and in the magic that he bestowed upon them.

"Naturally, they were shocked. They didn't know how to teach bone magic, for one thing. And how on earth was a creature like him supposed to increase their attendance before they had to shut their doors permanently? He told them not to worry about teaching magic. He would send his own teacher to help with that. I am the latest in a long line of such instructors." Tumulus's chest puffed a little in pride.

"All they had to do was give his students whatever they needed without question or complaint. They wanted a moment to discuss, of course. But it wasn't really a choice. Even if they hadn't been fighting to keep their heads above water, they couldn't say no to a supernatural entity. They weren't immune to the superstitions of the time and feared retaliation if they refused. So, they agreed. And he left. They watched him disappear into these woods." Tumulus nodded at the tree line.

I shivered, thinking about how many shadows clustered between those trunks. A pair of empty eye sockets could be staring out at us right now.

"It was the first and last time the Boneman showed himself to anyone who wasn't one of his own, as far as we know. They never saw him again. But by the end of the week, they had four dozen new students. Enrollment came steadily after that. The sudden influx of tuition not only saved the school but let it turn a profit.

"For a while those board members could convince themselves the Boneman's visit was some group hallucination. It was a couple years before they found the first of his students bundled up just outside the front door one evening. There was no explanation for her presence other than a tag tied around her wrist with her name on one side and the words "Remember your promise" on the other. The next day, their new professor showed up, courtesy of the Boneman."

Tumulus shifted on his feet. "They took the child in, followed the Boneman's instructions, and have done the same for dozens of his disciples since."

I swallowed the lump in my throat and peered at the thick forest. "How long ago?"

"Exact numbers are a little wonky, for some *mysterious reason*. It's been a couple hundred years at least."

Tumulus lovingly patted the grey bricks of the building. "The school has had its fair share of renovations since then and has expanded a great deal. The forest used to be farther away from campus. But the essence of this place never changed."

A couple hundred years. How many Bone Touched had come through this school since?

"How did the Boneman make people start enrolling?" The only persuasion skills I'd seen from the Boneman consisted of him using my fear against me.

"He erected a protective barrier around the school and posted Bone Touched in Noxier for one thing. Rumors of supernatural beasts run rampant in small towns, at least, back in the day they did. Noxier was no different. But with the Bone Touched and protective magic controlling the ghosts, the townspeople no longer had anything to fear. Safety is the number one thing parents look for if they're sending their children somewhere, and a town and school where people talk about the lack of evil rather than the presence of it is much more enticing than a place that's supposedly haunted."

"Are there others?" I asked.

Tumulus raised his bristly eyebrows. "Other schools like ours?"

I nodded.

He rubbed his chin, his hand scratching over stubble. "Not for Bone Touched. But the Boneman wasn't alone in adopting a school. There are other institutions where the followers of different deities are taught."

My jaw dropped like the blade of a guillotine. "Other deities?" Nicholas had briefly mentioned that there might be more than the Boneman but hearing it from him and hearing it from Professor Tumulus were two different things.

Tumulus chuckled at my shocked expression. "Yes. You didn't think the Boneman was the only one, did you?"

My mouth snapped shut. I'd never thought about it before. All anyone talked about here was the Boneman. Though it made sense. These sorts of entities tended to come in groups. Most mythologies had multiple gods. There was always a slew of legends to go with whatever religion someone converted to. What other beings were out there? What powers did they have? Did they make their students suffer the same way the Boneman did?

"Who else?" I whispered.

"There are three that form a sort of crooked trinity. The most important one for you to know is the Wind Whisperer. In many ways, it and the Boneman are connected. They're opposites, yet very similar. The Boneman holds domain over death. The Wind Whisperer is concerned more with life and the way people live it. A long time ago, it took a liking to Animos Prep, one of Mortorous Academy's biggest rivals."

I had a flood of questions. "What does the Wind Whisperer do?"

Tumulus smiled but it looked a little strained. "I don't know many details. The gods like to keep their demigods separate. But the Wind Whisperer deals in dreams, both sleeping and waking ones. It's attracted to lost souls, just like the Boneman, and calls its followers the Wind Dreamed. There's also Time and the Time Bent. All you need to know about them is that they cause trouble wherever they go. Stay away from them at all costs."

I frowned. "Why? What do they do?"

"They make a habit of causing chaos at the expense of others. If you ever encounter Time or one of their demigods, get as far away from them as soon as possible." Tumulus's hands were clenched into white knuckled fists. What was that about?

"Do they have a school like Animos Prep or Mortorous Academy?"

Tumulus grimaced. "No, and we should all thank the Boneman for that. Time destroys everything they touch. I would never wish to inflict them on an unsuspecting student body."

I bit the inside of my cheek. This changed things. What if this Wind Whisperer or Time could save me somehow? Get me away from the Boneman and this school.

It didn't sound like Time would be my best option, but the Wind Whisperer was a possibility.

Life and death were natural opposites, repelling each other in every way. Maybe the Wind Whisperer was the enemy of the Boneman. It had chosen an opposing school for its people, after all. If I could get to it, appeal to it...

"It's important to know these things." Tumulus was saying while my mind spun with the possibilities. "Our world is so much more complex than we know. We have to take whatever information we can get."

But who warned the regular people about these gods who

ran around and abducted kids and did unspeakable things to other people? Shouldn't *that* be the priority? To keep people safe from the things that went bump in the night. All people ever worked for was safety and security. Tumulus had practically said it himself just a minute ago. If they knew these deities could steal into their homes and take them out of their beds, they would never feel safe again.

Maybe that was another reason we weren't supposed to tell anyone aside from protecting ourselves from the nefarious machinations of ordinary humans. Ignorant bliss was better than anxious knowledge. Even if that was the case, I didn't like it.

Tumulus stretched his arms over his head with a groan. "I'm glad we got out here to discuss this. The fresh air does wonders. If it weren't for the potential of passersby spying on us, I would always hold our lessons outside. Being near the forest is nice. You can almost *feel* the Boneman's power lurking somewhere deep inside."

Was that what this feeling was? This faint sense of dread that wound around my neck, preparing to squeeze the life out of me?

Tumulus must have seen me wrinkle my nose, because he laughed. "You'll get used to it. The more you practice your magic, the more comfortable you'll get with being around him."

I didn't want to get used to being around him. I wanted him to stay as far from me as physically possible.

"Well, since you seem to be feeling like your old self, would you like to retire to your room for the day?"

I nodded. I could think of nothing I wanted more than to get safely inside and away from the haunted forest.

"Thank you for walking with me and hearing me out. I hope you learned a thing or two."

"I have." The number one thing being that the Boneman wasn't the only supernatural power out there. He might not even be the strongest.

"I will see you for our class on Thursday, then. Farewell, Ms. Ravena." He turned back in the direction we'd come.

I waited until he'd moved out of sight before I headed toward the girls' dormitory. It was eerily quiet in the common room, but that was to be expected since everyone was in class. I glanced at the enormous clock over the massive fireplace along the left wall. Its twin hung on the opposite wall, each side of the room mirroring the other.

Statistics would just be starting. Nicholas would be sitting at his desk beside my empty one. The students would hush as the lesson began. Nicholas might be wondering how I was. He probably wished I sat next to him.

I shook my head to clear the images and marched up the stairs to my room. The curtains had opened themselves again. I was getting really tired of that. My feet still carried me to them, and my hands still yanked them closed like they had this morning.

Would it be better if I had blinds? Maybe I could ask the admin about getting some. Would they jump at the chance to give me what I needed, or would they see my attempt to defy their patron god for what it was? I doubted they wanted to do anything that might upset the Boneman. And would blinds even make a difference? If he could open curtains, it stood to reason that he could open blinds too.

I sighed as I flopped down in my desk chair and started pulling out the homework I'd gotten that morning. It probably wasn't worth it to ask about the blinds. My head fell into my hand as I started scratching out responses to a worksheet from History.

* * *

A knock at the door a few hours later startled me out of my work-induced coma. I'd never had a visitor to my room before. Tumulus didn't count. He was just waiting outside to catch me coming back. And the Boneman hadn't knocked when he stole me out of my bed in the dead of night.

I got up and peeked out the peephole. The distorted image of Wren, glancing up and down the hallway, greeted me. I opened the door.

"Hey." Wren grinned up at me. "I have homework from the classes you missed. Can I come in?"

I held the door open wider for her, and she trotted inside.

She took a sweeping look around the room. "Someone's a minimalist. You don't have *any* personal items in here, do you?"

No. I didn't have any at all. Even the cloth in which the Boneman wrapped me up to deliver to the school and the name tag he tied around my wrist vanished during my first night on campus. No one had seemed surprised about it, though.

"Does anyone else live on this floor? It's so quiet and deserted. Kind of creepy, no offense."

I shrugged. There were only a handful of other rooms on the third floor, and they all lacked occupants. The admin seemed keen on keeping me isolated from the rest of the student body as if being Bone Touched was contagious.

"You have the homework?" I asked, not wanting to dwell on my gloomy living situation.

"Yeah." She slung her backpack off and propped it on an empty corner of my desk. "Nicholas caught me after I got out of book club, which you should really consider joining, and told me that you had to miss some of the day because you weren't feeling good. But he got all of the work from your teachers, so you wouldn't get behind."

Did he feel like he owed it to me for causing my panic attack? I would if our roles were reversed.

Wren held out a couple papers to me. "You didn't tell me you and he have the exact same schedule." The comment was offhand but charged with the need for an explanation.

I took the papers. "Wasn't my idea."

Wren snorted. "What? Did you two have another falling out? You're scowling."

I did my best to smooth my features. Wren was too perceptive, and I was too expressive.

"So, what did he do this time? Does it have anything to do with why you weren't in class?"

"Sort of." This girl was too smart for her own good.

Wren whipped out my desk chair and sat backward on it. "Spill."

My eyes focused on the worksheets in my hands. "I had a panic attack."

Wren straightened. "Like when we went to Noxier, and the seat belt locked?" I nodded. "And Nicholas had something to do with it?"

I spoke softly. "He didn't know. We were in the gym closet and...I felt trapped."

Wren rubbed her hands over her face. "I guess it's not

165

entirely his fault if he didn't know. It's not like you talk about your issues openly. Not that you should have to, of course. It's your business. But still, that closet is small enough as it is. Did you two get stuck in a corner or something?"

The memory of his dark eyes gazing into my soul in that dim room wormed into my mind. "Something like that."

"Well, he'll probably apologize in the morning. Unless you're too rattled to go to class tomorrow."

"I'm fine."

"Then you'll get your apology, and he'll know better, and everything will be fine again." Her gaze drifted to the homework I still held. *"That* is probably the start of it. It pays to have a friend who has all the same classes as you. That was nice of him to do. I wish a guy would do something like that for me."

I raised an eyebrow. "Give you a panic attack *and* homework?"

Wren barked a laugh as she got to her feet and pushed my chair back in. "I keep forgetting you have a sense of humor under that shy shell. Have you eaten yet? It's about time for dinner."

I glanced at the clock on my nightstand. She was right. My new homework would have to wait. I tossed it on my desk and followed Wren out the door.

18

Eighteen

Wren was right. Nicholas was quiet when he walked into Dr. Shalm's class, approaching his seat like he thought I might shatter if he moved too quickly.

Did he think I was that fragile?

"Sylvan," he started after a moment of silence then clenched his jaw. "What happened at gym yesterday... it was my fault, wasn't it?"

I opened my mouth to answer, but he charged forward. "I'm sorry. I wasn't thinking about how you would feel when I cornered you like that." His hands rubbed at his face, covering up his pinched expression. "I would understand if you changed your mind about being friends."

My brows rose. "You think I can't understand that it was an accident?"

He looked over at me. "That's not what I meant. I just... I saw what it did to you—what *I* did to you. It hurt just watching you go through that. It must have been horrible for you to actually experience. I wouldn't want to be friends with someone who did those kinds of things to me."

Wow. Nicholas told me on Saturday how much he wanted everyone to accept and like him, but I didn't think he would be so consumed by that desire that he would blame himself so much for something he never could have guessed would happen.

"You didn't know," I said.

His hands clenched into fists. "I should have. You've never liked being touched. You don't even like handshakes. Hemming you in like that was a stupid move."

I folded my hands in my lap and stared straight forward. "I forgive you." It wasn't like he had kidnapped, tortured, and kept me in a magic bathtub for what felt like forever.

"Are you sure? I don't want you to feel like you have to."

This was getting annoying. "You know better now."

"Yes, but—"

"Nicholas."

"Yes?"

"Stop."

He shut his mouth, his teeth snapping together with a loud click. His hands fidgeted.

"What?" I finally sighed.

"Did you get the homework I sent up with Wren?"

I nodded. "Thank you."

"It's the least I could do."

"You didn't bring it yourself."

"Boys aren't allowed in the girls' dorm. Besides, I didn't know if you'd want to see me."

He kept quiet for the rest of class and let me leave the room by myself. I recognized the pattern. He was trying to earn my trust by giving me space. Even though he didn't need to.

Once I'd gotten over my initial reaction, I could recognize that he wasn't entirely at fault for what happened.

If I didn't tell people what bothered me, they wouldn't know how to handle me. It still felt awkward to even think about trying to explain my triggers when I couldn't explain the reasons behind them.

Wren side-eyed Nicholas for the entirety of History class. Whether he'd caught Wren's reaction and figured out that I'd told her, or if he was still trying to give me space, we didn't see him at all during lunch. He left me alone in the rest of our classes, though his eyes burned into my back when the coaches asked how I was feeling at gym.

They told me they would no longer expect me to go into the closet when it was my turn to put away equipment. I suspected they felt a bit guilty about it too.

Did they know enough to worry about repercussions from the Boneman?

The professors of the classes I missed yesterday were surprised when I handed in the work on time with everyone else. They told me I hadn't been expected to complete it, even though they had given Nicholas the worksheets for me.

But weren't students supposed to hand in the work they'd missed? Or was I given an exception since I was Bone Touched? Did they think the Boneman would be angry with the school if I wasn't treated like the special snowflake he told them I was?

The thought annoyed me. I didn't want to be an exception because of what had happened to me. I just wanted a smooth, normal life separate from what the Boneman forced me or anyone else to do.

Over the course of the week, Nicholas calmed down and

started talking to me normally, walking with me to our classes, and sitting with me and Wren at lunch.

Normal. Regular. Average.

Perfect.

The next couple of weeks passed like that. Our little trio traveled between the library and the cafe on the weekends and evenings, doing homework, telling stories, complaining about whatever professor had gotten on our nerves that day.

I usually sat quietly and practiced my sketches while listening to the others talk. Nicholas had all the same classes I did, so he told whatever stories there were from any of those. And Wren never expected me to say more than a handful of words at a time. So, they made good companions, with Wren fielding any questions Nicholas directed my way and vice versa. Sometimes I wondered if they would even notice if I slipped away. They could get so invested in their conversations.

But one Friday afternoon at the cafe I brought out my phone and showed them the series of messages Nina kept sending me. They dripped with false sincerity, inviting me to her parties, and asking how I was doing with schoolwork. Stuff like that.

Wren scowled at all of it, but Nicholas had a different take.

"Maybe now that things have calmed down and she's gotten used to a new student in our classes, she wants to be friends."

Wren threw back her head and laughed so hard that the guy working behind the counter shot her an annoyed look. "I wouldn't trust a single word she has to say. She's either trying to uncover all your secrets to blackmail you, trick you into making a fool of yourself in front of other people, or wants to pretend to be your friend so she can get to Nicholas."

Nicholas frowned. "Nina can be self-centered, but she's not that conniving."

Wren narrowed her eyes at him. "How do you not see that girl is a literal demon? Whose side are you on anyway? Remember how she treated Sylvan when she first got here?"

"She just felt uncertain about the addition to our class," Nicholas grumbled. "She has problems of her own, you know. Her parents barely speak to her, and even if she brushes it off, I know it affects her."

Wren rolled her eyes. "It's no excuse. She would push us down the stairs if no one was looking. All her nasty little friends would too."

"She's never pushed *me* down the stairs."

"That's because you're the most beautiful person in a one-hundred-mile radius!" Wren clamped her mouth closed the second the words were out. Her face went white, then pink, then red. She turned away. "Objectively, I mean. Look, if you like her so much, why don't you go hang out with her? I'm sure she'd be more than happy for the chance to lie to everyone about dating you."

"Wren—" Nicholas started.

Wren focused on me. "I know this is your first phone, but seriously, don't you know how to block people?" She scooted her chair closer until it bumped into mine and leaned over to show me what to do.

I paid close attention but kept glancing up at Nicholas, who had turned to stare out the window with a hard expression. It wasn't his fault. He just wanted to keep the peace. But it seemed a little idealistic of him to want us to sympathize with Nina.

There were good people. There were traumatized people

who needed a little help. And there were people beyond redemption, stuck in their ways, reliving a cycle of pain and feeding themselves lies to survive it. Nothing could pull them out of it.

Sometimes, I suspected I might fall into that last category.

Like when I had panic attacks. Or I was too scared to be in the same room as a bathtub. Or when I went to my lessons with Professor Tumulus and had to actively concentrate to keep my hands from shaking around the bones I had to hold. He kept saying it would get better, that I'd get used to it. But it had been a couple months, and nothing had changed.

I'd gotten tired of 'eventually.' I'd lost faith in 'in time.' I'd abandoned 'be patient.' I'd given up on 'soon.'

"Are you going to the kickoff game tomorrow night?" Nicholas looked at me when he asked the question.

Kickoff game?

"The basketball game," Wren answered my silent question. She'd gotten good at picking up on what I didn't say. "Honestly, it's not that exciting. Playing games is so much more fun than watching someone else play them, no matter what form they take."

Nicholas, having recovered his humor, rolled his eyes. "You're just jealous you can't play as well as them. I know I am."

Wren raised her eyebrows. "Do my ears deceive me? Is Nicholas Ater admitting that there's something he's not good at?"

"Ha, ha. Not even *I* can be naturally gifted at everything. For example." He pointed the half-eaten remains of his donut at me. "Getting Sylvan to laugh is absolutely impossible."

Wren waved a dismissive hand. "I think that's just Sylvan.

172

I bet she has a really dry, messed up sense of humor, like cracking up when old people fall."

My head whipped around to glare at her.

She held up a reassuring hand. "I'm kidding! It was a joke. A bad one apparently."

I snorted and went back to the deer I'd started drawing. Its legs still looked too spindly to hold it up.

Nicholas jabbed his donut at Wren. "Anyway, you basically answered my question about the game." He swung the doughy half-ring back in my direction. "*You* have not."

I shrugged. I had seen plenty of references to basketball in the movies the admin showed me during my first days here, but I had no idea if I would enjoy the real thing or sports in general. There was still a lot that I didn't know about myself. There was so much time to make up and so many stones to turn over.

"You should seriously consider it. Our games with Animos Prep are always exciting." Nicholas leaned back and took a bite out of the donut.

I froze. Animos Prep. That's the school Professor Tumulus said the Wind Whisperer favored, where it sent its pupils.

"We're playing Animos Prep?" I asked, struggling to keep my voice steady.

Nicholas nodded. "Our kickoff games are always against them. There are usually a few other games in the season we play against them too. Keeps the rivalry alive and all. Plus, it's good for the student council to do some marketing. They always make the best shirts and banners, especially for home games."

Would any Wind Dreamed be there? Would I be able to tell who they were if they did show up? Would they be able to help me if I could find them?

"Can I take your shocked expression to mean you're interested?" Nicholas asked.

"Yes." I nodded so hard my hair, which I'd worn down, bounced around into my face, temporarily obscuring the world in a wall of wavy white.

Nicholas chuckled. "Are you a fan of the sport or just looking for yet another new experience?"

"Yes," I said again. That got a grin from both him and Wren.

"What about you, Wren? Want to join the party now that your best friend is interested?"

Best friend?

Wren sighed heavily. "I guess it would be more fun to go with you guys than to go alone. But if this turns out to suck, you owe me a week of free pastries from this place."

Nicholas lifted his chin. "Fine. I'll accept that deal, but only because I know you're going to enjoy it."

Wren shot back a reply, but I was no longer paying attention. This might be my chance. If I could appeal to the Wind Dreamed, I might be able to free myself from the Boneman. If I could free myself from the Boneman, I might be able to live the normal life I'd always wanted. There were still a lot of uncertainties, but I had to try.

Nineteen

No one told me how loud it was going to be. Everything made more noise than it should have. The announcer, the feet pounding against the waxed wood floors, the squeak of shoes. And don't even get me started on the voices of the crowd. They were loud even when there wasn't anything happening, voices overlapping and crashing into one another like ocean waves in the middle of a hurricane, drowning out anything that wasn't part of them.

Wren ran back to her room and grabbed some earplugs when she saw how much it bothered me. I could actually hear myself think after that. Every sound still reached me perfectly clearly, but they were now at a volume that didn't make my ears feel like they would rupture.

The second obstacle came in the form of the sheer number of people. I could barely take a step without having to dodge someone. The stands were worse. We were lucky enough to run into some of Nicholas's 'friends,' who had a spot near the aisle. Nicholas convinced them to scoot down to accommodate us, letting me sit in the relatively open space on the end.

I still tensed when people walked past me on their way up or down the bleachers, but it was much better than being stuck toward the middle, surrounded on all sides, the way it had been in the tub when I couldn't move, could barely breathe—

"Hey," Nicholas said as softly as he could while still making himself heard through my earplugs.

I glanced at him.

"Are you alright? This isn't too much for you, is it?" He gestured at our miniscule amount of foot space, and all the people sitting close enough to touch us.

"I'm fine." I had to be. I had to find those Animos Prep kids. I couldn't do that if I ran away or had a meltdown here in the stands.

He smiled a warm, quiet smile. "I'm proud of you for trying to stick it out, but you don't have to force yourself to stay if you don't want to."

I shook my head and flattened my hands on my lap. "I have to try."

Nicholas still had that smile on his face when he faced forward. We sat so close that it shouldn't have startled me when his thigh shifted to rest against mine. The contact was light enough that if I weren't on such high alert, I might have missed it.

I took a deep shuddering breath and tried to ignore it. I had other things that required my focus.

I spent the entire first half of the game studying the students of Animos Prep, both the players and the onlookers. They were easy to pick out in the crowd. All the people representing Mortorous Academy wore black or white or some combination of the two. But those from Animos Prep wore varying shades of pastel colors.

There were blues that looked like someone had cut a piece out of the sky. There were greens I was convinced were made with the tears of trees and bushes. There were yellows the color of the sun's rays when they speared through clouds. There were reds which must have been taken from the feathers of exotic birds.

Such whimsical colors.

The section of bleachers across the court from us was meant for the students of Animos Prep, but a few of them sat in our section too, clumped together against the jagged, black and white zebra stripes of the Mortorous Academy kids.

None of them escaped my scrutiny. But I had no idea what I was looking for. How was I supposed to know when I saw a Wind Dreamed? I couldn't even tell if another person was Bone Touched unless I caught a glimpse of their mark. No one was foolish enough to walk around with something like that exposed. Not if they were the real deal, anyway.

I kept watching for any sign, any indication that someone in the middle of all those soft, spring colors was different. For all I knew, they were *all* Wind Dreamed. Just because the Boneman only had one student at Mortorous Academy, didn't mean the Wind Whisperer operated the same way.

I'd found scattered reports about what the Wind Whisperer and Wind Dreamed did. From what I gathered, it had to do with entering and manipulating other people's dreams to change their emotions or motivate them or tell them something they needed to hear. I wasn't sure what that had to do with being the god of life, but it sounded much more relaxing than hunting ghosts.

"Finally!" Wren's exclamation made me jump. "Half time. I'm going to go get some food. Do you guys want anything?"

"Nachos would be great," Nicholas answered. "What about you, Sylvan? Want nachos?"

I shrugged. Another food I had no experience with. It had been an option in the cafeteria a few times, but so far, I'd been more intrigued by other foods.

"I think that was a yes," Nicholas told Wren.

She rolled her eyes but squeezed past us to go get food. We'd been sitting in a line, me at the end, then Nicholas, then Wren, then the boys Nicholas had sweet-talked into sharing their seats with us. The nearest boy, taking advantage of Wren's absence, scooted over to talk to Nicholas.

"Two girls at one time? I always knew you were a player, Nick. Never thought you'd go for the nerd and the mute though." He leaned around Nicholas to address me. "No offense."

My jaw tightened. *Offense very much taken.*

"She's not mute." Nicholas smirked like it was a joke, but his fists clenched in his lap. "She just doesn't waste her words on losers like you." The boy rolled his eyes, and his friends guffawed behind him. "And you shouldn't hate on Wren just because you're illiterate." More raucous laughter. "Besides, neither of them is my girlfriend."

"Sure, they aren't," called one of the boys further down the line. "You just spend every free moment with them." His companions murmured their agreement.

"Just because none of you understand good company, doesn't mean the rest of us don't," Nicholas shot back, still with that playful look on his face, still with that tense posture like he was restraining himself.

This was an interesting side of him. He was *almost* standing up for himself.

The nearest boy waved a dismissive hand. "Whatever. All I'm saying is you got it made." He leaned around Nicholas to address me again with an unsettling smile. "If you ever get tired of this guy, I could always use some company."

Nicholas stiffened slightly. I wouldn't have noticed it if his leg hadn't still been pressed against mine.

"If any of you think you're good enough for Sylvan, you need to get your brains checked. She deserves the world. Why would she settle for someone who thinks it's funny to bully her?" His voice had turned frigid. His smile was gone. He was dead serious.

The guy's eyes widened. "Whoa! You're awfully defensive of a girl you claim you're not dating. I bet Nina would throw a fit if she heard you saying things like that."

Nicholas narrowed his eyes. "Why should I care?"

They snorted and exchanged loaded glances. "You've been Nina's number one from the moment you stepped foot in this school and now you're throwing her away for a girl who just showed up out of the blue? What's gotten into you?"

Nicholas's jaw clenched. He opened his mouth to say something else, but I was done listening to them talk about me like I wasn't sitting right there. I stood and started down the steps. Waiting for food with Wren would be better than staying here while these boys fought over who was the better man.

"Sylvan, where are you going?" Nicholas caught up to me halfway to ground level.

"To find Wren."

179

"Hey." He stepped closer, only one step above the one I stood on. "Don't pay attention to what those guys are saying. They're just trying to get a rise out of both of us. It's what they do."

I glanced up to where the boys were watching us with knowing smirks on their faces. Of course, they were enjoying this. They were the kind of people who lived off the drama of others because they didn't have any lives of their own.

Leeches, all of them. I wouldn't give them the satisfaction.

"Go talk it out. I'll be fine."

It would also give me a chance to look at the Animos Prep students from a different angle. Of course, they would all act the same in the stands. They would put on a show of normality in front of a large group of people, but around a smaller crowd, they might let their guard down.

I didn't give Nicholas a chance to protest before I turned away and marched in the direction I'd seen Wren go. The path was only slightly less crowded than before the game. Most people still sat in the bleachers, but plenty moved about on the ground, visiting the restroom and getting food.

Wren stood at the edge of a cluster of people all waiting beside a counter with the word CONCESSIONS painted in big black letters on the white background of the wall. She spotted my approach and pivoted to face me. "Miss me? Or is my company just that much better than Nick's? Not that he's not fun to be around. I'm just better." She winked.

I shrugged but a half-smile tugged at my lips.

"It shouldn't be too much longer. They just handed out the order of the person who was in front of me in line."

I surveyed the crowd. Pastel clothing blended with black and white in a way that was almost pretty. I tried to take note of any odd behavior. But since I'd never been in a crowd like this, I hardly knew what was normal and what wasn't. This was getting exhausting.

Someone set a tray on the counter and shouted a number so loudly that I couldn't even understand what they'd said. But Wren stepped forward and claimed the tray. She returned and handed me one of the paper plates from it.

"Bon appétit," she declared.

I looked down at the chips dripping with cheese and weighed down by ground meat. It looked supremely messy. Thankfully, a handful of napkins sat on the tray along with two plates identical to mine.

"I thought I might as well jump on the bandwagon and get nachos too." Wren shrugged when my brows rose in silent question. "It helps that they were one of the best options on the menu. Which admittedly isn't saying much but this is still better than going hungry. They like to have these games at dinner time so people will be more likely to buy food."

Nicholas sat all by himself on the bench when we returned. The group of boys who bothered us before had vanished, leaving a healthy amount of space for the three of us. Nicholas scowled into the distance until he caught sight of us, and his face lit up with that brilliant grin.

I raised my eyebrows at him, but Wren voiced the question. "Where did your guys go?"

The smile vanished from his face. "They are *not* my guys."

"Oh?" Wren's eyes widened as Nicholas scooted down to make room for us. Wren now sat between him and me. "Did something exciting happen while I was gone?" She turned on me as if she thought I'd been part of it.

I shrugged, not knowing much more than she did, and she

focused back on Nicholas.

"They were being jerks," Nicholas said casually. "So, I asked them to leave."

Wren eyed him appreciatively. "And they listened to you?"

"I was very persuasive."

Wren leaned toward him, sea-green eyes glowing. "Teach me your secrets."

Nicholas chuckled and nodded back at the basketball court. "Maybe another time. The main event is about to start."

I went ramrod straight when someone dressed in a suit that disturbingly resembled the Boneman walked out onto the court. The Mortorous Academy students cheered, and the Animos Prep kids booed. Except for a handful that sat in the middle of the opposite set of risers.

I narrowed my eyes but got distracted when another person dressed in what looked to be long strips of multicolored pastel plastic ran out to join the Boneman mascot. This time, the Animos students roared in approval and the Mortorous kids jeered. All except that same group of students across from us.

"Ugh," Wren grunted, tearing away my attention. "Their Wind Whisperer costume gets more ridiculous every year. Don't they know you can't dress up as something that isn't even tangible?"

I blinked in confusion. *"Not tangible?"*

Wren explained. "Their mascot, the Wind Whisperer, is kind of like the Boneman is for us. It's another figure of myth and legend. Except the Boneman is made of physical bones, while the Wind Whisperer is just wisps of light and wind, like a counterfeit Aurora Borealis."

I wondered if she would talk like that about the god if she

knew it was real.

We watched the two mascots engage in what Wren called a dance battle. It was cute, I supposed. I just couldn't stop thinking about how these were powerful, real-life entities that these teenagers were dressed as. It ruined the playful atmosphere for me. The show almost felt disrespectful. Especially when Nina and her cronies, as well as a handful of Animos kids, joined them on the floor in cheerleading outfits that showed so much skin, I was surprised they were allowed on school grounds.

Nicholas and Wren were plenty into it though, if a little less vocal than everyone else. But I kept staring at that group of students across from us, who sat quietly and watched while everyone around them yelled. Was that them? Were those the Wind Dreamed I'd been searching for? Did they stay silent because they knew what a mockery everyone was making of such powerful beings?

I didn't pay any attention to which mascot won the dance battle or how the rest of the game played out. I barely registered the taste of the nachos as I mechanically shoveled them into my mouth. My eyes stayed glued to who I hoped— prayed would be my salvation.

There were three girls and two boys. Two of the girls had dyed their hair bright colors, blue and green. They wore clothes in colors that matched their hair. The others each wore a different color: yellow, orange, and purple. I memorized their outfits, their faces, the way one of the boys' cheeks dimpled when he smiled, the way the blue-haired girl played with the end of her high ponytail and leaned into the girl in yellow. By the end of the game, I knew their faces better than I knew my own, which wasn't saying much since

I tended to avoid mirrors.

When the players cleared the court and everyone started shuffling toward the exit, I shot to my feet and scurried down the steps, intent on catching those students before they left.

"Sylvan, wait!" Nicholas and Wren chased after me. "Where are you going?"

I barely spared them a glance. The Animos Prep students had already reached ground level and followed the crushing throng out of the gym. I jumped the last three steps and darted toward them. I probably would have lost them if it hadn't been for that one girl's blue hair. She was tall enough that it acted as a banner, leading me to them.

If I had been in any less of a hurry, I would have remembered that I hated crowds, hated being trapped by them, hated their noise and their smell and the feel of so many people brushing up against me. But there was no time for that. I fought the current of bodies, surging forward the way a shipwrecked man fights to stay afloat in stormy seas.

"Watch out!" The warning came from behind me too late.

A door opened and a flood of basketball players poured out. I slammed into one and went careening into a second before toppling to the ground. The players shouted in alarm as they tripped over me and each other, bodies falling in a heap.

As if triggered by my lack of motion, my fears caught up to me all at once. A tangle of limbs crushed me to the floor. Like the final blow from an executioner's ax, the memories of being stuck at the bottom of that tub, of being squeezed by a pair of skeleton arms until I passed out, of being held in place while my bones were systematically shattered and put back together, came down on me with deadly force.

I couldn't get enough air into my lungs. My vision darkened. Nausea rose out of the pit of my stomach. My whole body shook. I think I screamed.

It only got worse as the people on top of me struggled to get off, alternately alleviating and increasing the pressure. Someone yelled at me to stop thrashing. I wasn't aware I'd been moving at all until they said something. I clawed at the ground in a futile attempt to drag myself out from under the pile. My vision was going. I was losing any sense of my surroundings besides the fact that I couldn't move.

This was it. This was how I was going to die. Hyperventilating under a pile of sweaty teenage athletes. I would have liked something more peaceful, but this seemed in line with everything my life had been like up to this point.

I reached one final time for freedom.

And a hand wrapped around mine.

It gripped painfully hard and nearly yanked my arm out of its socket. But it bought me a few inches. I threw out my other hand, and another caught it. A third grabbed further down on my wrist. The combined strength of the people on the other side managed to pull me out and up onto my feet. My legs trembled under me as they herded me somewhere quiet. The world was still too blurry to make out details.

Some of the hands let go, but one set reeled me into a pair of warm arms and a solid chest.

"It's ok. You're safe. I've got you."

Nicholas.

I waited for the panic to consume me again at being so close, so wrapped up in him. But it didn't. Compared to where I'd just been, his arms were barely more than threads I could break whenever I wanted to. Unlike when I was trapped in the tub, I could still move. My limbs were still free.

I leaned into him, glad that my weak knees didn't have to hold my full weight, glad that I could take this moment to calm my breathing. My eyes slid closed.

"Is she alright?" An unfamiliar female voice asked.

"Yeah, I think she's calming down," Nicholas answered, his hand rubbing my back. "She'll be fine in a minute."

"Good thing we didn't lose our heads like the rest of these fools," said another new voice.

"She panics when she feels trapped." Nicholas cradled the back of my head. "Once she's out, she's ok though."

"Frida is similar, but opposite. She doesn't like being alone in large spaces."

"Thanks for spilling all my secrets to everyone, *Almos*. I happen to know that you are terrified of scorpions."

Nicholas chuckled, the sound rumbling from his chest into my ear like a tiny earthquake. I turned my head to try and get a look at whoever he was talking to. The movement seemed to startle him. He let go of me like I'd burned him and took a step back.

A faint flush crept up his face. "Hey, sorry for grabbing you like that, I'm—"

A dark arm, the color of trees from wild forests I'd never seen, shoved him out of the way. The girl who replaced him in front of me grinned, her bright white teeth creating a striking contrast with her deep brown skin. I was startled to recognize her as one of the people I'd been pursuing: the girl in yellow.

"She lives!" The exclamation startled me. "How are you doing, chickpea?"

Another girl, the one with blue hair and clothes, joined

her friend. "She looks good to me. Maybe a little more than good." She winked and my face heated.

"Didn't you two hear what her boyfriend *just* said?" I turned, recognizing the one they'd called Almos. He wore a shade of orange that reminded me of sunsets. And beside him stood the boy in purple.

The girl in green rolled her eyes as she closed in on me too. "Don't worry. We aren't falling on top of her like those clumsy basketball players." Frida.

Nicholas peeked over the yellow girl's shoulder. "Sylvan, are you alright?"

"Your name is Sylvan?" The blue-haired girl asked, not giving me a second to respond to Nicholas. "That's such a pretty name. I wish I had a name like that."

"There's nothing wrong with your name, Lorien," Frida assured her before turning back to me. "I'm Frida. This is Lorien and Imena. The boys are Almos and Reve. As I'm sure you can tell, we're from Animos Prep. Reve and I helped your boyfriend pull you out and get you back here."

Boyfriend? Back here?

I glanced around. A locker room. Maybe the one the players came out of when I ran into them.

Focusing back on the girls crowded in front of me, I remembered my manners. "Thank you."

They all beamed and started circling me like a pack of excited dogs.

"Your hair!" exclaimed Lorien as she combed her fingers through my wavy, white ponytail. "You could dye this all sorts of colors and it would come out so well."

"Not to mention, your eyes." Imena hooked a finger under my chin and tilted my face around to look at them from all angles. "Stunning. I've never seen anything like them."

I grew more and more confused as they continued to survey me and point out random features that they found interesting. Their fingers danced like butterflies across my skin and their voices buzzed like hummingbird wings. I didn't know how I thought my first meeting with the Wind Dreamed would go, but this certainly wasn't it. I thought there would be a lot more panting and pleading on my part. Maybe a few haughty looks from them.

That was what almost everyone at Mortorous would do. Plenty of them had done just that, and I didn't need anything from them.

The strangest part was, I didn't hate it. This attention. It felt affirming, like they actually meant what they said and cared about me. There were no backhanded compliments or barely concealed jealousy—though Lorien said multiple times that she wanted different parts of my body.

They had a pervasive calming effect on me. Like the Boneman's fear, but the opposite. One of the blogs I found had said something about the Wind Dreamed having a calming effect on people around them. That must be what was happening.

I wasn't used to this, but it was kind of nice. Even if I didn't know what to do with myself or how to respond to all the things they said. They didn't seem to expect me to. Like Wren.

Finally, Nicholas stepped forward, close enough to interrupt the girls' orbit. "I'm Nicholas, and this, as you've heard, is Sylvan. I'm sure you can tell we're from Mortorous Academy, both third years. It's nice to meet all of you."

"It's wonderful to meet you too," Lorien gushed, matching

Nicholas's charming smile. "Reve and I are also third years, but Imena and Almos are a year older and will graduate in the spring. Frida is our baby. She's just a first year."

Frida swatted at Lorien's hand when she patted her head.

I got the feeling Nicholas and Lorien were a pair of peas in a pod. She was gorgeous and probably had all the boys hanging off her every word despite what seemed like self-esteem issues. It might even help. The shy girls were always the ones that got the boy at the end of the movie.

Almos stuck his hands in the pockets of his pastel orange pants. "It's been a while since we've met anyone who is...not from our area. The rivalry always seems to come between us."

Could he have been talking about a rivalry between the Boneman and Wind Whisperer? He certainly chose his words carefully.

"It's a stupid rivalry," Nicholas replied. "It's not like we chose where we went to school. Our parents and guardians did that for us."

"It's just a way to make money." Frida crossed her arms. "The student council gets a lot of funding from these Mortorous vs. Animos events. We are nothing if not a capitalist society."

Imena rolled her eyes. "Please don't bore our new friends with your politics. *We* know we're on the same side, even if no one else does."

Was that another thinly veiled commentary on our supernatural patrons? It was hard to get a read on these people. Did they know about me, but were trying to keep quiet in front of Nicholas?

As if on cue, Nicholas stepped toward me so that his arm

brushed against mine. "Well, it was really nice meeting you all. Thank you again for helping me get Sylvan out of that tight spot. But it's getting late, and I wouldn't want you to miss your bus."

They stopped and looked at him for a moment. Frida bounced up on her toes, leaned into Nicholas's ear, and whispered something that made his face pale. I frowned at him as the girls drifted away.

Lorien smiled as they retreated. "You're so thoughtful. Watch over dear Sylvan for us. We look forward to seeing you at the next game."

They started heading for the door. This was it, my last chance.

"Wait!" I stepped forward and reached out as if I could grab them from halfway across the room.

The five paused to exchange glances. Imena broke off and came back to me. She leaned in just as Frida had done to Nicholas and whispered in my ear.

"We know what you dream of, chickpea. But we cannot take you from your creator. I'm sorry. I hope that with time you can grow to love him as much as we love ours."

20

Twenty

Imena darted back toward the group and with a final round of waves, they left, taking my last hope with them. Yes, they were Wind Dreamed. No, they could not save me from the Boneman. My sentence was irrevocable. Not even another deity could free me.

"Hey, Sylvan?" Nicholas touched my elbow.

I flinched, the calm feeling having left with the Animos Prep students.

"Sorry." Nicholas retracted his hands. "You don't look so good. Are you ok?"

I shook my head.

"Do you want to talk about it?"

"Where's Wren?"

"I lost her in the crowd." He rubbed the back of his neck. "She probably went back to her dorm. Or she might be outside. I don't know."

Right. I had run off without any regard for those I'd left behind. It wasn't that I didn't care about them. I thought they were both great. But if I had a chance to get away from all of this, I would. I would have been sad to leave them behind if the Wind Dreamed had said they could take me away, but I had to think about what was best for me. In the end, it didn't matter.

"We should go." I started for the door.

"Sylvan."

I didn't stop and Nicholas didn't try to come after me.

* * *

Wren gave me an earful about running off without her the next day at breakfast. I bore it patiently with a few muttered apologies and promised not to do anything like that again. But when she asked if I wanted to study or go into town, I told her I wasn't feeling good. She blamed seasonal allergies and left me alone after that.

During school on Monday, Nicholas talked to me sparingly and gently, like I might shatter if he spoke too loudly. Wren continued to chatter, but every once in a while, she would cast a suspicious glance at me like she could see that I wasn't really paying attention.

Funny how the loss of hope can make you feel worse than before you had any to begin with.

It was with this attitude that I walked into Dr. Shalm's class on Thursday and spotted Nina sitting in my seat. Lily, Vanessa, and a few others stood around her.

I paused at the edge of their circle. It didn't take Nina long to notice me. Her entourage parted to get a better view of what promised to be a spectacle.

"I was wondering when you'd show up." She leaned forward, planting her elbows on my desk. "You haven't been answering my messages lately."

I hadn't answered any messages she'd ever sent me, but it seemed pointless to bring up.

Nina picked at her nails. "I invite you to parties. No response. I ask how you're doing. No response. I even offer to study with you and still *no response*."

"I haven't been getting any messages. Maybe you saved the wrong number." My voice came out bored and toneless.

Even though she sat and I stood, she managed to look down her nose at me. "I sent myself a message from your phone. I know I have the right number. But even if ignoring me wasn't enough, I see you hanging around Nick all the time now. It's like you've glued yourself to him. Even after I told you how much trouble he was. Is my advice worth nothing to you?"

It's worth less than nothing. "I don't have control over what he does with his time."

"Maybe not, but you have control over what you do with *your* time. And believe me, your time would be better spent with someone else."

I kept having to remind myself that she wasn't worth a reaction. "You're in my seat."

"It's not yours anymore," Lily declared. She seemed pretty smug for someone who wouldn't benefit from this situation.

"Dr. Shalm changed the seating around a bit," Nina told me with a false smile. "You're over there now." She pointed at a seat toward the middle of the room, right in the center of a loud group of boys. "They're more your speed anyway. I'm sure you'll get along wonderfully."

I knew this was a power play. I knew she was trying to take advantage of me, put me in my place. Dr. Shalm might have changed the seating on her own, or Nina might have talked her into it. Either way, I doubted going against a teacher would look good. And it might be more satisfying to do what Nina wanted and act like it didn't bother me.

Besides, what did I care if I didn't get to sit next to Nicholas for *one* class when I sat next to him in all of the others? Nina could have her small victory. It would be her only one.

I pivoted smoothly and walked to the seat Nina indicated. The chair wobbled a bit when I sat down but it held firm. An overly muscled boy sat beside me. He eyed me in a way that probably wasn't appropriate for a school setting but didn't say anything. I did my best to ignore him. At least he was quiet. I could make this work.

Nicholas hurried in just as the bell rang. Would he be in too much of a rush to notice my absence until after the lesson started and he was trapped for the day with his new desk partner?

Dr. Shalm told us we were going to do more silent reading today by ourselves. That meant no getting up to talk to other students that sat halfway across the room because nasty girls had stolen their seats. I opened my book and began reading.

"Sylvan." The word tickled the back of my neck as it floated past my ear. *That didn't take long.*

I glanced at Nicholas. He crouched beside my desk low enough that Dr. Shalm couldn't see him. She was busy reading her own book, so she might not have noticed anyway.

"Why are you sitting next to…" He glanced at the boy beside me who was on his phone behind his book. "…him?"

I gave a pointed look at Nina, also on her phone behind her book. "Change in seating."

Nicholas glanced back at Nina and even from that side

view of his face, his deep scowl was visible. He took my wrist and pulled me out of my seat.

I flinched at the contact. "Hey!" I hadn't been one to shout over the course of what little of my life I could remember, but I certainly had no problem doing so now. The noise got the attention of everyone in the room *except* Dr. Shalm.

I scowled at her. There was no way that she hadn't heard me.

"I'll fix this." Nicholas held firm and somehow gentle at the same time. It surprised me that such a proprietary touch could be so tender. Almost the same way the Boneman held me right before he broke my—

No! I fought the rising panic.

Nicholas led me back to our seats and let go so he could lean toward Nina with both hands braced on his desk.

"Give Sylvan her seat back." His voice was sharp as knives and swords and all kinds of things used to disembowel a person.

Nina looked up, a little wide eyed at his tone, then glanced at me, massaging my wrist with one hand and holding my open book in the other. Her smug smile returned. "But she likes sitting next to Steven. She practically begged me to switch with her. Right, Sylvan?" Her words were sweet venom dripping from her mouth.

I rolled my eyes.

Nicholas didn't look the least bit deterred. He leaned in closer and whispered something in her ear. As I watched, her eyes went round, and her face drained of color. She leaped from her seat with her things like she was fleeing a burning building.

Nicholas took my hand, much more calmly, and guided me

around to my seat. I tried to wriggle free, but he didn't let go until I sat beside him once more.

Several pairs of shocked eyes stared at us, but no one made a move, and Dr. Shalm still hadn't taken notice. I looked at Nicholas who had resumed reading his book as if this was a normal day in class.

What just happened?

He'd never acted like this. He was the peacekeeper, the bright smile, the guy who built bridges. Not the one that burned them. This Nicholas sitting beside me was a completely different person. I clenched my hands in my lap to keep them from trembling.

I'd left my bag by the seat Nina glowered at me from. No doubt she would destroy whatever she could get her hands on now that Nicholas had humiliated her in front of everyone.

I started to get up. Nicholas caught my hand and didn't let go. My heart fluttered frantically in my chest. "You just got here and you're trying to leave again?" His playful smile did nothing to calm me down.

"My bag." I craned my neck to make sure Nina wasn't riffling through it.

"This bag?" Nicholas set down his book and held up my satchel.

"How...?" I breathed.

He set it on my desk. "I grabbed it on our way over here. No one's making you go anywhere if I have anything to say about it."

I put a hand to my mouth. My insides roiled. What was going on? I felt whiplashed from the sudden change in direction Nicholas's personality had taken.

He'd been moving closer and closer over the last couple

weeks that we'd been friends. At the game, he had no problem touching me, holding me.

Maybe a grain of truth lay in Nina's scathing words. I still didn't really know Nicholas. If he'd been putting on an act for so long to get everyone at school to like him, was it so hard to believe he'd been doing the same thing to me, and this was his real personality?

His behavior reminded me painfully of someone *or something*.

A different set of hands on me, forcing me to move how he wanted, do what he wanted, while I was powerless to resist. Breaking my bones and my spirit too many times to count.

My stomach lurched. I turned just in time to retch onto the ground instead of all over my desk. Several nearby students jumped up with disgusted exclamations. I bent over double as I expelled my considerable breakfast over the black and white tiles.

Someone, Nicholas probably, pulled my hair from my face as I heaved. My body shook through the last throes of it. When I was sure I was finished, I rested my head on my arms, folding them across my knees. My legs braced on either side of the puddle of sick. My breathing came in deep gasps.

"Are you ok?" That had to be Nicholas's hand on my back; his soft tone, inquiring after me.

I straightened and packed my things as quickly as possible.

"I can take you to the nurse." Nicholas started to get out of his seat after me.

"No!" It came out far too wobbly, too desperate.

It made him pause and that was all the time I needed to rush past Dr. Shalm's desk. She still hadn't noticed anything or even looked up from her book. What was wrong with her?

I fled to the bathroom. My mouth tasted foul and there was vomit on my lips. I washed my face as quickly as possible, then parked myself in a stall, locked the door, and tucked my feet up on the seat, for the rest of class.

* * *

I didn't know what would be worse: risking the wrath of the Boneman if I didn't go to the rest of my classes, or risking being near Nicholas again. Part of me knew it wasn't his fault, but that didn't quiet the instincts screaming at me to stay away from him.

Just thinking about it made me sick to my stomach all over again.

I found myself outside Professor Tilns's classroom when the bell rang. I drifted in and took a seat at the desk Wren usually occupied. She came in a moment later and frowned at me.

"Please switch. I can't sit next to him."

She flopped down in my seat. "What happened?"

I explained as quickly as I could. "And I panicked because—" I stopped. I couldn't tell her exactly why. I couldn't tell anyone what I was.

"Because it makes you uncomfortable," Wren finished.

Close enough. I nodded.

Wren smiled sympathetically. "I understand. We can switch but maybe you should try talking to him. Nina has always been like that. Nick… not so much."

I nodded again. Something was going on with him beyond Nina being a bully.

Wren shook her head. "I can't believe he would grab you

like that. He's always been so polite." She rubbed her hands over her face.

I wished I could tell her the real reason physical touch produced such a reaction in me. I didn't want to make Nicholas the bad guy when it was all in my head, but I had to protect myself.

"Sylvan."

I nearly jumped out of my skin. Nicholas stood on the other side of my desk.

"Is there a problem with a seating change again?" He eyed Wren, who reared back like he'd slapped her.

Wren would never do anything like that.

"I want to be here," I answered.

Nicholas gestured from Wren to his empty seat. "Then, Wren, would you mind—?"

"Yes, I would mind," Wren snapped. She must have taken his implied insult personally.

Nicholas blinked at her unforgiving response before turning back to me. "Is there something wrong?"

I tucked my knees to my chest.

Nicholas's face pinched. "Sylvan, please don't hollow out on me again. Can we work this out?"

My arms wrapped around my torso. My eyes fixed themselves on my desk.

He knelt down beside me, trying to catch my eye. "If this is about Nina, I promise you, she learned her lesson. She's not going to bother you anymore."

I shook my head.

"Sylvan, talk to me. I'm here." His hand reached up to grip the edge of my desk, the knuckles white. White like bone. *Bones, bones bones bonesbonesbonesBONES.*

I recoiled, leaning as far away from him as I could without tipping out of my chair.

Wren leaned forward. "She doesn't want to talk to you."

Nicholas looked from me to her then back to me before sighing, getting up, and going to his normal seat.

He stayed quiet for the next three classes and didn't even look at me. I didn't have anyone else to swap seats with, but I kept to the far edge of my chair as much as possible.

Lunch came and, thankfully, Nicholas was nowhere to be seen. Wren waited, by herself, at our usual bench.

"You doing ok?" she asked.

My lips pressed into a thin line, tighter than a lid on a coffin.

"As well as can be expected then," she muttered, picking at her food. "You know—"

"Scoot over." Nina planted herself forcefully between me and Wren.

Wren grabbed the back of the bench for stability. "Excuse you!"

Lily, Vanessa, and some other girls closed in and squeezed themselves onto the bench until Wren had to get up and I was surrounded. This had to be trouble.

"Do you mind?" Wren snarled. "No one invited you."

"Get lost." Vanessa made a shooing motion with her hand. "Go bury your nose in a book or something."

Wren turned red with anger. I tried to get up. If they wanted this bench, they could have it. There were plenty of other places to sit. But a girl I didn't know stepped in front of me.

Trapped.

"So, you and Nicholas, huh?" Nina spat.

I glared at her, focused on keeping my breathing steady. She might not know what she was doing, but I was *not* going to let her have the satisfaction of giving me a panic attack. I wasn't going to sit here and let her bully me without a fight either. "What did he say to you that made you move so fast?"

Her jaw tightened, but she ignored my question. "Obviously he doesn't care about you that much or he'd be here right now."

"I don't care about him," I replied.

"A likely story," Lily cut in. "He can't stay away from you, and he's not himself anymore. He *threatened* Nina." She deserved it. They all did. "Are you bribing him or something?"

"I don't have money." My fists clenched. My food lay forgotten on the tray in my lap.

Vanessa smirked and muttered under her breath. "A girl doesn't need *money* to bribe a boy."

"How are you here if you don't have money?" Lily demanded, either ignoring or not hearing Vanessa's comment. "The tuition costs more than most people can afford."

"Scholarship."

"I didn't think they made pretty nerds," Lily said.

I raised an eyebrow. "You think I'm pretty?"

Nina elbowed her friend for the unintentional compliment. "Look, if you don't care about him then prove it. Get with someone else. I'm having a party tomorrow, great place for hooking up, despite the adult supervision."

I didn't have time for this childish nonsense. If Nina wanted Nicholas, she was welcome to him. I couldn't even bring myself to be around him.

I opened my mouth to say as much. "I don't—"

My muscles stiffened. My eyes went wide. A pervasive fear spider-walked across my skin, chilling me to the bone. My breathing went low, and my heart rate accelerated. I knew that feeling. But he couldn't be here. There were too many people. I didn't do anything wrong. Why was he coming after me?

I realized I could still move. The terror was minimal, enough to feel but not enough to paralyze. I grabbed my satchel and shot to my feet, spilling my untouched food all over the ground, and sending the girl in front of me stumbling into Wren.

No matter how much they shouted after me, Nina and her friends did nothing to slow me down. The forest was in full view of the courtyard. People were everywhere, but I wasn't taking any chances. I darted inside the cafeteria and pressed my face to the nearest window.

The fear intensified. I had a view of the tree line, but nothing moved inside it except a slight swaying of branches in the breeze. My eyes scanned the forest's edge over and over until they fixed on a small, white figure.

It was too far to fully make out and half hidden behind a tree, but that had to be him. He stood there for a moment, looking at me. And in the time it took me to blink, he vanished.

Was he trying to tell me something? There had been no telepathic communication. Was he just there to spy on me? Was he here for Professor Tumulus?

It doesn't matter why he was here as long as he stays away from you.

Pounding footsteps heralded Wren's arrival. She bent over double to catch her breath.

"What…did I say…about running off…without me?" she wheezed.

"Sorry. I thought I saw something." I looked back out the window. Nothing but trees.

Wren straightened and followed my gaze into the forest. "Saw *what*? Another ghost?" The space between her eyebrows creased with worry.

"No. It must have been nothing." The last thing I wanted was to trigger her memories of our encounter with Lucas.

Wren heaved a relieved sigh. "Honestly, just when I think I've got you figured out, you go and pull something like this and confuse me all over again."

I winced. "Sorry."

She waved a hand. "Whatever. At least we ditched Nina. Let's go eat something before lunch is over."

After one last glance out the window, I followed her back toward the tables. We sat inside, hoping Nina wouldn't bother us with more witnesses around. But I was more concerned about the Boneman's appearance. No one else seemed to have noticed. As long as he stayed away from me, I supposed it wasn't too bad. I'd had enough of my past plaguing me today.

21

Twenty-One

Nicholas was markedly absent from the rest of our shared classes. Strange, but at least I was able to focus on my work and go to my lesson with Professor Tumulus in peace.

We had been progressing well. I could now view the entirety of a creature's life by holding its bone in my hand and channeling my magic. The test subjects had all been animals up to this point: pets and wildlife. But Professor Tumulus wanted to try something new.

My eyes widened when he put a human fibula in front of me.

I stared at him for a long moment. He couldn't possibly be serious.

"Go ahead. Tell me what scene first comes to your mind," Tumulus urged gently.

I wasn't so sure. Doing animals was easy. They didn't have complicated emotions. They had cute, endearing behaviors, like the mouse that enjoyed chasing its tail, or raw instincts, like the need to satisfy hunger.

Humans were vastly different. In the past, the first image I saw was always some emotionally charged moment in the animal's life—usually when it got treats or caught a particularly hearty meal. There was no telling what I would see from an actual person.

Not to mention morality. There was a reason dead men told no tales. Their lives weren't any of my business.

Then again, it's not like I had a choice in the matter. The Boneman had spoken, and his word was law. I certainly didn't intend to see him twice in one day. The first time had been a cryptic, narrow escape. I doubted I would get off so easily a second time.

I picked up the bone in both hands. It was spotted with age but not quite old enough that I worried I'd damage it. As before, my eyes slid shut and I centered myself, summoning the memories of this individual.

It came in a violent rush. Breaking glass and shouting, gunshots and a muffled thump. It was dark but hooded men hovered in my vision with shining metal in their hands. Then sirens and flashing lights. One of the men pointed his gun at me and discharged it.

I cried out and dropped the bone as the bullet tore into me. The images vanished and I was back in the classroom. My hands went to my torso, where a gunshot wound would have sent blood gushing down my shirt.

Nothing.

I was intact. It hadn't happened to me. My wide-eyed gaze went to Professor Tumulus.

"What...?" I could barely get the word out around my heavy breathing.

"That's what you're supposed to tell me." I hated the way

he obviously knew what I'd seen.

I looked at the fibula where I had dropped it on the table. "They got shot."

Professor Tumulus nodded with a small smile. "The biggest moment of his life. And unfortunately, the last. The man who owned this bone used to work at a convenience store. He was asked to close up late one night and got jumped on the way back to his car. One of the other employees called the cops while the robbery was taking place, but they arrived too late to help him. He bled out in the parking lot."

"Did they get them?" I asked. "The robbers?"

Professor Tumulus smiled at me. "Sometimes that's what we do. Those who are Bone Touched can see those last moments of a person's life and glean insight that is vital to solving crimes. The souls of people who were murdered tend to cling to life, which means they have a high probability of becoming ghosts. Solving the mystery and bringing their killer to justice can be such a powerful act that a ghost will pass on by itself."

It made sense. If someone found a way to kill the Boneman, I would definitely rest easier.

Tumulus sat back in his chair. "Not all Bone Touched are as combative and confrontational as Mallor had to be with that ghost you saw in Noxier. Some prefer a more pacifist approach. Many times, it's better for the area around them. Bone Touched are supposed to go unnoticed. But there are many eyes in a city, even at night. Avoiding detection gets hard. So, we kill two birds with one stone."

Huh.

Was that what I was supposed to do? Go out and solve homicide cases? I doubted I had the stomach for it. I had only just gotten comfortable enough to talk to people in full sentences without shutting down. How was I supposed to be a detective and catch murderers when I couldn't even face Nicholas? Being a freelance agent like Mallor didn't sit right with me either, though. It seemed like such a lonely existence. Nothing about being Bone Touched was appealing.

"Let's continue. I want to see if you can watch the whole of what happened that night. Maybe rewind to a happier time in this man's life," Professor Tumulus said.

I dreaded seeing that scene again, but my traitorous hand reached for the bone anyway.

The trauma of the moment I had to keep reliving over and over and over left me reeling each time I opened my eyes. I kept bracing myself for the bang of the gunshot and needed longer and longer to calm down afterward. I had to take a break half an hour through.

Professor Tumulus was patient with me. He said this was a difficult lesson for everyone. He disappeared into his office for a minute and came back with a black kettle filled with tea. It tasted grassy, but it was soothing and warm, so I didn't complain.

Tumulus sat across from me, watching the contents of his mug steam. "I suppose now would be a good time to warn you about your limits."

He didn't have to say anything. Over the course of the last few weeks, I'd become painfully aware of what I could and couldn't handle out in the real world. He didn't need to remind me.

"I assume you are unaware of how you came into possession of your magic, Ms. Ravena." It had something to do with the Boneman, and all that torturous time spent submerged in that milky fluid. "Your first memories are of lying in a tub filled with water, yes?" I nodded. "And of the Boneman visiting you periodically and breaking your bones into thousands of tiny pieces."

I nearly spit out my tea. He'd never been so forward about what had happened before I came to the school. As an unspoken rule, we didn't talk about it. Tumulus seemed to intuit how much I hated what little I could remember of my past and gave me space to deal with it in my own way.

Not anymore, apparently.

Tumulus handed me a napkin. "You see, there was a purpose behind all of the destruction and reconfiguring of your bone structure. The Boneman didn't just give you a different form. He *infused* your marrow with magic. He just had to take your bones apart to get to it first. That store of magic is what allows you to do what you do during our lessons. I've mentioned most of this before."

"We aren't sure, but we assume the bath all Bone Touched live in for the period of reconstruction has healing properties that help our bodies to recover from so much damage. Either that, or we're in there for long enough that the bones heal on their own."

"So, I could have been in the tub for *years*?" It had felt like forever, but the idea of losing so much of my life made my head spin. How old would I have been when the Boneman took me? I was only seventeen now. Was the Boneman snatching small children to be his servants?

He shrugged. "Who knows? There are still plenty of mysteries surrounding our little gang. But the important thing to remember is that the only reason the magic stays inside your bones is because they are intact. If you were to, say, fall down some stairs and break your leg, you would probably die."

My eyes went wide. "Die?"

Tumulus sighed and took a sip of his tea. "Yes. I have heard too many tales of Bone Touched who met with all-too-common accidents—accidents they could have survived had they been entirely human."

I looked down at my hands. I wasn't entirely human?

"Our magic is tied to our life forces. We cannot live without it. And since we don't have access to the Boneman's restorative tub, we can't heal ourselves in time to keep it from leaking out. Now, I'm not telling you this to scare you into leading a cautious life. Our bones are generally more durable than the average person's, probably for this specific reason. And small fractures are usually nothing to worry about. A broken finger bone will keep you lethargic and bed-ridden for a while, but you'll recover. It's the bigger bones in the arms and legs and torso that you need to worry about. And the worse the break, the worse for you."

So, when I collided with the basketball players after the game, I could have died for real if I broke something in the resulting dogpile? I had thought I'd meet my end under all of those students, but I was convinced that was just the panic talking.

"This is just something you need to be aware of going forward. I wouldn't recommend any extreme sports or getting into a car with people who might have questionable driving skills." I instantly thought of Wren. "But that shouldn't discourage you from going out and having fun with your friends when you want to."

Right. Nothing to worry about. I just might *die*. No

pressure. I threw back the last of my tea, relishing the warm path it traced down my throat. I *loved* being here.

Professor Tumulus took my cup once I set it down. "Are you ready to try again?"

No. I grabbed the bone anyway.

* * *

Two hours later, I trudged out of Professor Tumulus's classroom feeling tired and raw from watching the man die so many times. I hadn't been able to see anything but that moment in his life, those quick flashes before everything went black.

Professor Tumulus told me it was because it held such a strong emotional charge and had happened so quickly, but I just saw it as a reason to be concerned about getting a visit from a certain someone in the middle of the night. After the day I'd had, it would be just my luck.

I had closed the door behind me and didn't make it a single step before he spoke.

"I knew it."

I whirled around. Nicholas stood in the middle of the hallway blocking my exit. His black eyes bore into me like the darkness of an empty grave.

My hand went right back to the door. It was my only method of escape since Tumulus's classroom was the last at the end of the hallway.

Nicholas's eyes widened, and he raised his hands in surrender. "Wait! Please, let me explain."

My eyes narrowed. My hand clenched the doorknob. He was far enough away that I could whip the door open and lock it from the inside before he got to me. Tumulus would take it from there. He might not be willing to save me from the Boneman, but surely he would try to protect me from another student.

"I know what I did this morning made you uncomfortable." His words were rushed and breathless.

"'Uncomfortable' is a gross understatement," I muttered.

Nicholas grimaced. "I'm sorry. I didn't mean it that way. I don't want to make you feel unsafe. It just riled me that Nina was pushing you around and I thought you might need someone to stick up for you. You're new, and I thought that made you fragile the way I was when I first came here. I thought we were at a point where you would accept and appreciate that from me instead of being scared. After all, you let me hold you when you freaked out after the game."

"That had nothing to do with you." It had been more because of the Wind Dreamed than because of him. If they hadn't been there, I would have hated Nicholas's embrace.

He took a step toward me. I turned the knob and braced my feet to pull. He halted his advance and backed up a couple paces.

"I thought you needed someone who could be strong for you. I thought I was supposed to be that person because when I saw you sitting outside the office on day one, some part of me knew that we were the same. I wanted to be your knight in shining armor, because I didn't have anyone like that when I was new. But more than that I wanted to be there for you because I'm Bone Touched too."

My heart stopped in my chest. I wasn't sure if I was breathing.

I'm Bone Touched too.

211

Slowly, I let go of the doorknob. He clenched his jaw and swallowed hard, but kept his mouth shut, waiting for a reaction. We stared at each other for a long time, not knowing what to say.

"You're... Bone Touched?" It surprised me when Mallor showed he was Bone Touched but hearing it from Nicholas turned my brain to ash faster than a cremation furnace.

Rather than reply, he unbuttoned his shirt collar and pulled it back to reveal those inimitable marks below the left side of his collarbone: three, black fingers no more than bones.

My hand went to the spot on my chest where I had the same mark. Déjà vu washed over me. Mallor had done the same thing when he saved me from the ghost in Noxier.

Nicholas rebuttoned his shirt. "I've been leading personal tours of the school for new students since the beginning of last year, wanting to be the first point of contact for any new Bone Touched. I think I knew what you were the moment we walked through those doors, and you saw that statue of the Boneman. Your reaction was too genuine for someone who had never seen him in real life. Still, I worried I was just projecting my suspicions onto you. I didn't know if there could be multiple Bone Touched here. I didn't dare hope."

He raked his fingers through his hair. "But the more time I spent around you, the more things were adding up. You seeing Lucas, your panic attacks, your lack of family, your aversion to physical contact and small spaces were all too much to be coincidences."

He couldn't seem to look at me. "I didn't want to push you about it. I didn't know how you would react. The only thing I wanted when the Boneman brought me here was space to heal. I was afraid revealing what I was would bother you or

212

trigger some kind of relapse."

His eyes darted up to meet mine. "I was determined to be your friend regardless and tell you when the time felt right. But then there was this morning, and I couldn't stop myself." He rubbed the back of his neck with a guilty hand. "I'm sure you felt the Boneman when he came to reprimand me during lunch."

"He came for *you*?"

"He didn't take kindly to the way you felt about what I had done. He said I needed to be gentler with you. I know cornering you isn't exactly gentle." He glanced sheepishly at the door. "But I had to tell you. I needed you to understand that I want nothing but your safety and peace of mind. I think that's why we're here. I think the Boneman put us together to support each other."

I crossed my arms over my chest. Maybe. But I didn't want to think about the Boneman pulling the strings in my life like that. It meant he had the foresight to see that we might be friends and the power to push us together. It meant he might actually *care* about us.

It was too much. My time here had been such an over-whelming mess. I didn't know what to do about this new information. I leaned back against wall beside the door and slid down until I sat on the cold floor. My forehead rested on my knees. Nicholas's shoes squeaked as he parked himself on the floor down the hall, propping his shoulder against the wall to face me.

"Do you want me to leave?" he asked with trepidation, clearly not wanting to.

"I don't know," I mumbled into my lap. I didn't know anything anymore. How many times would my world get turned upside down before it finally settled?

A smile ghosted into his voice. "Is it too soon to hug you?"

I huffed a laugh. Definitely, and he knew it.

It made sense now that I thought about it. Nicholas said he didn't have a family either. He was also a transfer student. Nina said he was a bit weird when he first got here and that he disappeared and sometimes couldn't be reached.

In retrospect, I should have figured it out. But I was so wrapped up in my own pain that I hadn't even considered that someone so close to me might have had the same experiences.

I thumped my head back against the wall. "What now?"

Nicholas sighed. "I guess we go to school and eat regularly and learn bone magic. You know, normal people things."

I almost smiled at that. "I thought I'd be alone."

"Alone?"

"I thought I'd be the only one he'd—" I cut myself off. I couldn't even finish the sentence. "Admin had no idea what happened to me before I got here, and they said I wasn't allowed to talk about it with anyone. It's just been so... *suffocating*." I choked on the last word.

I buried my face in my knees again. He wouldn't see me cry. He could watch me panic, but he would *not* see me cry. His pants whispered against the floor as he scooted a bit closer but kept his hands to himself.

"It wasn't any different two years ago when the Boneman brought me here. I think admin are too afraid of messing up and making the Boneman mad. They aren't the only ones afraid of his wrath though. We've got our fair share of baggage."

"How does it get any better?" I whispered against my legs. "How do I stop being afraid of him?"

Tumulus said I'd get used to it, but it had happened so long ago for the professor that I didn't feel like he had a proper grasp on how I felt. Nicholas hadn't even done that much this morning and suddenly I couldn't stand being around him until he explained himself.

"You never stop being afraid of him and you never forget what he did to you. But after a while, it starts to fade. Wounds scar over time. You grow into it, around it, until it doesn't take up as much space in your life as it once did. It usually helps if you have someone to talk to."

I peered at him over my knees. He sat cross-legged a few feet away, dark eyes soft as silk. Either of us could have leaned across the space and touched the other, but we stayed still.

"Who did you talk to?"

"Mostly Tumulus at first. He was kind of preachy about it. But then I met some other Bone Touched that come around every once in a while. They helped me through it since I was the only Bone Touched student here for a while. But now you're here." His smile was warm and soft.

Yes. There was finally someone else. Someone who knew exactly what I'd gone through. Someone who could not only sympathize but empathize. Someone who understood my pain. I wasn't alone anymore. And while Nicholas still had plenty of his own issues to work out, maybe I now understood a few of them better.

We sat there for a long time. By some miracle, Professor Tumulus didn't come out of his room. Nicholas's chatty nature had abandoned him or perhaps he had cast it aside for the time being. It was nice to just sit there in silence with him, just to know that he was there but not have him trying to engage with me.

Finally, I stole a shaky breath that sounded more like a rattlesnake waiting to attack and stood up. Nicholas got to his feet too. I leaned my back against the wall and raked my hands through my hair.

"Do you want to go to dinner?" I asked, glancing out of the corner of my eye at him.

His answering smile lit up the hallway. "Yes, of course."

I had to bite my lip to keep from smiling too. I felt lighter like someone had been trying to bury me alive, but I'd finally managed to claw my way out of my own grave or at least shift the weight so it was easier to bear.

"You weren't in class after lunch," I remarked as we waited for cheeseburgers in the cafeteria.

He grimaced and glanced around to make sure no one was eavesdropping. "You know how I mentioned that you-know-who came and had a chat with me?" I nodded. "It was a long chat. Scaring you wasn't the only thing I did wrong, and he couldn't ignore my mistakes."

I frowned. "What did you do?" He'd been gone for hours. What could have warranted that long of a lecture? He barely said anything to me when he deigned to speak at all.

Nicholas crossed his arms and became very interested in his shoes. I barely heard him when he spoke. "I may have used my powers to keep Dr. Shalm out of our fight with Nina."

I was glad I hadn't gotten food yet. I probably would have dropped it in surprise. "How?"

"When you get into upper-level bone magic, you move from pacifist methods of passing on ghosts to more confrontational techniques, namely bone manipulation."

I tilted my head inquisitively, but Nicholas gestured for me to turn around. It was our turn to get food. I moved toward a table once I had mine.

"Bone manipulation," I reminded him once we sat.

"Right. Not only can we see memories imprinted on bones, but we can move them with our minds. Bones from deceased animals that are outside a living body are pretty easy, but we can also physically control the living, like puppets."

That wasn't spooky at all considering how long we spent as the Boneman's puppets.

He focused on his own food. "We're only supposed to do it if they're threatened by ghosts or are on the verge of discovering us while we're hunting. Which is why I got in trouble for doing it over some petty, high school drama. I should have just talked to Dr. Shalm about it instead of keeping the bones in her ear from registering the sound of our argument. I just got caught up in the moment."

I was more impressed than anything. Nicholas was so far beyond my level, but I supposed a two-year gap would do that.

"Bone manipulation is more commonly used on the bones of dead animals. Ghosts hate being trapped once they've been freed from their bodies, and the best way to trap them is with remnants that mimic the bodies they were once confined to. Some Bone Touched sharpen parts of skeletons into different weapons. Some just use the bones as they are. That's one thing I'm looking forward to after we graduate, finding my own style of ghost fighting."

My wrinkled nose had nothing to do with the taste of my burger. Part of me hoped I never had to graduate. Going out and fighting ghosts in any way didn't sound appealing at all.

"I know," Nicholas said around a bite of food. "But you have to admit, swinging around a bone sword sounds pretty cool."

"I suppose." This was another way I could tell Nicholas was farther along the path to becoming a full-fledged Bone Touched. He looked forward to parts of it. I couldn't find any redeemable aspect of this forced servitude.

After finishing our food, Nicholas walked me to the girls' dorm.

"Thank you for giving me another chance. I know I haven't given you much reason to trust me again, but I appreciate it, and I'll do my best not to mess up again." He put a hand to his forehead in a mock salute.

I rolled my eyes, but I was fighting a smile. My breath was a bit shaky when I faced the doors to the girls' dorm. I hoped Nina wasn't waiting inside to tear me apart. No matter what Nicholas had threatened her with, I wouldn't put it past her to try something nasty. All it would take was one push down the stairs, and she might very well kill me, depending on how many bones I broke.

Was this why Nicholas was usually so nice to everyone. For fear of retaliation? This was so stupid. If I knew how to manipulate bones like Nicholas, I might be able to defend myself.

I turned to him. "I want you to teach me how to manipulate bone."

Nicholas raised his brows. "Really? I'm not that far along yet. Tumulus would be better—"

"I don't want to wait for him to decide I'm ready."

He nodded appreciatively. "Alright. I guess I can try my best. We can start this weekend."

"Yes." The sooner the better.

"Great," Nicholas smiled softly. "Good night, Sylvan. Don't let the Boneman bite."

My eyes went wide.

He held up his hands. "Sorry, bad joke. If anything, he'll probably come visit me again."

I winced in sympathy. Hopefully, the Boneman would choose to only see the good that came out of Nicholas ambushing me outside of Professor Tumulus's room. I knew how terrifying it could be to wake up in the middle of the pitch-black woods with no one but the Boneman and no way to call for help.

He scratched his face. "Anyway, I hope you sleep well."

I inclined my head. "You, too. Thank you for telling me who you are."

"I should have done it a long time ago. I was just scared."

"We all are." The students, the Bone Touched, everyone. The world felt tired more often than not, like it was done fighting itself to try to find happiness and just wanted to sleep the bad days away.

Or maybe that was just me.

"Tell me about it," He sighed and started to back away. "Well, I won't keep you from sleep any longer. I'll see you tomorrow."

"See you tomorrow."

He pointed to the left end of the building. "By the way, there's a side door over there if you're trying to avoid running into a certain someone. She lives on the opposite end of the second floor, so she doesn't use that staircase."

"Thank you."

He smiled. "Any time."

He turned and started off as I headed around to the side entrance. The forest watched me dart into the building and up the stairs that just *had* to have windows that showed a sliver of the distant trees. I had to keep telling myself that it was better than running into Nina.

When I got up to my room, the curtains were closed. I had given up on trying to keep them that way and left them open when I went to class that morning but there they were, shut tight. Hopefully, it was a good sign.

22

Twenty-Two

Sitting down at my desk in the back corner of Dr. Shalm's class felt far less nerve-wracking than it ever had, even though Nina and her pack glared at me from across the room like I'd killed their dogs. They looked ready to start a fight.

I pulled out my sketchbook and tried to ignore them. Just as they started to get up to bother me, Nicholas sat down in his chair. Instantly, they backed off.

Interesting.

"Morning," he chirped, seemingly oblivious to their death stares. "Sleep well?"

"For the first time that I can remember," I replied quietly, biting down on the smile that threatened to spread across my face. No Boneman or dreams of my time with him had plagued me in the night. I'd slept like a rock and awoken refreshed and ready for the day.

Nicholas had no qualms about showing his grin. "That's good. Me too. I half expected a visit from *him*, but it was quiet."

I nodded my relief. Despite the apprehension of the moment, a lot of good had come out of Nicholas confronting me. Fear of another panic attack would have kept me from talking to him, and I wouldn't be nearly at ease if he hadn't explained things.

Nicholas leaned over to get a good look at the inside of my notebook. "How is it possible that you've gotten better at that? You were already great."

"Practice."

"You mean you just popped out of the tub already drawing full portraits like you did of Lucas and *this* is what it looks like when you actually work at it?"

I winced at the casual way he referenced my time with the Boneman. "Yeah."

Nicholas looked away, shaking his head. "Some people get all the talent."

The sound of Dr. Shalm calling out to the class made me jump to attention. "Alright, everyone, we're going to change it up a bit today. You will be reading alternately to your desk partner out of chapter ten. This *doesn't* mean you are to start up a completely unrelated conversation. We're only reading."

The class began to buzz with a low conversation I was willing to bet was not about the classical novel we'd started at the beginning of the week.

Nicholas turned to me. "I can read most of it if you're not comfortable with talking much."

I opened my book and scanned the lines before shaking my head. "I'm fine."

Nicholas raised his eyebrows. "Are you sure? You're always so loath to speak more than a few words. I can count the number of times you've said a complete sentence on one hand."

"Maybe to you," I muttered quietly enough that I thought he wouldn't hear.

His chortle proved me wrong.

"Mr. Ater!" snapped Dr. Shalm. "I don't remember this scene being that funny."

"Sorry, Dr. Shalm," Nicholas replied.

I couldn't help my smile at his sheepish expression. I rested a hand over my mouth.

"You don't have to hide it," Nicholas murmured. "You don't express happiness very often, not that I see anyway. You shouldn't cover it up when you're enjoying yourself."

I cast my eyes down at my book. Every time my mood took a turn for the better, something always happened to drag it down. That's how it played out with coming here to get away from the Boneman, hearing about the Wind Whisperer, and hoping it could save me. Nothing worked out the way I wished.

Happiness was such a fragile thing. To flaunt it by openly showing it felt like tempting the world to take it away.

Picking up on my unease, Nicholas cleared his throat and started reading.

Throughout the remainder of the class, I caught Nina staring at Nicholas and me. When she saw me looking, she would raise her chin and look down her nose as best she could before turning back to her book. She didn't intercept us at the end of class when we packed up. Nicholas followed me out into the halls and stuck close as we made our way to History class.

Wren stiffened when she saw us enter together. Her eyes darted from me to Nicholas, silently asking more questions than I could ever answer.

"It's ok," I said softly as I sat down in my usual chair.

Her eyebrows shot up. "You were terrified of him just yesterday, and now you're fine? Is that the truth or has he done something to you?" She leaned forward to glare at Nicholas, who did his best to pretend he couldn't hear every word she said.

"Nothing's wrong. He...fixed it."

I hated that I couldn't tell her what had happened. But the only way to keep a secret was to tell no one. I didn't think Wren would say anything to anyone else if we did tell her, but I doubted the Boneman would be pleased. What if he took her and transformed her? Or simply killed her to get rid of a loose end?

I didn't know the protocol for this kind of thing. There seemed to be a code of sorts between the deities, and surely, they'd had to deal with this problem before. I would never forgive myself if something happened to Wren because of me.

Wren leaned back. "You," she hissed, stabbing a finger in Nicholas's direction. He looked at her. "Watch yourself. If you hurt my friend, you answer to me."

He nodded gravely. "I know." He glanced at me, but I kept my eyes forward.

Wren didn't look satisfied, but she left it alone for the time being.

She came at us full force during lunch. Nicholas and I got to our usual bench first. The moment we sat down, Wren appeared out of nowhere and practically sat on our laps as she wedged herself between us. I tried to focus on my marinated chicken as she stared us down.

This was going to be fun.

"Hello, Wren," Nicholas greeted her.

She narrowed her eyes at him and started eating. Nicholas looked to me for help, but I had no idea what to do. Maybe she thought he was controlling me in some sinister way even though I told her everything was alright between us now.

I didn't know how to convince her without telling her the truth, the one thing I could *not* do.

At last, she spoke without looking up. "So, you just follow her around all day or what?"

Nicholas raised his brows at me and answered carefully. "We have every single class together, and I find that walking with a friend is better than walking alone."

I focused on cutting a piece of chicken instead of looking at him when he said it. Tension hung thick in the air like the stench of rotting bodies.

"But you *always* walk with Sylvan. Not that she isn't a superior choice in most situations, but surely you have no shortage of other friends," Wren said.

"Friends is not the term I would use to describe them." His voice took on a bitter tone.

Wren snorted. "Didn't seem to stop you from keeping them around before."

I picked at my food, acutely aware that I wasn't part of the conversation but was still meant to hear it.

Nicholas turned his black gaze on her. "I know what I did yesterday upset Sylvan. But I apologized." His gaze flicked back to me. "I explained myself, and I know that sounds a little vague, but I hope it repaired some of the damage."

I met his eyes, white to black, and let my expression soften. *It did.*

225

Wren scoffed. "A few words can't mend broken trust."

"Wren," I said softly.

"You can't treat her like a toy and follow her around like a stalker. She's new here, but that doesn't mean you can exploit her."

This was getting out of hand, but I had no idea how to stop it. In the movies I'd seen, arguments just played out and the characters dealt with consequences afterward.

Wren continued her interrogation. "What are your intentions toward Sylvan? You've been obsessed with her ever since she got here. As her friend, I have a right to know."

"My intentions?" Nicholas laughed. "What are you? Her mother?"

"You aren't answering the question."

Nicholas looked at me. I stared back, waiting for his answer. I had wondered the same thing since day one. He was Bone Touched and wanted to help me adjust to actually having a life. But was there more?

Wren snapped her fingers in front of his face. "Hey, I asked you a question."

Nicholas fixed his eyes on her. "I intend to be there for her, for whatever she may need. I think she deserves the world, and I want to give it to her."

It was similar to what he said to those guys we sat with at the basketball game.

Wren raised her eyebrows. "That almost sounded like a declaration of love."

Nicholas's jaw tightened. "I won't pretend I don't care about her if that's what you want."

"Are you in love with her?"

"Wren." I tried to step in again.

226

She ignored me. "If Sylvan asked you to be her boyfriend, would you say yes?"

Something in her tone resonated through my memory, reminding me of conversations I'd had with a very different girl. Nina.

It all made sense now.

Wren was jealous.

She thought Nicholas was interested in me while she was interested in him. She'd been holding out hope because I never told her that Nicholas said he didn't like her that way. I had encouraged her to pursue him. I'd given her the opportunity to be around him, flirt with him. And now she was realizing that her efforts had been in vain.

I was a terrible friend.

Wren wasn't satisfied by our stunned silence. "Because the way things are going now, I wouldn't be surprised if you two—Hey!"

I set my food aside, grabbed Wren's arm, and dragged her up, nearly upsetting her tray. Nicholas stood expectantly, but I leveled a look at him, and he sat back down. Wren kept squawking indignant questions as I pulled her behind a hedge that separated the courtyard from the rest of campus.

I ignored her until we were safely out of sight. "This is getting out of hand."

Wren crossed her arms, looking very much like a petulant child. "*You're* the one who decided to drag me away from my lunch."

I gestured back the way we came. "You're interrogating Nicholas."

She planted her hands on her hips. "So, it's my fault you let him back into your life after the way he made you feel

227

yesterday? After he was rude to me too?"

That's right. He'd thought Wren was pushing me around like Nina had. "He apologized."

"To you maybe. He probably doesn't even remember insulting me."

She might have been right. Between being defensive of me, the visit from the Boneman, and then trying to make things right, he could have forgotten about the careless comment he made about my seating change in History.

"Why don't you talk to him about that then instead of making it about what happened to me?"

"He only said it because he's so protective of you. He doesn't really care about me or my feelings. Just you. So, what's the point in bringing it up? Besides, shouldn't he have known better after he gave you that panic attack in gym?"

He doesn't really care about me or my feelings. Just you.

Wren sighed heavily. "Look, it's your business. But I don't think I want *him* around me anymore."

I stood there, stunned. Not long ago, she jumped at the chance to spend time with Nicholas, and now she hated him. This could be solved with a simple conversation between the two of them, couldn't it?

"I'll tolerate him during class because I don't have any other option, but I don't want him sitting with us at lunch or meeting up with us outside of class to study or go to the cafe or anything like that. You can do what you want but I'm done. Ok?"

I pressed my lips together. *Why are you tearing us apart?* "Ok."

Wren nodded in satisfaction. "Good. That starts right now, by the way. I want to be able to finish my lunch in peace. And if it turns out that this is a pattern of behavior for him and he's a piece of crap, I will not hesitate to tell you I told you so."

Fair. But Nicholas wouldn't push me anymore. Being Bone Touched leveled the playing field.

By the time we got back to our bench, Nicholas had attracted a crowd of people. We couldn't even see him.

Wren heaved an irritated sigh. "We should just go somewhere else. He's clearly forgotten about us."

As if determined to prove her wrong, the crowd shifted a little and, through the gap, Nicholas spotted us. He stood up, apologizing and saying goodbye to his fan club as he waded through them.

"Hey." He grinned at us, glowing from all the attention he'd received. I suspected he enjoyed it more than he said he did. "I was starting to think you two had run off without me."

"We should have," Wren mumbled under her breath.

Nicholas either didn't hear or chose to ignore her, fixing his eyes on me instead. "Lunch is almost over, and you've barely touched your food." He tilted his head to scrutinize me. "Are you alright?"

"Sylvan has to talk to you," Wren answered for me. "Go on. Drag him behind a bush, too."

She started back toward our bench, where the crowd had mostly dispersed. Nicholas watched her go before turning back to me.

His dark brows drew together. "Is this about how Wren doesn't seem to like me anymore?"

I jerked my head for him to follow, but instead of stopping behind the hedge, I kept walking, meandering around campus. Nicholas kept pace with mine.

"Is it that bad?" He asked grimly.

There wasn't an easy way to say this. "Wren doesn't want to be around you anymore."

"Because of what happened yesterday?" I nodded. "But didn't you explain that it's fine now?"

"She doesn't believe me."

"Because you can't tell her the truth." Nicholas went quiet for a long moment while we walked. "Is there anything I can do to convince her?"

"You could apologize for insinuating that she might bully me like Nina does. But I don't know how much it will help." Wren seemed determined to stay away from him.

"So…what? She doesn't want us to spend time together?"

I shoved my hands into my pockets. "No, she just doesn't want to spend time with you."

"I guess that's fair." He stared off into the distance. "I'll miss her though."

I would miss the three of us hanging out together too. One of my two friends no longer wanted to be around the other. I only had the pair of them.

He stuck his hands in his pockets. "This must be hard on you."

A little. "I'm sorry about Wren."

"Don't worry about it. I get where she's coming from."

My friendship with Wren was my first attempt at being normal. I couldn't lose her, but she couldn't be involved in the part of my life that was Bone Touched and she was broken up about Nicholas. I could still make this work. I just had to split my time between the two of them the same way I split my time learning bone magic from my normal schoolwork.

"For what it's worth, would you tell Wren I'm sorry?"

Nicholas said.

I nodded. I doubted she would care, but I'd tell her.

"I hate to have to tear you in half like this," he murmured. "You should prioritize her. It's my fault."

I shrugged. He wasn't wrong, but how I spent my time would be my choice, not his.

23

Twenty-Three

I ended up spending most of the weekend with Wren. She took Nicholas's apology as well as I expected and asked me not to mention him anymore. So, I didn't.

I met Nicholas at the library shortly before lunch on Sunday, though. Wren had been determined to go into town and tried to convince me to come. After the twentieth time I said no, she finally realized she wouldn't be able to change my mind and left without me.

Nicholas texted, asking if I wanted to work on homework together. I'd already finished it, but I went anyway, because I didn't want to be alone in my room.

He waited for me on a bench outside the library, despite the cold wind that had started up that morning.

"Hey." He grinned, turning away from the statue of a medieval knight that stood across the sidewalk from the library.

"Hi." I blinked back, my expression soft but far from smiling.

He got to his feet. "I was wondering when you would show

up."

I rolled my eyes, not dignifying his remark with a response, and made my way inside.

I thought the library was the one place on campus where no one would try to engage us. No one ever bothered me and Wren when we came.

But Wren wasn't Nicholas.

The girl behind the checkout called a greeting to him. He offered her a tight smile and turned away to follow me as I drifted toward the stacks. But the girl persisted, and he paused to give curt answers to her questions.

I didn't wait for their conversation to finish before wandering down the nearest aisle. Nicholas would catch up once he finished.

I was sitting on the thin carpet in the aisle, surveying the titles, when he found me.

"Sorry about that. I have something of a reputation."

"I hadn't noticed," I said without looking away from the shelf.

"Very funny." He leaned down behind me to look at the books. "I didn't know you liked to read."

I shrugged. *Neither did I.* I still didn't. But being around Wren made me want to try. Surely drawing and bone magic weren't the only things that could hold my attention.

"What book is your favorite?"

Another shrug.

"Right. I don't suppose you have one yet."

I reached out when a familiar title caught my eye. *Bone Spinner.* It was the book Wren had dropped that first day I met her. She said it was good. Where better to start than with a recommendation from a friend? I flipped it open to

233

the synopsis on the inside cover.

Nicholas peered over my shoulder. "Hang on. Isn't that about...?"

I snapped the book closed and shoved it sloppily back into place, standing quickly, and backing up.

Nicholas bent and straightened the book. He touched it carefully as if it were a highly venomous spider that needed special handling, or it would bite. "A few of the books in here are about the Boneman. Stories about the three gods are popular enough that people write all kinds of fiction about them."

I clutched the strap of my satchel.

"How long were you out of the tub before you started class? If you don't mind me asking," he said softly.

I lowered my head. "A few days." Four or five. I couldn't be sure. That time was a blur. I spent a lot of it sleeping. Thankfully, I'd grown out of the drowsy spells that had plagued me during that first week or two out of the tub.

"No memories from before him?"

I shook my head. "You?"

"It was more like a week, but yeah. Not one memory from before." Nicholas ran a hand through his hair. "After a while, the mention of him won't make you jump, and you'll get used to seeing his image around campus."

I heaved a sigh. That's what people kept saying. That moment felt farther and farther away each time someone told me I just had to hold on a little longer. Hopefully, having been through the same thing so recently, Nicholas knew what he was talking about.

"Hey," Nicholas breathed, extending his hand. "At least you have someone."

I peered up at him.

"I was the only one for a long time. But I'm here for you, Sylvan."

I glanced down at his hand. His fingers were long and slender. I found my own hand reaching out tentatively to rest in his. When his hand closed around mine, it didn't feel like he was holding tight enough to shatter my bones the way the touch of others did. He was gentle, soft, and warm.

"Come on, we have science homework to do." He gently tugged on my hand, pulling me toward the tables in the back.

"*You* have science homework," I corrected.

He put his free hand to his chest in a dramatic show of hurt. "You did it without me?"

I shrugged. "Yesterday." *With Wren.* But I didn't want to start that conversation again.

He huffed and pointedly looked away. "I can't believe you. After everything we've been through together, you go and do your homework *without* me."

I chuckled. He was absolutely ridiculous.

He stopped abruptly and turned on me, his face deathly serious. "Do that again."

My face went blank. "What?"

"Laugh. Smile. Do it again." He leaned closer, still gripping my hand.

I shook my head. Ridiculous. "Maybe you should say something funny again."

His lips twisted into a crooked grin. "You think I'm funny?"

"Maybe. Sometimes."

His mischievous smile spread.

"You have homework," I reminded him, wiggling my hand out of his and crossing my arms.

235

His eyes darted down to his now empty palm. He sighed. "Indeed, I do."

* * *

"This is going to be tricky. It took me a while to get my first bone to move. So, don't take it personally if you completely fail," Nicholas said.

"Thanks," I deadpanned.

The library had a few independent study rooms that students could use if they were working on group projects or wanted to curate their study environment. Nicholas and I had locked ourselves in one such room and pulled the curtain on the window in the door closed, so no one would be able to see inside.

Because it was high time I learned how to manipulate bones.

Nicholas pulled out a little box, opened it, and set the tiny bone inside it on the table between us. "I'm just trying to prepare you for what might happen. Seeing memories imprinted on bone is one thing. Moving them with you mind is another. It takes a lot of practice and precision."

He held his hand above the bone. His hand drifted slowly upward. The bone twitched and rose in sync with him. He turned his hand palm up, and the bone rotated to hover a few inches above it. The tiny white fragment began to orbit Nicholas's hand, weaving between his fingers without touching them, and twirling in circles until it came to rest on his palm.

I stared with wide eyes. "How long did it take you to learn how to do that?"

"Six months. And I practiced daily on my own." Nicholas set the bone back on the table. "I could move this bone across a table after a couple weeks, but it took much longer to learn how to do anything more elaborate."

I ran a hand through my hair. Six months was a long time.

"When you're starting out, it's easier to use your hand as a tether to help guide the motions of the bone. Once you get more experience, you can try just using your mind, but for now guide it with your own motion." He waved his hand over the bone. It followed the path of his fingers, staying in their shadow as he guided it back and forth across the table. "Like so."

He dropped his hand, and the bone stayed put. "Try to form an attachment in your mind between your body and the bone. It's an extension of you. It goes where you will it. Give it a try."

Nicholas sat back, and I scooted to the edge of my seat. I held my hand over the bone like he had. Making any kind of connection with a bone was the last thing I wanted to do. I didn't even want to have anything to do with my own bones—I barely considered them mine after what the Boneman did to them. But I refused to be helpless if I ever came face to face with another ghost.

The little white fragment was part of my body, and it would move as easily as my arm did whenever I told it to. My hand slowly drifted to the side. I willed the bone to follow my motion like a person's limbs following horses when they were drawn and quartered.

But just like a drawing and quartering victim, the bone

resisted my pull and sat perfectly still on the table below my hand.

I moved my hand back over it. This was fine. Nicholas said it would be hard. I tried again, moving in the opposite direction. Still nothing.

Maybe I needed to change my approach. My eyes narrowed. I commanded the bone to shift, pouring every ounce of concentration into making it move. It had to move. It *would* move. After all, it was just a bone, and I was a demigod. It had no choice but to obey me.

I swept my hand through the air with purpose. And the bone…

Stayed exactly where it was.

My hand dropped to the table and clenched into a fist. This was beyond frustrating.

"What am I doing wrong?" I demanded, spearing Nicholas in my gaze.

He sat calmly in his chair with his hands folded in his lap and a patient smile on his face. "You're not necessarily doing anything wrong, Sylvan. It's just that you've never done this before. You don't know what it feels like to do it right, so you don't know what to look for."

"What do I look for?"

His lips pressed into a thin line, and he frowned. "It's hard to describe. I guess it's a feeling of connection. You can sense that the bone is there beyond just seeing it and you make it move. Once you feel it, you'll know it, and it will be much easier to do it again. You just have to find that connection first."

He was almost as helpful as Tumulus.

I tried again and again and again, using different motions,

different mentalities, different angles. Nothing worked.

I sighed and rubbed at my scalp. All this concentration was giving me a headache. I had to be doing something wrong. There had to be more to bone manipulation than Nicholas was telling me.

"It's ok if you can't get it to move yet," Nicholas said gently. "I barely got it to twitch during my first lesson with Tumulus and that was after two hours of trying."

That didn't make me feel any better. "How long have I been going?"

Nicholas glanced at his phone. "A little over an hour."

"Then I still have an hour to go."

He grinned. "I admire your persistence, but there's no shame in taking a break, or stopping for the day and circling back to it another time."

I shook my head and jabbed a finger at the bone as I glared at Nicholas. "I *have* to do this."

The bone scooted an inch to the right. We both went silent and stared at it with wide eyes.

"Did you do that?" I whispered.

"No, that was you." He sat forward with a wide grin. "When you moved just now, it moved with you."

I blinked. "But I didn't do anything." I hadn't even been looking at it.

"Maybe that's the trick. You've been focusing too hard and need to relax into it."

That didn't make any sense.

"Try it again. Look at me and try to make it move," Nicholas urged.

I frowned but kept my gaze on him as I gestured for the bone to move. Out of the corner of my eye, I could see that it hadn't worked. I scowled down at the bone. Maybe it had just been a fluke. Maybe Nicholas had moved it to give me hope.

"Don't look at it, look at me." Nicholas moved to the edge of his chair and leaned close enough that I could feel the warmth of his breath. "Just focus on me and only think about moving the bone in the back of your mind."

I tried again, keeping my gaze fixed on Nicholas's fathomless eyes. Still nothing.

"It didn't work."

"Relax more, let your mind drift. Manipulate the bone as an afterthought."

But it couldn't be an afterthought. It was the whole reason I was here. The only reason the Boneman let me out into the world was to fight ghosts, and I couldn't do that if I couldn't manipulate bone. I only had a year and a half before I graduated and had to start hunting the restless dead. How was I supposed to learn what I needed to learn in so little time? How was I supposed to survive?

Nicholas gently took my hand, still staring deep into my eyes. "Good, now move the bone." He shifted our joined fingers to the side.

The bone followed for a couple inches. My breath caught in my lungs, and it stopped moving.

Nicholas's smile was blinding. "That was it. Did you feel it? The connection?"

"Yeah." For a moment there had been a faint tingle in the back of my mind, like a phantom limb.

"Perfect." Nicholas let go of my hand and sat back. "Now try again and search for that sensation."

I took a deep breath and centered myself.

We practiced for another hour. I couldn't do more than move the bone a couple inches at a time, but it was something. Nicholas theorized that I got too excited when I realized I was doing it and lost the connection.

"We'll work on maintaining that mental state next time. For now, how about you take a break. You've earned it." Nicholas placed the bone back in its box.

"Thank you."

He glanced up. "For what?"

"For teaching me."

The warmth in his smile could have heated the room in winter. "Of course."

I returned to my room that evening feeling drained but satisfied. I may not have been able to do all the tricks Nicholas showed me, but this was something.

I slumped into the chair at my desk and fished my phone out of my pocket. Wren had texted me some pictures of her at the bookstore to "show me what I was missing out on".

I rolled my eyes and told her I had a very successful day doing homework.

I thought we did all of the homework you had yesterday. She texted back.

I just got tired of doing it yesterday and needed a break. I responded. It still ate at me that I had to lie to her instead of telling her about being Bone Touched. With as many fantasy novels as she read, she'd probably be thrilled to learn that gods and demigods existed.

Are you done with all of it now? She asked.

Yes.

Want to come see the new books I got and watch a movie?

I sighed. I wanted to sleep, but I hadn't even had dinner yet, and hanging out with Wren shouldn't be too stressful. She was just going to talk about books and put on a movie. All I had to do was listen and watch and lose myself in a story.

Any time. I texted back, pushing off the chair and heading back out the door to go to Wren's room.

24

Twenty-Four

"Why are you following me?" I demanded as I headed down the sidewalk outside to my lesson with Professor Tumulus.

Instead of leaving Nicholas in Statistics like I usually did on Thursday afternoons, he'd trailed me out of the classroom and hadn't peeled off to go somewhere else.

"Because there was a change in my schedule that I have a feeling has something to do with us finding out about each other," he replied.

"We told no one." My grip on the strap of my satchel tightened.

"No, but he always knows," Nicholas replied gravely.

"He?" I hoped he meant Professor Tumulus.

Nicholas peered sideways at me. "You don't think it's a coincidence that we ended up having the same schedule, do you? The Boneman engineers this kind of stuff."

My shiver had nothing to do with the autumn chill. My mind went to the curtains in my room. How they had a nasty habit of opening and closing seemingly of their own accord.

The Boneman *had* shown up after I refused to practice bone magic. He watched, orchestrated, and executed. Like the god he was. Had he seen the times I'd tried to search for my family on my phone? If he had, he hadn't said anything about it.

I hoped he never did. Despite how poorly it had gone so far, it was the only way I could find out anything about what happened to me before the Boneman.

I was so absorbed in my own thoughts I barely managed to avoid stepping on the body of a sparrow that lay in my path. I flinched back. Nicholas didn't have the same reservations.

"Whoa!" He peered at it and grinned. "Is this your first?"

I frowned at him. "First what?" I'd had a lot of firsts since coming to this school. He would have to be more specific.

"The first dead thing that you've come across?"

I nodded, grimacing.

"How lucky. Birds have good memories. The Boneman must *really* like you right now."

"What?"

Nicholas produced a plastic bag from his backpack, flipped it inside out, fitted it over his hand, and used it to ever so gently pick up the bird. "The Boneman is the one that puts dead things in the path of his people. Birds are good because they fly, so seeing their memories is always fun. Bird bones are also good for fighting ghosts because they're hollow, so they trap spirits better. Something about how a bit of the ghost can get stuck inside, I think."

He zipped the bag closed and held it out to me. "Do you want to hold it?"

I cringed away from the carcass.

He chuckled, tucked the dead bird into his backpack, and

stood. "Yeah, it's not much to look at now. But Professor Tumulus can clean the bones for you. This is so exciting. The first in your collection, a sparrow."

"Why would I collect bones?" I'd passed out when I saw Tumulus's.

Nicholas started walking again. "How else are you supposed to get bones to fight ghosts? You can't just go around digging up graves and stealing bones out of their coffins."

My nose wrinkled. I definitely couldn't do that, but I also didn't want to keep a collection of the bones of all the dead animals I found. Wasn't it bad enough that I had to fight ghosts? Now I had to deal with animal bodies showing up wherever I went?

Nicholas burst into the classroom when we reached the thick wooden door, slamming it open so hard that it smacked into the wall. I flinched at the loud noise.

"Afternoon, Professor!" He greeted Tumulus with one of his shining smiles.

Professor Tumulus had his back to us, dropping food into an aquarium full of small fish. "Mr. Ater, we don't have a lesson until tomorrow. What are you doing—" He stopped when he turned and saw me beside Nicholas. "Ms. Ravena." He glanced between the two of us. "I suppose you've figured it out then."

My fists clenched. Of course, Professor Tumulus knew we were both Bone Touched. He was the only bone magic teacher at Mortorous Academy after all. Both of us had to learn from him. He probably knew we were in the same grade level too.

Had the Boneman told him to keep our shared secret from each other, or had the admin? Worse, had he decided for himself? He'd known how much I was struggling to adjust, or at least had some idea, and he'd kept this from me.

"Yup." Nicholas slung his backpack up on one of the tables in the front of the room.

Professor Tumulus looked at the half open black curtains over the windows. "I suppose that means *he* knows too."

"I can only assume since our schedules have been moved to coincide with one another's lessons." Nicholas pulled up a chair and started rummaging in his bag.

Tumulus focused back on us. "Wish I'd been informed. Doubling my class size without telling me isn't very polite."

I glared. Tumulus hadn't told Nicholas about me, either, even though Nicholas was so excited to have another Bone Touched at Mortorous. How did he expect us to trust him if he kept such important information from us?

"Don't look at me like that, Ms. Ravena," Tumulus scolded. "I make it a policy not to out any of my students to each other. Some people like to keep to themselves. Besides, you should be more concerned with your lessons."

What a stupid policy. How could knowing hurt anyone?

"Look what Sylvan found, Professor," Nicholas cut in, pulling out the bird bag.

Professor Tumulus scurried forward, looking relieved at the change in subject. "Ah, how wonderful. And in your first couple months, too. I didn't find my first sparrow until nearly six months in. And Nicholas here only found mice for—"

"Yes, well..." Nicholas interrupted. Was he blushing? "Can I remove the skeleton?"

Professor Tumulus narrowed his eyes at him. "The last time you removed a skeleton, you pulled the bones out of the body so hard they flew across the room and shattered against the walls."

Nicholas lifted his chin. "That was a while ago, and I've been practicing on my own with dead animals I've found. I've gotten so much better."

"If you've gotten better, why don't you show me on your own animal?"

"Because I haven't found any this week," Nicholas protested.

Professor Tumulus harrumphed. "That's what I thought. I will not have you ruining Ms. Ravena's first skeleton." He took the bird back into his office and returned a moment later with the human bone I had been practicing with last week in one hand and a rodent's cage in the other. "Try this again, will you? I'll need some time to fix up your bird and you need to practice. Mr. Ater, you will be continuing your lesson from last week as well." He set the cage on the table in front of Nicholas and the human bone in front of me and retreated to his office.

Nicholas sighed and glared at the rat inside the cage. I peered at it curiously.

"I'm supposed to make it move," Nicholas said when he caught me looking. "I'm good enough at manipulating bones now, that I'm learning how to move them while they're still inside a living body."

"You already did that with *Dr. Shalm*."

"This is more complicated. It's easy to control the movement of the bones in someone's ear because they're the smallest bones in the body. But getting an animal to move the way you want it to, especially when they're alive and their muscles are fighting you, is way more difficult. I've been trying to get this rat to do tricks for weeks with minimal success. And he's resisting me because it scares him that his body is doing something without his permission." He stuck his tongue out at the rat.

"I wonder what that's like," I muttered as I looked at the leg bone sitting in front of me on the table.

Nicholas put a hand on the table near me, not touching but close. "You know, supposedly, Bone Touched can't manipulate each other's bones. I think it has to do with the magic inside them. Not that the Boneman would ever tolerate us manipulating each other."

If we could, he might be able to keep me from having to listen to the droning of everyone else in our classes. Oh well. Nothing was ever that simple.

Nicholas jerked his chin at my bone. "So, you're doing the murder case, huh?"

I nodded.

"It can be a tough one. It took me a few weeks to figure out too." He sat back in his chair. "Just focus on slowing it down. Look for details and grab onto them before they escape."

I bit my lip and reached for the bone. Details. Right. My eyes slid shut.

It was dark. From the darkness came shouts, indistinct and muffled. There was the gleam of the gun pointed at my chest. Everything beyond it was hazy shadows. At the explosive sound of the shot, my eyes opened.

I sat in the classroom, unharmed. Nicholas glanced at me from where he was staring at the rat. I shook my head to ward off any of his questions.

Details.

I closed my eyes. Darkness. Shadows surrounding the gun.

The shadows shouting. What were they saying? I strained to listen, willing them to sound like words I could understand. They continued indistinctly until I caught the tail end of a sentence.

"...are coming. Let's go." The shadow to my left spoke in a distant, muffled voice that sharpened and faded at random intervals.

"And him?" The shadow behind the gun asked.

There came a snigger from the left. Then the shot.

Eyes open. I looked down at the bone. It was progress.

Eyes closed. I focused on the murmurings of the shadows once more.

"Your wallet, now!" The words came immediately.

"Ok, ok." Those words were coming from me, but they weren't in my voice.

"Your car keys too, while you're at it," the shadow behind the gun was saying. "Quick, we haven't got all night."

Night. Was that why they were just shadows? Or could I see them better if I concentrated? Sirens sounded in the distance.

"The cops are coming. Let's go," the left shadow said just as he had before.

"And him?" the silhouette behind the gun asked.

Again, came the snigger followed by the gun discharging. The second before the bullet hit and ended the vision, the features of my attackers came into focus. They both wore hoodies that hid their hair and cast shadows over their faces. The one with the gun was thin with a round face and dark eyes. The one on his left was more muscled and had a smirk that made his blue eyes dance venomously.

I didn't open my eyes between visions this time.

The scene came again and now the image had crystal clear resolution. The gunman had a shiny, gold watch on his outstretched wrist that looked expensive. His friend had a thin gold chain at his throat, a pair of gold studs in his ears, and a knife in his hand.

They had their dialogue and shot me. But the vision didn't end with the shot. I fell to the ground, asphalt cutting into my cheek, and stared toward the windowed front of a convenience store. A pair of feet came running toward me. Whoever they belonged to was shouting and sobbing.

"Hey," I whispered in the victim's voice.

"Don't," the man sobbed, tears streaming down his face and into the collar of his blue, button-up shirt. "You're going to be ok. You're going to live."

"We both know that's a lie. Tell my sister I forgive her."

"Live to tell her yourself."

The sirens blared all around us when the vision faded to nothingness. I opened my eyes to the familiar classroom scenery. Nicholas stared at me. So did Professor Tumulus, who must have emerged from his office while I was watching the vision.

I blinked a question at them. In answer, Nicholas leaned forward and brushed his thumb under my eye. I started at the movement but understood a moment later. Tears streaked silently down my cheeks.

I quickly wiped them away. "I saw it," I said to Professor Tumulus, trying to clear the emotion from my voice.

"All of it?" he asked.

"The killers. The friend. His sister. What did she do that needed forgiving?"

Professor Tumulus shook his head. "It's not our job to go

poking into their personal lives. But she seemed very happy to hear that she was forgiven for whatever it was when the friend told her at the funeral." He took the bone from my hands gently. "Well done. You mastered that quite quickly, sticking through to the end and remembering details. And you, Mr. Ater?"

Nicholas looked at the rat which twitched its nose in the air. The rat squeaked in alarm as it rose on its hind legs and raised its tiny arms over its head. It held the position for a second, during which it shook as it tried to rid itself of Nicholas's control. Then, it fell back to all fours and darted to the far corner of the cage where it crouched and hissed at Nicholas.

Nicholas sighed in disappointment.

"Well, you've only been working on it for a few weeks." Professor Tumulus placed a small glass box on the table in front of me. "This is for you."

I picked it up. Inside sat the perfect skeleton of a small bird, pinned to a bed of black foam. My sparrow. It had its wings tucked close to its sides and its legs lay below its spine. I thought it would be disgusting to have to keep a skeleton, but the bones shone perfectly white in their case. They were almost pretty.

Nicholas leaned over to get a good look at my bird. "That is the most beautiful skeleton I've ever seen."

"It's her first. It should also be her best," Professor Tumulus replied proudly. "Now, that's all the time we have for today. Get some good sleep and full bellies and be ready for next week."

He turned around and went right back into his office, leaving us to pack up and go by ourselves.

"I think he secretly has a gaming system in there that he's addicted to," Nicholas declared as we headed to the cafeteria for dinner. "He never sticks around long enough to do more than say goodbye before locking himself in his office."

I shook my head. I really couldn't see Professor Tumulus getting invested in something like that. I'd been in his office once for a brief period of time after I passed out the first day I was supposed to have a lesson with him. It just looked messy and stuffed full of the usual things you would expect to find in an office. No gaming devices anywhere I could see.

"Then what do *you* think he secretly keeps in his office that he can't stay away from?" Nicholas asked.

"A really comfortable chair."

He barked a laugh. "That's it? Not a secret girlfriend or a baby Boneman or anything like that?"

I shuddered at the thought of a tiny Boneman running around so close to where we had sat.

"I guess he is kind of old, so it would make sense that he'd value that sort of thing," Nicholas mused. "Still, it's fun to imagine what else he might have hidden away. Maybe he has a pulldown bed and just takes naps all the time."

That sounded plausible.

Nicholas switched subjects. "So, you mastered the murder case."

I shrugged. Professor Tumulus wanted me to practice looking into other memories, but the murder was enough for today. Part of me still worried each time I finished a lesson that it wouldn't be enough, and I'd wake up on the forest floor again. That fear calmed over time as I completed more and more lessons, especially now that Nicholas was teaching me bone manipulation on the side. But it still followed me around the way a wolf follows a lone deer, waiting to pounce.

"You were in it for a while," Nicholas said as we stood in line for beef stew. "And then you started crying."

I grimaced. In all honesty, I didn't know why the tears had started. I hadn't even realized they were there until Nicholas pointed them out. And after I promised myself that I wouldn't let him see me cry.

"Professor Tumulus seemed impressed with how quickly you grasped the memory," Nicholas continued. "Though it didn't surprise me."

I glanced up at him.

There was a strange gleam in his eyes as he spoke. "I think you were made into something special. Whether the Boneman was trying a new experiment with you or just wanted you to be stronger, I think you're going to be better than me before too long. You're already way past where I was after only a few weeks of practicing bone magic."

I wasn't sure how I felt about that. Part of me wanted to fail at all my lessons, so I wouldn't have to go out and hunt ghosts. Maybe then I could just live a normal life. But another part of me suspected the Boneman would know if I purposefully failed.

"I'll try not to get too jealous, but don't be surprised if I end up asking you to tutor me before long." He winked as we collected our bowls of stew.

I ducked my head, smiling faintly. It might be nice to have someone who wasn't an all-powerful god of death be proud of the progress I made. It was affirming to have another person at my side who cared.

My smile vanished when someone ran into me. My bowl tipped over and spilled steaming hot stew down my front. I gasped and dropped it reflexively. My tray and bowl crashed to the floor, splashing my shoes and pants. The person who ran into me fumbled for balance, grabbing the collar of my shirt and pulling making half the buttons pop off before they righted themselves.

I reflexively pulled the hot, soaking wet shirt away from my skin, realizing almost too late how it gaped open, showing not only way more bare skin than was descent for school, but also the three fingered mark below my collar bone. I closed it again, wincing when the steaming soup stains touched my skin.

"Oh, I am so sorry," Nina cried with false sincerity. "I didn't see you there."

Nicholas practically threw his food onto the nearest table, making everyone already sitting there cry out and retreat lest they also get hit with hot soup. He whipped the stack of napkins from his tray and slid them under my ruined shirt against my chest and stomach. I stiffened at the sudden and rather intimate contact, but he let go almost as soon as I had a grip on them.

He turned and spoke to Nina in a warning tone, while standing close enough to block my partially open shirt from all the eyes that had turned our way. "Go. Now."

"But I have an extra set of clothes in my bag. You can borrow them." She dug around in her backpack and offered a set of folded garments.

"We want nothing from you," Nicholas growled as he reached back to pull me closer.

"Are you sure? Sylvan, they're girl's clothes. The ones you *should* be wearing," Nina taunted.

I leaned forward to whisper to Nicholas. "Let's just go."

He glanced back at me, looking like he wanted to argue, like he wanted to make Nina regret what she did.

"Please." There were too many people watching the spectacle. I could feel the pressure of their gazes like six feet of dirt all piling on top of me, hoping for drama or maybe a glimpse of my bare skin.

Nicholas's gaze softened and he turned to help me arrange my shirt and give me more napkins so I didn't get soup all over my hands before leading me out of the cafeteria. Nina called after us, but I soldiered ahead.

Eyes followed us as we left. We made our way outside into the cold evening air and toward my dorm. The heat from the soup cooled quickly and left me freezing in my damp clothes.

"I'm sorry. I should have seen that coming," Nicholas said.

I shook my head. "It's not your fault."

"But it is. She targets you because we spend time together. The least I can do is protect you from her."

I paused outside my dorm to look at him. "Another woman's jealousy is not something a man can protect from." If I'd learned anything from all those movies the admin showed me, it was that.

"But you—"

I held up a hand. "It's fine. I'll be right back."

It didn't matter. She had tried to humiliate me, but it would take a lot more than ripping my shirt to make me cower. As long as no one had seen my mark, it would be fine. It would only take a moment to change my clothes and go back to the cafeteria. Nina wouldn't catch me off guard again.

25

Twenty-Five

When I opened the door to my room, a delicious smell hit me right in the nose. A pair of bone-white bowls sat on the desk, steaming with the same beef stew that had been dumped on me.

I glanced toward the window. The curtains were open.

I dropped my bag on the floor and scurried back downstairs, still in my wet clothes, still clutching my shirt closed.

Nicholas, who'd been waiting outside for me, took one look at my panicked face and instantly straightened. "What's wrong?"

"He was in my room," I panted.

"How do you know?" It didn't escape me that he didn't ask who. We both knew it could only be one person—if you could even call the Boneman a person.

"There's soup on the desk. Hot soup."

He looked up at the windows, even though mine didn't face this direction. "Can I see?"

I nodded. I didn't want to go back up on my own anyway. Technically it was against the rules for boys to be in the girls' dorm building and vice versa, but I didn't care. If we got caught, I might be able to play the Bone Touched card. The school seemed to offer special privileges to its magical students.

It was hard to tell if Nicholas followed me upstairs or if I followed him. We came to a stop outside my door. It was unlocked, but Nicholas still glanced at me for permission to enter before he opened it. I hesitated, not wanting to go in. But I couldn't just stay out here all night.

When I stepped over the threshold, Nicholas was bent over the bowls of soup. He picked one up and sniffed it. His fingers wrapped around the white spoon sticking out of it and lifted it to his mouth. I steeled myself for the worst.

His eyes widened. "It's delicious. I don't think the cafeteria makes anything near as good as this."

I continued to hover in the doorway, hardly able to believe he would willingly consume something that so clearly came from our tormentor.

He noticed me standing there, watching distrustfully. "I know you're scared of him," he said as he brought me the other bowl. "But you have to admit, he looks out for us from time to time."

I didn't take the food from him. I didn't have to admit anything. There was only one way this food could have gotten up here. And there was no way I was going to eat anything served in a bone bowl.

Nicholas sighed and set down the soup on my desk. He held out his hands to me, but I stayed where I was. The skin around his eyes tightened.

"Sylvan, I think he's trying to send us a message."

I shook my head. I didn't want to think about any message.

"It's like I told you." Nicholas took a small step toward me. "He wants us to become friends. I think this proves it. Don't you? Why else would there be two bowls?"

I eyed the steaming broth. Being friends with Nicholas was one thing. Eating food the Boneman himself brought us was quite another. How could he even cook? Much less do so quickly enough after I got the same food spilled all over me and deliver it to my room before I even got here.

"Please," Nicholas said softly, taking another half-step toward me, his hands still outstretched. "At the very least you need to change out of those ruined clothes."

My face flushed as his gaze darted down to the napkins sticking out of the split in my shirt then back to my eyes. That definitely needed to be addressed. Having a boy in my room while my shirt was falling open was a recipe for disaster.

I swallowed hard. Was it worse to eat the food or risk the Boneman's wrath by rejecting it? Nicholas thought it was ok, and he had been around a lot longer than I had.

Reluctantly, I let him have one of my hands. He smiled and gently tugged me into the room. The door shut behind me, sounding way too much like a tomb door sealing us in.

"Go get changed," he urged, nudging me toward the bathroom. "I'll be here when you're done."

I didn't want to go into the bathroom. The soup was scary enough. The tub, even hidden behind the curtain, was too much.

"Or I can leave," Nicholas suggested, misreading my hesitation.

My grip on his hand tightened slightly. "No."

"Here, I'll go in the bathroom, and you can change out here."

My head bobbed in agreement. I liked that idea much more.

"Ok." He lifted my hand to his lips and kissed my knuckles. "Come and get me when you're done."

I stared at my hand as he disappeared into the bathroom. It tingled a little where it had been kissed. I rubbed the sensation away as I went to the closet. I didn't see a point in putting on normal clothes since I wasn't planning on going anywhere else tonight. So, I opted for a red tank top and loose, grey pants made of a soft, silky material—the only thing I owned that could be considered sleepwear. A pair of fluffy red socks kept my feet warm against the chill of the hard wood floor.

I knocked on the bathroom door to let Nicholas know he could come out. He emerged as I turned away to fold myself into one of the chairs beside the window. Nicholas came up behind me and paused. I looked up. He had both bowls in his hands but just stared down at me.

I raised my eyebrows in question.

He shook his head. "Nothing, just your mark…"

I looked down. The top edges of the three skeletal fingers poked up over the edge of my top. I grimaced and pulled it up higher to try to cover the thing that branded me as the property of the Boneman. It didn't want to stay up. The neckline was cut too low.

"It's ok, Sylvan." Nicholas chuckled as he extended one of the bowls to me. "It looks nice on you."

I seriously doubted that. But the bowl hovering in front of my face distracted me from voicing any protests. I cringed as my hands closed over the ivory material. I set it in my lap and glared down at the brown contents.

"It's not poison I promise," Nicholas said as he settled into the armchair across from mine.

My hand shook slightly as I picked up the spoon and lifted it to my lips. I took one last steadying breath before I put it in my mouth.

Nicholas was right. It was delicious. Better than most of the other foods I'd tried so far. I hated myself for how easy it was to take another bite.

"I told you it was good," Nicholas said.

I scowled at him.

He laughed. "Yeah, I know. Still, it feels like he cares when he does stuff like this. There was one time a couple weeks after I got here when I found a tiny figurine made of bone sitting on my windowsill. I still have it in my room."

I grimaced. *As if dead birds weren't enough.*

I finished the soup as quickly as I could, not because I enjoyed it—though much to my dismay I did—I just wanted the experience to be over. I pulled myself out of the chair, tossed the bowl onto my desk, and went to where I'd dropped my satchel, intending to root around for my sketchbook.

The box of bird bones greeted me first. I picked it up along with my drawing supplies and headed back to my chair. I couldn't quite put aside the bird though. It sat in its glass sarcophagus, waiting to be unearthed. It didn't smell when I opened the lid the way I expected a set of bones fresh out of a dead body would. I gingerly picked up the skull. It felt so small and fragile even between my thin fingers.

I'd returned the skull Professor Tumulus lent me a couple weeks ago, so I hadn't viewed memories outside of my lessons in a while. I glanced at Nicholas, who watched me.

"Go ahead." He nodded his encouragement. "I won't intrude."

I gently folded my fingers over the bones and closed my eyes. Nicholas had been right; there was a lot of flying in this bird's life. My heart flooded with the thrill of it. It had nested a dozen or so times. Sometimes the babies died, but mostly they lived and grew to adulthood. I watched the bird tend to a clutch of eggs before taking off, and then the scene went dark.

My brow furrowed. That couldn't be right. I looked again, slowing the image down. Something in the undergrowth rustled before the vision cut off and I could have sworn I saw a fluffy tail swishing back and forth in the brush.

A cat.

We had a few cats around campus to make sure we didn't have problems with mice or rats. That must have been how the bird died. But then, the cat just left its body there on the ground. That was strange. Why hadn't it eaten it? And what about the eggs?

I rewound the vision once more. I knew that bush the cat hid in. I knew the path it grew beside. It was right outside this very building. My eyes shot open, and I bolted from the chair. I barely slowed long enough to deposit the bird bones on my desk before I flew toward the door. My socks made the ground slippery, so I paused to yank them off and toss them back on my floor.

"Sylvan!" Nicholas called after me through the open door.

I didn't stop until I found the tree from the bird's memories. My feet were bare, but I didn't care when the bark scraped against their soft soles. Those eggs were all alone and needed help.

Just like me.

There it was, at the edge of a branch. The nest. I had

to stretch precariously to peer inside without breaking the branch it rested on. The eggs were still there, five black-speckled shells.

"Sylvan!" Nicholas shouted. "What are you doing?"

Getting back down was a bit harder than going up, especially with just one hand, but I managed.

"Found something." I held out my prize to show Nicholas.

It had been a bother to hold the nest with the eggs inside while I descended the tree, a lot of bracing with my legs while I reached for branches with one hand, but there they were.

Nicholas peeked at them. "Those were its eggs, weren't they?"

I nodded and started back toward the dorm. The bottoms of my feet stung but I did my best to ignore them.

"Sylvan, you're bleeding," Nicholas said, stopping me in my tracks with a careful hand on my shoulder.

I turned back. Bloody footprints left a trail on the sidewalk. "Come here."

Nicholas gently hooked his arms around my back and beneath my knees. He lifted, and I clung to his neck with my free hand, startled to no longer be touching the ground. My nails dug into the fabric of his shirt. I tried to keep the images of a different time I'd spent in much more skeletal arms out of my head.

You can move. You can talk. Nicholas is not the Boneman. He is not the Boneman.

My heart rate still picked up. So much physical contact.

"I've got you," Nicholas soothed. "Just focus on your clutch, momma bird."

That helped distract me. I had to keep my hand steady, so the eggs didn't fall out. There would have been no point in running out to get them if they fell on the ground and cracked open.

Nicholas carried me up to my room, panting from climbing all those stairs with my added weight. I stiffened when he nudged open the bathroom door and set me down on the edge of the counter. He held out his hands for the nest and after a moment of doubt, I let him take it and set it on the other side of the sink.

He turned and whisked back the curtain protecting us from the tub. I didn't think. I grabbed my nest, jumped down from the counter, and ran to the far corner of my room, where I crouched with the eggs, huddling over them as if I could protect them from the memories of breathing that milky fluid in and out.

Bones breaking. Bubbles swimming to the surface when I could not. Screams that fought and failed to escape my throat.

My feet ached, but I didn't care. Why did he do that? Why did he uncover it right in front of me?

"Sylvan." Nicholas stood in the bathroom doorway. His eyes tracked the trail of blood spots I'd left on the ground, all the way to where I clutched the nest. He glanced behind him, and his mouth dropped open. "*Oh.* Sylvan, I wasn't even thinking."

He disappeared for a minute. There came the sound of the curtain drawing closed again. He came back and dropped to his knees a short distance from me.

"I'm sorry. I thought washing off your feet in the bathtub would be more efficient." He held out a hand. I tucked tighter around my eggs. "Please, we have to clean off your cuts. They'll get infected if we do nothing."

"No." I wasn't going anywhere near that tub.

263

"I won't put you in the tub, I promise. We can do the same thing in the sink just fine."

I relaxed infinitesimally. Nicholas slowly took the nest from me and put it on the desk. I got painfully to my feet as he did so and started toward the bathroom. Every step hurt.

Were the sidewalks made of broken glass? How badly had I cut my feet?

Nicholas caught me halfway across the room and scooped me up again. I dug my nails into my palms to keep the flashbacks from consuming me until I sat on the counter again.

"Feet here." Nicholas pointed at the sink while he rolled up his sleeves.

I obeyed and made the mistake of looking at the bottoms. They were a filthy, bloody mess.

I swallowed hard and focused on the mirror instead. My face stared back at me. I hadn't taken much time to look at it before. Only once, when I was staying with the admin, did I stop in front of a mirror to really examine what the Boneman had made me into instead of sparing a passing glance. I tried to forget after that moment, but the same visage stared back at me now.

My face was angular, almost gaunt from the way my cheek and jaw bones were accentuated. My skin was pale. My hair was even paler, snow, paper, bone—that breed of white—and wavy. It bordered on unruly if I didn't tie it back.

And my eyes. I suppose those were my most striking trait. They matched my overall color scheme with their silvery white hue. But when I looked closer, there were the tiniest bits of blue and green in the creases of my irises.

Why did the Boneman make me like this? What had I

looked like before?

I hissed as Nicholas turned on the faucet and cold water gushed over my feet.

He winced. "I know. I'm sorry. Do you want to wash them off, or should I?"

"I can do it."

I hunched forward, gritting my teeth through the pain, to gently rub away the bits of dirt and dried leaves and other disgusting things I didn't want to think about being in contact with an open wound. At Nicholas's urging, I put soap on the cuts too. I kept having to pause to let the pain subside a bit.

Nicholas passed me the hand towel to dry off before bending to poke around in the cabinets under me. Thank goddess the towel was black and wouldn't get stained. The bleeding had mostly stopped, but there were still some tacky spots left on the soft fabric. I made a mental note to throw it in a washing machine as soon as possible.

"Found it!" Nicholas emerged from the cabinet with a brown bottle in hand. "Good thing they keep you well stocked. Well, maybe not all good. This is going to hurt."

I drew my feet up away from him, suddenly suspicious of the contents of this mysterious bottle.

Nicholas leveled a disapproving look at me as he unscrewed the cap. "We have to make sure those cuts are clean. I promise you're going to be fine." He moved slowly to take my ankle and pull it back into the sink. "Take a deep breath."

Halfway through my long inhale, he poured a clear substance over the bottom of my foot. I shrieked and yanked my foot out of Nicholas's grasp. He let me go and waited with his lips pressed tight together as I calmed down and the stinging faded.

"We have to do it again," he said solemnly.

I shook my head, tucking tight in a ball. "No more."

"Would you like to do it?" He held the bottle out to me. I shrank away from it. "Then, I need your foot back."

I glared at the counter, regretting running outside. Why hadn't I at least kept my socks on?

"Sylvan." His disapproving voice wiggled into my brain like a maggot into a dead body.

I stretched out my foot, setting it in the sink again. I kept scowling at it as if my appendages were to blame for my rashness.

"What a mystery you are." Nicholas mused as he repeated the painful process with my other foot. "I don't know how you didn't notice you were hurt as you *walked on* your injuries."

I tucked my arms around myself and shrugged. "I was distracted."

He chuckled as he pressed gauze to the bottoms of my feet and wrapped them up in fabric bandages. "Sure. Now, the cuts aren't as bad as they looked. I think most of the discomfort you felt was because you had dirt and grit in the wounds. You should be mostly fine in the morning."

I carefully climbed down from the counter. They did feel a lot better than before Nicholas cleaned them.

"Thank you."

He smiled. "Of course. I just wish I could do more. I've heard Bone Touched can use their magic to heal surface wounds like this, but they can only do it to themselves. And unfortunately, I haven't learned how to do that yet, so I couldn't teach you."

I sighed. "Naturally."

His lips twitched into a half smile. "Now about those eggs…"

I swept back to my room and plopped myself into the chair in front of the desk. The tiny eggs stared up at me.

I put a hand over them. They were slightly warm, but how were they supposed to stay that way? I couldn't sit on them. I was too big. And I had class, so I couldn't be here to take care of them all day. I'd rescued them, but I had no idea what to do with them.

Nicholas came up behind me. "I bet we could find a ton of stuff on the internet on how to take care of these little guys."

Of course. That's where I'd found info on the Wind Dreamed. It hadn't been as helpful with locating my family, but hopefully that case was the exception, not the rule.

"Hang on." He dragged one of the armchairs from near the window to sit next to me. "Let's see what we can find."

We spent the rest of the evening scrolling on our phones, exploring the world of wildlife conservation. I found a tutorial on how to make a rudimentary incubator out of a box and a light, and we devoted the next couple hours to recreating it with a shoe box I had left over from my shopping trip with Wren.

Once we finished and put the nest inside, Nicholas glanced at his phone and cursed.

"It's so late." He darted to where he'd left his backpack across the room and stuffed his things in. "Time flies when you're having fun, I guess. I need to go if either of us are going to get anything close to a full night's sleep."

I got up as he started for the door. He paused with his hand on the knob.

"This was fun. We should do it again sometime."

"Ruin my feet saving a nest of bird eggs?" I asked. My feet still ached if I stood for too long.

He laughed. "Maybe not that part, but everything else, yes."
Maybe.

"Good night, Sylvan. I'll see you in the morning," Nicholas said with a smile as he opened the door, slipped through, and closed it behind him.

I looked at the box of unborn sparrows. I was a mother now. Sort of. And my feet...

They'd be fine.

* * *

My left foot was still a little tender that weekend. I took it easy after I returned to my room on Friday afternoon to find that the scrapes had started bleeding again at some point in the day, probably during gym.

I wasn't too concerned about it, but it wasn't like I spent all day on my feet. Saturday morning took some time to myself. It was one of those rare sunny days that helped keep the incoming fall weather from getting too cold and lit up the gothic structures that made Mortorous Academy.

So, I grabbed my sketchbook and pencils and made my way outside to see if I could draw some of the statues that decorated campus. Some of them were made of tarnished metal that still gleamed dully in the light. Others were carved of stone and looked like they had been here for hundreds of years.

It was those statues that caught my attention. In places, you could see where exposure to the elements had worn divots or smoothed sharp edges. Those parts would be particularly tricky to draw.

I parked myself on a bench in front of the statue of a rearing horse. Its mane and tail blew in an unseen wind. Its front legs lashed out as if it were trying to strike an enemy. Its mouth was open in a silent scream.

Perhaps it was the creature's soundless cry that drew me to it. I often passed this statue on my way between buildings on campus. While others depicted people in confident stances or majestic fictional beasts in elegant poses, this was the only one where the subject seemed to be anything less than at ease.

It looked like it was fighting for its life against an invisible foe. Maybe the foe I fought was a little more visible at times, but it didn't lessen the kinship I felt to the weathered stone horse.

I sat in silence, sketching and erasing, and resketching. A few students passed by on the nearby sidewalks, but I didn't pay them any attention, and they ignored me in turn. Until…

"Sylvan Ravena?"

I looked up at a tall woman with brown hair pulled back in a neat bun at the base of her skull. She smiled at me.

"Did I get your name right? I have a lot of kids to keep track of, so I'm never entirely sure."

I nodded.

She folded her hands in front of her. "Do you remember me?"

"How could I forget?" She was the headmistress of Mortorous Academy, Pine, the first human I had contact with after the Boneman dropped me off at the school three months ago.

She gestured at the empty stretch of bench beside me. "Do

you mind if I sit?"

I had wanted to spend the morning in solitude, but I scooted over a little to make room for her. Since it was probably rude to reject the woman who welcomed me to the first place I might consider home. I focused back on my sketchbook.

Headmistress Pine sat and sighed as she leaned back on the bench. "You enjoy drawing?"

I nodded, continuing to sketch.

She peered at my work. "You're very good. It's a shame this school is more focused on academics. I dare say you would have faired better at Animos Prep. They specialize in the arts and creative learning styles. You could have honed your talent there."

I could have done a lot more than get better at drawing if I'd gone to Animos Prep. I might have been able to escape my Bone Touched fate. But the Wind Dreamed refused me. Fleeing into the arms of another god wasn't an option.

Pine took a deep breath. "I've been meaning to check up on you, see how you're settling in, ask if there's anything you need."

"I have everything I need," I replied, still focused on drawing.

"I don't mean for school. I mean..." She glanced around like she thought someone might be listening. "I obviously have no idea what you went through before coming to us, but I'll admit those first few days before you started classes and had your own dorm room, I was a bit concerned. I've worked here for almost ten years, and I've never seen a Bone Touched as reluctant to talk or do anything really as you were when you first got here."

I stopped drawing and lowered my pencil. This was the first time someone who wasn't Bone Touched had talked about the supernatural world and believed it existed.

Of course, some of the staff would know that the Boneman existed. They had to deal with the Bone Touched that he left for them to take care of. They had to procure the school supplies and uniforms and cover our cost of living. They had to have someone like Professor Tumulus on staff to teach Bone Touched how to use their magic.

But none of them had breathed a word about it to me since I left that little cottage where I spent the first few days of my life out of the Boneman's tub. I'd almost forgotten that there were non-Bone Touched who knew magic and the gods were real.

"I understand if you don't want to talk about it with me, but know that if there's anything you need, I will do everything in my power to help," Pine continued.

I turned to look at her. "How much do you know?"

She sighed. "Probably very little in the grand scheme of things. The Boneman likes to keep normal people out of demigod business as much as possible. I just know that Bone Touched hunt ghosts with bone magic that they learn at this school. And that you essentially don't exist before being brought here."

"Don't exist?" I asked.

She nodded. "The Bone Touched that arrived at Mortorous Academy during my early days here, back when I was one of the lower administrators, didn't have any legal records or history. We have to bring in another Bone Touched who specializes in forging those kinds of papers to make sure we don't drawing attention from anyone who might wonder why we were giving full ride scholarships to undocumented students."

I'd suspected as much. I had no memory of my past, and any attempts I'd made to find out about it online led to dead ends. The Boneman had thoroughly and completely erased me from the world and made one of the other Bone Touched create a new identity for me.

"I've heard that when you graduate, whoever is in charge of forging legal papers outfits you with a passport and drivers license and anything else you need to go wherever you want." Headmistress Pine chuckled. "I'm a little jealous. You'll never have to wait in line for hours or have to pay money to get the documents you need. You can just travel the world whenever you want."

"Not *whenever* I want." My gaze returned to the horse statue. I'd still be beholden to the Boneman's will.

Pine cleared her throat. "Yes, well, it's still one less thing to worry about."

We sat in silence for a moment. I twirled my pencil between my fingers. The headmistress folded her hands in her lap.

"I take it you aren't fond of being Bone Touched." She spoke with the gravity such a statement deserved.

"My life is not my own and I can't remember a time it ever was," I replied.

Pine lowered her head. "I'm sorry. I wish there was something I could do."

"Me too." I'd tried everything only to hit dead end after dead end.

"The only thing I can offer is support. You, and any Bone Touched who needs it, will always have Mortorous Academy on your side." She offered me a smile.

"Because the Boneman commands it?" I wasn't interested in any help he offered.

"Because you deserve it. It can't be easy to go through whatever you've gone through, and everyone needs a support system. Sure, Mortorous Academy agreed to be that support system at the Boneman's urging, but that was over a hundred years ago. My predecessors may have acted out of some kind of duty to the divine. I act out empathy for the lost children in search of a safe place who are brought to my school. I don't do this for the Boneman. I do it for you. That might sound like propaganda, but it's true. So, when I say let me know if you ever need anything, I mean it. No matter how big or small it might seem."

She sounded sincere. Part of me wanted to distrust her the same way I distrusted almost everyone else. Another part of me desperately wanted to believe her. I wanted to have that support, especially from someone with the power to do something and the right motivations backing them.

Pine's watch chimed. She glanced at it and stood. "I'm sorry to have to run off, but I have a meeting starting soon and bureaucracy waits for no woman. Still, I'm glad I had a moment to talk with you. I look forward to seeing what you can do during your time at Mortorous Academy. And seriously, if you need someone to talk to or a schedule change or a new uniform, whatever, all you have to do is come to my office."

She held out her hand. I hesitated. Most of the people I'd shaken hands with had such firm grips, it felt like they were breaking the bones in my hand. But maybe…

I took her hand. She shook once, gently, and let go.

"I'll see you around campus, Sylvan." She flashed me a final smile and turned to head off toward the admin building.

When I focused back on my sketch of the stone horse, it looked stronger than I thought it had before, a little less lonely. I rubbed my eyes. Maybe I'd been staring at it too long. Maybe I was overthinking it.

I finished my drawing and went back to my room, only to find myself looking up pictures of horses on my phone and drawing them in a herd around the first rearing horse.

26

Twenty-Six

I stopped dead when Nicholas and I walked into Professor Tumulus's classroom on Thursday. I hadn't seen Mallor since that day in Noxier when Lucas's ghost attacked me. But there he stood, browsing the shelves of specimen jars, and bending to eye that black and red spider I'd noticed on my first day.

He straightened and faced us. "Hello, again."

Nicholas waved as if this was completely normal. "Taking us on patrol, Mallor?"

"Yeah, it's been long enough, and we've got fresh meat." Mallor looked at me.

Patrol? Fresh meat? What was that supposed to mean?

"Afternoon, Mr. Ater, Ms. Ravena," Tumulus called as he emerged from his office. "I have something a little different planned for our lesson. Instead of staying cooped up in here with little, old me, you're going to go out with Mallor for his evening patrol of the town and surrounding area."

I blinked. "Patrol? For ghosts?"

"No, I thought we'd look for trolls. I've heard they make

really good roast beef. And mutton. And fish. Any meat, really," Mallor said, sounding completely serious.

Nicholas leaned over to me. "Yes, for ghosts."

But I didn't know how to defend myself. Did they think I was prepared for this? Tumulus hadn't taught me how to do any kind of bone manipulation, and my lessons with Nicholas were slow going. We'd practiced this weekend, but I still couldn't move the bone more than six inches at a time. Wouldn't that make me vulnerable to attack?

"Don't worry, I've done this before. There's nothing to worry about." Nicholas's words didn't comfort me.

I stared at Professor Tumulus and Mallor. Even if we didn't run into any ghosts, and even if Mallor and Nicholas knew how to fight any we *did* encounter, wasn't it still dangerous? Why did I have to rely on them for protection?

"Well, come along, sunset waits for no one." Mallor stepped around us to head out the door.

I glanced at Tumulus one last time. He just smiled and said, "Good luck."

Nicholas held out a hand. I sighed and took it, allowing him to lead me out into the hallway. This was the lesson. The Boneman would be upset if I refused to participate, and I wasn't about to risk seeing him tonight.

We trailed Mallor down to the same parking lot where Wren's car lived. I found myself popping up on my toes to look for the beautiful green of the vehicle that had taken me into town last time.

I didn't find it before Mallor nodded at a nondescript, black car. Nicholas opened the back door and held it for me. I slid inside, hugging my satchel to my chest. Nicholas circled the car and scooted in beside me.

Mallor glanced at us in the rearview mirror. "Leaving me all by myself up here?"

"You're a big boy," Nicholas replied. "I think you can handle it."

Mallor snorted. "Yes, *that's* why you don't want to sit up here like you usually do."

I glanced between the two boys, trying to parse out what Mallor was implying. Had they had a fight or something? Neither seemed inclined to give me a hint.

"Tonight should go pretty smoothly," Mallor continued. "There haven't been any recent deaths in the area. And as far as I know, any spirits from previous deaths have been cleared out. So, unless we encounter a wandering ghost, it should be a quiet night."

I raised my eyebrows at Nicholas.

"Wandering ghosts usually come from people who died of natural causes. They're mostly peaceful since they just want more time on Earth, instead of seeking revenge like a murder victim. They're observers and typically pretty weak, so they'll probably avoid us if they see us," he explained.

Unlike Lucas.

Technically, Lucas had died by accident, but he was still killed by someone driving a car when he was young. It mildly pacified me that neither of them expected anything to come after us, but I was still apprehensive about ghost hunting before I could fight on my own.

Mallor drove so much more smoothly than Wren. I didn't feel the need to grab hold of the bar above the window at any point during the drive down the open country road.

"You do this often?" I asked the two boys.

"Not as often as we should," Mallor answered. "But since

Tumulus is too old to do field work, you get to have lessons with me about patrolling and fighting."

"Mallor is good at close combat. Obviously, getting near a ghost should be avoided, but you should always know what to do if the situation arises," Nicholas said.

Mallor sighed. "It'll happen more times than you want it to. Next year, I want both of you out with me at least three times a week. We can't have you graduating and going off to battle the restless dead without being prepared."

Next year.

I only had a year and a half before I had to catch ghosts on my own.

As the seasons changed, the nights waxed, and the days waned. Classes ended fairly late, so by the time we made it to town, the sun was only a distant light on the horizon. I pressed myself against the window when we slowed to enter the urban streets.

It looked so different in these late hours. The buildings were the same, but the lighting made all the difference. I wasn't a fan of the shadows where anything might hide, ghosts or the Boneman or even other humans. The brilliant electric lighting of signs and streetlamps fixed that. The contrast of the light battling the darkness entranced me.

It wasn't like the lights of Mortorous Academy at night. Those were too few and far apart to do anything but make me focus on the shadows around them. But there were so many more here, enough to hold the blackness at bay.

It was beautiful.

"You should probably close your mouth before you chip a tooth on the glass," Mallor said from the front seat.

I glanced over to see him watching me in the rearview

mirror. My jaw clicked shut.

"Let her have her fun," Nicholas's mouth quirked into a half smile. "Everything is shiny and new to her."

My expression softened, and I went back to staring out the window. My forehead made a smudge across the glass as I continued to absorb our surroundings.

We found a spot in a small parking lot, similar to the one in which Lucas's ghost had attacked me and Wren. I did my best to wipe the mark from the window. My efforts mostly just smeared it, but it wasn't as obvious now at least.

Nicholas grinned like a serial killer who'd just finished murdering someone as we climbed out of the car. I frowned a little at him.

"What?" He asked. His smile didn't falter.

"You're excited?"

Nicholas laughed. "I'm very excited. I can't wait to show you all my favorite places in town. We're going to have so much fun."

"You do know that we're going on patrol, not sightseeing, right?" Mallor deadpanned as he slung a backpack over his shoulders, locked the car and came to join us.

Nicholas crossed his arms. "You said yourself, there shouldn't be anything to worry about."

"That doesn't mean you get to goof off. Part of being Bone Touched is always being vigilant. You never know when you're going to run into something you're not prepared for. Besides, you know as well as anyone that Bone Touched attract ghosts."

I paled. "Will any come after us?"

Mallor shrugged. "There shouldn't be any close enough to sense us, but it's not impossible. Some know we pose a threat to them and stay away, but our power is like a homing beacon, drawing them in. It's useful if you're hunting them. Not so much if you aren't expecting them, like the last time you were here, and that poltergeist attacked you. Which is why *you* will not be wandering off." He stabbed a finger at Nicholas. "Neither of you will. I'm supposed to return both of you intact. And since we're not on school grounds, we're outside of the Boneman's circle of protection. This is serious business. Act like it."

"Hang on." Nicholas held up a hand as Mallor started toward the sidewalk. "You were there when Lucas's ghost attacked Sylvan?"

Mallor kept walking, and we had to jog to keep up. "Who do you think kept it from killing her and eating the magic in her bones? Thank the Boneman I was already on his trail, or she'd be in the ground, and I'd have to call in a host of reinforcements from places they might otherwise be needed to contain him."

"I'm sorry," I whispered.

Tumulus told me about ghosts craving our magic, but I hadn't realized how much trouble my presence and lack of experience could cause. It made me wonder again why I was here now. What if the same thing happened and Nicholas and Mallor weren't able to rein in the ghost before it got to me?

"Hey." Nicholas's hand brushed mine. I let him lace our fingers together. "It's not your fault, and no one blames you. Nothing happened anyway. You're safe."

"Yeah, I had a few words with Tumulus before you two showed up," Mallor grumbled ahead of us. "He has a problem about not telling new Bone Touched everything as soon as possible."

In my case, it hadn't entirely been Tumulus's fault. I'd run out on my first lesson, so he hadn't had a chance to tell me what I needed to know.

More people wandered about than the last time I'd been here. Despite the lack of sunlight, there was no shortage of bodies buzzing behind the lit windows of shops and scurrying down the sidewalks, hurrying between stores and to their cars. They all had their hoods and collars turned up against the chilly wind.

I wished we could go inside and hide from it too. But we had a job to do.

"Why would a ghost come here?" I asked. "Wouldn't it be able to sense Mallor and get scared off?"

"The lesser ghosts might," Nicholas agreed. "They'd stick to the outer reaches of town. It's the stronger, more destructive ghosts that would be this close. But think about it, they've had their lives taken from them. Maybe it was their time, maybe it wasn't, but the reason they're the *restless* dead is because they're still clinging to life.

He gestured around us. "They want to be walking these streets, talking to these people, shopping in these stores. You know, *living*. They don't want to move on and leave it all behind. It's all they know. People go their whole lives fearing death and the afterlife. Of course, they're going to try living in houses or eating in restaurants—though ghosts can't eat. Only the strongest ones can even interact with objects. The point is, they're clinging to what they know, what they want."

"But it turns them rotten," Mallor interjected. "They become consumed with the need to live again. They lash out at people and objects, especially the stronger ones. They become a danger to the population. That's why we hunt them, aside from the fact that they belong on the other side."

"What is the other side like?" Was it really as scary as the ghosts seemed to think?

Mallor shrugged. "The only person to go there and return is the Boneman."

Well, I definitely wasn't going to ask *him* about it.

We walked a full minute in silence before Nicholas changed the subject. "Patrols are always boring. Unless there's a ghost, it's mostly sightseeing. Like that park over there."

He pointed to the left. A stone arch with the words 'Noxier Park' chiseled into it spanned the length of a wide sidewalk that led into a sprinkling of trees. I imagined it must be nice during the day, but right now, with shadows clinging to the trunks like hands to prison bars, it only reminded me of the Boneman's forest that bordered Mortorous Academy.

"There's a dog park a little way down that path, and hiking trails run out to the edges of town, and into the forest beyond. They're really pretty on the rare occasions when the sun comes out," Nicholas explained.

"A mile or so back that way"—he jerked his thumb behind us— "is the community garden where all kinds of flowers and fruiting plants are grown. They even have a peach tree that looks amazing when it blooms in the spring. It's right next to the old library that has a lot of manuscripts from the town's earlier days as well as more modern stuff. But I'm sure you've heard all about that from Wren."

I chewed on my lower lip. I hadn't actually. She only ever talked about buying books in Noxier, not borrowing them from the town library. She liked the Mortorous Academy library, but she never mentioned any others. I might not get the chance to hear about anything like that from her anyway, now that she was shutting down on me.

This last week, she'd been quiet. Even when I sat with her at lunch, she didn't start conversations much. It was feeling less and less like she was my friend.

"If you didn't have a sacred duty to protect the people of the world from undead spirits, you would make a terrific tour guide." Mallor smirked over his shoulder at Nicholas.

Nicholas puffed up his chest. "Maybe that's what I'll do in my free time. I bet it's more fun than trying to sell people technology they don't need."

Mallor pointed a warning finger at him. "Maybe, but at least I get to play with the display devices. You'd just be listening to yourself talk all day."

"He already does that a lot," I offered.

Mallor barked a laugh as Nicholas put his free hand to his chest in mock outrage. "I will have you know that I do not talk all day just to hear my own voice—though it is a very nice voice if I do say so myself—I do it to entertain you, Miss I-Don't-Want-To-Talk-To-Anyone."

The corner of my lips quirked up. "Like you don't want to entertain yourself too."

Nicholas stuck his tongue out at me.

Mallor was still laughing ahead of us. "How long ago did you put a leash on that boy, Sylvan? Or did he put it on himself and give it to you?"

I snorted.

Nicholas tried to kick Mallor in the back of the knee. Mallor stepped away, crouched, and swept Nicholas's remaining leg out from under him faster than I could react. I let go of Nicholas's hand as he tumbled into a bike rack.

283

Mallor stuffed one hand in his pocket and offered the other to Nicholas. "That was sloppy. How long has it been since you practiced?"

Nicholas took his hand. "Probably since the last time you came up to the school."

Instead of pulling himself all the way upright, Nicholas dropped halfway up, yanking Mallor off balance. Nicholas rolled, planted his feet against Mallor's chest, and flipped him up and over, onto his back in a patch of grass. Nicholas sprung to his feet and smirked down at Mallor, who coughed from having the air knocked out of him.

I stared in shock. They were throwing each other around like they weighed nothing. Weren't they going to break something? Just how strong were our bones?

"Maybe not as sloppy as you thought." Nicholas looked down his nose at his defeated opponent, but his goofy grin ruined any air of superiority he might have been trying to put on.

Mallor got back up. "Not bad. Was that your plan from the start, or just revenge?"

"A man never reveals his secrets."

Mallor rolled his eyes and started walking again.

We made a long, looping route around and between buildings. I kept an eye out, not because I wanted to find a ghost, but because everything was so fascinating. My eyes lingered on the lights of store signs. My ears followed snatches of conversation as people passed. And when the aroma of roasted beef and savory sauces curled out the door of a small restaurant, my head snapped to follow it.

A dozen or so tables occupied the open space, half of them filled with people enjoying their dinners. A pair of double doors swung open in the back as a waiter walked through them, and I caught a glimpse of a spotless kitchen beyond. My stomach growled at the thought of sitting down and enjoying a warm meal that didn't come from the school.

"Sylvan is hungry," Nicholas announced, also coming to a stop in front of the restaurant.

I rolled my eyes. Of course, he would say something.

Mallor paused and glanced at him, then at me. "I guess you haven't had dinner yet." He looked around the street as if a ghost might appear and attack us that very second. "We've almost made a full round, so now would probably be the best time to get something, but it has to be quick." He pointed a threatening finger at Nicholas. "We eat and get out. No playing around."

Nicholas put a serious hand to his heart. "No playing around."

Mallor circled back toward the doors and the inviting smell coming out of them. I might have followed a little too close behind. I hadn't planned on saying anything, but I was starving, not to mention cold. Even with my school-issued jacket, the autumn winds whipped around me. Sitting down in a warm restaurant with a hot meal sounded heavenly.

At first, I didn't know what to order, but Nicholas was more than willing to make recommendations. The pork chop I chose oozed butter and spices. I couldn't get enough of it. Nicholas let me try some of his chicken, which was also incredibly delicious. Both meats were so juicy and tender.

Nicholas wanted to get dessert, but Mallor barely had the patience to stay long enough to pay for our meal. Nicholas grumbled about not getting any cheesecake as we once again patrolled the streets of Noxier. I would have liked to get some too, but Mallor had looked ready to burn Nicholas at the stake when he asked, and that wasn't a hill I was prepared to die on.

Dinner was enough for me. Too many good things in a row meant an equal amount of trouble later, like drinking all the water when you're only halfway across a desert. You're satisfied, but you run out of supplies. The world always balanced itself out like that.

We completed the rest of our circuit through town without incident. No ghosts. No feeling of being followed. Nothing out of the ordinary.

I was glad for it. A quiet walk through town was just fine by me, even if it only got colder the longer the sun stayed down. I buried the lower half of my face into the collar of my jacket.

"Just one stop left," Mallor called back to us. "The cemetery."

I almost tripped over my own feet. "Cemetery?"

"Of course. If there are ghosts around, they'll be at the cemetery. It's sort of a home base for them, even if their bodies weren't buried there," Nicholas explained with a casual wave of his hand.

Naturally. "I hate this job."

Nicholas chuckled softly and offered a hand. "I don't know. It has a few perks. Like hanging out with amazing people."

I took his hand. "I guess."

"You wound me."

"Your ego is too big for me not to hit it whenever words come out of my mouth."

Mallor laughed while he walked. Nicholas rolled his eyes at me, but there was a faint smile on his lips when he turned away.

27

Twenty-Seven

The cemetery was exactly what I expected. Large tombstones marked graves instead of flat plaques. Flowers in various states of decay and unlit candles decorated the spaces in front of them. A handful of angel statues stood watch over the field of dead bodies. The whole thing was almost comically gothic down to the poor lighting and the way our breaths plumed in the air.

I wondered if any movies had been shot here.

We walked more slowly through the well-kept grass than we had on the sidewalks, partially to make sure we didn't trip over any stray grave offerings, and partially out of reverence. We didn't carry any flashlights. Given the setting, flaming torches might have been more appropriate anyhow. The moon was bright overhead. And I doubted all those moving shadows would have eased the feeling of my blood jumping beneath my skin, trying to get out, to run away.

"There shouldn't be anything here, but it never hurts to check," Mallor whispered as if he thought someone else might be listening.

I hunkered down in my jacket and eyed the shadows like they might snatch me up and drag me into one of the graves. Nicholas gave my hand a light squeeze and smiled at me when I glanced at him out of the corner of my eye.

"Looks like the kind of place *he* would like," I whispered so softly I didn't expect him to respond.

But he nodded anyway. "Aside from forests, graveyards are one of his favorite places. He meets Bone Touched in them after they've caught a ghost, so they can hand it over."

"To do what?"

"Take them to the afterlife. No one ever sees him do it." He dropped his voice to an ominous tone and leaned in close. "At least, no one who's lived to tell the tale."

I jerked my hand out of his and tucked my arm against my body.

"Sorry." Nicholas winced, letting his hand fall away. "Bad joke."

I chewed my tongue. I didn't find anything funny about what we were doing. Not even close. I would take a night alone in my room over this—at least I'd have the bird eggs for company. Walking through the town wasn't too bad, but this felt like inviting trouble. Especially since I still didn't know how to defend myself from a ghost other than by running.

Grass crunching softly underfoot was the only sound. No other human was crazy enough to be out here in the middle of the night. No ghosts charged at us from the darkness.

A cloud of mist rolled along the ground several feet away. I paused to watch it. It should have been way too dry and windy for fog. It moved slowly, almost crawling over the grass.

"What is it?"

Nicholas's whisper in my ear made me jump. I hadn't realized he stopped too. My finger lifted toward the mist. He leaned over my shoulder, practically resting his chin on it.

"An apparition," he murmured. "Mallor."

Mallor was at our side in an instant, following my still pointing finger. "Good eye. Those ectoplasm types are hard to see since they look so normal in such a misty climate." He unslung his backpack and rummaged through it.

"These kinds of ghosts are relatively docile. If it sees us, it'll try to run," Nicholas said. "Or attack. But there are enough of us that it will think twice about fighting."

"Can't it feel us?" I asked. Mallor said ghosts could sense Bone Touched.

Mallor shook his head. "At this distance it might not. Ectoplasms, the formless, misty blobs, are pretty low level. It's only poltergeists and others that can take a full human form that have a wide range on them. This one looks small, so it won't be very strong. But I'm going to need a bit of help." He handed Nicholas a large, flat, white piece of something and a handful of smaller white objects.

"Bone," Nicholas said when he caught me looking. "Manipulated into a different shape. Some Bone Touched fight with unchanged bones, but most shape them with their powers. It's a difficult skill to learn though."

I could only imagine. Moving bones was hard enough.

"Stop talking. You're going to scare it," Mallor hissed. "Sylvan, you stay here and take notes. Nicholas, you know what to do."

My eyes widened. "Wait."

Mallor had already vanished between the headstones and statues. Nicholas put a reassuring hand on my arm. "Don't worry. It won't sense you as long as it's distracted with us. Just stay here, stay quiet, and watch us do what we do best." He flashed me his trademark grin, pressed something into my hand, and ducked away into the shadows of the graveyard.

I crouched behind a tall gravestone and looked at what Nicholas gave me. A small, white blade sat in my palm. A bone knife.

I'd never been happier to hold a bone. He'd given me something to defend myself. I may not be able to guide it through the air, but I could certainly stab with it.

I peered out from behind the stone slab to watch. The mist sat still, gently roiling against the ground. From here it looked completely harmless.

It wasn't attacking, like Lucas had. It wasn't even near any people. It was minding its own business out here. And Nicholas and Mallor were about to capture it and take it somewhere it didn't want to go.

I leaned a cheek against the cold gravestone. This story felt too familiar. I tried to stifle my sympathy. This ghost wasn't supposed to be here. It might start hurting people if it stayed in the world of the living too long. It should have moved on to a better place by now. But it was still here, desperately clinging to what it knew.

There wasn't any warning. Nicholas materialized out of the night.

The mist reared up as he charged toward it and hurled a piece of bone like a frisbee. The makeshift weapon lodged into the cloud of fog, sticking halfway out of its side. The ghost let out a high, keening sound that had me clamping my hands over my ears.

But Nicholas was still running, pulling another bone

fragment out of his jacket. The mist darted in the opposite direction. The bone slowed it down. It rolled over the ground but had to lift itself to keep the weapon from pressing into the dirt and getting driven further into its body.

Despite the injury it still moved faster than Nicholas. It hurtled toward the edge of the graveyard, where an angel statue watched the commotion impassively. As it passed under the stone creature, Mallor appeared between the rocky wings.

Sometime in between disappearing a minute ago and now, he had produced a series of interlocking bones that formed a net. He tossed it with both hands, the way a fisherman would. The bones crashed down onto the foggy ghost and curled to form a complete sphere.

The ghost screamed and thrashed around inside. Its cage shook and rolled but held.

A completely unconcerned Mallor climbed down from the statue. I stood up slowly and stared. It had all happened so fast.

Nicholas jogged up beside me, panting slightly. His eyes were bright from the thrill of the chase. "That was fun."

Not the words I would have used.

He turned a wild grin on me. "What did you think?"

I watched the raging spirit. "It ran away."

"As we suspected. This is a small ghost, maybe an older person who died without getting to travel the world or something. Those sorts of little regrets tend to keep spirits from being too powerful or malevolent but don't let them move on."

Mallor gestured with a hand. The ball-like cage started to roll on its own despite how the ghost struggled. Nicholas followed and nodded for me to join him.

"It didn't sense Mallor even when he was right on top of it?" I asked.

Nicholas shrugged. "The weaker a ghost is, the less intuition it has. It was also distracted by me. Ghosts don't know exactly what Bone Touched are or what they can do, but the bigger, stronger ones have some sense. They instinctively know that they are the prey, and we are the predators. The smaller ones are in the dark unless a bigger one tells them."

"They do that?" Why had it never occurred to me that ghosts could communicate with each other?

"It's pretty rare. But yeah, mostly if there are no Bone Touched in the area. Ghosts build up and congregate. Sometimes they form packs that travel together and look out for each other. Those packs are led by stronger ghosts, mostly poltergeists, who might have experience with Bone Touched. They communicate with the others, so they can all have each other's backs. It sounds wholesome except that they wreak havoc everywhere they go. And that cooperation makes them more difficult to subdue. Taking down just one ghost can be hard enough. We got luck with this one."

I pressed my lips together. "You caught it. What now?"

"Now," Mallor answered as he rolled the bone cage to a relatively open area at the edge of the cemetery beside a tall lamppost. "We wait."

I frowned. *Wait for what?*

Nicholas drew closer, his hand brushing mine. I let him take it. "You aren't going to like this part."

His grim expression made me want to crawl into an empty grave and pull the dirt over myself. The prospect of catching a ghost had excited him, but now he looked like he was preparing for his own funeral.

My heart jumped into my throat. "Nicholas, what—?" A familiar chill crept over my skin. I tried and failed to swallow. My hands shook. "No," I whispered.

"Come here." Nicholas knelt and sat back on his heels. "It's easier if you sit."

I wanted nothing more than to run as fast and as far from what I knew approached us. But my limbs were already growing stiff with that terror-inducing aura so close. I could only fall to my knees, gripping Nicholas's hand like it could keep me from drowning in all the fear.

Mallor stood beside the ghost's cage with his head bowed. The ghost had gone deathly still as if it knew what was coming. Or maybe the Boneman's paralysis worked on it too.

My eyes stayed fixed on where a dim pool of light from the lamp dissipated into darkness. I should have known this was how tonight would end. Nicholas said the Boneman met Bone Touched in cemeteries to collect captured ghosts, but I hadn't thought that meant immediately after they were captured. I thought I'd have time to leave and Mallor would handle it.

The low rattle of very large bones moving against one another, and a deep thudding of feet sounded from the darkness. The artificial light from the lamp caught and shone on an elongated snout full of sharp teeth.

My breaths turned shallow and quick as the enormous skeleton emerged fully into the light. The Boneman stalked toward us with long, slow strides, as if he had all the time in the world. If he was a god, he probably did.

He stopped once he towered over Mallor. The ghost was so quiet and motionless in its cage that I started to think it was trying to hide. If ghosts could sense the power of the Bone Touched, how did they feel when they met the Boneman?

The Boneman eyed Mallor long enough for me to wonder if they were having one of those quiet conversations the Boneman had with others in their minds. Then he turned his attention to me and Nicholas.

The Boneman's patented terror locked my muscles. He came toward us, stopped, crouched. The position almost made him look human. He swiveled his head from me to Nicholas to the sliver of space between us, where our hands lay clasped in the cool grass. His skeletal fingers reached out and rested over our joined hands.

You found each other.

My breath stuttered on its way in.

Good. Stay together.

He retracted his hand, stood, and walked back to the ghost in its cage. I tried not to think about how that exchange could have been worse in case I jinxed it.

The Boneman stopped at the ghost's cage. He pulled it open like it was made of cobwebs. The spirit inside didn't move a single tendril of mist.

The Boneman cupped the ghost in his hands the same way I'd held the nest of bird eggs when I pulled it out of the tree, heartbreakingly gentle. The misty soul didn't try to dart away as the Boneman scooped it out of the cage and hugged it until it seeped through the spaces between his ribs. The ghost swirled gently inside his rib cage.

With one final look at the three of us, the Boneman turned and stalked into the darkness beyond the graveyard.

295

My breathing evened out and feeling slowly returned to my body. Mallor blew out a breath and turned toward the grotesque cage. With a flick of his wrist, it folded into a much more manageable size.

That broke the spell of silence and stillness. I shot to my feet, whirled, and stormed off between the gravestones toward the street.

"Sylvan?" Nicholas stumbled when he got up. I ignored him as he chased after me. "Sylvan, wait."

I halted once I reached the glow of the streetlamps outside the cemetery and spun so fast that he nearly slammed into me. "Why didn't you tell me we would be there when he came?"

Nicholas's throat bobbed as he swallowed hard. "I'm sorry. I thought you understood that we would be when I told you about handing ghosts over in graveyards."

"You should have clarified. I didn't have to be here for *that*." I jabbed a finger in the direction we'd come. "I didn't even help catch the ghost."

"You pointed it out. That counts as helping."

I turned my face away. My fists burrowed into my pockets. I could still feel the Boneman's touch on the left one. He'd left me alone for so long that I almost forgot what it felt like to be in his presence, how much it reminded me of my oldest and worst memories. The encounter had been short, but it was enough.

"Please," Nicholas breathed. "Don't hollow out."

When I looked at him again, tears streaked down my cheeks. "Then don't keep me in the dark," I whispered back.

"I won't." He said it the way one makes a vow to a person who's on their deathbed.

One hand emerged from my pocket. Nicholas took it almost before I could offer it to him. His smile was a bit shaky, but my features smoothed out in response.

"Kiss already, why don't you?" Mallor grumbled as he shuffled through the grass past us.

Nicholas looked up to issue some kind of retort, but I squeezed his hand and tugged him onto the sidewalk.

"*You* didn't tell me *he* was going to show up," I said darkly to Mallor.

"You didn't ask. And honestly, shouldn't Tumulus have lectured you about that already?"

"Don't deflect."

"Don't blame me for getting distracted by the need to do my job."

I let go of Nicholas's hand and shoved Mallor sideways into a building. He grunted and swore. Nicholas stared with eyes wide enough that I was surprised they didn't pop out of their sockets and go rolling across the ground.

Mallor watched me warily as he straightened.

I stood my ground, fists clenched, feet braced. "*Your job* tonight was to teach us, not throw us in blind."

If he wanted to make fun of the fact that I had no idea what was going on in this supernatural world unless someone told me, he could eat concrete. I wasn't going to stand for this when he had probably been in the same situation a few years ago.

Instead of retaliating, Mallor grinned at me. "I knew you had a spine buried somewhere under all that anxiety. Nice to finally see the real you." I said nothing. He jerked his chin up the street. "Let's get you back to the Academy before you start a brawl."

Twenty-Eight

I checked on the eggs as soon as I got out of bed the next morning. A tiny crack had formed along the side of one. At first, I was distraught. We had been so careful with them. We'd gone through all the trouble of making the incubation box, and it didn't even matter. One of them had already died. Bone Touched *did* attract death.

Then I looked closer and noticed a bigger crack toward the bottom of another. Through that crack, a sliver of grayish beak poked through. As I watched, the beak moved, tapping at the crack, trying to make it bigger.

The eggs weren't breaking. They were hatching.

Nicholas and Wren would have had simultaneous heart attacks if they could see how widely I smiled. I couldn't remember ever being so excited. Finally, something in this land of death was coming to life, and at my hands no less.

My good mood must have shown as I sat in class, even after I'd managed to calm down enough to stop grinning.

"Someone looks happy." Nicholas slid into his seat next to me.

"The eggs are hatching." I barely restrained the smile that threatened to break across my face.

"Already? That was fast. Though, I guess since they were laid at the wrong time of the year, anything goes. What are you going to do about feeding the chicks?"

Any traces of a smile melted from my face. That's right. I had to take care of the babies after they hatched. I couldn't just release them into the wild in their helpless, featherless, newborn forms.

"I don't know," I finally said. I hadn't thought that far in advance.

"Well, they usually eat half-digested bugs. I'm assuming you don't want to chew up worms and beetles and spit them into their tiny mouths." My scrunched-up face drew a laugh out of him. "Yeah, I didn't think so. It probably works fine if we just crush them up, add a little water, and feed it to them like that. We can go bug hunting after classes are over."

I nodded, my excitement spiking again.

"Great! We might need to improvise a shovel though. I'll poke around my dorm during lunch and see what I can come up with."

Nicholas wasn't the only one to notice my change in mood.

"Spill," Wren ordered when I found her at our usual spot for lunch.

She hadn't said a word about it during History, but she rarely said anything more than absolutely necessary to me in front of Nicholas now. It was getting tiresome, the way those two would cast wary glances at each other during class.

Nicholas was still looking for a way to patch things up. Wren was warning him not to. And I… I was in the middle, trying to block out the tension between them. At least we only shared a class with Wren once a day. I couldn't imagine putting up with her silence for longer.

When the two of us were alone, things were better. It gave me hope that everything could be set right. She was coming back to her normal, perky, talkative self. So, I told her about the chicks, leaving out the part about how I'd first found out about them or anything having to do with Nicholas. Thankfully, Wren was too excited about the prospect of playing with baby birds to dig too deeply into it.

"There is so much to do," she gushed. "You were right to keep them warm, but they'll need enrichment of some kind. They'll have to learn how to fly once they get old enough. And they need food, of course. Can't let the little guys starve to death. We should go to the library and do some research today. I can meet you there."

Uh oh. "Actually, I'm going with Nicholas."

The smile vanished from her face at the mention of his name. She got like this whenever he came up in conversation. "Going with Nicholas to do what?"

"Forage for food for the chicks."

Wren pressed her lips together. "Of course, you are. I'm sure you told him all about it in your first class, and he just *insisted* that he help you out because he's such a *nice* guy."

I stared down at my food to avoid her spiteful gaze and murmured. "You can come too if you want."

Wren snorted. "No, by all means, go dig around in the mud for bugs with your boyfriend."

He's not my boyfriend.

"Did you even think that I might want to come along before you invited him?"

I tried again. "You can still come."

Wren crossed her arms. "You know how I feel about him. And you for that matter."

My head jerked up. *"What did I do?"*

"Don't give me that." Wren stabbed a finger in my face. "You're keeping secrets. You've *been* keeping secrets for about as long as I've known you. It was fine when we barely knew each other, but now it feels like you're keeping them from me out of spite or something."

I took a deep breath. "Wren, there are things I can't talk about—"

"Do you talk about them with *him*? With Nicholas?" She made a face when she said his name like she was eating roadkill.

"Please, don't do this."

Wren reared back as if I'd slapped her. "You *have*. Why? Why does he get to know, but I don't? Does this have something to do with why you won't tell me what made you forgive him for how he treated us?"

I dug my hands into my hair. It would all be so much simpler if I just told her. What would be the harm in it anyway? If I explained, she would understand. She wouldn't spread it around, right? If I told her why it needed to be a secret, surely she wouldn't say anything to anyone else.

"Sylvan, I don't want to fight with you about this." She suddenly sounded exhausted. "But friends share things with each other. All relationships are built on trust. Why don't you trust me?"

I swallowed. *Because I don't know how. I've only really lived for a few months. I'm new to everything. I'm just learning what it feels like to have friends.*

I wanted to tell her all of that, but only two pathetic words

301

came out of my mouth. "I can't."

Wren sighed and stood up with her tray. "Well, maybe you should eat lunch with a friend you *can* trust. Let me know when you're ready to talk."

And just like that, she was gone, breaking my heart as she went.

Nicholas barely looked at me after I came out of the girls' locker room in my gym uniform before his brow furrowed with concern.

"What's wrong? Did something happen? Is it the chicks?" He scooted closer to me on the bench.

My knees went to my chest. In the basketball shorts and T-shirt, I felt naked and cold.

"Sylvan, please." Nicholas held out a hand, palm up, between us, offering but not pushing.

I stared at it. "I don't think Wren wants to be friends anymore."

The hand dropped. "What? Why?"

"I keep secrets."

"About being Bone Touched?"

I nodded.

"But you *have* to keep those secrets. It's not a choice."

I shook my head. "She doesn't know that."

"And you can't explain it to her without telling the secrets," he sighed and ran a hand through his hair. "This is why I always wore a mask around people before you came. They can't understand without knowing and they *can't* know."

"What do I do?"

"I don't know. It's always going to get messy like this if you try to have legitimate relationships with people who aren't... like us. I don't like it any more than you do, but that's how it goes."

I hated that. I refused to accept it. I would think of something. I couldn't lose the first friend I'd ever made. The Boneman might as well take me back to the tub if I did.

"If it makes you feel any better, I'm never going to leave you over something so petty." Nicholas offered his hand again.

I rolled my eyes as I took it. "You know the truth, though. You've *lived* the truth."

"And that's why I'll never leave." He squeezed my hand.

I was still wondering at the impression that squeeze left when we found ourselves out in the small field between the academic building and the forest after classes ended. I'd been hesitant about going out there, but Nicholas managed to convince me that it was the best place to dig around for the bugs we wanted. Besides, it was the most private place we could think of. The rapidly setting sun didn't do anything to assuage my anxiety, though.

I kept glancing at the tree line ahead of me as I stabbed at the dirt with a pair of scissors. It was the best we could find without asking for help from one of the staff. And since we didn't know how they would feel about me keeping baby birds in my room—whether I was Bone Touched or not—we didn't want to raise any suspicions.

The trees looked so much taller from down here on the ground, darker too, more alive. They almost appeared to be leaning toward me, reaching out to grab me and pull me into their midst.

"You're letting them escape!" Nicholas cried, lunging after a small crawly insect I had unearthed without realizing.

He managed to catch hold of it and toss it in the little glass jar he found in his room.

We'd gotten a bit of rain last night, so the wet ground was ripe with worms and small scurrying beetles. One took flight as I grabbed for it. I crawled after it, but the thing was fast and refused to give up. Nicholas chuckled as I chased the bug, half falling over myself to catch it, almost all the way back to the path behind the admin building.

I caught it in my hands just as a voice said, "So this is how the two of you spend your afternoons?"

Professor Tumulus stood on the sidewalk with a bemused look on his face. I shot to my feet. The beetle squirmed in my cupped hands, trying to push between my fingers.

"Afternoon, Professor." Nicholas jogged over to us. "What brings you out on this fine autumn evening?"

"Nothing as interesting as catching insects." Professor Tumulus still watched me curiously.

Nicholas handed me the jar so I could deposit my wriggly treasure inside. I scrambled to keep our other crawlies from escaping their glass coffin while I dropped the new one down. The worms were no problem, wriggling together at the bottom of the jar but the other beetles tried to use my fingers as an exit ramp.

"Sylvan found the nest of the dead bird from the other day, and the eggs just hatched," Nicholas explained.

"Ah." Professor Tumulus still frowned in mild confusion, but he didn't ask why I had become so invested in a nest of baby birds. Maybe part of him understood that I needed this. "Well, I was hoping to find you two anyway. Are you ready for tonight?"

"Tonight?" I asked.

Tumulus smiled at me, then focused on Nicholas. "You remember what tonight is, right?"

Nicholas stared blankly for a long moment before his eyes widened. "Is that tonight? Already?"

Tumulus nodded. "I came to make sure you were prepared."

"Of course, I've been looking forward to it since the beginning of summer." His smile glowed with excitement.

I looked between the two. "What's tonight?" I asked again.

Nicholas turned his jubilant expression on me. "Oh, Sylvan, this is going to be your first one, isn't it? You're going to love it. It's—"

"A surprise." Tumulus cut him off. "One I'm sure you'll enjoy, but you need to get ready first. Mr. Ater, I trust you can help her."

Nicholas looked like he might burst at the seams. "Of course!"

"Excellent. I'll see you both in the auditorium at sundown, then." Professor Tumulus turned and scurried off faster than I'd ever seen him move.

I whirled on Nicholas. "What is going on?"

"Nuh uh. No way am I spoiling this for you. I want to see your face when you walk into that auditorium and see all the—" He stopped and shook his head to clear it. "Come on, we've got to get ready. Showing up in our school uniforms will get us laughed at."

"Laughed at by who?"

He just put a finger to his lips and smirked.

My eyes narrowed at him. I had limited experience with surprises, which made me naturally suspicious of them, especially since the first one I could remember was getting kidnapped by the Boneman.

But Nicholas knew me. He wouldn't knowingly lead me into anything like that. Not after last night. Right?

I crossed my arms. "You have to tell me *something*."

He pressed his lips together, thinking hard. "There will be people there I think you'll become good friends with."

That wasn't much to go on. But if there were other people there, then the chances of the Boneman showing up were practically zero. That was enough for now. I could interrogate Nicholas more on the way. My arms uncrossed.

I had barely taken a step before Nicholas shot off. I had to run to keep up with him and even then, he kept urging me to go faster. We were both panting by the time we reached my room.

After setting the jar of bugs and improvised digging tools on my desk beside the box of slowly hatching eggs, I turned on Nicholas. "Ok, what else should I know?"

He leaned against the door. "You should probably change into something comfortable."

I narrowed my eyes but grabbed a pair of black pants that hugged the thighs and loosened at the knee, a blood-red tank top, and my black, school-issued jacket with the words 'Mortorous Academy' stamped over the left breast.

"Good enough?"

"Perfect. I'll meet you outside in fifteen minutes. Don't be late." And he was gone.

I spared a moment to check on the hatching eggs. Bugs scuttled around in the glass jar beside it. The shells had fully split open. Tiny pink blobs lay among the twigs and leaves of the nest. They didn't look like much, all motionless and naked without their feathers. But I imagined I looked similar to all those members of the Mortorous Academy staff when they found me lying outside on the ground in the dead of the night a few months ago.

My gaze turned to the outfit in my hands, and I scowled. Nicholas was going to talk whether he liked it or not.

Twenty-Nine

I had half a mind to go back up to my room, grab my bed sheets, and tie Nicholas up until he told me what we were walking into. He kept bouncing ahead, then pausing to wait for me to catch up, then jumping away again. It made it impossible to ask him about what he was leading me into.

My shirt was cut low enough that I had to wear my jacket zipped up to cover the mark below my collar—I thought it came up higher when I picked it. Nicholas seemed to have copied my outfit. I didn't know what was under his school jacket, but he wore his black uniform pants.

"Come on! Hurry up!" He bounded back to my side this time instead of waiting for me to catch up. "We're going to miss dinner at this rate, and the food is always to die for."

"What dinner? Where are we going?" I asked again.

He smirked, walking backward to look me in the eye. "The auditorium. Didn't you hear Professor Tumulus? Now, let's go." He offered a hand to me.

I took his hand, but before he could start pulling me along,

I yanked him around and pushed him against the side of the library. Nicholas's eyes widened. His playful mood died as I stepped close enough to hear his breath hitch.

"Tell me where we're going," I ordered quietly.

It took him a second to respond. "It-It's a surprise." He tried to slip away, but I pressed a hand to his chest to hold him still. His heart pounded under my fingers at the strange reversal of what happened a few weeks ago when he manhandled me in English class.

"I don't like surprises." The last surprise I'd gotten from my fellow Bone Touched was the night before when the Boneman showed up after we caught the ghost. Even if the Boneman himself wasn't there, I refused to walk into anything unprepared again.

Nicholas tilted his head closer, hovering inches from my own. "This isn't like the surprises *he* gives. I would never do that to you. You're going to enjoy this, I swear."

"And if I don't?"

"If you don't…" He licked his lips, eyes darting over my face. "I'll make it up to you. I will do anything you want, give you anything you want. Just say the word, and it's yours. I'll put the world in the palm of your hand if that's what it takes."

That seemed a bit excessive. I could barely handle my own life. How was I supposed to handle the whole world? It stood as a testament to his confidence, I supposed, that he was willing to make such grand promises.

My hand dropped from his chest, and I backed up. He stumbled forward as if I'd been holding him up. I shoved my hands in my pockets and continued walking toward the auditorium. Behind me, Nicholas let out a breathy laugh, then followed.

A sign warning students not to enter because of a "private event" hung on the doors to the building. I glanced at Nicholas, but he grinned at me and opened the nearest one, holding it for me. Darkness suffocated the interior. Only the emergency lights illuminated the ground every few feet, bathing most of the branching hallways in shadow. It would have put me on edge if I hadn't been distracted by a distant sound. A faint thrumming came from the auditorium as we approached.

Nicholas paused with his hand on the door handle. "You might want to unzip your jacket now."

I put a hand over the place where those three skeletal fingers permanently marred my skin. "I can't."

Nicholas shrugged as he used his free hand to unzip his own jacket. Underneath, he wore a white tank top that also exposed his mark. "Fine, but since you're new, it'll look weird if you don't identify yourself."

My hands itched to rip the zipper back up on his jacket. How could he be so reckless? Even if people thought it was fake, it wasn't worth the risk. "I don't…"

"Everyone here knows what you are, Sylvan. And it's nothing to be ashamed of."

He pushed open the doors and music, deep and thrumming and ancient, pulsed out. Red and white lights faintly illuminated the dark auditorium. The seats had disappeared somewhere, and the room was full of people. Dimly lit bodies milled around, talking, eating off plates they held in their hands. A few pairs of eyes slid our way, but we went mostly unnoticed.

Nicholas leaned in close to be heard clearly over the music. "We're all the same here."

That's when I caught sight of the first mark, on a brawny man a few feet from the door. Another sat in its spot below the collar of a woman who threw her head back and laughed explosively at whatever her companion, who also bore the mark, had said.

The more I looked, the more I saw. Everyone wore low-cut shirts that displayed the symbol like they were proud of it, like they hadn't been tortured and forced into servitude to a dark god to get it.

All of these people were Bone Touched.

"There you are!" Tumulus shuffled over to us, a bright smile on his face. "I was wondering if you'd manage to get Ms. Ravena here on time," he said to Nicholas.

Nicholas grinned back. "No problem, Professor."

"Excellent, excellent. Everyone is looking forward to meeting her. Come in." He gestured for us to step out of the doorway and turned away without waiting for a response.

Nicholas leaned toward me again as we walked. "Still feel like keeping that jacket zipped up?"

I shot him an irritated look but reached to open my jacket. It felt like unzipping a body bag, exposing myself and what I was to all these people. But everyone else looked so comfortable showing off their marks, even Nicholas. Maybe I was just so used to hiding what I was that openly admitting it didn't feel right.

"There's our little swimmer!" A young woman in a black camisole and black, skintight leather pants with a halo of curly pale blonde hair materialized out of the crowd and looped an arm around my shoulders. "Welcome to the club, sweetheart."

I stiffened under her touch, instantly freezing to the spot.

Nicholas swung around. "Hey, Nex. I had a feeling you'd be the first to ambush us."

The woman, Nex, disengaged from me and went over to pinch Nicholas's cheek. "Look at you being all grown up and getting yourself a girlfriend. It's about time, Nicky." *Nicky?* Nex spun back, putting an arm around my shoulders again and leaning close as if we were best friends. "If he ever gives you trouble, darling, you let me know, and I'll come take care of him for you."

"Give the kids a break, Nex." Someone grabbed Nex by the back of her neck and pulled her away from me. "The swimmer's still soaking wet, and Nick's just trying to look out for her."

Swimmer? Was I the swimmer they kept talking about?

I spun to get an eyeful of a tall, lanky man with the hood of his white jacket pulled over his head. Nex whirled and put him in a headlock before I could blink.

"I told you to stop doing that to me, Aeron," she growled, turning from overly friendly to feral in a matter of seconds. "Try it again, and I'll send you back to the Boneman the old-fashioned way."

"Can't you two show an ounce of decorum?" sighed a second woman dressed all in red with hair to match. "We aren't in the wilds of the north anymore. You can't just act like animals." She glanced at us. "Apologies."

I backed up a step. Nicholas came to my side, close enough to brush arms. "And so, it begins," he muttered. "If you need to step outside for a minute, just let me know. Being new kind of makes you a celebrity."

"Why are they calling me a swimmer?" I asked, still watching the woman in red scold Nex and Aeron, who had managed to wrestle each other onto the floor. A crowd was forming around them, pushing us back in their eagerness to watch the brawl.

"It's slang for a new Bone Touched. You've just finished your time 'swimming' in the tub." He made finger quotes around the word 'swimming'. "They might also call you wet or damp."

Tumulus had told me about the "wet" thing, but this was new. Bone Touched had a whole slang vocabulary. Interesting.

This room housed so many more Bone Touched than I ever imagined. The auditorium was packed with people who all bore the same three-fingered mark on their chests. It made me feel simultaneously bigger and smaller.

Nicholas jerked his chin at the far corner of the room. "Come on. Let's get our hands on some food before things get started."

I took his offered hand, not wanting to get separated in the crowd. Some people danced to the chilling music. Some just stood around, talking and eating. Some sulked by themselves against the walls. They were all shapes and sizes, ages and ethnicities. At one point, I spotted Tumulus with a handful of similar-aged men and women, all laughing and chatting.

A wall of tables held enough food to feed a herd of starving wildebeests. I hardly knew where to start after Nicholas handed me a plate, so I followed his lead and began in the middle.

I was eyeing a tray of assorted fruits when a soft crack sounded over my head and delicate pieces of black and white and red paper rained down around me. I turned, bewildered, to face a black-haired woman in all white.

313

Her face split into a grin and she held up a triumphant hand. "I got her first!"

A few cheers sounded around the room. I picked one of the pieces of confetti from my hair and frowned at it as the woman trotted away.

Nicholas glided over and started brushing the debris from my hair. Why did I have to wear it down? The paper practically melted into its wavy mass.

"A tradition," he explained. "When there's a brand-new swimmer, everyone takes turns cracking confetti eggs over their head during the course of the meeting. It's supposed to be good luck for you and anyone that cracks an egg on you."

"I should have brought an umbrella," I said as I combed out my hair.

Nicholas laughed. "It wouldn't have mattered. These people are relentless. You're lucky they didn't ambush you on the way here."

Great. Maybe I'd get buried alive under all the paper scraps.

I finished piling my plate with food and followed Nicholas to a relatively quiet corner. I watched everyone mingle and socialize with fascination. They all looked so normal. How did they smile so easily when they were all in the same, unfortunate boat?

"What do you think?" Nicholas asked after a long moment.

"There are so many."

"The world is a big place, and there are a lot of people in it. There have to be many of us to deal with the inevitable ghost activity."

"So, this is a regular thing?" I gestured at the gathering around us.

"It happens four times a year. Always here. This is the

center of everything for us. Everyone went to school here. Coming back reminds them how far they've come and how far they still have to go. Besides, it gives the recluses some much-needed social time." Nicholas nodded at the people who lingered along the walls, watching quietly, like us. "Some Bone Touched work in pairs or small groups. Some work alone. But even lone wolves need to be reminded that they have a pack that's there for them if they need it."

That sounded nice. As someone who once thought they would be completely alone, I knew finding others who understood was invaluable.

Crack.

Confetti rained down around me. I had to jerk my food away from my body to keep the paper from contaminating it. When I turned to confront my assailant, a familiar face greeted me.

"Welcome to the party." Mallor grinned at me.

My expression softened. "Hi, Mallor."

Nicholas poked his head over my shoulder. "You're not looking too bad for a guy who got shoved into a brick wall by a swimmer."

"Hey, don't discount her strength. If she'd been prepared, I think she could have taken on that ghost that attacked her when we first met all by herself."

Lucas. Ghosts should have been the first thing I learned about once I got to Mortorous Academy. Even the admin could have told me. It was at least partially their responsibility to keep me safe.

But no. No one wanted to tell me anything.

Even this gathering had been a secret. It wasn't as bad as previous ones, but I still had no idea anything like this took place. Was that part of being new, or was it just about being me?

A hand clamped over my mouth and yanked me away from the boys. I struggled to stand my ground, but whoever held me was strong. We moved rapidly through the crowd. Nicholas and Mallor disappeared as I was hauled across the auditorium.

Not again. I will not be taken away again.

I threw my head back into the face of my assailant. They cried out and let go. I whirled to see the now bloody face of Nex, the woman who'd cornered us earlier.

She held a hand to her bleeding nose and chuckled. "Good to see the old skeleton's still churning out fighters. Man, that stings. Almost broke my nose."

"I told you kidnapping her wasn't a good way to go." The girl in red handed Nex a white handkerchief. "You deserved that. She's probably still reeling from her time in the tub."

"Oh, she looks a lot tougher than that, Keres." Nex held the cloth to her nose. "She didn't completely panic. She fought back. Which means you deserve this."

Her hand disappeared into her pocket and came out with a black egg. She smashed it down on my head, sending eggshell shards and confetti raining down around me. I shook my head to get the majority of it off, but the woman in red, Keres, came in and cracked an egg on me too.

Just when I thought she was on my side.

"So." Nex slid an arm, which felt way too much like an anaconda preparing to choke the breath out of me, around my shoulders. "How are you adjusting to life on the other side of the tub?"

"It's... ok."

I brushed shreds of paper off the shoulders of my jacket, covertly trying to dislodge Nex. I needed to get back to Nicholas or at least find Professor Tumulus. I didn't trust her at all. She oozed chaotic charisma. But she seemed to be steering me in the opposite direction of where I wanted to go.

"'Ok' as in you're settling in or 'ok' as in you hate being Bone Touched but you don't want to bring it up because you think we're going to lecture you about how you'll get used to it and like it eventually?" Keres asked.

I opened my mouth but couldn't find the words, so I shut it with a sharp click of my teeth.

"We won't get all defensive on you like the older Bone Touched might. All of us go through that phase," Nex sighed as she kept guiding me through the crowd to the opposite side of the auditorium.

"Just because most of us are out of it doesn't make it any less valid," Keres continued. "I remember trying to figure out a way I could kill the Boneman when I was your age."

I straightened. "That's possible?"

Keres laughed. "No. That's what I found during my research. He's a god. He can't be killed."

My shoulders slumped. I picked at my food. Of course, a potential solution would get thrown in front of me only to be yanked away in the next moment.

Nex gave me a squeeze. "Don't worry, little swimmer. Our big, bad bone daddy is a lot more caring than he might seem."

I choked on the piece of cheese I'd just put in my mouth. Keres patted me on the back until I regained my breath.

"What are you talking about?" I rasped. Sure, he'd brought soup to my room and chastised Nicholas for what happened in English class, but none of that made up for what he'd done to me before I came to Mortorous Academy.

Nex took a step back, keeping one hand on my shoulder. "Well, you know, he wants us and him to be…" She crossed the fingers of her free hand and clicked her tongue. "You feel me?"

Absolutely not.

Keres rolled her eyes. "What Nex is trying to say is that it's going to be hard to reconcile what he did when you were in the tub with acts of kindness he might do now, but the Boneman wants a relationship with his children. And he wants his children to have relationships with each other, like how he put you and Nicholas together. He knew you would need one another."

Nex nodded. "It's cute how close you two are. But you have the rest of us too. We may not be around as much, but that makes it all the more important that we steal you away from Nicky when we are."

I narrowed my eyes at her like she's just confessed to murder. "You abducted me."

"Of course!" She took her hand off my shoulder to throw both arms in the air. "How are we supposed to have girl time if Nicky's hovering around you like a vulture over roadkill?"

"Girl time?"

"You're stuck in this school where the only Bone Touched within a fifty-mile radius are boys," Keres explained. "You must be starved for female company."

I opened my mouth to protest that I did have a female friend until I remembered that Wren didn't want to talk to me anymore. Spending time with Nicholas was nice, but Nex and Keres were right. It wasn't the same.

"Let's start with names." Keres smiled. "I'm Keres. This is Nex. And you are…?"

"Sylvan."

"Man, where was the Boneman hiding *that* name when I came out of the tub?" Nex whined. "I want a cool name like that."

The line sounded almost exactly the same as what Lorien from Animos Prep had said when we met. It put me more at ease and I smiled a little.

30

Thirty

I spent the next several minutes in the company of Keres and Nex, mostly letting them talk but supplying answers when they asked questions.

When I brought it up going to find Nicholas, the girls assured me that Mallor and Aeron were hanging out with him, so he couldn't possibly be that miserable.

"Actually, if he's with those two, who knows how he is," Nex snickered.

Keres suppressed a laugh of her own. "You're terrible, Nex. I'm sure they're more than fine."

Hopefully, Nicholas enjoyed spending time with the older Bone Touched as much as I did. I liked hearing about Nex and Keres's recent ghost hunting adventures and what it was like to be Bone Touched out in the world. The two of them usually partnered with each other and Aeron, but sometimes they split off with others or on their own. I wondered if I'd be able to partner with Nicholas on missions once we graduated.

No sooner had the thought crossed my mind than I was

trying to shake it out. I still didn't want to hunt ghosts at all. But since there seemed to be no way out of it, at least none that I'd found, it would be much more enjoyable to do it with someone I had already befriended.

Someone behind me smacked a confetti egg over my head, snapping me out of my reverie. The culprit vanished before I fully turned around. Nex and Keres giggled.

"Come on, I think we're about to start." Nex hooked an arm through mine and hauled me toward the front of the auditorium. Keres followed.

Several dozen chairs remained standing in front of the large stage. The crowd around us moved toward them, occupying whatever empty seats were closest. Nex and Keres pushed me into the middle of the front row, taking a seat on either side of me.

Nowhere for Nicholas to sit.

I tried to turn to see if I could spot him, but Nex grabbed the confetti-covered crown of my head and twisted until I faced forward again. I glared at her out of the corner of my eye.

She grinned and winked. "Pay attention."

A man with silver-streaked brown hair came to stand in front of all the now-filled chairs. He stood at ground level, not up on the stage. A bit strange. He surveyed all the Bone Touched before him. They fell into a collective hush. The music cut off, leaving the auditorium eerily quiet.

"That's Ajal," Nex muttered to me. "One of our leaders."

"One of?"

"There's sort of a council of the more experienced and talented Bone Touched. It's not super formal. They just help keep us organized," Keres answered.

"Good evening, brothers and sisters!" Ajal called with more gusto than I anticipated. "It's wonderful to see so many healthy, living faces tonight."

A cheer went up in the crowd. Ajal grinned at the response, letting them make noise for a while before raising a hand for silence. Everyone quieted rather quickly.

"As welcome as it is to be surrounded by so many of you, not all of us made it through the last few months of battling the raging tide of death. For our fallen comrades, we will have a moment of silence."

He bowed his head. The other Bone Touched followed suit. I fixed my gaze on my lap. How many had died? Was I replacing one of them? Ajal lifted his head and, as one, we all looked up.

"We have a spot of good news, though. We have a new member. This is Sylvan Ravena's first gathering." He looked me in the eyes. "Welcome. I hope we haven't scared you too much. It seems as if a few people have gotten your egging started."

A ripple of laughter echoed around the room. I didn't doubt that my hair was thoroughly covered in red, black, and white confetti. Many eggs had broken over my head while I talked with Nex and Keres. I'd stopped trying to do more than brush the excess off, so it didn't fly into my mouth or onto my food.

"We all wish you well in your training and look forward to the day we can bring you fully into our fold," Ajal continued. "The Boneman knows we need all the help we can get."

More chuckles.

"Speaking of which, we have business to attend to, as always. Sectors 7, 18, and 42 need a few more hands on deck. There was a mass shooting and a flood that left a nasty amount of spirits floating around. If anyone from Sectors 14, 26, 63, or 67 would like to volunteer to transfer, please speak now."

A few hands rose, including Keres's. I glanced at her.

"Disasters like this happen from time to time," she told me. "Sector 63 is out in the countryside, so I don't get a lot of action unless something truly terrible happens."

It must be common, this shifting of assignments, if she hadn't even hesitated. Ajal went on to list a few more areas that needed additional help and which others they might take people from.

After that, we held a memorial service for the two Bone Touched who had died over the course of the last few months. It was a quiet, solemn affair where candles were passed out and lit. Then we went up on stage and poured out some of the melted wax on two boxes, which I assumed contained the cremated remains of the deceased.

I lingered for a moment in front of the boxes. They were smaller than I would have thought they'd be. How was it possible that a person's entire body could be held with just two hands? That a living, breathing, thinking, feeling person could be so easily turned into a pile of dust?

Keres gently nudged me from behind. Right, I was holding up the line. I tilted the melted wax out of my candle over the two boxes and made my way back to my seat.

One of the older Bone Touched took the wax-covered boxes away once we were done. I watched her until she disappeared through a side door.

"They'll bury them in the forest to be returned to the Boneman after the gathering is over," Nex informed me.

We come from the Boneman and to the Boneman we return. I thought sourly. Even in death we couldn't escape him.

Once the service concluded, it was back to business. Some Bone Touched were being partnered up or split apart to do specific missions. There was a discussion of methods that should be used in each scenario. The teams were encouraged to talk amongst themselves, and the individuals were encouraged to use their best judgment or to seek counsel from others.

Ajal declared. "We will take a short break and reconvene in half an hour. Feel free to mingle and talk amongst yourselves. We haven't picked the food tables clean yet, so if you're feeling peckish, help yourself."

The Bone Touched stood and started moving toward the back of the auditorium. Nex and Keres guided me toward the food. Nicholas appeared beside me not a moment after we reached the buffet.

"There you are. You are *covered* in confetti." He chuckled while brushing off the top of my head and shoulders.

Nex grabbed him in a bear hug, ripping him away from me. She lifted him clean off the ground and swung him in a circle. I slipped a hand over my mouth and laughed at his shocked expression. Nex dropped him, and he staggered a bit.

"You're so cute." She patted his cheek. "Taking care of our little swimmer."

The low light made it hard to tell, but I swore a blush crept up his cheeks. "I'm just doing what neither you nor Keres had the courtesy to do—"

"I'm sure it had nothing to do with how distracted you were before the meeting started," Mallor interjected.

"What is a bone without its shadow?" Keres grinned.

Nicholas glared at them. "I hate all of you."

Nex laughed. "Speaking of bones and shadows, you must have been swimming in the tub for a long time to get hair like that." She stepped forward and flicked a strand off my shoulder. "Not to mention your eyes."

I tucked my hair behind my ear self-consciously. It was my most distinguishing characteristic. I couldn't hide anywhere with it. It made me look more like the ghosts we were supposed to hunt than a Bone Touched.

"It just means you're strong," Aeron said. "The Boneman has three baths to keep us in while he remakes us. White, black and red."

"You can usually tell which color a Bone Touched was made in based on their hair and eyes," Nex continued. "Obviously, Nicky here was black. So was Mallor. Keres was red. And Aeron and I were white, but we didn't spend as much time there as the three of you." She gestured at me, Nicholas, and Keres. "So, I only have blonde hair and blue eyes and Mallor is just brown all over."

"Each of the colors has a meaning." Keres picked up a cookie from the table and popped it in her mouth. "The bone, the bone's shadow, and the bone's blood—or marrow if you want to be scientifically correct. White, the bone, is the warrior, the strongest fighter. Those are the ones who go out to meet the ghosts where they are, no matter how far they have to go. Black, the bone's shadow, is the protector, the defender. Like Mallor, they tend to stay in one place and fight to keep it safe at all costs. And red, the bone's blood, are the strategists, the smart ones. They're more likely to set up traps for ghosts than hunt them. Or, in special cases, like with Tumulus, they're the ones that teach the swimmers how to use their bone magic."

I was fairly sure my eyes were wide enough to pop out of my head. Not all Bone Touched had the same experience? And they had different specialties?

"What if a bone wants to be a bone's shadow or a bone's blood?" I asked.

Nex snorted. "The Boneman doesn't make mistakes, little swimmer. He knows us. He knows what roles we are best suited for. All we have to do is carry them out."

But what if I don't want to fulfill my role?

"Better hurry up and take what you want," Mallor warned, glancing over his shoulder. "It looks like we're starting up again soon."

Annoyed at not being able to ask more questions, I turned and piled some sweets on my plate, before starting back toward my seat. Nicholas stayed close this time, refusing to let the older Bone Touched separate us again. I was glad for the small comfort of his familiar company.

He claimed a pair of chairs for us in the middle of the crowd. The other four filled in around us.

Nicholas offered a hand. I took it. Nex, who sat beside me, dug an elbow into my arm and flicked her eyebrows up and down rapidly when she saw. I rolled my eyes and stuffed a brownie in my mouth.

They could think whatever they wanted about us. It didn't change anything.

The rest of the meeting was a lot of bureaucratic fluff about a census of the Bone Touched population and an open forum for the audience to voice any concerns, which were then addressed by anyone who cared to suggest a solution.

Once, Nex snatched a bite-sized cookie from me and

inhaled it. Nicholas leaned across me to hiss a warning at her about taking things that weren't hers.

She flashed him a grin. "You should really give her more credit, Nicky. She almost broke my nose when I stole her away from you. I think she can defend her food herself."

Nicholas glanced at me. I shrugged. I had more food on my plate than I could eat anyway. What did I care if Nex took a piece? More than one might be pushing it though.

Nex stretched. "She's more of a fighter than you think. I wouldn't be surprised if she's hunting ghosts within the month."

I didn't want to fight ghosts at all, much less within the short span of a month—that was almost a third of my lifetime out of the tub. Couldn't I take over for Tumulus and teach others? Or even just stay in town, like Mallor, and not have to deal with much?

"I don't know why I hang out with you guys," Nicholas huffed. "All you ever do is make fun of me and now you're dragging Sylvan into it."

"Love you too, Nicky," Nex crooned and blew him a kiss.

He leaned in and whispered in my ear. "Can you fake a panic attack or something so we can get away from these lunatics?"

I chuckled. "But this is so much fun."

His eyes darted over my face. Heat started to rise to my cheeks. In an effort to distract him, I held up the last of my cookies between us. He took it gently from my hands and took a bite, licking the crumbs from his lips.

I looked away quickly before he could catch me staring.

It wasn't long before Ajal brought the meeting to a close. "It's been wonderful to see everyone together again. As always, feel free to stay and socialize until Tumulus kicks us out." Laughter rippled across the crowd. "Until we meet again in three months, remember that you are the bridge between the worlds of the living and dead, the protectors of all souls whether they reside in a body or wander restlessly without one until the day that you return to the Boneman."

"Until we return to the Boneman," Everyone echoed. Even Nicholas.

"And take some of the leftover food with you," Tumulus called from the front row. "I don't want to see so much as a crumb left on those tables."

The music started up again and several Bone Touched closed in to raid what remained of the feast. In the rush, several eggs cracked on my head. I was fairly sure there was more confetti than hair on my head at that point.

Nicholas had given up trying to clean me off and just shook his head whenever a new egg opened on me.

The others started saying their goodbyes. Nex wrestled Nicholas away from me, the two flipping each other around into different holds. The rest of us enjoyed the spectacle. Keres hugged me, which I didn't panic about thankfully, but weirdly that didn't surprise me. Mallor shook my hand, and Aeron tipped the edge of his hoodie at me like a hat.

"Give us a call if you need anything." Keres handed me a slip of paper with four phone numbers and their names beside each one. "And good luck with…" She trailed off as she gestured toward where Nicholas had pinned Nex to the ground. "…that."

I pressed my lips together to hide my smile. "Thanks."

"By the way, you two should stay out of Noxier and the forest for a while," Mallor said. "There was an accident this afternoon that resulted in a lot of people dying. I haven't gotten the chance to check for ghosts, but I'd be surprised if there weren't a few hanging around. So, stay at school where it's safe."

I nodded. "Ok." I couldn't go to Noxier unless Mallor gave me a ride, and there was no way I'd go into the forest on my own anyway.

"Well, we have places to be, people to see, ghosts to hunt," Aeron said. "See you at the next meeting, swimmer."

I raised a hand in farewell as they left. Keres separated Nex and Nicholas as if it were the easiest thing in the world. Nex grinned like a fiend and waved goodbye, before following the others out. Nicholas approached me, panting slightly. There were a few dark smudges on his white top, but other than that, he looked no worse for wear.

"Who won?" I asked.

Nicholas frowned. "I would have if Keres hadn't broken us up."

I smiled. "I'm sure." Against a seasoned Bone Touched, I didn't like his chances, but he grinned anyway.

"Are you ready to go?" He held out a hand.

I took it and let him lead me out into the chilly night. It had to be past midnight. Other Bone Touched flooded out with us, laughing, talking, pushing each other around. But they all headed toward the parking lot while we ventured back toward the dorms.

We zipped up our jackets to hide our marks and keep us warm, but I still shivered until Nicholas pulled me closer and hugged an arm around my shoulders. It wasn't as casual as with Nex. It felt more personal, more proprietary. But he was warm, so I had nothing to complain about.

"They didn't bother you too much, did they?" he asked. "They can get pretty...excitable, especially when there's someone new around. They practically mobbed me at my first meeting. It was disconcerting since I didn't know anyone there except Tumulus."

"They're cool," I replied.

Sure, Nex had the personality of a lit stick of dynamite inside a gas tanker sprinkled with gunpowder, but it made her more fun. Besides, Keres's cool composure balanced it out. I hadn't spent as much time around Mallor and Aeron that night, but I knew Mallor before this and Aeron seemed interesting in his own way.

I wasn't sure if I was ready to deal with so much complicated energy on a regular basis, but it would be nice to have people I enjoyed spending a few hours with four times a year in a crowd of otherwise unknown faces. Just like how I had Nicholas and Wren in the sea of uninterested students during school.

Nicholas raised an eyebrow at me. "They are mostly. Nex doesn't understand personal space though."

I shrugged, his arm bobbing up and down with the motion. "She makes me smile."

He huffed. "That happens so rarely, I suppose I *have* to cut her a little slack."

"They also told me more about being Bone Touched. Tumulus never mentioned that bath stuff."

"Yeah, the bone, shadow, blood thing should definitely be covered on day one of lessons."

I pressed my lips together. Warriors, protectors, and strategists. I couldn't think of myself as a warrior. I'd only ever run away from or watched others fight ghosts. But

Nicholas was definitely a protector.

"Keres said bone shadows stay in one place and defend it from ghosts. Do you think they can pick a person to stay with and defend them instead?"

Nicholas was uncharacteristically quiet for a long moment. His grip tightened on my shoulder. "Maybe." His voice was low and a little hoarse.

I studied his face, but he was looking pointedly away from me. "Would you want that?"

"It would depend on who the person was," He answered carefully.

"Who would you want it to be?"

"Birds."

I frowned. "What?"

He cleared his throat. "Do you think the birds are going to finish hatching soon? I don't think it's supposed to take them more than a day, so they might already be out."

What a tactless change in subject.

"Nicholas."

He plowed on. "I read something about them not needing to eat for the first twenty-four hours because they're still running off the nutrients of the yolk. So, we can probably go look for more bugs tomorrow before they need food. I don't know how much they eat in one sitting, so I'm not sure if we need more."

"Nicholas."

He still refused to look at me, even as we approached the side entrance to the girls' dormitory. "And of course, they'll need a regular source of food for a few weeks before they're able to leave and hunt on their own."

I sighed. He was really making me do this.

"Speaking of which, I have no idea how to teach a baby bird to fly. Are we supposed to show them somehow? Or just throw them in the air and hope for the best? Maybe we can coax them out if they imprint on you as their—"

I grabbed his face in both of my hands and pulled him toward me. His face registered shock half a second before our lips crashed together. I didn't have much of an idea of what I was doing—other than imitating something I'd seen in all those movies—but it sure did the trick. He shut up so thoroughly that you could have heard a heart stop beating.

He didn't move when I released him and stepped back. He just stood there, frozen to the spot, staring at me.

"I think there was something to what the others were saying when they teased us," I murmured and stuffed my hands in my jacket pockets, suddenly unsure of my actions and feeling the need to justify them. "I think there has been for a while." *I was just too wrapped up in my problems to notice.*

I turned toward the door. He could think about this for the night, for the weekend if he wanted. He didn't rush me into things, so I wouldn't rush him. It was fair, and we were tired from our eventful night.

I made it three steps before Nicholas grabbed my arm, spun me around, and kissed me. A startled sound escaped my throat, but he held me so gently like I was one of the freshly hatched baby birds that probably waited on my desk in their incubation box. One hand cradled the back of my neck. The other plastered itself to my cheek.

Nicholas pulled back enough to whisper. "I think you're right." Then his mouth was on mine again, a soft, coaxing pressure.

And I was kissing him back, in the dark of the night,

with the Boneman's forest visible just past the corner of the dormitory. My eyes closed. My hands traced up the front of his jacket and fisted in the warm material, pulling him closer.

The hand on my cheek moved to my lower back. Nicholas maneuvered us over to the wall beside the door. He leaned his back against it and held me as close as possible, still kissing me. I slid an arm up around the back of his neck. He made a noise deep in his throat that sent heat shooting through me.

I broke away to steal a gasp of air. He moved to press his lips to my cheek, my jaw, my throat, the patch of skin just below my ear. He rested his face in the crook of my neck, panting lightly, holding me tight.

He chuckled breathlessly. "I don't know whether I want this to be real or not." His hand moved to the back of my head, pressing my face into his shoulder. "It feels so right, and I'm terrified you're going to start having a panic attack because I moved too fast or I'm holding you too tight or it's too dark and we're too close to the forest—"

The arm I had around his neck clamped over his mouth. "If I didn't know better, I'd say you were *trying* to make me panic by reminding me of all of that."

He shook his head against my hand and kissed my palm. I removed it. "I would *never*."

"I know." I snuggled into his warmth. "I trust you. I think that's why I'm not panicking."

He combed his fingers through my hair. A few pieces of confetti fluttered into the grass at our feet. "Thank you for trusting me. As someone who has been through what you've been through, I know how big of a deal that is, and I'm honored." He pressed a kiss to my temple.

I smiled into his jacket. That was part of the reason I trusted him. He understood me and my…eccentricities. He was always there, even if I didn't need him to be, and I had a feeling he always would be.

"Speaking of what you've gone through…"

Nicholas shifted, putting a foot of space between us. I blinked up into his eyes as black as the night around us. His hand dipped into his jacket pocket. I braced myself subconsciously for whatever he might pull out. If it had to do with my past, it couldn't be good.

He moved fast, whipping his arm over my head. A *crack* sounded, and more black and white and red paper rained down around me.

I caught one of the pieces and glared at it. "I take back what I said about trusting you."

He laughed. "Come on. It's good luck." He took my hands and leaned closer. "Besides, I had to be the last to get you. It's *extra* good luck for the ones who get you first and last."

I rolled my eyes and gave his shoulder a shove as I moved toward the side door again. He wrapped both arms around me from behind and hugged my back against his chest.

His chin rested on my shoulder. "Can I come back tomorrow? I want to visit the birds."

"Just the birds?"

"No."

I smiled. "Meet me at breakfast."

"Perfect." He spun me around, hooked a finger under my jaw, and kissed me. "I'll see you then."

He didn't move though, just kept staring at me, grinning as wide as a skull. I had to step away, toward the door.

"Good night, Nicholas," I said as I opened the door.

"Good night, Sylvan."

He was still standing there when the door swung shut between us.

I trotted up the stairs to my room, forcing myself not to look back, not to run back, fling that door open, and drag Nicholas up the stairs with me. If Nex could see us now, she'd laugh herself to death.

31

Thirty-One

It was freezing cold on Monday morning. I hadn't gotten out of bed yet, but I could tell. Autumn had taken a sharp turn with a front that came in the night before. The heat trapped in my cocoon of blankets beckoned me back into unconsciousness, but school would start before long and I hadn't even gotten dressed yet.

My phone vibrated on my dresser. My hand darted out to snatch it before snapping back into the protective warmth of my bed. The screen bore one notification: a message from Nicholas.

Good morning.

I smiled. That was a good reason to drag myself out of bed.

I donned a white sweater and my thick black jacket over my button up, each with *Mortorous Academy* embroidered under an image of the Boneman's skull on the left breast. I put on a fleece-lined pair of leggings under my uniform pants. I wished I had thicker socks, but I would have to make do with what I had for now. The layers made me feel like a mummified corpse, all wrapped up in cloth, but they helped enough with the cold that I didn't die of hypothermia on the way to Dr. Shalm's class.

Fewer people were on time, perhaps for the same reason I was reluctant to emerge from my warm blankets.

Nicholas didn't look at all troubled by the weather as he breezed through the door. His jacket was unzipped, and he didn't even have a sweater on under it. He stopped beside his desk and leaned toward me. I leaned back until I had to grab the back of my chair to keep from falling onto the floor.

He pulled back, pressing his lips together. "Sorry, I guess you're not into public displays of affection."

I blinked. *I hadn't really thought about it before, but it did feel weird to put something so precious and new on display.*

He sat down beside me. "There's no pressure, obviously. We can take this at whatever pace you want."

I caught Nina watching us from across the room with a handful of her cronies.

"Maybe not with an audience," I murmured and faced forward.

Nicholas cast a glance in Nina's direction and looked about ready to get up and say something to her when Dr. Shalm entered the room, uncharacteristically late, and started the lesson.

When class was over, Nicholas made a move to follow me, but I put a hand on his shoulder.

"There's something I need to do. Can you give me a minute?"

He rested his hand over mine. "This isn't something I should be worried about, is it?"

I shook my head. "I can handle it."

"Ok." He took my hand and kissed my knuckles. "I'll be

337

along in a minute. I think there's something I need to do too."

He turned toward where Nina was not-so-covertly watching us. I was more than happy to let him take care of whatever that was. I had my own drama to deal with.

Wren sat in her corner seat in Professor Tilns's classroom, with her nose in a book, as usual.

I sat down beside her as calmly as possible. She said nothing, but her eyes stopped moving across the page. She had been pretending I didn't exist recently, and I hadn't wanted to cross boundaries by pressing her. But now I looked directly at her instead of playing along.

"Wren," I said softly.

"Sylvan." She said my name reluctantly.

I wasn't one to beat around the bush, so I went straight for it. "I need you."

The book lowered a fraction of an inch. She definitely wasn't reading it now.

She turned a page anyway. "Are you practicing lines to say to Nicholas? I hear he's been glued to your side. There's a picture of you two cuddling in the cafe going around social media."

My jaw clenched. Nicholas and I had gone to the café that weekend a couple times. Nina or one of her gang must have seen us.

"I'd rather do this with you."

Wren raised her book, pointedly looking at it, even though she still wasn't paying attention to the words on the page. "What a shame. I did say you wouldn't be able to count on him."

"It's not about that. It has to do with… my past."

She finally looked away from the book. Not fully at me,

but close enough that I knew she was listening.

"I don't think he would get it. From what he's told me of himself, I'm not sure how he would take this."

"Take what?" she asked, suspicious curiosity slithering through her tone.

"I want to find my parents."

A beat of silence. "You don't know where they are?"

This was the tricky part. I was telling the truth. I wanted to find out if they still lived and if I could somehow go back to them, even if I had to keep doing chores for the Boneman. I'd run into a wall trying to do this on my own, but if anyone had an idea about how to do this, it was Wren. She was the smartest person I knew—the smartest person I knew who wouldn't try to talk me out of it at least.

"This isn't the place to have this discussion." I glanced around, expecting Nicholas to walk in any second. "Can we talk at lunch? I don't know what I'm doing, but I have a feeling you would. Besides, I miss you."

Wren finally turned to look at me. "This has something to do with why you act all..." She gestured vaguely in the air. "Doesn't it?"

I nodded.

"And you'll tell me about it?"

Another nod. I would tell her as much as I could without revealing the secret I was supposed to guard with my life.

Wren closed her book and set it slowly on the desk. "We can talk at lunch. I can't promise anything right now, since I don't know anything, but I *might* be able to help."

A wide grin broke across my face. "Thank you."

She fidgeted with the pages of her book. "You-know-who won't be there, right?"

339

"No. He won't."

Nicholas would understand. Rekindling my friendship with Wren should be enough to keep him away. I doubted he would approve of my search since he was so much closer to the Boneman.

And if the Boneman himself tried to interfere...

There had to be a reason he separated us from our loved ones and wiped our memories of them. Nicholas said something on the first day we met about the Boneman not wanting us to have preexisting attachments so we could serve him alone.

But Keres and Nex also said he cared about the Bone Touched. He had to know how much this would mean to me. I could have a relationship with my family and hunt ghosts at the same time. The Boneman should know that.

The bell rang, and Nicholas's seat remained empty.

"Did you put him out of his misery, or what?" Wren asked.

I shrugged. He'd gone to talk to Nina after class, but I didn't know any details for certain. Though since Wren mentioned a photo on social media, I had my suspicions. He generally seemed to know what he was doing around them, so I couldn't imagine what took him so long.

The whole class passed without a sign of him, but when Wren and I crossed into the hall, he was waiting outside the door, leaning against the wall. His eyes darted between the two of us as we approached him, a hesitant smile on his face. Wren continued walking, barely sparing him a glance. I stopped in front of him.

Nicholas glanced at Wren's retreating form before focusing on me. "Is it safe to assume that was what you wanted to do without me?"

I nodded and started toward our next class. He followed.

"So, you two are on speaking terms now?" His hand brushed mine, and I let him take it.

"We're working on it." I didn't want to get too confident. I was still mulling over what exactly to tell her about myself without mentioning the Boneman.

"That's good. Maybe someday the three of us can be a trio again."

Maybe. That might take a while though. I could tell Wren what I wanted about myself, but there was no way I would risk telling her anything about Nicholas.

"You missed class," I remarked.

Nicholas frowned. "Yeah, things didn't go exactly the way I expected. Nothing to worry about, but I thought it would be better to skip class and cool down."

I raised my eyebrows, but he didn't elaborate. He just squeezed my hand and kept walking.

"What are you doing tonight?" he asked abruptly.

"Probably nothing." I was hoping to get started on things with Wren after school, but hopefully that wouldn't take long. I imagined we would just make a plan and start actually looking at some other time.

Nicholas had that bright, excited grin on his face. "Would you like to watch a movie?"

"What movie?"

"Whatever movie you want."

"Ok."

"That's a yes?"

I nodded.

"Perfect." I jumped a little when he leaned over and kissed my temple. "Meet me in the auditorium after dinner."

My brows creased into a frown. "Why the auditorium?"
"Trust me," he whispered as we turned into our class.

Thirty-Two

Nicholas didn't fight me when I told him I wanted to eat lunch with Wren instead of with him. He just wished me luck and headed in the opposite direction.

Wren held my gaze as I approached with a tray of roast beef in hand. Her food appeared untouched, like she still hadn't decided if she would stay long enough to eat it. I took my usual place beside her and started sawing at the meat with my knife.

"Now would be a good time to explain," she prodded.

I took a moment to chew on the first bite. The flavor fled as my nerves set in. I'd had time to craft my story, but I still didn't know how she would take it.

"When I was younger, I got kidnapped," I started.

Wren inhaled sharply.

I kept my eyes on my food, slicing it into small pieces. "I don't remember much, and I *really* don't want to talk about what I do remember. But that's why I'm so jumpy and quiet. Why I don't usually like it when people touch me or try to

343

force conversation."

Wren swore sharply.

"I only got out recently. I don't know my parents or if they're even alive. I've been poking around on the internet, but it hasn't yielded any results. I thought you might have an idea about where I could continue my search."

"The authorities aren't trying to locate them?" Wren's voice rang with her rage.

"I don't think they care." The roast beef sat in ribbons on my plate.

The admin could be under all kinds of instructions from the Boneman. Despite my heartfelt conversation with Headmistress Pine, they might try to steer me away from finding my family. They certainly didn't seem to be looking. They didn't act concerned about the possibility that I might have parents out there who might want to find me as much as I wanted to find them.

"I know it doesn't make anything better, but I'm sorry all of that happened to you," Wren murmured. "It sounds terrible."

It was.

She took a deep breath. "I'm also sorry that I blew up at you about Nicholas. I kind of regretted doing that even before you told me about this. It was stupid. I should have known you had your reasons, and I shouldn't have pushed you to talk about your past, especially when it was this traumatic. I guess I thought it was something trivial."

I set my food aside, no longer hungry. "I should have said something anyway. It sounds really cliché, but I've realized that talking about it does help. Besides, you were my friend. I should have known I could trust you with this."

"Were?" Wren whispered. "Or are?"

I looked at her. Some fragile mix of hope and dread swam in her sea-green eyes.

The smallest of smiles curved my lips up. "Are."

Wren smiled. "Good, cause it would be awkward for me to help someone who isn't a friend with such a personal project. Not that I wouldn't, of course. It would just be a bit weird if we weren't close."

I smiled back. "Yeah. Can we meet in the library after school to start?"

"Yes, of course. This will be fun, like a case from one of the crime thriller novels I've read. I'll do some brainstorming and see you then. I'm sure we can do this, even if we have to DNA test everyone in the world!"

That sounded a little ambitious, but it was a good sign when Wren got motivated like this. It gave me hope. Even if I couldn't escape the Boneman, maybe I could reclaim something he'd stolen from me.

"One question though." Wren held up a finger. "Not that you don't have terrific judgment when it comes to asking people for this kind of help, but why didn't you ask Nicholas?"

I pressed my lips together. She had a point. He always paid attention to me and my needs, often putting them above his own. It felt strange to have someone so dedicated to me after thinking I was so alone. Honestly, he should prioritize himself more.

But this was the one thing I didn't want to trust him with. I had a feeling he would try to talk me out of it.

Besides, I had to learn how to do things on my own eventually. I couldn't keep relying on the school, or the Boneman, or Nicholas to provide for me. I wouldn't have those things forever. At some point, after I graduated, they would throw me out on my own and expect me to not only make a life for myself but also hunt ghosts whenever I was told to do so.

I finally answered. "I don't think he would get it."

Wren frowned but left it alone. "Well, I can't promise anything. There are billions of people in the world, and we don't know if we're looking for someone living or dead. But I'll do what I can."

"Thank you."

"Yeah, yeah." She waved a hand. "Just so you know, I'm not doing this because you told me your sob story. To be honest, I kind of missed you too."

* * *

Nicholas's gaze found me the moment I stepped out of the locker room in my gym uniform.

"How did it go?" he asked cautiously.

I sat down before I answered. "Good. We're hanging out in the library after school."

He nodded. "Good. I knew you would patch things over. You were so close in the beginning that I would have been surprised if you didn't."

"She still doesn't like you."

"It's ok. We can work toward that, take baby steps." He captured my hand in both of his. "We're still on for tonight, though, right?"

"Yes."

"Excellent." He squeezed my hand lightly.

"Nicholas."

"Yes?"

"Is this a date?"

A beat of tense silence ensued, punctuated only by the low chatter of the others. "Did you not want it to be? Cause it can be casual. I don't mind—"

I shook my head. "I want it to be a date."

His gaze softened. "Then it's a date. Would you like me to bring you chocolate and roses so you can have the full experience? Maybe I should wear a suit and tie."

I rolled my eyes and shook my head. I was smiling as I faced forward, though.

He leaned his shoulder heavily into mine. "Is that a yes? I think that was a yes."

I snorted. "Do whatever you want."

His voice dropped. "Can I do you?"

My gaze snapped to him. He seemed to realize what he'd just said, and red flooded his face.

"I mean, I can do what you want, too. If it's more casual, then I should probably just wear a shirt."

"And pants," I supplied, feeling equally flushed.

"Yes, of course."

One of the coaches blew her whistle, saving Nicholas from further embarrassment.

~~~

Wren had already parked herself and her laptop at a table in a back corner by the time I made it to the library.

She started speaking the second I sat down across from her. "Short of sending in a DNA test, which would take a while, we can check through police records or search up your name. I'm sure it wouldn't be too hard to find something about a girl with white hair and eyes getting kidnapped. It's not like there are a ton of you out there."

I winced. "I already looked up my name." It was the first thing I'd tried. No luck. "And I didn't have white hair and eyes before."

Wren looked up at me, gears turning almost visibly in her head. "I thought you said it was natural."

I shrugged. "I think it was the stress."

She took a deep breath. "Ok. Do you remember what you looked like before?"

I shook my head. The Boneman completely altered my appearance during my time in the tub. If I had to guess, I would have said I had brown hair and eyes since those seemed the most common, but I couldn't remember.

"Do you know what your family did or where they lived?"

Again, I shook my head. I knew I remembered when I was in the tub—it was one of the last memories to go. But I'd completely lost hold of it.

"So, we have basically nothing to work with. No wonder you didn't get very far on your own," Wren sighed. "Not that it's your fault, of course. None of this is your fault. It just makes it hard."

"That's why I came to you." I had faith in her intelligence.

She smiled. "I appreciate your confidence, but this is a pretty tall order, even for me. We could contact a foundation. I know there are a few organizations that help reunite kids with their families. I don't know if they'd be able to do anything with the limited amount of info you have, but they probably have better resources than we do." She scowled at her computer. "Like I said, we can look through old police reports, but to do more I'm afraid we'd need to get someone else involved."

I was loath to bring in anyone else. The more people who

got involved, the higher the chance that the Boneman would protest my little project. Then, it would be over.

I scooted my chair closer to Wren. "Let's look."

33

Thirty-Three

I stabbed at the chicken on my plate during dinner. Sometimes my hand slipped, and the fork hit the plate with a dying screech, making me flinch. But I couldn't help it. Wren and I spent three hours poring over regional missing persons reports in the library to see if anything looked right.

Even though I had no memories of my parents or myself before I was taken, I held out hope that I would recognize something if I saw it. Surely, knowing your family members, people you've spent time with since birth, was instinctual, something the Boneman couldn't touch.

But either my instinct hadn't kicked in or we hadn't found the right report, despite going through *years* of material. Everything from the last seventeen years, my entire lifespan. Nothing.

Wren suggested I might have been taken from somewhere further away. I might have lived on the other side of the ocean for all we knew.

This was a lot harder than I thought it was going to

be. I hadn't considered how many possibilities there were. Some naive part of me wanted to believe that this massive puzzle could be solved in one afternoon. But children went missing all the time all over the world and not all of those disappearances were reported. I could be any of them.

We put in a request for a DNA test from an ancestry website, but the materials probably wouldn't arrive for a few days.

I took an angry bite out of my chicken. The longer this took, the more opportunity the Boneman had to stop me. He hadn't appeared during the day, but there was still tonight. I hated that I could only sit here and wait.

At least I had my date with Nicholas to look forward to.

Date.

The word only existed in my mind as an abstraction. I hadn't considered that it might apply to me. Not anytime soon at least. But half an hour later, after consuming my mutilated chicken, I found myself nudging open the door to the auditorium.

Unlike the night of the Bone Touched gathering, all the seats were in their rows. Only some low lights illuminated the edges of the walkways. I crossed my arms and surveyed the dark room. I couldn't see more than the faint outlines of the seats at the edges of the rows. Terrific. It wasn't like anything could be hiding in the darkness waiting to—

"Sylvan."

I whirled. No more than a pair of shins clad in black slacks were visible, but that was definitely Nicholas's voice. He stood in the middle of the auditorium.

"Come here," he murmured.

My feet drifted along the dark, carpeted aisle and stopped short of his shoes.

351

"Here, let me just…"

I squinted as the projector up in the viewing box flipped on and illuminated a long, white screen hanging over the stage. The bright light reflected back at us, showing me the rest of the auditorium with its hundreds of foldable chairs spread across the ground floor and the ascending steps behind.

I turned my attention back to Nicholas in time to catch him slowly looking me up and down.

I knew it was overkill to go back to my room and change into the dark green, one-sleeved top. My grey pants hugged my thighs and loosened at the knee. My black, school-issued jacket hung over one arm.

The three black skeletal finger marks below my collarbone stuck out against my pale skin like a severed head on a silver platter. I itched to put the jacket back on to cover it, but it was warm in the auditorium compared to the chill outside. I would end up sweating before long.

Nicholas continued to stare at me, taking in my clothing. Compared to his school uniform, I felt overdressed. I'd told him to wear whatever he wanted and then went and changed into something nice.

I reached for my jacket. I'd barely worn any of the clothes Wren bought for me other than weekends. But this had felt like the right occasion. Clearly, I misread the situation.

I had the jacket in my hand, ready to put it on, when Nicholas finally spoke.

"You look beautiful."

My hand fisted in fabric. I watched it crinkle in my grasp, unwilling to look at him. I didn't want to see his expression. I shouldn't have done this. The attention was too much. I took a deep breath.

"Sylvan." He nudged my face up to meet his eyes. "You are amazing. You're stunning. Thank goodness we have to wear uniforms to school. If you got to wear this on a daily basis, I never would have stood a chance of capturing your attention. You'd have so many boys after you."

"I don't want boys after me."

I'd been trying to blend in and disappear from the moment I got here. I liked the background. It was nice and quiet and full of people who weren't afraid to be authentic and friendly. Nicholas knew the popular crowd. He knew there was no way I would ever be interested in that life. I liked my circle tight and my relationships deep.

"Is it ok that I'm after you?" he asked.

My expression softened, giving way to a small smile. "Yes."

"Good." He kissed my forehead. "Because I'm not going anywhere any time soon. Unless you want me to."

I glanced away and my eyes snagged on the blanket behind Nicholas. It looked like a bigger version of the comforter that I liked to snuggle into when I went to sleep at night. A handful of tiny plastic candles dotted its surface, accompanied by a three-tiered, silver tray covered in various types of desserts.

Nicholas caught me staring. "I know it's kind of cheesy, but you seem to like food, so I thought you might enjoy this."

He stepped aside and let me walk to the edge of the blanket. I stood there, staring down at the arrangement, while he circled around to the other side and sat down on the fluffy surface. He patted the blanket beside him, inviting me to join. I folded myself onto it and eyed the food.

"This isn't even the best part." Nicholas picked up each of the battery-powered candles and flipped them on while he spoke. "I didn't sneak all this stuff into the building with the best audio and visual setup for nothing."

He set the last candle down and pulled a remote out of his pocket. He directed it toward the viewing box in the back and hit a button. The projection on the screen changed to the main menu of a movie. Music blasted through the speakers. I flinched and clamped my hands over my ears.

Nicholas frantically pounded the buttons until the noise subsided to a volume that wouldn't burst our eardrums. "Sorry, I didn't check the sound before you came in. Anyway, is this ok? Or would you rather watch something else? I brought a few options."

"What is it about?" The title on the screen wasn't telling me anything.

"It's about ancient mythology. There are all kinds of deities and demigods with powers and stuff."

I raised an eyebrow at him.

He winced. "Too close to home?"

I shook my head. "No. I want to see." If anything that made me more curious.

His face brightened. "Ok. Let's do it."

A press of a button later and the opening credits scrolled across a scene of ancient ruins. I leaned back against the row of chairs behind us and watched the names fade in and out of view to the lively tune of trumpets and harps. Ten minutes into the film, I was more focused on the action than a coroner on an autopsy. I fixated so effectively that I jumped when Nicholas's hand appeared under my nose, holding a small, bready confection.

"Sorry." He retracted his hand slightly. "It's just that you haven't touched any of the food. I thought you might have forgotten about it."

I had. I'd gotten sucked into the movie and completely forgotten anything else existed in favor of the sword fights and epic chases. Even Nicholas.

My fingers brushed the palm of his hand as I took the treat and took a bite. Fruity jelly exploded out of the center as I bit down. It soaked the soft bread in sweetness. My mouth watered as I continued to chew. How had I not tried any of these yet?

Nicholas chuckled when I snatched a chocolate from the tray. "I guess that means you liked it." He reached for a sweet himself.

I nodded. *Very much.*

The movie continued to play. I continued to graze on the desserts. At the end of the film, as the characters were settling into their lives again, I caught Nicholas watching me instead of the screen. I raised an eyebrow in question.

"Are you going to share?" He jerked his chin at the tiny cinnamon roll in my hand.

At least one other sat on the tray. So, I popped the treat into my mouth while maintaining direct eye contact with him. He smirked and leaned over. I stilled as his mouth met mine.

He kissed me deeply. I leaned into him.

He sat back and licked his lips clean of the sugar that had transferred from my mouth to his. Completely forgetting the movie, I stared at him. He winked. My face burned as I turned back to the movie, finding it much harder to focus on the ending.

"What did you think?" Nicholas asked as he walked me back to my dorm.

"Interesting." The difference between this fictional representation of gods and demigods and the real ones I knew gave me a lot to think about.

Nicholas smirked. "Loquacious as always."

"How horrible that demigods have to struggle whether they're fictional or not."

Nicholas's expression grew grim. "Magic doesn't make life easy the way people like to think it does. It just makes everything more complicated."

I tilted my head back so I could stare at the cloud covered stars above. "At least the demigods in the movie were abandoned by their gods, not tortured by them."

"Do you still have trouble with your bathtub?" Nicholas asked softly.

My arms folded tightly around me. "I use the showers in the girls' locker room to bathe instead of my own."

It was kind of pathetic if I thought too long about it. The only similarity was the color, and even then, the Boneman's tub had been much whiter. Like bleached bone. That's probably what it was. It was *always* about the bones.

My bones, other people's bones, animal bones. Just bones, bones, *bones*. It was enough to drive me mad. My brain couldn't even register that my bathtub was made of porcelain because all it could see were bones!

Nicholas paused at the side door of the girls' dormitory. "This was fun, we should do it again sometime soon."

I nodded absently, still lost in my thoughts.

Nicholas frowned. "Is something wrong? Did you not enjoy yourself?"

"No, I liked it, I just…"

It was just the pressure of everything getting to me. Maybe it had something to do with how frustrating the search for my family proved to be. Maybe it was how trapped I felt without a way to escape the Boneman.

Sure, the Bone Touched I'd met so far had been great. I was starting to settle into life and learn how to use my powers. But a cage filled with friends and magic was still a cage.

"It's ok. I can tell you need some time. Maybe it was a mistake to watch a mythology movie," Nicholas continued.

I raked a hand through my hair. "Maybe."

"Good night, Sylvan."

"Good night, Nicholas."

He turned and trudged into the night, still wearing a faint frown.

I slipped into the girls' dorm and paused to put my face in my hands. There I went ruining my date over my own circular thoughts. Everything had to be about stupid bones!

I took the stairs two at a time. My door slammed against the wall when I shoved it open and slammed closed again. My jacket made an unusually loud noise when I threw it at one of the armchairs by the window—the curtains had cracked open to reveal a sliver of the darkness outside. The seams of my shirt and pants almost ripped as I yanked them off.

The sparrow chicks were chirping in their box, but I ignored them. My downstairs neighbors probably weren't happy to hear me stomping to the bathroom. I opened that door more gently, but it still smacked into the door jam. I glared at the black and white polka-dotted shower curtain.

"This is your fault," I snapped as I yanked it back.

The gaping, white tub smirked up at me. I clenched my hands into fists to still the trembling.

"I'm sick and tired of letting you control my life."

I plugged the bottom and turned both knobs as far as

they would go. Water thundered down. I spun toward the mirror, gripping the counter with white knuckles, fighting the flashbacks.

I glared at myself. "I'll learn the stupid magic. I'll fight the stupid ghosts. But I will not let you ruin the few good things I get to have when I'm not being a hunting dog."

I yanked the tie out of my hair and raked my fingers through the braid until nothing but loose, white waves remained. I shed what little clothes I still had on and faced the wretched tub. My hands shook as I turned the water off.

My feet stayed rooted to the cold bathroom tiles for a long time. The sight of the glassy smooth surface of the water froze me to the floor.

Hours and days and weeks and months and years breathing that white fluid and waiting for my body to be destroyed and put back together.

I shook my head.

It isn't the same tub. It isn't the same liquid. It isn't even the same room.

I kept telling myself those things. I would be fine if I climbed in. I wouldn't lock up and drown or stay there until the Boneman came to reconfigure my body. I could get right back out and only be wet from the water. But the memories still lingered.

I would always be a slave to the fear if I didn't get a handle on it.

So, I braced a hand on the wall.

Stepped one foot in.

And halted once more.

The water came halfway up my calf, lukewarm and still. So still. Just like all that time spent in that other tub.

I gritted my teeth and swung my other foot in.

Water lapped against my legs and the sides of the tub. My fingernails bit into my palms as I clenched my fists, one fist braced on the wall. I turned slowly to face the rest of the water.

This was good. This was very good. My chest heaved with the force of my breaths, but my vision was clear, and my legs were stable.

My feet shuffled along the bottom of the tub until I stood in the middle, my heart in my throat. This was the hardest part. I don't know how long I stood there, staring at the water, before I finally let my legs fold. I sat down hard and sprang back up almost instantly.

Too much. Too much, too much too muchtoomuch!

My knees shook under me. Water droplets cooled against my skin. I gripped the walls. My forearms braced against the tiles. My forehead leaned against them. A lonely tear streaked down my cheek.

But I could do this. I had to do this. I couldn't move on with my life if half the things in the world sent me into a spiral of panic. That wasn't how normal people lived their lives, and I was determined to be at least partially normal. I wanted to take control of myself.

I sat down again. Water rippled around my ribs. No matter how swiftly and completely the fear rose, I ordered myself to stay. For Nicholas. For Wren. For myself. To spite everyone who had wronged me. To prove to the Boneman that he didn't own every part of my life. To strengthen my will, I could do this.

I sucked in a deep breath and lay down. The water stung my eyes, but I blinked it away. It was blurry, reminding me of how little I could see through that milky fluid, reminding me of how many times I had to lay there and listen to the Boneman breaking my limbs apart. How many times I wanted to scream from the pain.

So, I opened my mouth.

And *screamed*.

Bubbles erupted from my mouth. The sound reverberated through the water, filling the space with all that pent-up rage and pain.

My face only broke the surface once I ran out of breath. I gasped, not because of the terror crowding my chest, but because it felt good to let it all out after keeping everything trapped inside for so long.

I ducked back under the water and screamed again, before shooting back up to breathe. I did the same thing over and over until my lungs ached and the tub full of water was just a tub full of water instead of the torturous place where I'd spent so much of my life.

Slowly, I stood and faced my reflection in the mirror across from me. I was soaking wet and breathing hard, but I looked alive. Maybe not whole, but alive.

34

Thirty-Four

Nicholas was almost late to Dr. Shalm's class on Monday. I hadn't seen much of him over the weekend, instead I perused more missing persons reports with Wren. The search had yet to reveal any leads, but I found myself relaxing in Wren's company, nonetheless.

We'd gotten the DNA test kit and sent it back already in the hopes that one of the ancestry websites we'd found could fill in some missing information. Apparently, Mortorous Academy was close to one of their bases, so we shouldn't have to wait as long as we thought. We'd eaten out at the café. We'd talked for hours—Wren was surprised when I consistently spoke more than one sentence at a time. I'd even gone down to her room on Saturday night to learn how to play a card game and just talk.

Things were finally starting to feel normal between us again. But of course, that meant Nicholas had to stay away. I'd messaged him a few times but hadn't seen him in person.

I had decided not to let it bother me. If I could overcome my fear of the bathtub, I could handle a few days without

Nicholas.

I spent the time before class drawing. Today's image was an overflowing bathtub. *My* overflowing bathtub.

I'd repeated the process of filling up the tub and slowly submerging myself every evening. I even took an actual bath afterward. It was nerve-racking but had gotten easier and easier.

I used my phone to take a picture of the tub last night as a reference, but I was having trouble getting the fluidity of the water right. It always looked a little too cartoonish or flat.

I pretended not to notice when Nicholas walked in.

"That's pretty," Nicholas said as he sat down in his chair. He sounded hesitant. No doubt he remembered how heavily our last conversation featured tubs.

"Thanks." I erased another line. Maybe if it curved a little more at the sides...

Dr. Shalm announced a free work class period. We could talk as long as we kept the noise down. I had already read ahead and completed all the accompanying work in between boughts of looking through police reports, so I just kept drawing.

"I missed you this weekend. How are things going with Wren?" Nicholas asked.

"Much better."

"And how are you? Our conversation on Friday night got pretty heavy right before I left."

I curved the line. *That looks better.* "I'm fine."

He scratched his neck. "You know you don't have to act tough in front of me, right? I don't blame you for wanting to keep your struggles to yourself. I spent years doing that before you came along and even now it's hard to open up sometimes. I won't push you on it, but I want to know how you are even if you're struggling."

I side eyed him. "I really am fine. I can take baths now."

He visibly stiffened. "You... can?"

I nodded as I put the finishing touches on the drawing. "I just needed to *push* myself." I briefly explained the process of disconnecting my past associations from present circumstances. "A lot of good experiences can override a bad one. I think the same might be true with other things." I put down my pencil and slid my hand into his.

He chuckled and gave it a squeeze. "I'm glad you're overcoming it. Just try not to get too carried away. I'd hate for you to have a panic attack and drown in your bathtub."

I rolled my eyes. "I would never."

"Class, I have an announcement!" Dr. Shalm called over the drone of conversation in the room. "This is very important, so I need you to listen."

It took a couple minutes for everyone to quiet down and get to their seats. I exchanged a glance with Nicholas. It was rare for Dr. Shalm to preface the class with anything other than a reminder about upcoming tests or quizzes.

Once everyone looked like they were paying attention, Dr. Shalm continued. "This is an Academy-wide notice. A man was found dead in the forest only a couple miles from the school early this morning."

Whispers started up immediately. Nicholas took my hand.

For everyone else in the room, this was a scandal, a mystery, something to gossip about.

For me and Nicholas, it was a potential threat.

Death meant a strong possibility of a ghost. Even though Mortorous Academy was under the Boneman's protection, the thought of a ghost wandering so close to the school didn't sit well with me. Especially since Mallor warned us at the Bone Touched gathering that there had been some kind of accident in the area and people had died.

Could the two be connected?

Dr. Shalm spoke over the hushed voices of the students. "The poor man was a tourist doing some hiking, not anyone from Mortorous or Noxier. But the police have yet to release information about the cause of death. So, until that time, no one is allowed to enter the forest."

Muted cries of outrage flew around the room.

"I know some of you like to go looking for the Boneman in the evenings, but this is serious. We don't want anyone else to get hurt out there. If you are caught going into or out of the forest, you will be barred from any extra curricular activities for the rest of the semester and have detention for a month."

The frustration in the room was palpable.

"This may seem extreme to some of you, but this is how seriously we at Mortorous Academy take your safety. You may still drive to Noxier in the afternoons or on weekends, but everyone needs to stay out of the forest. No exceptions. Is that understood?"

Grumbles of acquiescence echoed around the room.

"Good. Now, let's get started with today's lesson." Dr. Shalm rifled through her desk.

"Should we be concerned?" I murmured to Nicholas.

Nicholas's brow furrowed. "I'll text Mallor on our way to History, but I'm sure he's already on it."

I hoped so. It was his job to keep us safe after all.

* * *

Wren wasn't in Professor Tilns's class. I stared at her empty seat for half of the lecture, but no amount of wishing brought her through the door. I sent her a message as soon as the bell rang. There was no response until lunch.

Our usual bench out in the courtyard lacked her distinctive presence. I sat down anyway, hoping she was just late. Perhaps she hadn't felt well this morning or something— there *was* some kind of seasonal bug going around the school. I did my best to cut off thoughts about the man who died in the forest. What if Wren...

No. I refused to believe it. When I checked my phone a notification with her name on it waited for me. I opened it as quickly as the phone would allow.

Sylvan, I have transferred schools. Do not attempt to contact me. You will not see me again.

I stared at those three sentences, so cold and sharp like a knife sliding between ribs. That wasn't how Wren usually texted. She rarely even said my name unless she was trying to get my attention. It wasn't like her to just cut contact, either, especially after we had patched things up between us.

We were smiling and laughing just yesterday. Now she didn't want to talk to or see me again and wasn't even giving me a reason. When she was mad at me before about Nicholas, she came right out and said so. She wasn't afraid to confront me about it.

What happened between yesterday afternoon and now that made her say this? Why was she transferring schools? None of it made sense. Why was I losing my friend again?

"Sitting all by yourself like the lonely loser you are?" Nina's

365

harsh voice cut through my thoughts.

She was alone this time. That didn't stop her from having the gall to sit down, pick my pizza off my plate, and take a bite.

"Go away, Nina." I really wasn't in the mood for this.

"No, *you* go away." She jabbed the pizza at me. "Ever since you got here, you've been ruining my life. You get Nicholas's attention without doing anything. You turn him against me. And then he turns all *my* friends against *me*!"

I blinked. Was that what Nicholas had been doing when he missed Tilns's class that day? Staging a coup against Nina with the popular girls?

Nina took another bite of my pizza. "You aren't even that special. You've got weird hair and weird eyes and that's it. You're basically a carbon copy of that Wren girl you're always hanging around with. An awkward mess. Speaking of which, where is she? Did she leave you all alone because *you* finally got the guy she's been not so secretly pining after all these years?"

I clenched my hands into fists around my phone. "Now isn't the time for this discussion."

"No, now is the perfect time for this discussion. Did you get everything you wanted in your miserable, little, nobody life? Was it worth it to dethrone me? Cause I can guarantee that wherever you're planning to go after this, my family can stop you. We have connections all over the place. I can personally make sure you never get into any colleges or get even a halfway decent job. You don't get to come in and pretend like you're on top just because you have that new girl allure. You'll see. Nicholas will get tired of you eventually and then you'll be stuck with nothing."

She took an aggressive bite of my pizza to punctuate her rant.

"Maybe if you put as much effort into treating people with respect as you put into being a bitch, you'd still have friends," I hissed.

Her eyes widened. "How dare—?"

"All this little speech of yours has proved is how jealous of me you are. Of my authenticity. Of my real friendships. Of my ability to succeed where you've failed for years. You are nothing without your family behind you. If they cut you off for being the stuck-up, self-centered jerk you are, you'd have no money, no future, no hope. You pretend you're better than me, but you're just intimidated by the fact that I am twice the woman you are with half the resources."

Nina's mouth hung open, occasionally closing and reopening like she wanted to retort but couldn't think of anything to say.

"Now, get out of my face. If you ever bother me or anyone else again, I'll make sure everyone knows who you truly are, and you'll have no hope of rebuilding your friend group."

She chuckled. "I could convince them otherwise just like I have so many other times. It's your word against mine."

"Want to bet?" I held up my phone and pressed play on the recording I'd just taken of her trying to give me a verbal beat down.

Nina's face went pale. "You can't record me without my permission!"

"Too late. Now, leave me alone." I snatched my half-eaten pizza out of her hand and stood up with my things. "And don't even try to run crying to anyone about this, because the admin will side with *me*. You aren't the only one with

367

connections."

I stalked away without waiting for her response. My pizza went right in the trash can. No way was I going to touch it after she had. I found Nicholas in a corner of the cafeteria, sitting by himself.

"Hey," he said when I sat down next to him. "I thought you were going to try to find Wren. What happened?"

I buried my face in my hands as tears burned my eyes. "She's gone."

Nicholas settled a hand on my back and spoke in a low soothing voice. "What do you mean she's gone?"

I opened the message from her and passed it to him. He read it and frowned. "This doesn't make any sense."

I knew it didn't, but I didn't know how to handle this situation if she didn't want me to contact her.

"I'm sorry." Nicholas gently folded me into a hug.

My arms snaked around him and my face fell into the crook of his shoulder. I was sorry too.

I visited her room after school, but her roommate told me all her things were packed up and gone by the time she came back from classes.

"She didn't even say anything about it. It's like she just vanished."

I chewed my lip. "Thanks anyway."

"No problem. If you hear anything from her, would you mind letting me know? I'm kind of worried something happened at home that made her leave."

"Yeah, sure." I was worried too.

Thoughts of Wren infected my mind while I tried to manipulate bones under Nicholas's watchful eye. I couldn't move any of them an inch. After twenty minutes of nothing,

I sat back in my chair and stared at the ceiling.

"Let's stop there for today," Nicholas said gently. "You have too much on your mind to focus on bone magic."

Unfortunately, he was right.

35

Thirty-Five

I dropped by the main office the next day before class.

The woman at the reception desk frowned at me when I asked if she knew what happened to Wren. "We're not allowed to disclose the private information of any of our students whether they're still enrolled here or not. Why don't you ask her yourself?"

"I can't." *She told me not to.*

"I'm sorry, but I can't help you," The woman said patiently as if I were a child she had to handle carefully.

I gritted my teeth. Of course, the admin would be useless. They always were. Why had I expected anything more?

"Ah, Ms. Ravena, so nice to see you." I turned to see Headmistress Pine walking in the door. "It's been a while. How are you doing?"

Maybe this secretary would refuse to tell me anything, but Pine knew what I was. She told me to tell her if I needed anything. "I need your help."

She smiled indulgently at me. "How about you come in my office, and I'll see what I can do."

370

"Headmistress, I don't think—" The secretary started.

"It's fine, Amy. I'll take care of it."

Amy eyed me as I followed Pine to her office, but I didn't spare her so much as a glance.

Once we were shut in Pine's office and could talk freely, she smiled brightly at me. "I'm glad you took me up on my offer. What can I help you with?"

"I have a friend who said she transferred schools, but it was so sudden. I think something might have happened to her." Even though I had a message from her proving otherwise, I still worried that she might have met a similar fate to the tourist Dr. Shalm told us about the day before.

Pine frowned. "Well, I can certainly check our records for you."

It would have to be good enough. I waited impatiently as she booted up her computer and sifted through the files for any relevant information. If something had happened to Wren, how would I even find her? What would I do to help?

I tried to fight off the onslaught of questions. *One thing at a time*.

Finally, Headmistress Pine said. "It looks like she submitted paperwork to transfer to Animos Prep on Sunday evening. Was she in class yesterday?"

"No."

She sat back with a contemplative expression. "Well, that's a little unusual. Normally, a transfer takes a few days. We have to send transcripts and letters of recommendation and Animos would have to figure out what classes to put her in and set her up with an ID number. It's a very long, painful process. But I'm not privy to the details of her personal life. Maybe her family waited till the last minute to file the paperwork. I'm sorry, but that's all I know."

Animos Prep. The Wind Whisperer's school. It wasn't much, but it was something.

"Thank you."

* * *

"What do you know about the Wind Dreamed?" I asked Nicholas before he even sat down at his desk in English class.

He shrugged. "Probably about as much as anyone else. They're the Wind Whisperer's demigods. They go to Animos Prep and learn their magic the same way we do here. It has something to do with entering and changing people's dreams while they're sleeping. Why?"

I think they have Wren. But I couldn't tell him that. Not without telling him that I thought she was with them because she and I had been trying to find my parents.

That was the only explanation I could think of. Wren had gotten the DNA test results and she'd figured out I was Bone Touched. Had it scared her, so she'd run away? Did the Wind Dreamed take her?

I had so many questions and no way to answer them unless I managed to get into contact with the Wind Dreamed I'd met weeks ago. But would they even help me? They hadn't when I'd tried to escape from the Boneman. They'd rejected me before I even asked.

I ran my fingers through my hair. "No reason."

Nicholas didn't look convinced, but he didn't push it.

Unfortunately, it looked like I had to abide by Wren's message and leave it alone. For now, at least.

36

Thirty-Six

Someone tumbled through the door to Professor Tumulus's room when Nicholas pulled it open for us on Thursday afternoon. That someone let out a sharp curse. Nicholas flinched back as Nex's wild, blue eyes stared up at us from the floor.

Her face split into a grin as she popped up to push the door all the way open. "Look who decided to finally show up!"

"What are you doing here, Nex?" Nicholas asked. "I thought you were supposed to be halfway around the world in a different sector."

"They had to bring in the big guns." Nex flexed her arms, which, even with the padding of her leather jacket, didn't look big at all.

"For what?" Nicholas asked.

Keres's red-nailed hand grabbed the back of Nex's collar and hauled her out of the doorway. "Let them come in first."

Nex swatted at her as we shuffled in. Keres and Nex weren't the only other Bone Touched in the room. Mallor and Aeron stood against the opposite wall, locked in conversation with another man I didn't recognize. A handful of other people, who I assumed were also Bone Touched, huddled in pockets around the room.

This couldn't be another meeting. Nicholas said those only happened every few months, and there weren't nearly as many people as last time. So, why were they all here?

Tumulus came scurrying out of his office and raised his arms. "Quiet, please. It looks like we're all here now, so we might as well get started."

Silence fell almost immediately. Everyone migrated toward Tumulus. If the Bone Touched could be granted one thing, it was their ability to listen to instructions—fitting given that we had to constantly be at the beck and call of the Boneman. I glanced at Nicholas, but he just shrugged and followed the crowd.

"Most of you know, or at least have an idea why you're here," Tumulus began. "A little over a week ago, a bus carrying twenty-seven people crashed and exploded on the way into Noxier. We were hoping this wouldn't be much of a problem, but Mallor has done some scouting and reports that the spirits of at least twelve of those who died in the collision have formed a pack."

The Bone Touched shifted warily.

That didn't sound good. Nicholas and Mallor had told me about how packs of ghosts sometimes gathered and used their numbers to gain power and even take down Bone Touched. If a group that big had gotten this close to us, it would spell disaster for those living in Noxier. Would the ghosts get bold enough to approach the school, even though it was supposed to be warded by the Boneman?

"They have taken up residence in the forest and have

already turned extremely hostile. We've even had a death."

That was the man we'd heard about. I'd wondered if the two incidents were connected. Mallor said ghosts grew hostile towards people, but it surprised me that they would turn to murder so quickly. Obviously, they would try to kill Bone Touched, but I would have thought regular people who didn't have magic in their bones wouldn't be in as much danger.

"This is a dire problem, especially so close to the school. So, you have all been summoned to bring down this pack before anyone else gets hurt."

What?

I barely knew how to move a bone a few feet across a table— a skill I hadn't even told Tumulus about—and they expected me to go fight a horde of ghosts?

"Since Mallor is most familiar with the area, and has been observing the ghosts, he will present his plan." Tumulus gestured for Mallor to join him in front of everyone.

My heart pounded in my ears. I took a half step back. Nicholas glanced at me, brushing his hand against mine. It wasn't as reassuring as he meant it to be.

"The ghosts have set up camp in a thicket not far from where the crash occurred," Mallor said. "We'll have two groups a quarter mile away on opposite sides of their base. Group Bone to the east and Group Shadow to the west. A couple of us will escort our swimmers right into the heart of enemy territory, where we will leave them as bait."

He gestured at me and Nicholas. A disturbing amount of eyes shifted to us.

"We'll call this Group Blood," Mallor continued. "Nicholas, once the ghosts are following you, you'll run west to Group Shadow and Sylvan will run east to Group Bone. That is your only job. You are not expected to fight. Your escorts will keep tabs on you in case something happens. You will not be in danger." Mallor looked at me when he said that. "Just get the ghosts to split up and follow you to your respective group so they're easier to catch, then get back to the vehicle where it's safe."

Safe? Did he think it was going to be that easy?

Mallor turned away to start assigning the others to the three groups.

Nicholas slipped his hand into mine. "It's not going to be a big deal, Sylvan," he said softly. "These ghosts are smart and can sense how powerful a Bone Touched is. We have power, but we're young. We're easy prey to them, so they'll come after us and we'll lead them right to their doom."

"But what if they catch us?" I hissed. "What if we die?"

"That's what the escorts are for. They'll protect us. Everyone here is capable, but they need to split the pack to pick off the ghosts."

I didn't like that at all. It felt too much like they were sacrificing us to the angry apparitions.

"Won't the Boneman be upset that they put us in danger?" I asked. I never would have thought I'd come to rely on the Boneman's mercy, but maybe it could spare me now.

On the other hand, would we be in more danger if we let the ghosts run wild? Especially for the rest of Noxier. All those people would be sitting ducks.

"He wants us to be safe, but he also wants this taken care of. It's literally the reason he created us." He faced me fully and took my other hand. "They aren't going to force you to do this. It'll mean they have to change their plans, but if you don't feel confident that you can do it, there's no shame in backing out."

I surveyed the others, so invested in their planning, so ready to put their lives on the line. None of them so much as questioned it. They just agreed to fight. Even Nicholas was prepared to play his part, and he was still learning, too.

Someone had died, Tumulus said. An innocent person who had no idea what they were walking into. A person who relied on us to keep them safe whether they knew it or not. And we had let them down.

Just like I had been let down when no one protected me from the Boneman.

"No," I said, gripping Nicholas's hands tight. "I can do this." No one else would die at the hands of these ghosts if I could help it. What were my efforts to make a life worth if it came at the expense of others' lives? If I couldn't do it, why had I left the Boneman's tub? Why had I wasted my time overcoming my fears?

Nicholas blinked in surprise, then grinned wide. "Really? I honestly didn't expect you to agree this easily, but ok. Great. I'm going to be there for most of it, so I'll help when I can. There's nothing to worry about."

I nodded. "I know." There wouldn't be anything to worry about, because I wasn't going to let those spirits take me down, even if I didn't know how to defend myself as well as most of the other Bone Touched. I could run. There would be other Bone Touched to cover me. "Don't worry about me."

Nex, Keres, Aeron, Mallor, and two other Bone Touched were part of the Blood Group that would follow me and Nicholas when we led the ghosts to their respective ambushes. Nex hooked her arm in mine and tugged me down the hall, shouting something about how I simply *must* ride with her and Keres to our meeting point near the ghost hideout.

Nicholas looped an arm around my middle from behind to keep her from stealing me away. "What a great idea, Nex." His voice dripped with sarcasm. "How about I come with you?"

Nex scowled at him. "No boys allowed in Rhonda."

"Rhonda?" I asked.

"That's what she named her car," Nicholas murmured in my ear.

Ok then.

Nex let go of me but continued to glare at Nicholas. "Rhonda doesn't like boys. She's only for girl time."

"Rhonda's a *car*," Nicholas said, his arm still wrapped around my waist, as we walked. "And aren't we supposed to use her as our safe haven after we lure out the ghosts? As far as I know, you're the only Bone Touched crazy enough to get a custom paint job that includes powdered bones to protect against ghosts. I think it's *you* who doesn't like boys."

Nex snorted. An evil gleam entered her eye. "I like boys just fine. Looks like Sylvan does too." Her gaze dropped to where Nicholas's hand gripped my side.

He glanced down as if just realizing he was holding me and let go like I'd burned him, murmuring apologies. I missed his warmth once it was gone.

"Has he been treating you right, little swimmer?" Nex asked, dropping back to walk beside me as we descended the stairs and drifted outside. "Spoiling you rotten and kissing you silly? Those bone shadow types tend to be like that. Always wanting to protect and provide. Kind of stifling, but sweet. Have you slept with him yet?"

"Nex!" Nicholas barked.

She waved a hand at him while keeping her eyes on me. "I wasn't talking to you."

"He sleeps in his own bed," I replied evenly.

"A shame, he seems like the ravishing type."

"Nex." This time Keres stepped in to scold her. "We're in a school. You could at least pretend to be a civilized human being." A knowing smile curled across her lips. "Besides, you know he would be gentle with her. Based on how he looks at her like she's stolen half of his heart, I'd say he really loves her."

The two women giggled. I glanced up at Nicholas. His face was red, whether from anger or embarrassment or both, I couldn't tell.

Clearly, we needed to change the subject. "You have bones in your car paint?"

"It's my own little stronghold," Nex declared proudly. "Even the tinting on the windows and a heat-resistant coating on the undercarriage are treated with bone dust. No ghost can get in or out, though I haven't figured out how to keep them from slashing my tires yet."

"Even so, Rhonda has saved a few lives in her time," Keres said.

Impressive.

Nex turned out to be an even crazier driver than Wren. Nicholas and I braced ourselves across the backseat. The ride didn't smooth out until we hit the open road. Keres, seemingly unaffected by the hairpin turns and sudden stops, glanced back at our strained positions and laughed.

"Believe it or not, Nex has never gotten into an accident before," she told us as she turned back around.

"I'll have to check the police records to believe it," Nicholas shot back, not daring to relax.

Nex smirked. "Good luck. Bone Touched don't leave records."

It was just like Headmistress Pine said. No borders could hold us back with the Boneman on our side.

"You have all the weapons you need, or do you need to borrow something?" Nex asked us.

I certainly didn't have anything that could stand against a ghost. It wasn't like I carried bones on me at all times.

"Isn't the point that we *don't* have weapons, so we look like easy targets?" Nicholas replied.

"That doesn't mean you can't carry them concealed. Ghosts can only sense your power, not how many bones you have on you. Here, let me make you something."

I watched in fascinated horror as Nex took hold of one of her teeth and *ripped it out*. Nicholas and I flinched at the squelch it made when it pulled free of her gums. She ran her tongue over the bloody gap as she rolled the tooth between her fingers. It stretched and thinned like dough.

"There's one." Nex tossed the needle-like tooth into the backseat. I leaped as far away from it as the confines of the car would allow. "We've got at least fifteen minutes until we reach the rendezvous point, so I can make a decent arsenal for you. Any requests?"

Nicholas picked up the shard of bone with the tips of his fingers like it was covered in poison. "Maybe something that wasn't just in your mouth."

"Picky Nicky." Nex grinned, displaying a full set of teeth. The gap had vanished. She must have noticed my stare because her eyes found mine in the rearview mirror. "The Boneman breaks apart every bone in our body and puts them back together during our time in the tub. Every bone, except our teeth. They're the only exposed bones in the human body, so keeping them together while they heal is pretty much impossible even in the tub. The Boneman would have to sit there and hold them himself, and he doesn't have time for that."

She paused to pull another tooth out of her jaw. "It's probably a good thing, though. They make decent weapons in a pinch. You can pull them out and regrow them with healing magic just fine. Since they don't have magic in them, it doesn't affect us the way surgically removing a leg or arm bone would. It doesn't drain our life."

"It just hurts a normal amount," Keres grumbled. "Yanking teeth isn't pleasant unless you have no nerve endings in your mouth. And if you're not practiced with healing magic, the holes bleed a lot and you can be left toothless for days. It's ok as a last resort, but I don't recommend making a habit of it."

Nex rolled her eyes. "So sensitive."

"So insensitive."

"Hey, it helped us get out of that jam in the savannah when that troupe of ghosts had us trapped in a cave for two days. I didn't see you complaining then."

Keres jabbed a finger at her. "That was different. We were about to die, and if I recall correctly, you cried the first time you pulled a tooth."

"But then I got used to it and look at me now." Nex tossed a tiny throwing star made of bone at us with a deft flick of her wrist.

Nicholas barely avoided getting sliced across the arm with it.

"Watch where you're throwing your bloody mouth detritus!" He snapped.

"Do you hear these swimmers?" Nex asked Keres as if we weren't sitting right there. "A couple of ingrates."

I rolled my eyes and Nicholas huffed out an exasperated breath.

Thirty-Seven

We pulled off the side of the road at a seemingly random spot. Trees loomed all around us like an army of grim reapers, watching and waiting. The air was cool but not as cold as it had been in the last few days. A light mist threaded through the trunks to our right. We parked behind a couple of cars. Beside one, stood Mallor, Aeron, and the two other Bone Touched who made up our little team. Nex popped out of the driver's side door and waved at them.

Mallor was too deep in conversation with the other two to acknowledge us, but Aeron made his way over, damp leaves squelching under his feet.

"Nice to see you made it in one piece." He grinned at me and Nicholas. "Nex's driving didn't shake you up too much, did it?"

Nex threw an elbow into his side. "If you get cornered by ghosts out there, I will *not* be saving you."

"Good thing I won't need you to. If anything, I'll be the one coming to *your* rescue."

"In your dreams." Nex took a swing at him, but he dodged and spun her into a headlock.

"Save that energy for when we're in the thick of things," Mallor ordered as he finally joined us. Surprisingly, they broke apart without complaint. "The others will be in place soon. You know what you're doing?"

"We all go in together," Keres said as if reciting a speech from memory. "Half a mile out, we drop away from the swimmers and let them go on by themselves. Once they lead out the pack, we follow them to make sure the ghosts don't catch up. The swimmers run past the ambush and keep going. Once we make sure they're safe in Rhonda, we double back and join the fight. And the rest is standard procedure."

Mallor nodded. "Keep your phones on in case we need to amend the plan." *In case something goes wrong*, he meant. His gaze shot to me and Nicholas. "Do you need anything before we go in?"

Nex ran her tongue over her fresh set of teeth. "They're fine. I outfitted them on the way in."

"Gross," Aeron muttered.

I had to agree, but having a pocket full of bone shards was better than nothing as long as I didn't accidentally stab my hand on the sharp points when I reached for one. I might not be able to control them as well as the others could, but I could always throw or stab with them if I had to.

"Everyone ready?" Mallor's eyes lingered on me.

I nodded as the others muttered their ascent. Nothing but determination filled my mind. I wasn't going to let them down, not just because it might mean my death, but because there was a town full of people at stake. The margin of error was nonexistent.

Nicholas's hand brushed mine but didn't take it. I glanced at him. We had a plan. All we had to do was stick to it and we'd be fine.

"The other groups are ready. So, it's showtime," Mallor declared.

As one, we turned and headed into the woods. Two miles of forest separated us from the ghost camp. Damp leaves and sticky mud clung to our shoes with every step. There wasn't much low-growing vegetation to be seen, but plenty of mushrooms and shelf-like fungi sprouted from the ground and tree trunks. The branches overhead fractured the already low light, turning our surroundings dusky grey. I half expected to see the Boneman peep out from behind one of the trees at any moment.

For once, no banter came from Nex and Aeron, or anyone else for that matter. Silence suffocated our group. I doubted the ghosts could hear us all the way out here, but I supposed it never hurt to stay alert. For all we knew, they'd abandoned their base and were stalking us at that very moment.

We spent so long in tense silence that I jumped when Mallor finally spoke even though he only whispered. "This is where we leave you." He and the others came to a stop. "Keep walking for another half mile and you'll run into a clearing full of bramble thickets. The ghosts should be camped out there. Hopefully, you won't even need to get close enough to see the thicket."

We nodded. Nicholas pivoted and gestured for me to follow. It felt wrong to leave the safety of the group, but we had to play our part. I turned my back on the others and set off with Nicholas, praying this wouldn't be the last time I saw them.

We walked in silence for a long moment. I cast a glance over my shoulder toward where we'd left the others. Even though we hadn't gotten that far away, they were nowhere to be seen. I imagined they were hiding behind the trees so as not to alert the ghosts to their presence. I forced my eyes forward. Looking for them would give them away, and we needed every advantage we could get.

"Do you think they're going to be there?" Nicholas asked in a low murmur.

I shrugged. I wasn't going to pretend like I knew anything for certain. The ghosts could be all around us, closing in, preparing to attack at any moment.

Nicholas heaved a breath. "It's going to be ok. We aren't actually going to be in any danger."

"Are you trying to convince me or yourself?"

He chuckled. "Both, hopefully. I don't like this any more than you do."

My eyes darted between the trees, searching for any sign of movement. "You were fine at the graveyard in Noxier."

"It's one thing to go up against a low-level ghost with a fully trained Bone Touched at your back. And quite another to let a horde of ghosts chase you through the woods, knowing that the smallest slip up could mean your long and painful death."

I swallowed. "It would be long and painful?"

He chewed his lower lip. "I mean, I would hope not, but I'm not optimistic. They're after the magic in our bones after all. I doubt they would care if we were alive or dead when they took it."

My hands clenched into fists. This wasn't the kind of thing I wanted to think about as we marched closer and closer to the ghost's hideout.

Nicholas ran a hand through his hair. "We'll be fine. The others will swoop in and call for backup if we get overwhelmed."

"You really trust them, don't you?" I murmured.

Nicholas smiled to himself. "They can be a mess sometimes—who isn't—but when you need them, they come through for you. That's the Bone Touched bond."

And I was a part of that now. I wasn't alone anymore.

We drew up short as a bramble thicket materialized out of the light fog ahead. That was it. If our information was correct, the ghosts would be waiting for us there.

I wasn't sure who reached for whom first, but Nicholas's hand ended up in mine. He squeezed. I squeezed back. I wasn't ready, but I never really would be. Now was our time. We had to do our duty and protect Noxier, Mortorous Academy, and the rest of the world from these ghosts.

In tandem, we walked up to the thicket. It had to be fifty feet wide, roughly circular, and high enough to swallow a small bear. Nicholas kicked at the net of thorns. Nothing happened.

"This has to be the right spot," he whispered.

I frowned. "It's deserted."

"It's too quiet."

He was right. I hadn't realized it until I listened. Not so much a cricket stirred in the bushes. No birds chirped in the trees. Not even the wind rustled the fallen leaves at our feet. That silence couldn't be natural.

My blood chilled.

I started walking to the right and released Nicholas's hand to give him a light shove to the left. We were supposed to head in these directions anyway. Maybe if we made a circle around the thicket, the spirits would take the bait and jump out at us.

Nicholas and I started a slow circle around the brambles. How long had these been growing here? The bushes all knotted together and overran each other. Branches grasped at branches, trying to choke one another out in a desperate bid for more space. The ground underneath was all but invisible.

I squinted into the bushes, trying to see through the thorns and fog to spot any ghosts. But that couldn't be right. The thorns were one thing, but the fog shouldn't be thick enough that I couldn't see through it. Had it been there a moment ago?

I leaned over the thicket to get a better look.

The fog *looked back*.

A scream wrenched out of my throat as a ghostly face lunged through the tangled brambles. I threw myself back just in time to avoid its grabbing hands, stumbling into a tree. Once the apparition emerged from the bushes, it solidified and colored its lines in until it could have passed for a living woman in jeans and a long-sleeved blue shirt. Shoulder-length blonde hair swayed around her face as she lurched for me again. I ducked and her fingers swiped through tree bark, sending bits of wood flying.

Behind her, more ghosts drifted out of the thorny branches, dozens of them. More than the twelve Mallor said he'd seen. It almost looked like all twenty-seven of the passengers from the bus crash were here.

I backed up slowly. Where had they all come from? We weren't prepared for this.

Across the thicket, Nicholas screamed my name. I dared to glance in his direction. No ghosts stalked him. They all surrounded me. That wasn't how it was supposed to happen. They were supposed to go after Nicholas, too. Our plan hinged on our ability to separate them.

"Daughter of death," hissed the woman, drawing my eyes back to her. "You have something we want." Her hand lifted to point at me as her eyes turned dark as graves. "Something buried deep in your BONES!"

She charged. The rest of the ghosts came crashing around her in a screaming wave of reaching limbs and snapping teeth.

I spun and took off. The cries of the dead followed close behind. I didn't know if Group Bone could take on so many, but *I* certainly couldn't. Hopefully, Mallor and the others were relaying the situation to Group Shadow and getting them over to help us.

My feet flew over the ground. Mud sucked at my shoes. Leaves slipped under me. I managed to stay upright by some miracle. Surely, the ground hadn't been this uneven when Nicholas and I headed to the thicket. Surely, there hadn't been so many loose branches to scratch at my legs or trip me. Surely, all the small rocks now under my feet had rolled into my path for the sole purpose of sending me flying.

My breath came in sharp gasps. My heart pounded against my rib cage like a prisoner against the bars of a cell.

Still, I ran. A quarter mile had never seemed so far when we ran in gym class.

A hand grabbed at my braid. I yanked away. The elastic ripped from my hair, and it went flying out in a white banner behind me. Other fingers brushed my clothes. They were

389

practically on top of me. Their screams reached a fevered pitch.

My legs and lungs burned. The ambush had to be close. I was running out of energy and the ghosts seemed inexhaustible. If my body gave out now, not only would I die, but any chance of taking the ghosts out easily would die too. The ghosts would glut themselves on the magic in my marrow and become even stronger.

I couldn't stop, but I couldn't run forever, either.

Please, I begged. *Please, be here.*

I shot between a pair of trees growing ridiculously close together. The ghosts parted around them and were met with a barrage of flying bones. From behind and above, the other Bone Touched sprung their trap.

Ghosts wailed as shards of bone sunk into their bodies. Bands of white snapped around their limbs. They went down into the mud and leaves, tearing at their shackles.

I spared a glance over my shoulder to see the Bone Touched descending upon them. There were probably more than twice as many ghosts as Bone Touched, but my people held their own against the rushing tide of the dead. For now.

With my eyes momentarily averted, I missed a large tree branch lying on the ground. My feet connected with it, and I went sprawling. A hand appeared in front of me as I scrambled upward.

Nicholas's worried face stared down at me. His chest heaved as he panted, having run all the way here too. He must have been right behind the horde that followed me. "Come on, we need to go!"

I grabbed his hand and hauled myself to my feet. We had to get out of the line of fire before any of the ghosts noticed us.

But as we turned to head back to the cars, our way was blocked by a trio of spirits. Two were people, a little boy, and an older woman. The third was a floating orb that darted at us faster than we could think.

We ducked and spun out of the way and came face to face with the boy and woman. Nicholas drew a handful of the throwing stars Nex had made from her teeth out of his pocket and sent them flying. The little boy took two to the chest and fell back screaming and clawing at himself. The old woman was faster. The orb didn't have a problem weaving in the air to avoid the projectiles either.

I searched for a way around the two as Nicholas drew more bones from his pockets and tried again. The orb moved too quickly, and the old woman was surprisingly nimble. I feinted right and the orb swooped to intercept me. I swerved and headed left, racing around it and the woman, who was preoccupied with Nicholas. I raced back toward the rest of the ghosts and Bone Touched. Hopefully, someone would see and help us.

The orb shot forward, slamming into my back, and sending me into the mud. The breath rushed from my lungs. I coughed, spitting the forest floor out of my mouth, and tried to get back up, but a second orb joined the first and rammed into my side, rolling me over. Another ghost, one that looked like a person, stood over me. It was the woman who first came out of the bushes and led the charge.

She slammed her foot into my stomach, pinning me down, and grinned at me, her eyes wholly black. "Give me your life."

She reached for my face. The orbs hovered behind her, vibrating with excitement.

My breath came fast. I pushed at her leg, but she didn't budge. This was it. I was trapped. Hands reaching to take everything from me, just as a different set had before. My vision blurred as panic wrapped around my throat like the suffocating coils of a snake.

I wasn't going to come back from this. There would be no tub, no Academy, no chance at another life. I would die. But I could at least go down screaming.

My mouth opened and I let out the loudest, most ear-splitting screech I could muster. I poured all those weeks of pain and fear and loneliness from my time in the tub and at the Academy into that one note. Just like I did when I made myself lay down in the bathtub in my dorm room.

My pockets exploded. The bone shards from Nex hurtled out. They lodged deep in the ghost woman and both orbs. The woman fell, clutching the leg that had held me to the ground. Half a dozen white fragments poked out of it. She snarled at me, even as I scrambled to my feet.

But my work was done. I tried not to get too excited about how well I'd just manipulated bone. I tried to push down the thrill of having finally touched that power. Just because I did it once, didn't mean I could do it again. Besides, my shredded pockets told me enough about how many bones I had left.

I ran to where Nicholas had finally subdued the old woman. She leaned against a tree with a bone needle in her throat. She tried to gasp around it, which didn't make much sense to me since she was already dead and therefore didn't need to breathe, but I didn't stop to question it. I just grabbed Nicholas's arm and started running.

A handful of other ghosts tried to jump in our path, but reinforcements had arrived and kept the spirits occupied while we made our escape.

I'd lost track of where we were in relation to the cars, but Nicholas managed to guide us back. No ghosts followed, but neither did any Bone Touched. We were supposed to have an escort. They were probably overwhelmed by the ghosts, too busy fighting for their lives and ours.

Rhonda was unlocked when we reached it, and we dove into the back. Nicholas lunged around the driver's seat to hit the button that locked all four doors. We were safe. As long as Nex made it out alive and brought her car keys to drive us out of here.

I pressed my face to my window, leaving condensation all over the glass as I panted. "We're clear, right? They didn't follow us?"

"No." Nicholas's breaths came as hard and fast as mine. "We're ok. We got away. By now, the others will have the ghosts mostly under control. Probably."

"Probably."

We sat in silence for a moment, letting our breathing even out and our heart rates calm.

"You aren't hurt, are you?" I asked Nicholas.

He smiled. "A few bruises, but otherwise no. That was one tough old lady. If you hadn't taken care of that orb, I might not have made it."

"You mean how it pushed me into the mud?" Thin streaks of it still clung to my clothes. I wiped my face with what clean portions of my shirt I could find.

"I mean how you manipulated those bones into it and two other ghosts." Nicholas plucked a leaf out of my hair and let it flutter to the floor. "I've seen some pretty cool bone magic, but never anything like that."

"I'm just glad it happened. I guess all your lessons paid off." I grabbed a half-empty water bottle from the cup holders in the front seat and used it to rinse out my mouth, which still tasted a bit earthy.

Nicholas shifted in his seat to face me. "I think you could have done it without my lessons. I think you *can* do anything. I have a feeling I'm going to have the privilege of saying I'm friends with one of the most powerful Bone Touched in the world pretty soon."

"Friends?" I slipped the bottle of now dirty water back into the cup holder.

His eyes softened, like a summer night's sky. I could almost see the stars glittering in them as he slid his fingers across my face to cup my cheek. "Maybe a little more than friends."

I leaned into his touch. "Maybe a little more than a little."

We met in the middle, pressing our lips together in a kiss hotter than a cremation furnace. Nicholas slid closer across the back seat cradling my face with both hands as he deepened the kiss. I gripped one wrist, bracing my other hand on the back of the seat.

Nicholas broke away an inch. "You're...ok with this, right? You're not going to freak out?"

I huffed an exasperated sigh and swung myself up into his lap. My knees touched the seat backs on either side of his hips. Nicholas stared up at me, hands hovering in the air as if he were afraid to touch me.

"I'll be fine," I murmured and sealed my mouth over his.

His eyes slid closed, and his hands found a home on my waist. My fingers tangled themselves in his dark hair. The sensation of his tongue sliding over mine lit a fire under my skin. He tasted like chocolate. He'd probably been eating it before we got here. He must have been more nervous than he looked about this mission if he was stress-eating.

My fingers trailed down the back of his neck, feeling the residual tension from our ghost encounter slowly melt from his muscles. I continued down the back of his shirt. He made a noise deep in his throat and pulled me closer, forcing my legs to part further to avoid cramming them into the seat behind him. I withdrew my hand and brought my lips to his throat as I reached for the buttons of his shirt.

"Sylvan," Nicholas panted when I exposed the muscles of his chest and stomach.

I kissed a path down his collarbone, over the wretched mark on his chest, lingering as if I could erase it. Nicholas swore sharply as he pulled at my shirt buttons. I giggled against his skin. He got impatient once half the buttons were open. His hand caught my chin and tilted it up.

I groaned as his lips blazed a trail down my throat, mirroring the places I'd kissed him a minute ago. I plastered one hand to his chest under the fluttering halves of his shirt and wrapped the other around the back of his neck. His own hands wriggled under the back of my shirt to grip the smooth skin of my back.

"Keres said I looked at you like you'd stolen a piece of my heart," Nicholas breathed into my half-open shirt. "But she was wrong. You've stolen all of it. And I don't want you to give it back."

I dragged his mouth back to mine. "I wouldn't even know how," I whispered against his lips.

His eyes flickered open long enough to meet mine. "I hope you never find out."

The click of the doors unlocking made us both jump. I

tried to slide off Nicholas's lap, but he crushed me against him, covering our bare chests, I realized.

The driver's side door opened and Nex poked her head in. "By all means, don't stop on my account." Her grin was indistinguishable from a shark's. "Please, consummate this relationship before your little teenage loins explode."

"Shut up, Nex," Nicholas hissed, still clutching me to him to preserve what remained of our dignity. It probably didn't do much good. His hair was a mess, and he was still breathing hard. We were flushed and pressed together in a compromising position. There was no denying what we'd been doing or where it might have gone.

Nex plopped down behind the wheel. "Listen, Nicky. This is my car you're making out in. You don't get to tell me what to do. And if you've gotten any kind of bodily fluids on my upholstery, you're going to deep clean the whole thing from top to bottom. Understand?"

Nicholas heaved a sigh into my shoulder. "Don't worry. You interrupted before we got that far."

"Good." Nex yanked her door closed.

I cleared my throat and pushed myself upright. Nicholas let his hands drop to my thighs. The pressure of his frustration could have crushed the car flat. I didn't move from his lap as I refastened the buttons on his shirt.

His thumbs moved idly over the soft fabric of my pants, and he didn't take his eyes off me when he spoke to Nex. "Where is everyone else? I take it since we aren't speeding out of here with a mob of ghosts on our tail that everything went alright."

"Yup." Nex stretched her arms out. She would have smacked me in the head if Nicholas didn't slip a hand around the back of my neck and pulled me away. "They're just wrapping things up, making sure the Boneman comes to collect the ghosts. Mallor made me miss the party to come find you guys and make sure you were still alive."

Nicholas rolled his eyes. "Thanks for caring so much."

"Hey, you made it back to Rhonda, so you did just fine."

"I guess," Nicholas said as I finished buttoning his shirt and he started on mine.

Nex snorted. "You're just upset you didn't get to stay for the main event."

"Right." Nicholas snuck in a kiss against the base of my throat as he fastened the last button.

My breath caught. He grinned. I slid off his lap into my seat and caught Nex watching us in the rearview mirror. She smirked but didn't make any further jabs.

We waited until Keres and the others trickled out of the forest and slunk into their cars. Keres had a long scratch on her cheek and her clothes were muddier than mine. Nex frowned at the mud as Keres sank into the passenger seat with all the grace of a corpse.

"Everything ok?" Nicholas asked.

"Yeah, just a busier night than I'm used to. There were *so many* ghosts." She leaned back and closed her eyes. "Mallor and Aeron are going to that little restaurant in Noxier. The one right across from the library. They said we should join them. Honestly, after that fiasco, I could use a warm meal. And a drink. And something sweet, too." She pulled at her filthy shirt. "Definitely a change of clothes first though."

Nex already had the car in gear. "Then what are we waiting for?"

38

Thirty-Eight

Nex pulled out on the road, throwing Nicholas into me and nearly hitting Mallor's car as they tried to pull out too. Nex slammed on the horn and Mallor responded in kind. Nicholas and I braced ourselves for the turbulent ride back.

Keres seemed impervious to the laws of physics that sent the rest of us careening around in the car. She sat as still as a cadaver the whole way, no matter what crazy turns Nex took. I envied her for it.

Despite the odds, we got to the restaurant in one piece.

Mallor and Aeron already had a table. Nex flounced up to them and called loud enough for half the restaurant to hear, "Man, hunting the dead really makes a woman hungry!"

"Could you not go around screaming about what we've been doing?" Aeron hissed at a much more reasonable volume.

"You should already know the answer to that question," Keres snorted as she claimed the head of the table and rummaged around in a plastic bag she'd fished out of Nex's trunk.

"A guy can hope he's wrong," he muttered.

Nex smacked him in the back of the head while Keres handed me a clean set of clothes. "We should get changed before the restaurant staff have a collective heart attack about how much mud we've tracked in."

She and I retreated to the bathroom in the back to change and wash up as much as possible in the sink. I winced when I realized how much dirt clung to my hair. It didn't seem to have mattered to Nicholas, but what state must Nex's back seat be in?

Keres glanced at me in the mirror as I did my best to wash out my hair. "I'm proud of you."

My pale eyes darted to her face. "For what?"

"For everything really. You seem to be taking to the Bone Touched life better than I thought you would." She stuffed her dirty clothes in the plastic bag. "I don't usually like being wrong, but this is an exception."

I frowned at the sink. "I don't know if you're that wrong."

"You're progressing quickly in your magic studies. You're making friends with other Bone Touched. You're going on missions and excelling at them. Sounds like you're settling into your demigodhood to me."

I wrung out my hair as if I were wringing someone's neck. "What if I still don't like the Boneman?"

Keres chuckled. "I know some Bone Touched who are years past graduation and still hate him. Forgiving him for all that pain will take a while. If it happens at all."

"How long did it take you?"

"Years. There's still a bit of resentment, a part of me that questions if it was really necessary, but it doesn't do to dwell on the past for long."

I grabbed some paper towels and pressed them to my hair. "But doesn't he want us to like him? Doesn't he want us to see him as a father figure?"

Keres turned to face me fully. "He understands. The Boneman can't control your feelings or personality. That's why he takes people who have lived for a little while instead of snatching babies from their cradles. He chooses his children based on their character. Just because he pushes you to do what he wants doesn't mean he can force you to love him— none of the gods have the power to do that. He's willing to wait for you. He's a hopeless romantic, not a twisted puppeteer."

The Boneman had done his fair share of puppeteering, but I didn't press that point. "You're sure?" He didn't seem that patient. When I'd refused to learn bone magic, he hadn't wasted time confronting me about my defiance.

"Yes. You probably won't believe me because of the stage you're at in your journey, but he genuinely cares about all of us and wants us to be happy. He would never do something to hurt you just for the sake of hurting you."

Nicholas had said something similar once. So had Tumulus. I didn't want to believe them at the time. I was still hesitant to fully credit Keres's words. But if she told the truth, that meant there was a lot more to the Boneman than I thought when I first came out of the tub.

I tossed the paper towels in the trash. "Thanks, Keres."

"Any time, Sylvan." She beamed at me. "Now, let's go get some dinner. I'm starving."

Nicholas got up and pulled out a chair for me when we returned to the table, but I took the one beside it that he'd just gotten out of. The others chuckled. Nicholas feigned offense but sat down and scooted his new chair closer to mine so our joined hands could rest on my thigh. He didn't let go of me through the entire meal, even though I held his dominant hand. It made him a little clumsy while he ate, but when I tried to release him, he tightened his grip.

We ended up getting dessert this time, mostly because Nex insisted. Mallor wanted to take us back to the Academy, but she had other ideas.

"Don't you remember being all cooped up in that school with nothing to do? Have mercy on our poor little swimmers." She grabbed Nicholas and hugged him like he was a starving child. "They'll waste away in those colorless halls. It's our duty to bring life to their dead world."

Nicholas struggled against her. "Let go of me, Nex. Don't pretend like you're doing this for anyone but yourself."

"Maybe." She let Nicholas go and sashayed over behind me. Her arms squeezed me in a tight hug from behind. "But think about little Sylvan. She got chased by all those ghosts today. She deserves a special treat for not only surviving but taking down a few of them." Nex leaned down to talk directly into my ear. "I saw what you did out there. It was magnificent, Sylvie."

Nicholas frowned. "Sylvie?"

"Of course. You're Nicky. She's Sylvie. It fits perfectly. And it's about time I gave her a nickname. It's practically a rite of passage." Nex stuck a self-important finger in the air.

"I think it's nice," I murmured. I liked feeling like I was one of them.

Nicholas raised his brows. Nex squeezed me tighter. "I knew you would. Now, desserts all around!" She released me and went back to her seat to look at the menu.

Nicholas leaned toward me. "If you wanted a nickname, you should have asked someone with taste."

I smirked. "You can give me one if you want."

Nicholas rolled his eyes. "I happen to like your name just the way it is. And don't be surprised if you get tired of *Sylvie* really fast."

"At least I'm not *Nicky*."

He shuddered. "Please, don't ever call me that. It sounds so juvenile. I deserve something stronger and more elegant that fits my character."

I folded my other hand around his. "I like Nicholas just fine."

"Is that why you never call me Nick like everyone else?"

I nodded. He leaned to kiss my temple, and the table erupted in a collective *aww*. Even Mallor smiled a bit. Nicholas and I rolled our eyes and looked at the dessert menu.

"So, why did all the ghosts go after you, anyway?" Nex asked.

I shrugged. "I thought you guys were supposed to have all the answers."

"It could be because Nicholas has had more training— I've heard some ghosts can sense that—so, they thought you would be an easier target," Keres suggested.

"It's more likely that they were attracted to your power," Aeron countered.

"They're attracted to the power of every Bone Touched, genius." Nex swatted at him.

He ducked. "I'm talking about the fact that she probably has more magic in her arm than most of us have in our whole bodies."

My brow furrowed. "What do you mean?"

"Aeron has a theory that the closer the pigmentation of the Bone Touched is to the bath they were reformed in, the more magic they have," Keres explained.

"And that since the white bath creates warriors that utilize every one of our skills, it's the most magical," Mallor continued. "By that logic, your white hair and eyes mean you're an incredibly powerful Bone Touched even before getting fully trained."

"It would make sense seeing as how you manipulated bone after such a short time," Aeron said. "And naturally, the ghosts would go after whichever one of you had the most magic. They'd rather go after the five-course feast than the microwave dinner."

"I'm sitting right here." Nicholas protested.

Mallor considered me. "It would certainly explain how the ghost of that boy found you when you visited town. I'd been trying to pin him down for weeks, and he just walked right up to you."

I ran my free hand through my wet hair. I hadn't thought about the possibility of one Bone Touched being created stronger than another. Sure, there'd be slight differences. Even a god couldn't create two things exactly the same. But it kind of made sense. Both Tumulus and Nicholas were impressed with the speed at which I learned bone magic.

Nicholas bumped me with his shoulder. "I keep telling you you're going to be one hell of a ghost hunter."

And I was starting to believe him.

All too soon we found ourselves outside the restaurant, saying goodbye to Aeron, Nex, and Keres. Nex wrapped me up in a bone-crushing hug, telling me to give her a call if

Nicholas ever broke my heart, so she could personally break every one of his bones and watch the magic leak out of them.

She also squeezed Nicholas in a tight hug and whispered something to him that made his face go red. Aeron nodded his head at us, and Keres gave me a warm smile, both saying they would see us at the next Bone Touched meeting.

"Don't be strangers!" Nex called as she skipped off with the other two following.

"Alright, you two." Mallor shoved his hands in his pockets. "Time to get you back to the Academy."

39

Thirty-Nine

Nicholas sat in the middle seat, right next to me, on our way back to school. The sun had gone down, leaving a thick chill in the air. Even with the heat on, it felt better to have Nicholas's warm body so close to mine. We didn't talk, but the silence was far from uncomfortable.

Mallor took a back road to drop me off closer to the girls' dorm. Nicholas tried to follow me out.

"No, you don't." Mallor grabbed the back of his shirt and yanked him back into his seat. "She'll be fine for the two minutes it'll take to get to her room. You need to rest after such a big mission, not stay up with each other."

I bit my lip to suppress the smile that rose at the sight of Nicholas's pout. "I'll see you tomorrow."

"Yeah, see you tomorrow." He grabbed my hand and pulled me down for a quick kiss. Mallor made some grumbling noise in the front seat as Nicholas whispered. "I'll find you later once I ditch him. After all, the birds miss me, don't they?"

"Terribly." The smile that tugged on the corners of my lips was hard to control.

I ducked out of the car again, closed the door, and watched Mallor peel away from the curb.

The wind had picked up while we were in the restaurant, probably the beginnings of another cold front. It blew straight through my clothes to chill my bones on the way back to the dorm.

I'd gotten used to taking the side entrance to avoid people, but Mallor had dropped me off at the back doors that opened into the common room. I might as well use them. Nothing in there could be as scary as what I'd faced tonight.

I was wrong.

Deafening music assaulted my ears the moment I entered. How had I not heard it before? Perhaps I was too lost in thought.

I'd forgotten it was a Friday night, which meant the common room turned into a nightclub.

The noise wasn't the only thing that startled me. The common room wasn't decorated in the usual bright colors, but in our school's black and white. And there were bones *everywhere*.

Plastic bones hung from the ceiling. Bone garlands made of paper wrapped around the columns. Fake skeletons leaned against walls and in corners. Tissue paper skulls served as centerpieces on tables. And in the center of the common room stood a life-size sculpture of the Boneman.

Black and white streamers hung over his shoulders and ribs. His eyes lit up with little red bulbs.

My hands clenched into fists. This was fine. I was fine. I just survived a massive ghost attack. This didn't even compare to that. Besides, I'd been desensitizing myself in my bathtub. I could walk through the common room when it was full of fake bones without any trouble.

I forced my feet to move. Students kept stepping in my way, their laughter and conversations far too loud for comfort. I gritted my teeth. If the music weren't blaring, maybe they'd actually be able to hear each other without shouting.

The real scare came when I passed the fake Boneman. Its jaw unhinged with a mechanical roar that sent me jumping away. I couldn't hold it together after that and raced across the room to the stairway door as fast as the crowd would allow.

I only dared to breathe easily once the door closed between me and the party. I didn't usually pay attention to the conversations of my classmates, but I thought I would have heard something about a bone-themed party. Maybe they were celebrating some competition event, or it was spirit day or something. Regardless, it completely ruined the triumph from earlier this evening.

I reached for the handrail to steady myself, but someone grabbed my arm and yanked me out through the side door into the rapidly chilling autumn air. I stumbled and spun to face my assailant.

Nina's sharp eyes raked over my oversized clothes. Keres's spares weren't my size.

Nina glared at me. "You still don't have the decency to dress well, do you?"

I frowned and opened my mouth to ask what this was about as her fist snapped across my face. I stumbled to the side and stared at her with my mouth wide open. She didn't give me a moment to comprehend what was going on before she punched me in the stomach. My body folded in half. The air rushed from my lungs.

"What…?" I wheezed.

Her foot connected with the side of my head, and I hit the ground.

"Did you honestly think you could ruin my life, destroy my reputation, and then talk to me like I'm not worth ten times more than you ever will be?" She stomped on my hand as I tried to push myself back up.

I cried out, but not loud enough to cover the sound of my fingers breaking under her heel. My hand started to go numb, not the way it did when I was cold, more like the nerves in my hand were shriveling up and dying.

No, no, no!

Breaking bones was bad. That's where my magic, my life force lived. I could die if enough damage was done to my bones.

Nina kicked me in the side. I rolled, trying to scramble up and away. She just kicked me again.

"No one can hear you scream over the music in there." She grinned down at me. "And even if they did, no one cares what happens to you."

When she kicked me next, a rib fractured. Numbness spread across my side. Nina stomped down on my leg and that broke too. Everywhere her foot connected, my bones cracked. I could barely feel my body enough to curl into a defensive ball. Weren't my bones supposed to be stronger than this? How did she have the strength to incapacitate me so easily?

"How…are you…so strong?" I managed to ask between blows.

Nina paused and grinned wide enough to show molars. "The Boneman isn't the only god who likes to hand out powers."

But the Wind Dreamed were at Animos. And they didn't interfere with the Bone Touched. A vague memory of Tumulus telling me about another god the day I had a panic attack in the gym closet reached out of the murk of pain clouding my mind. He said there was a god of time. He also said to stay away from them at all costs.

Was Nina one of their demigods and using the power she'd been given to kill me?

Oh no.

This was no better than when I'd been stuck in the tub, listening to the Boneman take me apart, unable to move, to fight. I tried to scream, but as the feeling in my ribs disappeared, so did the muscular control over my torso. I could barely breathe.

I was going to die this time. No one knew what was happening to me. No one was coming to my rescue. I couldn't focus enough through the pain to even try to control Nina's bones in her body. This was my end.

I'd had such a short life. If only I'd had time for more. I wanted to travel the world like the other Bone Touched and save people's lives without them ever knowing they'd been in danger. I wanted to see my baby birds grow up. I wanted to stay with Nicholas, so we could work out this blossoming romance between us. I wanted to find out what happened to Wren.

Tears ran down my face. I hoped I wouldn't become a ghost that haunted this school. Nina deserved it, but it would be so much trouble for Mallor and Nicholas and Tumulus.

I'm sorry.

A shout stopped the steam of blows from continuing. Nina stopped, looked behind me, and took off running. A moment later a pair of black-clad knees fell to the ground in front of me. I glanced up into dark eyes that swam with worry.

Nicholas.

"No, no, no, no, no." His hands skimmed over my body like flies over a carcass, trying to decide what to do. "Oh, Sylvan. It's gonna be ok. I—" He looked up, eyes darting. There was no one out here to help us.

"Nicholas," I croaked, reaching for his hand with my good one.

He grabbed it and squeezed lightly. "I'm here. It's ok. I've got you."

I stared up at him, trying to focus on the lines of his face. "You're really pretty."

He let out a hoarse laugh. "So are you. We're going to get you help." He stood up, jogged a few paces away, looked around, and came back.

"It's ok. There's nothing you can do," I whispered.

"*No.*" He took my hand again. "You're going to be fine."

"I'm dying. No one can put my bones back together."

"Don't say that. We have to try." He scooped his arms under me as gently as possible. I still cried out as the broken fragments of my bones shifted under my skin. "I got you." He looked around some more and started walking as fast as he could, determination burning in his eyes.

The numbness spread to take over my whole leg and torso. My left arm, tucked against my chest, didn't respond when I tried to move it. I had to make a conscious effort to breathe. "This is it. I'm sorry we didn't have more time together."

He growled. "We're going to have plenty of time. Don't you dare say goodbye."

My head fell against his shoulder. "I'll miss you."

"I'll miss you too. Always remember that, and remember me, ok?"

My eyes drifted closed. "Not even the Boneman could take my memories of us."

"I hope not."

My eyes slit open in confusion. I drew breath to ask what he meant when our surroundings finally registered in my pain-addled brain. Trees towered over us, blocking nearly all of the moonlight. On what little I could see of Nicholas's face in such deep shadows, there was nothing but unmovable determination. He looked chiseled out of stone, like a grave marker.

"Where...?" But I already knew. There was only one place with this many trees close enough for Nicholas to carry me from the girls' dorm. "Nicholas, why are we here?"

Instead of answering, Nicholas shouted into the dark forest around us. "Help! Please, help us!"

"What are you doing?" I gasped.

"I know you're in here. She needs you. She's dying, and you're the only one who can do anything about it." He turned in a full circle, eyes searching the trees.

I clutched his shirt with my good hand. "Stop, Nicholas. You can't!"

He looked down at me, a tear streaking down his cheek, catching the light. "I don't care what it takes. I don't care if you hate me for this. I am *not* letting you die." He raised his head. "They say you care about us!" he screamed. "This is your chance to prove it. Please, I'm begging you, save her!"

"Nicholas, no." I tried to cover his mouth, but he shook me away.

He was trying to call the Boneman. He thought the Boneman could fix me. But he would only break me further. I would rather die like this, in Nicholas's arms, than go back to that solitary existence in the tub.

Nicholas didn't stop yelling into the forest until a chill that had nothing to do with the weather ran over us. The beginnings of that devouring terror crept in, stealing our breath, demanding all of our attention.

Nicholas dropped to his knees and set me gently on the ground. I whimpered from both pain and fear and grabbed his hand, uselessly trying to pull myself back into his arms. We could still move. We could still get out of here. The last thing I wanted was to have my final moments of life tainted by the Boneman's presence. Nicholas gripped my hand in return but didn't pick me back up.

"Please, don't let him take me again," I whispered.

"I'm sorry." He looked up as my muscles stiffened, the terror freezing them in place. The deep rattle of bones knocking against each other sounded to my left, growing louder.

"Please, save her," Nicholas breathed as fear closed both of our throats.

I could only feel one arm, one leg, and my neck and head now. The rest of me might as well not exist. I wished I would die before the Boneman ruined my last view of Nicholas, even if he was staring at our creator instead of me.

The rattle stopped right beside me. The white of the Boneman's snout hovered in my peripheral vision. The great thump next to my shoulder would have made me jump under normal circumstances. Skeleton fingers grasped my face and turned it away from Nicholas.

The Boneman knelt on my left, looking down with those empty eye sockets. His thoughts wound through my mind sadly. He turned his head to take in my broken body, then fixed his gaze on Nicholas.

I will take care of her.

No. I wanted to scream, to fight, to run. This was my worst nightmare coming true.

The Boneman was taking me back and no one could do anything about it. Nicholas was just handing me over to him as if he hadn't walked with me on my journey to recover from the last time the Boneman held me prisoner. As if he didn't know how much this betrayal hurt.

The Boneman gently removed my hand from Nicholas's. A tear escaped my eye. Another raced across my other cheek. The Boneman scooped me into his arms, tucking my head into his shoulder so I couldn't see anything but his bones.

Bones, bones, bones.

But I make no promises.

And with that, he turned and stalked off into the forest, taking me away from my school and my life. Most sensation had left my chest, but I could still feel my heart shattering into tiny, scorched pieces.

40

The Boneman

The girl was barely alive when the Boneman brought her into the black-tiled room with its empty, white porcelain tub at the center. Usually, he had time to prepare the bath and make sure everything was perfect before he put his children in it. But this was an emergency.

He set the girl's limp body in the bottom of the empty tub and pressed the bare bones of his hands to the smooth surface beneath her. The walls of the tub began leaking a milky white fluid.

The Boneman moved quickly, stripping the ill-fitting clothes from the girl's body, and arranging her on her side as the liquid pooled in the bottom of the tub and rose around her. Her pale eyes stayed fixed on the oozing walls of the tub, half-lidded from the pain, both internal and external.

There had been no mistaking the moment when all the fight left her. Her despair exploded through every bone in her body, broken or otherwise. The boy had begged for her life, but she never wanted to return to this place.

The Boneman didn't blame her. There were days when he

hated this room almost as much as she did. He hated feeling his children's agony as he tore them apart and put them back together. They had no way of knowing that was the only way they could ever live again.

There was no shortage of dead or dying, but he picked his followers with care, taking them from the moment right after their bodies stopped being capable of housing their souls and reforging that connection between flesh and spirit.

They never remembered. They *couldn't* remember. Dying wasn't an experience the human mind could come back from in one piece. It was better to erase and start over.

This girl, rattling her way through every breath as liquid slowly engulfed her body, had a completely different life than the one he gave her after her transformation. Pulling her ghost into the cage of his ribs after that man beat her to death outside her family's inn had been the best thing to happen to her and she didn't even know it.

He knew she would make a perfect Bone Touched when, instead of being frozen like other spirits were when they traveled inside him, she'd wrapped her ghostly arms around his spine and hugged him.

It pained him to feel her fear once he brought her soul and body to this room and unified the two in the tub using the mark he made on her chest. She deserved more. All his children did.

But the Boneman had to do more than resurrect dead kids. Order demanded they have a divine purpose to escape their mortal fates. So, he gave them one. And once their time was up, they returned to him, ready to rest after truly living.

The Boneman looked down at the girl in the tub. The white water had risen over her mouth and nose. She breathed much more easily now. Her eyes widened, having heard every one of his thoughts, now knowing the story of her beginning and his purpose in creating her.

Do you see now? he asked.

A gleaming tear escaped the one eye that remained above the liquid's surface. *You're doing it again.*

The Boneman rested a hand on her head, and she didn't squeeze her eyes shut in terror the way she and so many others had before her.

Yes.

He stepped out of the tub as the magical fluid closed over her head. He would let her rest for a while to absorb the things he'd told her and allow her body to stabilize before he began the long process of putting her bones back together. She deserved some time to herself anyway.

As the Boneman closed the dark wood door to her room, he didn't see the fingers of her unbroken hand slowly clench into a fist.

Acknowledgments

I'm speechless.

Day dreaming a silly little story in your head is one thing. Writing it down is another. But publishing it and being able to hold the book in your hands is a whole other can of worms. This book is four years in the making. In that time, a lot of people have helped or supported me during my writing and publishing journey.

I'd like to thank all the members of my undergraduate creative thesis class. I wrote the first couple of drafts of *Bone Touched* alongside you all. You were my first writer friends and helped shape this story into what it is now during our critiquing sessions.

Damaris Martinez, I hope Wizard Larry is still inspiring you. Matthew Vieyra, it's your turn to publish your creative thesis manuscript. Cesar "CJ" Loya, I'm going to hold you to what you said about making this book into a famous TV show/movie. And Professor Jason Harris, I never would have thought my thesis could win an award, but you did, and you were right, thank you.

Jeff Hart, your editing notes told me things I didn't want to hear, but need to in order to make this book as good as it could be. I'm glad that you enjoyed reading *Bone Touched*. Emma, thank you for your work on this beautiful cover and other art associated with this or any of my works.

To all my family and friends who believed in me every step of the way and are almost as excited about this as I am, you're support over the years means everything. To Briscoe, my fluffy, little writing buddy, even though you mostly just slept on the floor while I wrote, your presence was a comfort.

To everyone who heard about *Bone Touched* through social media, thanks you for taking a chance and reading this book.

And for anyone who identifies with Sylvan's struggles on any level, know that you are not alone and that you still have people rooting for you.

About the Author

F. R. E. (Rita) Kinney grew up and lives in Texas and is the author of *Bone Touched*, the first in the *Crooked Trinity* series. When she isn't writing books inspired by weird dreams, she is taking long walks with her dog, crocheting, knitting, or lurking around her local Catholic church.

You can connect with me on:
🌐 https://frekinney.org

www.ingramcontent.com/pod-product-compliance
Lightning Source LLC
Chambersburg PA
CBHW020009120726
47903CB00004B/1200